"THE ULTIMATE THRILLER WRITER."
—*SUSPENSE MAGAZINE*

**Praise for #1 *New York Times* bestselling author
Brad Thor's *The Last Patriot***

"Stunning."

—*Publishers Weekly*

"Wow, this guy can write."

—*The Atlanta Journal-Constitution*

"A thoroughly researched, high-fueled thrill ride . . . 'National Treasure' meets 'The Bourne Identity.'"

—*The Tampa Tribune*

More acclaim for Brad Thor and Scot Harvath, "the perfect all-American hero for the post–September 11th world" (Nelson DeMille)

Praise for *Near Dark*

"Fast-paced . . . pulse-pounding . . . supremely entertaining. . . . His best ever."

—*The Washington Times*

"If you love thrillers . . . if you've ever read a thriller you enjoyed . . . if you think you ★might★ like a thriller . . . you HAVE to order Brad Thor's *Near Dark*. This might be the single greatest thriller I've covered on *The Real Book Spy*. It's amazing!"

—*The Real Book Spy*

"Not since Ian Fleming rendered James Bond a mere shell of himself in the wake of *From Russia, With Love* has an author pushed an icon to such depths."

—*Providence Journal*

"Brad Thor has mastered the art of the thriller cliffhanger."

—*New York Journal of Books*

"Brad Thor thrills yet again with *Near Dark*."

—*The San Diego Union-Tribune*

Praise for *Backlash*

"As close to perfect as a thriller can be."

—*Providence Journal*

"*Backlash* is a triumph."

—BookReporter.com

"*Backlash* is the best thing Thor has ever written."

—The Real Book Spy

Praise for *Spymaster*

"A modern Cold War 2.0 thriller . . . impossible to put down."

—*National Review*

"Thor convincingly portrays Russia as a reborn Cold War–era evil empire hell-bent on reconquering its former territory."

—*The Washington Post*

"A master of action and pacing, Thor continues channeling the likes of John le Carré in crafting a thinking-man's thriller packed with as much brains as brawn, making *Spymaster* a must-read."

—*Providence Journal*

"A terrific, terrific read."

—KKTX

BRAD THOR

A THRILLER

THE LAST PATRIOT

EMILY BESTLER BOOKS

—

ATRIA

New York   London   Toronto   Sydney   New Delhi

EMILY
BESTLER
BOOKS

ATRIA

An Imprint of Simon & Schuster, Inc.
1230 Avenue of the Americas
New York, NY 10020

Copyright © 2008 by Brad Thor

This Emily Bestler Books/Atria Paperback edition April 2021

For information about special discounts for bulk purchases, please contact Simon & Schuster Special Sales at 1-866-506-1949 or business@simonandschuster.com.

The Simon & Schuster Speakers Bureau can bring authors to your live event. For more information, or to book an event, contact the Simon & Schuster Speakers Bureau at 1-866-248-3049 or visit our website at www.simonspeakers.com.

Manufactured in the United States of America

1 3 5 7 9 10 8 6 4 2

ISBN 978-1-9821-4831-7
ISBN 978-1-4165-8039-3 (ebook)

For Jeff and Jennifer, Jean and Dan—
four of the most courageous people I know

"Let no one of you say that he has acquired the entire Koran, for how does he know that it is all? Much of the Koran has been lost; thus let him say, 'I have acquired of it what is available.' "

—Ibn Umar al-Khattab, 7th-century companion of
Mohammed and 2nd Muslim Caliph

PROLOGUE

Andrew Salam stepped out from behind the bronze statue of Thomas Jefferson and asked, "Are you alone?"

Twenty-three-year-old Nura Khalifa nodded.

Her thick, dark hair spilled over her shoulders, stopping just above her breasts. Beneath her thin jacket, he could make out the curves of her body, the narrowness of her waist. For a moment, he believed he could even smell her perfume, though it was more likely the scent of cherry blossoms blown by a faint breeze across the tidal basin. He shouldn't be meeting her at night and alone like this. It was a mistake.

Actually, the mistake was allowing his lust for her to cloud his judgment. Salam knew better. She was a gorgeous, desirable woman, but she was also his asset. He had recruited her and he was responsible for the tenor of their relationship. No matter how perfect he thought they could be for each other, no matter how badly he wanted to feel, just once, her lips and that body pressed against his as he buried his nose in the nape of her neck and drank in the smell of her, he couldn't crumble. FBI agents controlled their emotions, not the other way around.

Shutting out his desire, Andrew Salam remained professional. "Why did you contact me?"

"Because I needed to see you," said Nura as she moved toward him.

He thought about holding out his hand to stop her. He was afraid he wouldn't be able to control himself if she got any closer. Then he saw the tears that stained her face and, without thinking, opened up his arms.

Nura came to him and he pulled her into his chest. As she sobbed, his head fell to the crown of her head and he allowed his face to brush against her hair. He was playing with fire.

As quickly as he had allowed her to come to him, he knew it was wrong and he gently pushed her away until he was holding her by both shoulders at arm's length. "What happened?"

"My uncle's the target," she stammered.

Salam was stunned. "Are you sure?"

"I think they've already hired the assassin."

"Hold on, Nura. People just don't go out and hire assassins," began Salam, but she interrupted him.

"They said the threat has grown too great and it needs to be dealt with, now."

Salam bent down so he could look into her eyes. "Did they mention your uncle by name?"

"No, but they didn't have to. I *know* he's the target."

"How do you know?"

"They've been asking lots of questions about him and what he's working on. Andrew, we have to do something. We have to find him and warn him. *Please*."

"We will," said Salam as he looked around. "I promise. But first, I need to know everything you've heard, no matter how small."

Nura was trembling.

"How did you get here?" he asked as he removed his coat and draped it over her shoulders.

"I took the Metro, why?"

Though the couple had the memorial all to themselves at this time of night, Salam was uncomfortable about being out in the open. He had a strange feeling that they were being watched. "I'd feel better if we went someplace else. My car is parked nearby. Are you up to taking a walk?"

Nura nodded and Salam put his arm around her as they exited the statue chamber.

While they walked, Nura began to fill him in on what she had learned. Salam listened, but his mind was drifting.

Had he been paying attention to more than just how good she felt pressed up against him, he might have had time to react to the two men who sprung from the shadows.

CHAPTER 1

The Italian Centre for Photoreproduction, Binding, and Restoration of State Archives, also known as the CFLR, was located in an unassuming postmodern office building three blocks from the Tiber River at 14 Via Costanza Baudana Vaccolini. It boasted one of the world's leading archival preservation facilities, as well as a young deputy assistant director named Alessandro Lombardi who was eager to begin his evening.

"Dottore, mi scusi," said Lombardi.

Dr. Marwan Khalifa, a distinguished Koranic scholar in his early sixties with a handsome face and neatly trimmed beard, looked up from the desk he was working at. "Yes, Alessandro?"

The Italian adopted his most charming smile and asked, "Tonight, we finish early?"

Dr. Khalifa laughed and set down his pen. "You have *another* date this evening?"

Lombardi approached and showed the visiting scholar a picture on his mobile phone.

"What happened to the blond woman?"

Lombardi shrugged. "That was last week."

Khalifa picked his pen back up. "I suppose I can be done in an hour."

"An *hour*?" exclaimed Lombardi as he pressed his hands together in mock prayer. "Dottore, if I don't leave now, all of the good tables outside will be gone. Please. When the weather is this nice, Italians are not allowed to work late. It's state policy."

Khalifa knew better. No matter what the weather, there were always people working late in the CFLR building—maybe not in the Research and Preservation department, but there was almost always a light burning somewhere. "If you want to leave your keys, I'll lock up the office when I go."

"And my time card?" asked Lombardi, pressing his luck.

"You get paid for the time you work, my friend."

"*Va bene,*" replied the young man as he fished a set of keys for the department from his pocket and set them on the desk. "I'll see you in the morning."

"Have fun," said Khalifa.

Lombardi flashed him the smile once more and then made his way toward the exit, turning off any unnecessary lights along his way.

Dr. Khalifa's desk was a large drafting-style table, illuminated by two adjustable lamps. His time as well as Lombardi's was being paid for by the Yemeni Antiquities Authority.

In 1972, workers in Yemen had made a startling discovery. Restoring the aging Great Mosque at Sana'a, said to have been one of the first architectural projects of Islam commissioned by the prophet Mohammed himself, the workers uncovered a hidden loft between the mosque's inner and outer roofs. Inside the loft was a mound of parchments and pages of Arabic texts that at some point had been secreted away, and were now melded together through centuries of exposure to rain and dampness. In archeological circles, such a discovery was referred to as a "paper grave."

Cursory examinations suggested that what the grave contained were tens of thousands of fragments from at least a thousand early parchment codices of the Koran.

Access to the full breadth of the find had never been allowed. Bits and pieces had been made available to a handful of scholars over the years, but out of respect for the sanctity of the documents, no one had ever been permitted to study the entire discovery. No one, that is, until Dr. Marwan Khalifa.

Khalifa was one of the world's preeminent Koranic scholars and had spent the majority of his professional career building relationships with the Yemeni Antiquities Authority and politely petitioning it to allow him to review the find. Finally, there was a changing of the guard and the new president of the Antiquities Authority, a significantly younger and more progressive man, invited Khalifa to study the entirety of what the workers at Sana'a had uncovered.

It didn't take long for Khalifa to realize the magnitude of the find.

As Yemen didn't have the proper facilities to preserve and study the fragments and as the Yemeni government was absolutely opposed to Khalifa taking the items back to the United States, an arrangement was made for the complete contents of the grave to be transferred to the CFLR in Rome where they could be preserved and studied before being returned to Yemen.

With the blessing of the new Antiquities Authority president, Khalifa oversaw the entire process, including the technical side which included such things as edge detection, document degradation, global and adaptive thresholding, color clustering, and image processing.

His anticipation grew as each scrap was preserved and he was able to begin assembling the pieces of the puzzle. A significant percentage of the parchments dated back to the seventh and eighth centuries—Islam's first two centuries. Khalifa was handling pieces of the earliest Korans known to mankind.

A billion-and-a-half Muslims worldwide believed that the Koran they worshiped today was the perfect, inviolate word of God—an *exact* word-for-word, perfect copy of the original book as it exists in Paradise and just as it was transmitted, without a single error, by Allah to the prophet Mohammed through the Angel Gabriel.

As a textual historian, Khalifa was fascinated by the inconsistencies. As a moderate Muslim who loved his religion, but believed deeply that it was in need of reform, he was overjoyed. The fact that he had found, and was continuing to find, aberrations that differed from Islamic dogma meant that the case could finally be made for the Koran to be reexamined in a historical framework.

He had always believed that the Koran had been written by man, not God. If such a thing could be proven, Muslims around the world would be able to reexamine their faith with a modern, twenty-first-century perspective, rather than the outdated, unenlightened perspective of seventh-century Arabia. And now it seemed that he had just the proof he needed.

It was such a powerful discovery that Khalifa could barely sleep at night. It dovetailed so well with another project his colleague Anthony Nichols was working on back in America, that he felt as if Allah himself was steering his research, that this was His divine will.

All Khalifa could think about when he wasn't at work was getting back to the CFLR facility each day to further investigate the fragments.

Though on evenings like this Khalifa missed Lombardi's companionship as well as his expertise with the technical equipment, the truth was that he hardly noticed when the young Italian was gone. In fact, he was often so engrossed that he barely noticed Lombardi even when he was standing at the desk right in front of him.

Turning to the voluminous collection of information he had stored on his rugged Toughbook laptop, Khalifa pulled up one of the thirty-two thousand images the CFLR had already digitally archived. While he could have crossed the room and retrieved the fragment itself, he often found it unnecessary as accessing the digital images was much easier.

Khalifa was working on lining up six slivers of text written in the Hijazzi script when a shadow fell across his drafting table. "What did you forget this time, Alessandro?" the scholar asked without looking up.

"I didn't forget anything," responded a deep, unfamiliar voice. "It is you who have forgotten."

Dr. Khalifa looked up and saw a man in a long, black soutane with a white collar. It was a common sight throughout Rome, particularly near the Vatican. But even though the CFLR did a certain amount of work with the Holy See, Khalifa had never seen a priest inside the building. "Who are you?"

"That's not important," replied the priest as he moved closer. "I would rather discuss your faith."

"You must be confused, Father," said Khalifa as he sat up in his chair. "I'm not a Catholic. I'm Muslim."

"I know," said the priest softly. "That's why I'm here."

In an explosion of black cloth, the priest was suddenly behind Khalifa. One of his large, rough hands cupped the scholar's chin while the other gripped the side of his head.

With a powerful snap, the priest broke the scholar's neck.

He stood there for a moment, the corpse clutched tightly, almost lovingly to his chest, then stepped back and let go.

Khalifa's head slammed against the table before coming to rest beneath it.

The priest dragged the body across the floor and positioned it at the bottom of a set of stairs which led up to a small archival library. From there, it took only moments to set the fire.

•   •   •

Two hours later, having showered and changed, the assassin sat in his hotel room and studied Khalifa's laptop. Connecting to a remote server, he had the Koranic scholar's password program cracked within fifteen minutes. From there, one e-mail confirmed everything he needed to know.

> Marwan,
>
> Finally, good news! It appears we have located the book. A dealer named René Bertrand is bringing it to market in Paris at the Antiquarian Book Fair. I will be meeting him there to negotiate the purchase. As you know, my funding is limited, but I have faith that barring an all-out bidding war, the book will be ours!

As planned, I will see you next Monday at 9:00 a.m. in the Middle
Eastern Reading Room of the Library of Congress—although
now we'll finally have the book and can begin deciphering the
location of the final revelation!

Anthony

The assassin had had Khalifa under surveillance long enough to
know who the sender was and what he was referring to. It was a
parallel and potentially more damaging project, which up until this
point had appeared stalled. Obviously, things had changed—and not
for the better.

The assassin shut down the laptop and spent the next several hours
pondering the implication of what he had learned. He then started
formulating a plan. When all of the angles had been considered and
tested in his mind, he reactivated the computer.

Attaching the relevant e-mails between Khalifa and Anthony
Nichols, he composed his report and delivered his assessment to his
superiors.

Their response came back twenty minutes later, hidden in the draft
folder of the e-mail account they shared. The assassin had been cleared
for the Paris operation.

At the end of the message, his superiors instructed that funds would
be transferred to Paris and all necessary arrangements would be made.
They then congratulated him on his success in Rome.

The assassin deleted the message from the draft folder and logged
off. After reciting his prayers, he disconnected his phone and hung
the Do Not Disturb sign on his door. He would be leaving early in
the morning and needed to rest. The next several days were going to
be very busy. His superiors were in agreement that the prophet
Mohammed's lost revelation needed to stay lost—forever.

CHAPTER 2

T hirty-seven-year-old American Scot Harvath studied the amazing woman sitting at the café table next to him. Her blond hair had grown back and came to just below her ears.

"We need to make a decision," she said.

There it was—the topic he'd been trying to avoid since killing the man who had shot her nine months ago.

"I just want to make sure that you're fully—" he began, his voice trailing off.

"Recovered?" she asked, finishing his sentence for him.

Harvath nodded.

"Scot, this stopped being about my recovery the minute we left the United States. I'm fine. Not one hundred percent, but as close as I'm probably going to get."

"You don't know that for sure."

Tracy Hastings smiled. Prior to being targeted by an assassin bent on revenge against Harvath, Tracy had been a Naval Explosive Ordnance Disposal technician who had lost one of her luminescent, pale blue eyes when an IED she was defusing detonated prematurely. Though her face had undergone significant scarring, the plastic surgeons had done a remarkable job of minimizing the visible damage.

Hastings had always been in great shape, but after the accident she had thrown herself into her fitness routine. She had the most perfectly sculpted body of any woman Harvath had ever known. Self-conscious about her disfigurement and the pale blue eye given to her by her surgeons as a replacement, Tracy had been fond of joking that she had both a body to die for and the face to protect it.

It was a joke that Harvath had worked hard to wean from her repertoire. She was the most beautiful woman he had ever met, and slowly his hard work had paid off. The closer they grew and the safer Tracy felt with him, the less her self-deprecating humor seemed necessary.

The same could be said for Harvath. Ten years Tracy's senior, he had used his sarcasm largely to keep the world at bay. Now, he used it to make her laugh.

With his handsome, rugged face, sandy brown hair, bright blue eyes, and muscular five-foot-ten frame, they made a striking couple.

"You want to know what I think?" she asked. "I think this is more about your recovery than mine. And that's okay."

Harvath started to object, but Tracy put her hand atop his and said, "We need to put what happened behind us and get on with our lives."

They had been together less than a year, but she knew him better than anyone ever had. She knew he'd never be happy living an ordinary life. So much of who he was and how he saw himself came from what he did. He needed to get back to it, even if that meant her nudging him toward it.

Harvath slid his hand out from under hers. He couldn't put what had happened behind him. No matter how hard he tried, he couldn't shake the picture of finding Tracy in a pool of blood with a bullet in the back of her head, or the memory of the president who had stood in his way while the person responsible continued to target those closest to Harvath. A couple of friends suggested that maybe he was suffering from PTSD, but in the words of an Army colonel he once cross-trained with, Harvath didn't get PTSD, he *gave* it.

"We can't be gypsies forever," Tracy insisted. "Our lives have been on hold long enough. We need to get back to the real world, and you need to think about going back to work."

"There's about as much chance of me going back to work for Jack

Rutledge as there is of me going to work for a terrorist organization. I'm done," he said.

A Navy SEAL who had joined the president's Secret Service detail in an effort to help improve the White House's ability to stave off and respond to terrorist attacks, Harvath had grown to become the president's number one covert counterterrorism operative and was exceptional at what he did.

So exceptional, in fact, that the president had created a top-secret antiterrorism effort known as the Apex Project specifically for him. Its goal was to level the playing field with international terrorists who sought to strike Americans and American interests at home and abroad. That goal was achieved through one simple mandate—as long as the terrorists refused to play by any rules, Harvath wouldn't be expected to either.

The Apex Project was buried in a little-known branch of DHS known as the Office of International Investigative Assistance, or OIIA for short. The OIIA's overt mission was to assist foreign police, military, and intelligence agencies in helping to prevent terrorist attacks. In that sense, Harvath's mission was in step with the official OIIA mandate. In reality, he was a very secretive dog of war enlisted post-9/11 to be unleashed by the president upon the enemies of the United States anywhere, anytime, with anything he needed to get the job done.

But that part of Harvath's life was over. It had taken him years to realize that his counterterrorism career was incompatible with what he really wanted—a family and someone to come home to; someone to share his life with.

Starting relationships had never been his problem. It was keeping them going that he never could get right. Tracy Hastings was the best thing to ever happen to him and he had no intention of letting her go. For the first time in he couldn't remember how long, Scot Harvath was truly happy.

"We don't have to go back right away," said Tracy, interrupting his thoughts. "We can wait until November, after the elections. There'll be Christmas and then the inauguration in January. Unless the Constitution has been rewritten and Rutledge is elected to a third term, you'll be dealing with a completely new president."

Harvath was about to respond when he looked out across the street and noticed a well-dressed Arab man remove a "Slim Jim" from beneath his blazer.

Popping the lock on a faded blue Peugeot, the man climbed in, shut the door, and disappeared beneath the window line.

He didn't know why, but something inside Harvath told him this was more than just a car theft.

CHAPTER 3

Car thefts probably happened all the time in Paris, but Harvath had never seen one. He had also never seen such a smartly dressed criminal before.

As much as he was trying to escape his old life, his instincts were still attuned to the world around him. Just because a sheepdog had grown tired of fighting off wolves, it didn't mean that wolves had grown tired of preying on sheep.

"What is it?" asked Tracy, as she followed his gaze across the street.

"Somebody just broke into that Peugeot."

They both listened as the car's engine came to life and the thief's head popped back up from beneath the dashboard. Instead of driving away, though, the man just sat there.

"What's he doing?" she asked.

Harvath was about to answer when he saw a silver Mercedes sedan approach. The thief must have seen it too because he immediately applied his blinker and pulled away from the curb, leaving the parking space to the Mercedes.

Harvath had spent enough time in cities like New York to know the lengths people would go to for a parking space, but stealing a car? This was ridiculous.

As the Peugeot slipped away, the Mercedes took its place.

No sooner was it parked than another well-dressed Arab opened the door, looked both ways up and down the street, climbed out, and walked away.

Tracy looked at Harvath again. "What the hell was that all about?"

"I've got no idea," he replied. "I didn't see that guy arm his car alarm, though. Did you?"

Tracy shook her head.

For a second or two, Harvath studied the Mercedes. Then he removed a twenty-euro note, laid it on the table, and said, "Let's go."

Tracy didn't argue.

On the sidewalk, Harvath took her arm and picked up the pace.

"Shouldn't we do something?" Tracy asked.

"We are," responded Harvath. "We're leaving."

"I mean, report what we saw."

Since retiring from the counterterrorism arena, Harvath had kept an exceptionally low profile. He loathed bureaucracies more than ever, and the Paris police had one of the worst.

Nevertheless, Tracy was right. What they had just seen didn't make sense. It could, of course, be nothing, but Harvath doubted it. "The next phone we see, we'll call it in," he said.

In front of them, the door of a small bookshop opened and a man in his early fifties with a gray beard, wavy salt-and-pepper hair, and a blue blazer hurriedly stepped outside. Nearly bumping into Harvath and Tracy, the man excused himself in French and continued off in the direction of the café.

Normally, Harvath wouldn't have given it another thought, but then he caught sight of the driver of the Mercedes standing near the corner. He watched as the man appeared to study a photograph and then raised a cell phone to his ear.

The Arab spoke no more than two words. When he nodded and hung up the phone, Harvath suddenly realized what was going on.

Letting go of Tracy's arm, he spun and took off after the man in the blazer, praying he could reach him in time.

CHAPTER 4

Harvath landed on top of the man just as the Mercedes in front of the café exploded.

Acrid, black smoke blotted out the sky as red-hot shrapnel rained down upon the street.

The violence of the explosion made Harvath's entire body feel as if it had been crushed in a vise. The air was forced from his lungs and his ears rang with such piercing intensity he felt for sure they had to be bleeding.

Reaching to the side of his head, he touched one and then the other. Thankfully, there was no blood. He did a quick assessment of the rest of himself and when he was certain he was okay, he turned his attention to the man in the blue blazer.

Supporting his head, Harvath carefully rolled him onto his back, making sure not to move his neck. He was bleeding from a laceration near his scalp. Removing the man's handkerchief from his breast pocket, Harvath used it to apply light pressure to the wound. He knew he needed to be careful not to exacerbate any spinal injury.

"Stay still," Harvath said in French. "Don't move. Are you hurt anywhere else?"

The man stared at him blankly.

Harvath was about to repeat the question when Tracy raced over to him. "Are you okay?" she asked, out of breath.

"I'm not hurt," replied Harvath, who then motioned at the man in the blazer and said, "We need to immobilize his neck."

Tracy knew he was right, but her EOD training had kicked in. "There could be a secondary device. We need to get away from this area before first responders arrive."

Harvath was well aware of terrorists waiting for help to arrive at the scene of a bombing before setting off another, even deadlier explosion. "He needs an ambulance, though."

"No," replied the man suddenly in English. "No ambulance. No hospital." He was trying to get to his feet.

"Stay still," ordered Harvath.

"Scot, we need to get out of here, now," insisted Tracy.

Harvath looked down at the man in the blue blazer and made a decision. Grabbing his upper arm, he helped him stand.

No sooner was he up than his knees buckled. Harvath caught him around the waist and with Tracy's help, kept him upright and began to move him away from the flaming café toward the corner. All the while, Harvath kept his eyes open for any of the Arabs who'd been involved in the bombing. If they were smart, they'd be long gone, but Harvath had a very bad feeling there was more to all of this than met the eye.

There were numerous dead and wounded scattered along the sidewalk, as well as inside what was left of the café. Though Harvath and Tracy both wanted to help the others, they knew they couldn't stop.

Making it to the end of the street, they turned the corner and could hear the wail of klaxons as first responders raced toward the scene.

Harvath and Tracy made their way halfway up the block and found a place to set the injured man down. He was shell-shocked with his eyes semi-glazed over and still bleeding from the gash above his forehead.

After easing him onto a set of weathered stone steps and making sure he wasn't going to tip over, Harvath and Tracy left him staring into the street as they moved far enough away so they could talk without being overheard.

"How'd you know that bomb was about to go off?" asked Tracy.

"The Arab who dropped the Mercedes was standing across the street. When the guy in the blue blazer passed us, the Arab looked at some sort of photo and then dialed his cell phone."

"So it wasn't a random attack. They had him under surveillance. He was the target."

Harvath nodded.

"But why? Who is he?"

"That's what I want to know," replied Harvath as he produced the wallet he had taken from the man.

"You picked his pocket?"

"Call it professional curiosity," he said as he withdrew the man's driver's license. "Evidently, our bombing target is fifty-three-year-old Anthony Nichols of Charlottesville, Virginia."

Tracy looked over her shoulder to make sure Nichols couldn't see what they were doing. *"Virginia?* What is he, CIA?"

"According to his business card he is Professor Emeritus and Resident Scholar in the Corcoran Department of History at the University of Virginia."

"Which could mean anything."

Harvath kept looking through the man's wallet. It contained everything one would expect it to—credit cards, various membership cards, a small paper envelope with a hotel key card and room number written on it, as well as a smattering of other people's battered business cards.

Harvath was just about to give up when he recognized something about the last card. Removing it from the stack, he studied it once more. It was for an insurance agent with an address in Washington, D.C., but that wasn't the important part. What had caught Harvath's attention was the phone number.

He had seen those ten digits before. In fact, he had them committed to memory. "I know this phone number," he said.

"What's it for?" asked Tracy.

"A private voice mail box belonging to the president of the United States."

And with that Harvath knew that whoever Anthony Nichols was, he was a lot more than a professor of history at UVA.

He was about to say as much to Tracy when she looked over at where Nichols had been sitting and said, "He's gone."

CHAPTER 5

WASHINGTON, D.C.

At just over six feet tall with dark hair, dark eyes, and a strong jawline, thirty-five-year-old Aydin Ozbek looked more like someone from the pages of *Esquire* magazine than one of the Central Intelligence Agency's most proficient field operatives.

A second generation American of Turkish descent, Ozbek had grown up in a tony suburb of Chicago, where he was a high school wrestler of considerable note. With an intense intellect and outstanding SAT scores, he attended the University of Iowa on a full academic scholarship and wrestled all four years; attaining repeated all-American status as his team took three Big Ten titles.

Wanting to serve his country after college, Ozbek, or "Oz" as his friends called him, joined the United States Army with his sights set on the Fifth Special Forces Group. He excelled at everything the Army threw at him and broke several records in Ranger School.

Then came the Special Forces Selection and Qualification courses, which were some of the most physically grueling and mentally demanding experiences he had ever undertaken. Being awarded the Green Beret was one of the greatest accomplishments of Ozbek's life.

Prior to 9/11, he had served as a medical sergeant, known as an 18 Delta, under a president and national defense strategy that didn't allow the Special Forces community to carry out the kinds of missions they had been trained for. In short, they didn't see much action.

With his Special Forces, medical, and Arabic training, it wasn't hard for Ozbek to find exciting employment elsewhere. He worked extensively for the State Department, operating out of embassies around the world, and even did a short stint with storied U.S. operative Painter Crowe and his elite Sigma Force unit before landing at the CIA with the National Clandestine Service.

The mission statement of the NCS, formerly known as the CIA's Directorate of Operations, was to coordinate human intelligence, known as HUMINT, between the CIA and other agencies like the FBI, DIA, DSS, INSCOM, Marine Corps Intelligence Activity, and the Office of Naval Intelligence.

In addition to eliminating turf battles with the FBI, State Department, and Department of Defense, the NCS's mission included conducting covert operations and recruiting foreign agents. The NCS oversaw a myriad of units for political, economic, and paramilitary covert action. It also housed a group responsible for counterterrorism tasks known as the Special Activities Division.

Special Activities was run by and composed of former Special Operations soldiers highly trained in weaponry, escape and evasion, covert transportation of men and materials, guerrilla warfare, explosive ordnance, counterinsurgency, and counterintelligence.

This was the area of the Central Intelligence Agency that Aydin Ozbek called home. His office was in the heart of a highly classified NCS/Special Activities program known as the *Dead Poets Society*. Its focus was the capture or termination of rogue intelligence officers.

If an American or allied intelligence officer went freelance or went missing, especially if they were in possession of information critical to the interests of the United States, it was Ozbek's job first to find out why. Had they been captured? Had they gone rogue?

If the operative in question had in fact been captured, his or her dossier was turned over to a Special Activities "recovery" unit. If it was determined that the operative had gone rogue, Ozbek's team then created two folders—one blue, one black.

Placed in the blue folder was a full operational blueprint for locating the target and bringing him or her back to the United States, or another suitable facility overseas, for interrogation and an assessment of the damage they had or may have caused.

The black folder included plans for locating and terminating the target.

Both folders contained suggestions for damage control and additional mop-up operations, which sometimes called for elimination of persons the rogue intelligence officer had been in contact with.

It wasn't a game. Ozbek didn't like killing people. But sometimes it was necessary.

Stepping off the elevator on the fourth floor of CIA headquarters in Langley, Virginia, Ozbek had almost made it to his office when he was spotted by his teammate, Steve Rasmussen, a five-foot-eleven wiseass in his late twenties with red hair and blue eyes.

"Well, look who's finally here," chirped Rasmussen.

Ozbek didn't feel like getting into it with him. His fifteen-year-old Labrador, Shelby, had cancer. She had been up most of the night in pain. Her medication wasn't working anymore. Even upping the dosage hadn't helped, so Oz woke his vet and convinced the man to meet them at his office first thing in the morning.

Shelby meant the world to Ozbek. She was the only woman in his life who didn't complain about the insane hours he kept. For the time being, the vet was holding her for observation, but Oz knew he was going to have to start facing the inevitability that she would need to be put down soon. Rasmussen wasn't a dog person, and Oz doubted he would understand.

"Actually," said Ozbek as he brushed past his colleague and stepped into his office, "early mornings seem to be the only time your wife and I can be alone anymore."

Rasmussen followed him in and sat down on the couch. "That's not true, Oz. If you came by on Saturdays, you could have the whole day together and I could get some golf in. We'd all be winners."

Their status as CIA operatives notwithstanding, if Patricia Rasmussen heard either of them talking like this, she'd kick both their asses. "What's up?" asked Ozbek, changing the subject.

Steve Rasmussen was silent for a moment and then dropped a black file folder on the coffee table. "Someone from the Transept program needs to be dealt with."

CHAPTER 6

O zbek walked over and picked up the file. The ultra-secret Transept program was responsible for producing the most proficient killers the Central Intelligence Agency had on its payroll. And, as the American government and the CIA didn't condone assassination, technically the Transept program didn't exist.

"Selleck wants you on this personally," said Rasmussen, picking up the intricate wooden puzzle Ozbek kept on his table.

The NCS Director. Ozbek raised his eyebrows as he perused the file. "Why me?"

"Because it's complicated."

"Obviously, but complicated how?"

"Sunday night there was a murder at the Jefferson Memorial," said Rasmussen.

Ozbek finished scanning the file and handed it back to his colleague. "And?"

"Somebody whacked an employee of the Foundation on American Islamic Relations. Are you familiar with them?"

Ozbek was. The Saudi-funded Foundation on American Islamic Relations, or FAIR as it was ironically known, was one of the biggest Islamist front organizations in the United States. It had offices across the country with representatives who rushed to the microphones any time a Muslim was accused of anything. They were knee-jerk reactionaries who trotted out the dreaded Islamophobia slur before knowing any of the facts of a case.

Muslims pulled over with pipe bombs in their trunk? Those are just fireworks and the law enforcement officer responsible is nothing more than a bigoted Islamophobe.

Muslim imam airline passengers praying loudly right at the gate, deriding America in Arabic, switching seats to configurations similar to the 9/11 hijackers, and asking for seat belt extenders that could be used as weapons although they are not overweight and simply leaving them at their feet? These poor men are guilty of nothing more than flying while Muslim. And FAIR will help coordinate the imams' lawsuits against the Islamophobic passengers who were unnecessarily frightened and reported the men's completely normal activity to the flight crew.

FAIR's efforts had had a chilling effect across the country. The FBI was openly attacked for publishing pictures of Middle Eastern men wanted in connection with unusual surveillance of ferry boats in Washington State. The cowardly *Chico Enterprise Record* newspaper refused to publish any description further than the ages of numerous men who were actively surveilling fire stations across northern California with cameras, video cams, and sketch books. When asked by firemen what the hell they were doing, the Middle Eastern men fled in waiting vehicles.

As far as Ozbek was concerned, there was nothing "American" about the Foundation on American Islamic Relations and the word should be stripped from their name. They were an Islamic supremacist organization pure and simple who wanted to see the American government overthrown and replaced with an Islamic one governed by sharia law. They made him, as well as the overwhelming majority of responsible, law-abiding Muslims in America, sick.

What's more, they were entirely too well connected in Washington. Though Ozbek couldn't prove it, he was certain that FAIR's chairman, Abdul Waleed, had been strategic in one of the most egregious scandals to come out of the Pentagon in decades.

The Defense Department's sole advisor on Islamic law and Islamic extremism had been recently terminated because a high-ranking Pentagon official, who also happened to be Muslim, found his opinions too critical of Islam. It was like firing the government's only advisor on Nazism right in the middle of World War II, or sacking its lone Communism advisor in the middle of the Cold War, just because a German or Russian staff member was upset that the advisor wouldn't tone down his opinions of the enemy and what drove them.

Ozbek had seen FAIR's chairman photographed with the Muslim Pentagon official, Imad Ramadan, too many times not to believe that the pink-slipping of the Islamic law expert didn't in some dark way bear FAIR's fingerprints.

The entire event was insane, even for the PC quagmire that was Washington politics.

But be that as it may, Ozbek didn't see what FAIR or a murder at the Jefferson Memorial had to do with the Special Activities Division. "What's all this got to do with the CIA and the Transept program?" he asked.

"This is where it gets complicated," replied Rasmussen. "First of all, the suspect arrested at the scene, an Andrew Salam, claims he didn't do it. He says he was framed."

Ozbek rolled his eyes.

Rasmussen set the puzzle down and raised his palms. "I know. I know. But listen to this. He claims he's a NOC for the FBI."

NOC, pronounced *knock,* was an espionage term largely used by the CIA that stood for *non official cover.* It designated a covert operative who had no official ties to the government he or she served. The problem was that the FBI didn't use NOCs.

"Let me guess," said Ozbek. "The FBI disavows any knowledge of this guy?"

"According to them, Andrew Salam has never had any connection to the Bureau whatsoever."

"Maybe he's making it all up. He wouldn't be the first law enforcement impersonator who got caught. Maybe the guy's delusional."

"I don't know," said Rasmussen. "He interned in the Near Eastern section of the Library of Congress and graduated top of his class at the Georgetown Center for Arabic Studies."

Ozbek knew Georgetown's Arabic Studies Program. It was a prime recruiting pool for many of the intelligence agencies, particularly the CIA, but that didn't mean this guy wasn't unbalanced. "Fast-forward to where Transept plays into this," he said.

"Salam claims he has been running an FBI-sanctioned operation to infiltrate and develop intelligence assets in radical mosques and Islamist groups across the country.

"One of the groups he infiltrated was the Foundation on American Islamic Relations. He had turned an employee inside the organization and was meeting with her at the Jefferson Memorial."

"Where she wound up dead," said Ozbek.

"He claims he and his 'asset' were attacked," replied Rasmussen.

"And he survived."

"He says that when the attackers saw Park Police approaching, they bolted before they could finish him off."

"Lucky for him. Did he get a look at them?"

Rasmussen shook his head. "They were supposedly wearing masks."

"What about CCTV footage? The Park Police have cameras at the Jefferson Memorial."

"They were down at the time the crime occurred. They've been 'looking into it.'"

Ozbek was getting more interested. "Any romantic history between him and the victim?"

"Investigators are looking into that too."

"What else do you have?"

"Park Police are confident that they caught him *in flagrante delicto*—blood on his hands, clothes, everywhere," said Rasmussen. "Salam says he was trying to save the victim's life."

"Was there a weapon?"

"A knife, but it was wiped clean. No prints. The D.C. cops have been sweating him since he was brought in. He's been shut up tighter than a clam and just when they thought he was about to break, that's when the NOC story surfaced."

"What was his alleged asset meeting with him to discuss?" asked Ozbek.

"According to Salam, she had stumbled across something pretty substantial. Supposedly, FAIR had hired an assassin."

"And this assassin graduated from the Transept program?"

Rasmussen nodded. "Whether this guy is full of shit or not, he did mention Transept, and you know as well as I do what a closely guarded secret that program is. He couldn't have made that up."

"No, he couldn't. Obviously somebody has been talking about things that they shouldn't."

"I'll tell you something else. The D.C. cops might not be overly impressed with this guy, but he really talks like an intelligence operative."

Ozbek looked at his colleague. "Maybe he actually thought he was working for the FBI."

Rasmussen nodded again. "I spoke with our liaisons at the Bureau and a contact I have with D.C. Metro police who are heading the investigation. Because the Agency has come up in the interrogation and they can't make heads or tails out of this guy, they're prepared to let us have access to him."

"When?"

"As soon as we want."

"All right," replied Ozbek. "Let's pull everything we have on the Foundation on American Islamic Relations, Andrew Salam, and especially the Transept program."

Rasmussen picked up the folder. "That's fine, but as far as the FBI,

D.C. Metro, and this Salam guy are concerned, we've never heard of
the Transept program. That's the word from on high."

CHAPTER 7

A ghost in his mid-forties wearing tan corduroys and a navy
blue cashmere sweater sat on a narrow green bench admiring the medieval ruins of the Parc Monceau. He hadn't been
seen by anyone from his past life in over five years.

His brown hair was medium in length and his wire-rimmed glasses
framed a rather unremarkable face punctuated by two sharp green
eyes. When standing in his brown leather shoes he came to just over
five feet nine inches tall. He had the trim frame of an endurance
athlete.

In a discreet pocket inside the man's Barbour jacket was a passport
that bore a false name. It was as good a name as any—no better or
worse than any of the names he had assumed throughout his career.
Distinctly Anglo-Saxon, like the name he had used for his assignment
in Rome, it suited him, as had his true Christian name, Matthew
Dodd.

He had renounced that name when he embraced Islam. It wasn't
hard to let go. With all of the different aliases he had assumed over his
career, it was difficult to remember who he really was anyway.

The only things that had ever grounded him and given him a true
sense of purpose were his beautiful wife and his little boy, but they
had been gone from his life for almost ten years now; killed in a car
accident by a spoiled, drunken teenaged girl in her brand-new BMW
while he had been away on an assignment.

His handlers hadn't even had the decency to tell him when it happened. They had waited until the operation was complete and then informed him—a full month after his wife and son had been buried. One week later, the teenaged girl who took his family from him walked out of the substance abuse program her well-connected family's slick lawyer had arranged with the court and picked her life back up where it had left off. The girl had never spent a single day in jail. It was not only wrong, it was immoral.

When he found out, the assassin had felt as if hooks on long chains had been sunk into his skin, tearing the flesh from his body in sheets. After the pain had come a disturbing numbness. In a culture of gray where anything could be justified, rationalized, or spun to mean just the opposite, he longed for a line to be drawn between black and white. More than that, he longed for someone to explain how all of this could have been allowed to happen. Some placed the blame on the driver's parents, some on her peers, and others still on society in general. Dodd just slipped deeper into depression.

His employers put him on medical leave and then, when they needed him back, shuttled him through a battery of tests, rated him ready to return to the field, and dispatched him once again to do what they needed him to do.

He had drowned his sorrows in booze and blood, taking chances and assignments no one else wanted to take. There was nothing else for him in his life anymore. Or so he had thought.

He could still remember the day he became a Muslim. That's when he had chosen for himself the Muslim name of Majd al-Din—*Glory of the Faith*. It was a good name and one that suited his new life.

Through the bitter anguish of losing his wife and son, Dodd had realized that the Muslims had something in overwhelming supply that his countrymen were very quickly running out of. That something was faith. More than that, Muslims abided by a clear moral code that delineated the difference between what was right and what was wrong.

Up until the 1950s, American children yearned for adulthood. When their time came to be adults they stepped into the role proudly, leaving childhood behind and taking up the mantles of responsibility, honor, and dignity. They embraced and championed the ideals of those who came before them while valiantly tackling new ideas and problems that their families, communities, and nation faced. Those days were long gone.

Americans now shunned adulthood, preferring to remain in a state of perpetual adolescence. By failing to move forward with grace and dignity, they left a gaping hole in American society. They treated relationships like disposable lighters, tossing marriages away when they ran out of gas. Children were left without families, and even worse, they were left without adults who could be role models of responsible behavior.

With this lack of willingness to step forward and embrace adulthood, the nation had lost sight of its core values and ideals. In its place had morphed an *every man and woman for himself* mentality in which materialism was placed before spirituality and submission to God.

Dodd saw it as a lack of respect and a lack of order in American society and therein lay the appeal of Islam for him. Skeptical at first, the more he witnessed the lives of the devout Muslims he came in contact with in Afghanistan, Pakistan, and the other places his assignments took him, the more he realized Islam was the answer he'd been seeking.

Islam provided honor. It provided a code by which to live with dignity and in peace. It wasn't the problem—it was the solution, and it was the only thing that would save the United States.

CHAPTER 8

To hasten America's salvation, Dodd had given himself wholly to Allah. He viewed himself as a precision instrument which would be guided as Allah saw fit.

That guidance arrived quickly in the form of a soft-spoken imam in Baltimore where Dodd kept a small apartment. The imam had been suspicious at first, but when he realized that Dodd had truly embraced Islam he looked into Dodd's background and then introduced him to another imam he thought Dodd could be useful in serving.

The imam's name was Mahmood Omar. Dodd had never met the man before, but he was immediately impressed. Not only did the Saudi-born, forty-something cleric's penetrating eyes and large stature contribute to a commanding presence, but he was well schooled in the ways of the West and America in particular.

Dodd was determined to put his unique skill set to work for the betterment of America, and Sheik Omar was pleased to have such an experienced warrior fighting on behalf of Islam.

Omar was a facilitator of international jihad and started Dodd out on small operations, always outside the United States. As both his confidence and trust in Dodd grew, so too did the scope of the assignments he was being sent on. More often than not, Dodd was carrying out sanctions on behalf of Omar's colleagues and benefactors in the Middle East.

It was tedious work that Dodd began to chafe under. After a time, he could see no benefit to America in any of it, nor could he fathom how it might be advancing the Muslim cause in the U.S. As corrupt and decadent as it was, Dodd still loved America and he missed it. He wanted to be back home. He was tiring of death and wanted to get on with living. Then the Khalifa assignments had come up.

Omar had assigned him to Rome and used two other men for Washington. Though Dodd had consulted on the assignment at the Jefferson Memorial, it had not worked out as planned.

The Park Police had apparently altered their patrol patterns. Omar's men should have had twenty minutes, but another patrol unit had been right on their heels.

If the men had been allowed to take Nura and Salam at one of their homes as Dodd had suggested, they wouldn't be having this problem right now. Sheik Omar, though, had had other plans. His greatest flaw was that he liked to make statements.

When Omar discovered that Nura and Salam already had a rendezvous planned at the Jefferson Memorial, he decided that would be the perfect place to kill them. He saw it as laden with ironic symbolism.

In reality, it had been laden with incredible complications, not the least of which was the security camera system. Salam had survived and was in police custody, but Omar didn't seem to be losing any sleep over it. Dodd could only trust that the evidence they had planted would be enough to convict Salam for Nura's murder.

The car bombing outside the café in Paris had also been overkill, just as Dodd had said it would be. Omar still didn't care. Once he set his mind on a course of action, he stuck with it regardless.

Killing Anthony Nichols up close in his hotel room would have made more sense. It would have been quiet and efficient—the way these things should be done. But Omar didn't want quiet and efficient. He wanted to send another message that would be heard loud and clear. It was loud and it was clear, all right. The problem was that car bombs were not Dodd's area of expertise.

Dodd was an assassin, not a bomber. And despite Omar's justifications backed up with extensive recitations from the Koran and Hadith that non-Muslims could never be considered innocents, Dodd disagreed. He didn't like killing civilians. What's more, the bombing was excessive. It was using a sledgehammer when all that was needed was a flyswatter.

To pull off the bombing, Omar had reached out to people he knew who had contacts in France. It was too many degrees of separation and had all been one big clusterfuck from the get-go.

Omar's local talent had been able to get only half the amount of explosives they needed. When they finally were ready to pull off the attack, the trigger man had gotten jumpy and had blown the Mercedes prematurely. As a result, Nichols had survived.

The entire operation had been a waste of time and money and now Nichols was spooked instead of dead.

But no matter how incompetent the team had been, it was still Dodd's assignment and he took responsibility for it. He was nothing if not a man of honor.

The first few drops of an approaching rain began to fall and Dodd turned up the collar of his coat. He was in the process of considering moving to one of the cafés along the edge of the Parc Monceau when the prepaid cell phone he'd purchased that morning vibrated.

"Yes," he said as he activated the call.

The deep voice of Sheik Omar resonated from the phone as if he were sitting right there on the bench next to him. "How were the lines at Versailles today?" he asked.

"Not as bad as the Louvre," replied Dodd.

With the authentication between them complete, Omar inquired, "Did the flight take off on time?"

"No," replied Dodd. "It actually took off early. *Before* all the passengers were able to board."

Though the cleric said nothing, Dodd could feel Omar's anger building from almost four thousand miles away back in America. "Tell me what happened," the sheik finally said.

Dodd filled him in as ambiguously as he could, ever leery of the U.S. government's eavesdropping systems. Both were on chat-n-chuck, throwaway phones purchased strictly for this conversation, but if the NSA had his voiceprint and the ECHELON system registered a match, it wouldn't do them much good.

"We need to make sure any passengers that missed the flight are rebooked as soon as possible," stated Omar.

"Same airline as before, or can this be a private charter, as I originally suggested?"

It took a moment, but the cleric relented. "Private charter will be fine. Just make sure that our passengers get to their destination."

"Understood," stated Dodd. "Anything else?"

"Yes," replied the sheik, almost as an afterthought. "You mentioned another man who was rushing for the plane as it left the gate."

"I did. He had a woman with him. Do I need to be concerned about them?"

"I'm not sure," said Omar. "I'll leave it to your discretion, but should you happen to see them again, I'd like them treated as VIPs."

"Understood," replied Dodd as he stood up from the bench. "I'll make sure they're booked on the next flight as well."

He ended the call and removed the phone's battery and SIM card, then broke the phone into several pieces, all of which he dumped into a series of storm drains as he exited the Parc Monceau.

Dodd had his orders. He needed to find Anthony Nichols and finish the job. If the man and woman from outside the café got in his way again, he would kill them too. And this time, he would do it his way.

CHAPTER 9

Harvath glanced at his Kobold Chronograph. He and Tracy had spent twenty minutes searching for Anthony Nichols. They had no way of knowing if he'd walked away of his own accord or if he'd stumbled off as a result of his head wound and was bleeding in a doorway somewhere. Harvath, though, had a hard time believing it was the latter.

He stopped walking and turned to Tracy. "This guy obviously doesn't want to be found. I'm inclined to support his wish."

"Then what do we do now?"

Harvath could see a Metro stop at the end of the block and he pointed at it as it began to rain. "How about onion soup? I'll take you to a nice little restaurant called The Foot of the Pig in Les Halles."

"Scot," insisted Tracy. "We have to find this guy."

"No, we don't," replied Harvath. "Maybe he was CIA after all. But whoever he is, he's a grown man and he can fend for himself. He didn't come about the president's private phone number for nothing. He'll have people who can help him out."

"And who's going to help us out?"

"Out of what?"

"Out of what?" repeated Tracy incredulously. "I'm suddenly the only person who knows how the investigation into that bombing is going to unfold? In that block alone, there were two banks—each with ATMs and a hotel. Once the area is secure, the French police, or more likely the internal intelligence service, the Renseignements Généraux, is going to pull all the surveillance tapes from their cameras.

"They'll see the car get stolen, the Mercedes come in and take its place, and then they'll see you and me beating a hasty exit from the café, only to have you rush back and knock that Nichols person to the ground a split second before the bomb goes off. Then they'll see us help him up and evac him from the scene."

Tracy didn't say anything else. She just closed her mouth and waited.

"Shit," said Harvath. This wasn't his fight and he didn't want any part of it, but Tracy was right. The French authorities were eventually going to be looking for the two of them whether they liked it or not.

They hadn't done anything wrong, but their behavior was suspicious and could be construed as an indication of foreknowledge of the attack. Whether "gut feelings" counted as a reasonable defense in France was not something Harvath was terribly eager to find out.

Nichols was the reason the attack had happened. Harvath was sure of it. He was also sure that without Nichols, he and Tracy were going to have a lot of trouble with the French authorities.

For a moment, he thought they might be able to hop onto a train and leave the country, but Harvath knew he was deluding himself. This was a major terrorist attack. French citizens were dead and France would stop at nothing to get to the bottom of it.

Harvath knew how good the French intelligence services were. He and Tracy might make it out of the country, but they wouldn't be safe anywhere. Besides, running would only make them look guiltier.

They needed to track down Nichols. Harvath looked at Tracy. "How long do you think until they have our pictures isolated from the CCTV footage?"

It was a rhetorical question and Tracy knew it, but she pieced it together for him anyway. "They'll take witness statements from as many people as they can. If someone mentions our behavior as being out of the ordinary, that'll make them instantly scrutinize the camera feeds for more than just who the bombers were.

"Once they've got our faces, they'll enhance them and then run them through every database they have access to while simultaneously sending our pictures out to every law enforcement officer up and down the chain of command in France. At best, we've got two, maybe three hours."

"And at worst?"

"I don't want to think about it," responded Tracy. "It's giving me a headache."

Harvath retrieved Nichols' hotel key card from the man's wallet and said, "Then I guess we need to get moving."

CHAPTER 10

The Hotel d'Aubusson was located on the Rue Dauphin in the Paris neighborhood of St. Germain des Prés. Stopping at a nearby department store, Harvath and Tracy purchased a change of clothes and wore them out of the store.

They carried their old clothes in the shopping bags they had received from the department store. Though the hotel probably wouldn't have stopped them from passing through the lobby, Harvath felt that by carrying the bags, they looked even more like hotel guests.

Just to be sure, Harvath had Anthony Nichols' key card out and in hand as they crossed the Hotel d'Aubusson's stone lobby and headed for the elevator. The only interaction they had was a quick smile from a harried front desk clerk.

Harvath and Tracy got off the elevator on the third floor and walked down the hallway to Nichols' room. They had decided that Tracy would knock and pretend to be a staff member with a fax for him from the front desk. If Nichols answered, Harvath would take him. If he didn't, Harvath would use the key card to let them in.

After listening at the door for any signs of life, Tracy gave the door three sharp raps. She announced in both French and lightly accented English that she had come with a fax. There was no response. She repeated the procedure once more and then stepped back.

Harvath dipped the key card into the reader. The mechanism beeped twice and the door unlocked. Slowly, he pushed it open and stepped inside.

The bathroom was to his right, its door slightly ajar. Harvath nudged it open with his foot and his eyes were immediately drawn to the marble vanity. Sitting on top of a plastic pharmacy bag were a bottle of antiseptic, some gauze pads, a box of bandages, and an open package of Steri-Strips. Nichols had obviously been back to his room, and recently.

But if that was the case, the key card shouldn't have worked. Any new card issued by the front desk would have come with a new code, rendering the previous card inactive. Harvath was wondering how the hell Nichols had gotten back inside his room when he heard Tracy scream.

Harvath turned just in time to see the lamp come crashing down. Raising his left arm, he absorbed the brunt of the blow with his forearm as the lamp shattered against it. Instinctively, his right hand drew back in a fist and came sailing forward, connecting with his attacker's jaw and sending Anthony Nichols to the bathroom floor.

They both looked at him.

"He sure fights like a history professor," Tracy said finally as she stripped the cord from the lamp and tied Nichols' hands behind his back.

Harvath helped carry him to a chair, where they threaded his arms over the back and secured his feet to the legs with drapery ties. Tracy found a bathrobe hanging on the back of the bathroom door and used its belt as a gag.

Once they had him secure, Harvath checked the hall to make sure no one had heard the commotion. Confident that they were safe, he hung the Do Not Disturb sign on the door, turned on the television set, and prepared to interrogate the man named Anthony Nichols.

CHAPTER 11

Harvath pulled up a chair and placed it in front of Nichols. He was not happy at the thought of having to interrogate him, but he'd been left with little choice. This was all supposed to be part of his old life; the life he had given up in order to begin anew with Tracy. But here he was.

Though Harvath tried to ignore it, he had a deep-seated fear that he would never really be free of his old life. It would follow him like an overzealous bill collector and haunt him until the day he died.

He'd been lucky for a while; happy. But then the specter of his past had found him sitting in a Paris café with the woman he loved, minding his own business, and decided to pull up in a bomb-laden Mercedes and say hello.

Even so, Harvath wasn't ready to give up yet. Once he got the information he and Tracy needed from Nichols to clear themselves in the bombing, he could go back to trying to live a different life; a life that would make him happy, which meant putting as much distance between himself and his old ways as possible.

As Nichols began to come around, Harvath lightly slapped his face to get him to focus. Tracy knew the game and sat behind Nichols where she couldn't be seen.

When Harvath felt the man had regained enough of his senses he said, "I'm going to start by telling you three things that are true. I want you to listen very carefully as your life depends on remembering them."

Nichols' eyes were slow to focus, but then suddenly went wide with fear as he realized what was happening. He tried to move, but was bound to the chair too tightly. His face paled and his breathing became rapid.

"One," said Harvath, continuing. "I know a lot more about you than you think I do. Two, I will only ask my questions once. If at any point you lie or refuse to answer me, I will break a bone of my choosing. And three, if you attempt to cry out for help at any point, I will cause you a pain so intense that you will beg me to go back to breaking your bones.

"Now if you understand me, I want you to nod once for *yes.*"

Nichols nodded repeatedly.

Harvath placed his hand atop the man's head to stop him. "I said *once* for yes. Pay attention, or things are going to get ugly very fast."

When Harvath removed his hand, Nichols nodded once and stopped.

"Good," said Harvath. "I'm going to take your gag off now. Remember, the only sounds I want to hear coming out of your mouth are the answers to my questions. Do you understand?"

Nichols nodded once for yes.

Harvath nodded and Tracy undid the man's gag. Nichols opened and closed his mouth and then worked his jaw from side to side.

Though Harvath had hit him pretty hard, the man's jaw didn't seem to be broken. "What's your name?" asked Harvath.

The professor spoke slowly. "Anthony Nichols."

"Where are you from?"

"The United States. Charlottesville, Virginia."

So far so good. "How'd you get into this room?"

Nichols looked at him. "With my key card."

"Your key card was in your wallet," stated Harvath, "and you left your wallet behind."

"The hotel gave me two. I had the other in my trouser pocket."

Silently, Harvath chastised himself for the mistake. He should have anticipated that. "Who do you work for?" he asked.

There was a slight pause before Nichols said, "The University of Virginia."

During his time with the Secret Service, Harvath had been trained to detect microexpressions, subtle facial cues and body movements that suggested a subject was under stress caused by lying or an intent to do harm.

Both the pause and a shift of Nichols' eyes told Harvath the man wasn't being completely honest with him. "Who else do you work for?"

"*Who else?* What do you mean?"

Nichols was stalling, trying to buy time while his brain raced to come up with an appropriate answer, and Harvath knew it. This guy was not an operative. Even the greenest of field agents would have been much better trained. This guy was a civilian.

Looking at Tracy, Harvath instructed, "The gentleman obviously needs to be convinced that we're serious. Put the gag back on him. I don't want anyone to hear him scream when I go to work on him."

Nichols started thrashing against his restraints as he tried to turn his head to see what Tracy was doing behind him. "No, no, no. Please don't hurt me," Nichols shouted. "I work for the White House."

The man's eyes dropped with shame at his admission and Harvath waved Tracy off with the gag. "You mean you work privately for the president."

Nichols looked up at him but said nothing.

"You had a card in your wallet with his voice-mail number."

"How do you know that?"

"Because," replied Harvath, "only a handful of people have ever been given that number, and I'm one of them."

"You work for the president?" asked Nichols.

"I used to. Now, I'm retired."

"Then what's this all about?"

"That's what you're going to tell me," said Harvath.

"I can't do that," replied Nichols.

"Then you can tell the French police."

"I can't tell them either."

Harvath puffed up his cheeks like a blowfish before slowly letting the air escape. "Then you're in a very tough situation."

Nichols' mind was racing to find a way out of his predicament. "Call the president," he said. "He'll vouch for me. He'll also tell you to let me go."

"I'm sure he will," chuckled Harvath. "The thing is, my girlfriend and I like to make sure all of our bases are always covered. We're going to need you to explain to the French that she and I knew nothing about that bombing until it happened."

"If you let me go," implored Nichols, "the president will help you both. You can trust me."

"I'm sure I can trust you," said Harvath, reading the man's face and seeing the truth, "but I don't know that I can trust the president."

"So you'd hand me over to the French police just to save yourselves?"

"Let me think about that," replied Harvath as he paused less than a millisecond in thought. "Yes. *Yes,* we would." Turning to Tracy, he said, "We're done talking with this guy. Bring me the phone. I'd rather take my chances with the French police. Besides, we don't have anything to hide."

"You're making a big mistake," pleaded Nichols.

"I'm sorry, Professor," said Harvath as he began dialing. "You had your chance."

Nichols tried a different tack. He remembered back to when the president had given him that number and all the things he had said to him about being of such important service to his nation. Finally, he hit on something. Looking at Harvath he said, "If you were close enough to the president to have been given that number, then you must have been someone he trusted; someone who cared very much for your country."

"I still do," said Harvath, and then he switched to French and began speaking to someone on the other end of the phone.

Nichols was in a panic. If he got handed over to the French authorities, it would all be over. He had to make a choice—either spill it all to the man in front of him or save it for the very interested French police. He prayed to God he was making the right decision. "Stop. I'll tell you everything. Just hang up the phone."

"You've got five minutes," said Harvath as he hung up on the automated, Paris version of Moviefone and looked up at Nichols. "I suggest you make this worth my while."

Nichols waited, hoping his captors would loosen his bonds a bit more, but when they didn't, he began talking. "The president has brought me on board to help him take down fundamentalist Islam."

Harvath looked at Tracy with a smile and then back to Nichols. "You've got to be kidding me."

Nichols shook his head.

"How could a professor of history be capable of anything even remotely resembling counterterrorism work?"

Nichols was about to answer when his hotel room window erupted in a hail of broken glass.

CHAPTER 12

Dodd's men had jumped the gun, again. Their only job was to keep Nichols in their sights until the assassin could get there. Instead, the men had shot up Nichols' hotel room from across the street.

The men had seen three figures through the draperies and fearing it was the French authorities, had decided to act. If Nichols broke and told them what he knew, there'd be no containing this thing. It was a rash decision, worse than the car bombing, but he realized the men had been left with little choice. That didn't mean, though, he had to like the situation. Now he had to play clean-up and make absolutely certain that Nichols was dead.

As far as Dodd's men could tell, no one had been left alive inside the hotel room. Dodd ordered one man to keep an eye on the hotel while the others sanitized the apartment they'd been using for surveillance. It wouldn't take the French police long to figure out where the shots had come from and he wanted to be long gone before they got there.

Dodd crossed the street and walked into the lobby of the Hotel D'Aubusson. Everything appeared normal; the staff oblivious to what had transpired only moments ago upstairs. Dodd kept moving and strode right to the elevator.

As the car ascended, he removed a .45 caliber Heckler & Koch pistol from a holster at the small of his back. From a pocket in his Barbour jacket came a Gemtech suppressor, which he affixed to the weapon's threaded barrel.

When the elevator doors opened, Dodd tucked the hand holding the pistol inside his jacket and stepped out into the hallway. Had the pistol been out and ready, he might have been able to get off a clean shot.

All he caught was a shadow of a figure as it disappeared into the far stairwell. Dodd raced for the stairs at his end of the hall and burst through the metal fire door. He pounded down with tremendous force, taking the stairs three and four at a time.

At the ground-floor level, he tucked his pistol back beneath his jacket and stepped out into the lobby. He searched for Nichols, but didn't see him.

Crossing the lobby, Dodd reached the far stairwell and opened the door, but no one was there. *How was that possible?*

Then he realized how presumptive he'd been. Maybe whoever he'd seen hadn't gone down, but rather up. *But what was up?* There was only the hotel's pitched roof.

He took the stairs just as fast going up as he had coming down and considered stopping on the third floor to check Nichols' room. *Maybe*

Nichols was still there? Maybe, but he doubted it. Dodd didn't believe in coincidence. If he found the person he'd seen entering the stairway, he'd find Nichols, he was certain of it.

Dodd kept moving, picking up speed as he rushed up the stairs—his body in exceptional physical condition. At the top floor he raised his pistol, eased open the door, and swung out into the hallway. *Nothing.*

He found the roof access, but it was locked. The only way Nichols could have made it through was if he'd had a key, which Dodd considered highly unlikely.

Taking the stairs back down, he checked each hallway for signs of his prey. Finally, he reached the third floor, and Nichols' room.

There was broken window glass everywhere. Pieces of a shattered lamp littered the bathroom floor and there was blood in the sink, but that was it.

Whoever had been in this room had gone and they had taken Nichols with them.

Dodd began tossing the room only to be interrupted by a blaring alarm.

CHAPTER 13

Harvath had acted quickly. His first instinct had been to grab both Tracy and Nichols and get out of the hotel as quickly as possible, but he knew better. The shots had been fired from a suppressed weapon, most likely from a building or rooftop across the street.

With the hotel room's sheer draperies drawn, the shooter couldn't have had a very good picture of what was going on in the room. Even so, he had taken the shot anyway. In fact, he had taken several. Whoever these people were, they seemed quite intent on making sure that Nichols and anyone else with him be taken out.

First the car bomb and now the shooting. Someone was trying very hard to kill Anthony Nichols, and Harvath wanted to know why. But before he did that, he had to get all of them to someplace safe.

While the shooter had probably packed up and taken off already, Harvath had to operate under the assumption that the threat still remained and that it might very well be closing in on them. Complicating matters was the fact that he was unarmed and the only backup he had was Tracy, who was also unarmed. Thankfully, none of them had been wounded in the shooting. Things could have been worse, much worse.

They avoided the elevator and ran into the stairwell closest to Nichols' room. Harvath fought the urge to race all the way to the lobby. Whoever was gunning for them could have posted men down there. Instead, Harvath had them descend one level and enter the second-floor hallway.

There they saw signs pointing toward the hotel's conference room and Harvath headed for it.

Inside, a large U-shaped table had been set for an afternoon session with pads of Hotel D'Aubusson paper, ballpoint pens, and pitchers of water. At the back of the room was a sign marked *Sortie de Secours,* Exit.

The door opened onto a service area with a narrow set of stairs that led into the bowels of the hotel.

When they got to the bottom, they moved quickly through the basement. The whole time, none of them spoke.

A small service elevator brought them up to the receiving area at the south corner of the building. It was as far from the front of the hotel as they could get without going outside.

Near the door, Harvath discovered a clutch of chairs that sat among a handful of discarded cigarette butts. Atop a nearby time clock were stacks of matchbooks from the hotel bar. *Must be the employee smoking lounge,* he said to himself.

Scanning the loading area, Harvath got an idea that he thought might help cover their escape.

He dragged a large metal trash bin filled with newspapers and other paper products into the center of the room. Into it he dropped several oily rags he'd found in the corner.

Wrapping the last of the rags around a broom handle, he then tossed Tracy the matches and held his makeshift torch out for her to light.

Once it was going, he tilted it into the trash bin and set the contents on fire. It took a few moments, but soon the room was filled with thick gray smoke. Seconds later, the hotel fire alarm went off.

They stayed in the receiving area for as long as they could. When it became too difficult to breathe, Harvath opened the door and they exited onto Rue Christine.

People were already spilling out of the nearby shops and businesses at the sound of the alarm to see what was going on.

Tracy took Nichols by the arm, turned left, and headed away from the hotel toward Rue Des Grands Augustins. Harvath crossed to the other side of the street and hung back to make sure they weren't being followed.

They met up at the corner and moved quickly to Place St. Michel. There, they hid themselves among the throngs of tourists who clogged the narrow streets around Rue St. Séverin.

Harvath kept Tracy and Nichols moving as he doubled back three more times over the next twenty minutes. When he was convinced no one was on their tail, he purchased an international calling card and found a telephone.

They needed to get off the streets as soon as possible. Harvath had no desire to go back to their hotel, and checking into a new one was too risky. They needed someplace safe; someplace where nobody would know who they were or why they were there.

For that kind of anonymity, there was only one person Harvath trusted enough to call.

CHAPTER 14

P ort de la Tournelle," said the voice on the other end of the phone, "lower quai, facing the Ile Saint Louis."

Ron Parker was director of operations for a private intelligence organization known as the Sargasso Intelligence Program. Its chairman and founder was a successful hotelier and former no-holds-barred fighting champion named Timothy Finney. Harvath had a long history with both of them and he trusted them with his life. They were also the unofficial dog-sitters for Harvath's Caucasian Ovcharka, Bullet, whom he had left with them when he and Tracy had decided to leave the country six months ago.

Sargasso was one of several heavily guarded, highly secretive programs Finney ran behind the scenes of his private, five-star Elk Mountain Resort outside Telluride, Colorado. Much like private military corporations augmenting American forces in different hot spots around the globe, Finney had decided to do the same thing, but in the intelligence arena. He had been after Harvath for years to come to work for him.

It was a tempting offer. Sargasso's elite client list read like a who's who of the American intelligence community. Not only did Sargasso collect and analyze information, they also developed assets, fielded operatives, and ran operations around the world. They were a first-class outfit, run by two patriots who put their love of country above their bottom line and in doing so had become more successful than they ever could have imagined.

The key to their success was giving their people every tactical and operational advantage needed to get the job done. To that end, Sargasso had been developing a string of safe houses around the world, including one in Paris.

"I know you wanted to get away from the St. Germain area," Parker added, "but it's the best we can do for you."

Harvath memorized the rest of the information, thanked his friend, and hung up.

Fifteen minutes later, he, Tracy, and Nichols arrived along the Seine and laid eyes on the Sargasso safe house. She was known in French as a *péniche*—a sleek, decommissioned barge—which had been painted jet black. He found it just a bit ironic that the Arab World Institute—an organization created to disseminate information about Arab cultural and spiritual values—was headquartered just above the boat at street level.

Harvath punched a code into the recessed keypad near the wheel-house and the lock released with a hiss. The door was very heavy, and Harvath guessed that it had been armor-plated. He rapped on one of the windows as he stepped inside and noticed that they were not made out of actual panes of glass, but heavy sheets of bulletproof Lexan. Finney and Parker had done an excellent job up-armoring their barge.

Down a short flight of steps were a kitchen, three staterooms with baths, and the main living and dining space. Harvath excused himself and headed toward the main cabin in the stern.

He closed the door behind him and crossed to a built-in bookcase. Running two fingers along the top, he found the hidden hasp and pushed down. A section came forward on hinges and Harvath opened it the rest of the way. Inside was an airtight plastic Storm case. Harvath lifted it out and placed it upon the bed.

The case held a loaded .45 caliber Taurus 24/7 OSS pistol with a sound suppressor and two spare magazines. There was also a small manila envelope with ten thousand euros in cash. The Sargasso program was prepared for any eventuality.

Harvath divided the gear amongst his coat pockets and then put the empty case back where he'd found it.

After powering up the stateroom's laptop and sending an encrypted message to Finney and Parker to let them know they'd made it safely aboard the péniche, he rejoined Tracy and Nichols in the living area.

Nichols was sitting on the couch with a bag of ice clutched against his jaw with one hand and a glass of Scotch from the barge's well-stocked bar in the other. Tracy was at the varnished kitchen counter holding an orange bottle of prescription medication.

Harvath slid into the galley beside her and quietly asked, "What are those? Are you okay?"

"I'll be fine," she replied as her hand closed around the bottle of painkillers. "They're just for headaches."

She shook two tablets into the palm of her hand and popped them into her mouth. "Excuse me," she said as she nudged Harvath out of the way to get to the refrigerator.

Reaching inside, Tracy removed a small bottle of Evian, unscrewed the cap, and took a long swallow.

"Since when have you been taking the pills?" he asked.

"Don't worry about it," she said as she brushed past him and walked into the seating area. "Really, I'll be fine."

The headaches had come and gone ever since she'd left the hospital, but they had been mild and Tracy had a very high threshold for pain. The bottle was half-empty, and he wondered how long she had been hiding the severity from him.

It was a talk they would have to have later. Right now, he needed to focus on Nichols. Removing a bottle of Evian for himself, Harvath joined Tracy on the short couch across from the man who'd been the target of both a car bombing and a sniper attack all in the space of one day.

As they had already explained to the professor who they were, formal introductions were not necessary.

"So, Mr. Nichols," said Harvath. "Let's talk about what you and the president are working on and why someone apparently wants you dead."

"It's a long story."

Harvath fixed his eyes on him. "Try to make it short."

CHAPTER 15

"Why don't you start with how you and the president got together in the first place?" said Harvath.

Nichols knew that he had no choice but to comply. His mind was drawn back to the night he was summoned to the White House to meet with the president. "The president said he had read several of my books and had selected me because of my expertise as a Thomas Jefferson historian."

"Selected you for what?"

"To act as his archivist to help organize his papers and other things for his presidential library."

"Isn't that what the National Archives is supposed to do?" asked Tracy.

"That's correct, but most presidents have someone on their staff or someone they bring in from the outside go through the materials before the National Archives comes in. It allowed me to come and go from the White House and the residence without arousing any suspicion."

"Suspicion over what?" asked Harvath.

Nichols took a deep breath. "In the wake of 9/11, the president sought to comfort a grieving nation, but he also needed comfort. More importantly, as he explained it to me, he needed guidance. And he found it in a White House diary Thomas Jefferson had kept during his presidency.

"President Rutledge had believed that fundamentalist Islam was an enemy the likes of which no other American president had ever experienced before, but he was wrong."

With those words, it dawned on Harvath. "Because Thomas Jefferson was the first American president to have gone to war against fundamentalist Islam."

Nichols nodded. "The tradition of keeping a private, presidential diary was begun by George Washington and was known only to successive American presidents and their naval stewards. Rutledge had gone to the diaries after 9/11 to seek guidance from his predecessors and that's where he encountered Jefferson's experience with fundamentalist Islam.

"Jefferson was convinced that one day Islam would return and pose an even greater threat to America. He was obsessed with the subject and had committed himself to learning everything he could about it."

Harvath was struck by how prescient Jefferson had been.

"It was in going through Jefferson's diary," said Nichols, "that Rutledge discovered something extraordinary."

CHAPTER 16

Most Americans were unaware of the fact that over two hundred years ago, the United States had declared war on Islam, and Thomas Jefferson had led the charge. For that reason, Professor Nichols felt it important to set the backdrop for what he was working on.

"At the height of the eighteenth century," he began, "Muslim pirates were the terror of the Mediterranean and a significant swath of the North Atlantic. They attacked every ship in sight and held the crews for exorbitant ransoms. The hostages were subjected to barbaric treatment and wrote desperate, heart-wrenching letters home begging their governments and family members to pay whatever their Mohammedan captors demanded.

"These extortionists of the high seas represented the Islamic nations of Tripoli, Tunis, Morocco, and Algiers—collectively referred to as the Barbary Coast—and presented a dangerous and unprovoked threat to the new American republic.

"Before the revolutionary war, U.S. merchant ships had been under the protection of Great Britain. When the U.S. declared its independence and entered into war, the ships of the United States were protected by France. Once the war was won, America had to protect its own fleets."

"Hence the birth of the U.S. Navy," added Tracy.

Nichols shook his head. "It didn't happen as quickly as you might think. Beginning in 1784, seventeen years before he would become president, Thomas Jefferson left for Paris to become America's Minister to France. That same year, the United States Congress sought to appease its Muslim adversaries by following in the footsteps of European nations who paid bribes to the Barbary States, rather than engaging them head-on in war.

"But then, in July of 1785, Algerian pirates captured two American ships and the Dey of Algiers demanded an unheard-of ransom of nearly $60,000.

"It was extortion, plain and simple, and Thomas Jefferson, now U.S. Minister to France, was vehemently opposed to any further payments. Instead, he proposed to Congress the formation of a coalition of allied nations who together could force the Islamic states into perpetual peace."

The plan sounded all too familiar to Harvath, who remarked, "A coalition of the willing?"

"Quite," said Nichols, "but Congress was disinterested in Jefferson's plan and decided to pay the ransom.

"In 1786, Thomas Jefferson and John Adams met with Tripoli's ambassador to Great Britain to ask him by what right his nation attacked American ships and enslaved American citizens.

"He claimed that the right was founded on the laws of their prophet and that it was written in the Koran that all nations who didn't acknowledge their authority were sinners, and that it was not only their right and duty to make war upon these sinners wherever they could be found, but to make slaves of all they could take as prisoners, and that every Muslim slain in battle was guaranteed a place in Paradise.

"Despite this stunning admission of premeditated violence on non-Muslim nations, as well as the objections of numerous notable Americans, including George Washington, who warned that caving in was both wrong and would only further embolden their enemy, the United States Congress continued to buy off the Barbary Muslims with bribes and ransom money.

"They paid Tripoli, Tunis, Morocco, and Algiers upwards of one million dollars a year over the next fifteen years, which by 1800 amounted to twenty percent of the United States government's annual revenues.

"Jefferson was disgusted. To add insult to injury, when he was sworn in as the third president of the United States in 1801, the pasha of Tripoli sent him a note demanding an immediate payment of $225,000 plus $25,000 a year for every year thereafter. That was when everything changed.

"Jefferson let the pasha know, in no uncertain terms, what he could do with his demand. The pasha responded by chopping down the flagpole in front of the U.S. Consulate and declaring war on the United States. Tunis, Morocco, and Algiers immediately followed suit.

"Jefferson had been against America raising a naval force for any-thing beyond coastal defense, but having watched his nation be cowed by Islamic thuggery for long enough, he decided that it was finally time to meet force with force.

"He dispatched a squadron of frigates to the Mediterranean to teach the Muslim nations of the Barbary Coast a lesson they would never forget. Congress authorized Jefferson to empower U.S. ships to seize all vessels and goods of the pasha of Tripoli and also to 'cause to be done all other acts of precaution or hostility as the state of war would justify.'

"When Algiers and Tunis—who were both accustomed to American cowardice and acquiescence—saw that the newly independent United States had both the will and the might to strike back, they quickly abandoned their allegiance to Tripoli.

"Nevertheless, the war with Tripoli raged for four more years and flared up once more in 1815. The bravery of the United States Marine Corps in these wars led to the line 'to the shores of Tripoli' in the Marine hymn and they would ever after be known as 'leathernecks' for the leather collars of their uniforms that prevented their heads from being chopped off by Muslim scimitars when boarding their ships.

"Islam, and what its Barbary followers justified doing in the name of their prophet and their god, disturbed Jefferson quite deeply. America had a tradition of religious tolerance, in fact Jefferson himself had coauthored the Virginia Statute for Religious Freedom, but fundamentalist Islam was like no other religion the world had ever seen. A religion based upon supremacism whose holy book not only condoned but mandated violence against unbelievers was unacceptable to him.

"As I mentioned, one of Jefferson's greatest fears was that someday this brand of Islam would return and pose an even greater threat to the United States."

"He was definitely ahead of his time on that one," remarked Tracy.

"Long before leaving for France," Nichols continued, "Jefferson had committed himself to learning everything he could about the tenets of Islam and also about how its radical, warlike doctrine could be defeated without another shot ever being fired."

"Which is why he owned a copy of the Koran," added Harvath.

"Perhaps," said Nichols. "But it has also been suggested that Jefferson's copy of the Koran may have been purchased in 1765 while he was studying law at the College of William & Mary. It's possible he was studying it as a legal text or for comparative religion purposes. We don't know for sure."

"Is that the same Koran a Muslim congressman used for his swearing-in ceremony a couple of years ago?" asked Tracy.

"Yes, it was. You see, Jefferson wasn't anti-Islam. He was anti-Islamist. There's a distinction. He didn't give a damn whether his neighbor claimed there were twenty gods or no God, as long as the man neither picked his pocket nor broke his leg. Fundamentalist Islam, though, picks pockets *and* breaks legs and that's why Jefferson had to find a way to stop it. He was the father of the separation of church and state, after all.

"But the underlying problem with fundamentalist Islam is that it is both political *and* religious. It teaches that the two cannot be separated. The Islamists believe that man-made laws are inferior and must be replaced with God-given Islamic or sharia law and that all governments worldwide should be Islamic."

"I wonder how that would go over in Washington," said Harvath.

"Probably not very well," replied Nichols. "Coupled with the mandate that violence be wreaked upon all unbelievers until they capitulate to Islam's yoke, fundamentalist Islam is anathema to everything Jefferson stood for. That's what makes his discovery even more exciting."

"Then you believe he found something?" asked Harvath.

Ever so slowly, Anthony Nichols nodded.

CHAPTER 17

A ndrew Salam was sick and tired of talking. Ozbek could see it in his face the minute he walked into the D.C. Metro interrogation room. The man had been repeatedly grilled since being arrested. His eyes were puffy and bloodshot. He looked tired, he looked angry, and he looked hungry. What he didn't look like, though, was a killer.

He appeared to be of Pakistani descent, with dark skin, dark hair, and brown eyes. He was around five-foot-six, five-foot-seven, max. He had a thin scar that ran through his left eyebrow.

"Have you had anything to eat today?" asked Ozbek.

Salam shook his head. "Only some stale coffee."

Ozbek waved Rasmussen over. "Tell us what you want and my partner will go get it for you."

"Seriously?" asked Salam, his eyes brightening a bit.

Ozbek nodded. He learned a long time ago that the most productive way to start an interrogation was to build rapport by trying to give the prisoner something he wanted.

Once Rasmussen had left to get the food, Ozbek asked Salam how he had been recruited.

The man took a moment before replying. It was obvious that he was having trouble coming to terms with the fact that he had been duped. Finally, he replied, "It seemed so real to me. Just like out of a movie. Three years ago I was on my way to my internship at the Near Eastern section of the Library of Congress when this guy approached me, flashed his FBI credentials, and asked if I could be free for lunch."

"And you said yes."

Salam nodded.

"Then what happened?" asked Ozbek.

"We met later that day. I ate and he talked."

"What was his name?"

"Sean Riley," the man replied.

"So what did you and Sean Riley talk about?" asked Ozbek.

"Like I said, he did most of the talking. But the subject was the growing threat America faced from both Islamic extremist ideology and legal 'Islamism.' "

"Meaning political Islam," clarified Ozbek.

"Right," replied Salam. "Riley described an active campaign by Muslim extremists to destroy Western civilization from within—quietly, peacefully; even legally. He explained how they were working to destabilize America and ultimately replace the U.S. Constitution with Islamic sharia law."

"And that bothers you?"

"Of course it does. It should bother every American. And it's already happening. They have brought about women-only classes and swimming times at taxpayer-funded universities and public pools. Christians, Jews, and Hindus have been banned from serving on juries where Muslim defendants are being judged. Piggy banks and Porky Pig tissue dispensers have been banned from workplaces because they offend Islamist sensibilities. Ice cream has been discontinued at certain Burger Kings because the picture on the wrapper looks like the Arabic script for *Allah*. Public schools have been pulling pork from their menus. Women have been beaten, strangled, and killed by their husbands, brothers, or fathers for 'dishonoring' their families. It's death by a thousand cuts, or sharia inch-by-inch as some refer to it, and most Americans have no idea this battle is being waged every day across America.

"By not fighting back, by allowing groups in particular like FAIR to obfuscate what is really happening, and not insisting that the Islamists adapt to our culture, the United States is cutting its own throat with a politically correct knife and helping to further the Islamists' agenda."

"And that's why this Sean Riley wanted to recruit you? To take the fight to the Islamists?" asked Ozbek.

"Exactly."

Ozbek had seen a chilling collection of classified evidence before it was made public in a terrorism financing trial in Dallas which laid out the Islamist agenda to take over the United States. The evidence contained a detailed strategy memo from the Muslim Brotherhood—the oft-cited parent organization of Hamas and al-Qaeda which was intimately tied to FAIR—laying out steps for how the U.S. Constitution and Western civilization could be destroyed from within and replaced with sharia law.

Ozbek remembered the words of an audiotape he'd heard played that detailed the Brotherhood's paranoia about "securing the group" from infiltration by "Zionism, Masonry . . . the CIA, FBI, etc." so that they could detect any outside monitoring and get rid of any such enemies.

The FBI had already floated a cursory theory of theirs to Ozbek and Rasmussen that Salam's job was just that—to discover where American Islamist organizations were vulnerable and to infiltrate them in order to shore them up. The only thing was that Salam didn't know it. He'd been purposely kept in the dark.

"Why did they pick you for this assignment?" asked Ozbek.

"I asked Riley the same thing," replied Salam. "He said my thesis caught his attention."

"What was it about?"

"It was about how the Islamists were slowly creating a specialized victim status for themselves whereby discussion of Islam, as well as their motives for Islamic supremacism, were quickly becoming no-go topics. I entitled it *The Quiet War* and paid special attention to how the Islamists had realized that they could further their agenda by playing upon Americans' natural distaste for racism. They did it by creating a label that smacked of bigotry and which could be applied to anyone who called into question their true loyalties, motivations, religious texts, or ultimate end game— *Islamophobia.*"

"And what were your conclusions?"

Salam looked at him. "They weren't good. The United States is doing nothing but ceding ground to the Islamists. It would rather be politically correct than victorious, and as long as it refuses to engage its enemy on every single front it will never win."

"That's a pretty serious charge," said Ozbek.

"Sure it is. But it's right on the money," the man responded. "For the majority of its adherents, Islam is a beautiful religion. We not only don't want to commit acts of violence, we don't want anyone else to either, especially not in the name of our religion. If it were up to us, we'd gladly see the violent passages the extremists use to justify their actions removed from the Koran.

"The majority of Muslims in America and around the world are moderate *and* peaceful. Islam brings comfort and provides a noble path for over a billion people on this planet. It is the source of incredible goodness. We want to live in harmony with our neighbors, regardless of what their beliefs are.

"Everyone wants us, the moderate Muslims, to reform Islam, but no one does anything to help. They don't seem to understand that the moderates who are brave enough to stand up are constantly drowned out by the Islamists who are more media savvy, better organized, and considerably better financed."

Ozbek referred to his notes. "So that's where this Operation Glass Canyon that you told the FBI about came in?"

"Yes," said Salam. "Operation Glass Canyon was supposed to take the fight directly to the fundamentalists."

"This was headquartered out of your firm, McAllister & Associates?"

"My part of it was. I thought the rest was being handled by the FBI."

"What is McAllister & Associates?" asked Ozbek.

"It's a P.R. and lobbying firm that specializes in Muslim clients. It was my cover, which allowed me to infiltrate the Islamist movement in America."

"And were you successful?"

"Very," replied Salam. "I placed or turned people in almost every hard-core Islamist organization in the country."

"Didn't you ever get suspicious that you weren't really working for the FBI?" asked Ozbek. "According to what I was told, you didn't even train at the FBI Academy in Quantico."

"Riley trained me at an Islamic compound in upstate New York called Islamaburg. He said it was for my protection because the FBI wanted to keep my identity a secret, even from other FBI agents."

"But here you are," pressed Ozbek, "feeding all of these reports to Riley and nothing is happening. Doesn't that set off any alarm bells for you?"

"Are you asking if I got frustrated?" asked Salam. "Of course I did. But what did I know? Government is famous for being slow. In fact Riley always liked to calm me down by joking that the FBI put the 'bureau' in bureaucratic. No matter how hot a piece of intel was that I gave him, he always assured me that it was being passed up the chain of command and being acted upon."

When Steve Rasmussen returned with the food, Ozbek gave the prisoner a few moments to begin eating before turning the conversation to the heart of why they were there.

CHAPTER 18

Let's talk about the Foundation on American Islamic Relations," said Ozbek.

Salam shook his head with disgust. "They are the worst

thing to have ever happened to American Muslims. You know FAIR's director, Abdul Waleed, actually boasted at a conference once, not knowing that there was a reporter present, that Islam wasn't in America to be equal to any other faith, but to become dominant. He said he believed that the Koran, not the Constitution, should be the highest authority in America, with Islam as the only accepted religion on earth. And he said he would not rest until he made that happen. That's not the kind of Islam I practice. In fact, that's not the kind of Islam the majority of Muslims practice."

"Tell me about Nura Khalifa and the assassin FAIR supposedly hired."

Andrew Salam suddenly grew much less talkative. It was obvious to Ozbek that he had touched a nerve and he felt he knew what it was. He had seen a picture of Nura Khalifa. She was stunning.

Finally, Salam said, "She was a good woman. She didn't deserve to die."

Ozbek had never lost anyone close to him—not in the Army, not at the CIA, not even in his regular personal life. He could only imagine how the man felt and trod as delicately as the situation would allow. "Were you two intimately involved?"

"No. It was strictly business between us."

"Did you have feelings for her?"

Salam looked at his interrogator. "Even if I had, I would never have compromised such a valuable asset. If nothing else, at least I can say I was professional."

"She fed you a lot of information on FAIR?"

"Tons."

"Which you fed to Riley?" asked Ozbek.

"Yes."

"And he was the only person claiming to be with the FBI that you ever had contact with?"

"Correct," said Salam, "but no matter how much information about FAIR and its activities I gave him, nothing ever seemed to be done about it. I got the same line about investigations being in the works and it taking a lot of time to build strong cases and then one day Riley told me to sever all ties with Nura and back off the Foundation on American Islamic Relations."

"Did he say why?"

"Riley claimed that the Bureau was finally beginning a full-blown investigation of the organization and that any further work I did could jeopardize my cover. I agreed. The only problem was that Nura didn't. She was convinced by what she was seeing and over-hearing that something very big was afoot."

"What was she seeing and overhearing?" asked Ozbek.

"Abdul Waleed began having more and more meetings with a radi-cal Saudi imam who ran several mega-mosques across the U.S. named Sheik Mahmood Omar. According to Nura, the two men seemed to be carrying the weight of the world on their shoulders.

"She had overheard them complain on two separate occasions that if the threat wasn't halted, Islam, as well as everything they had been working for, could be seriously compromised."

Ozbek interrupted him. "What *threat*? What are we talking about?"

"That's exactly what I wanted to know," replied Salam. "Nura said they had begun asking a lot of questions about her uncle, who is a Koranic scholar from Georgetown."

"What's the uncle's name?"

"Dr. Marwan Khalifa."

"Where at Georgetown did he work?"

"The Center for Arabic Studies."

Ozbek looked at him. "The same place you studied."

"True, but I've never met him. He's one of those Indiana Jones types who's always off on some archeological dig or research project."

"Do you know where he is now?"

"He has been bouncing around a lot working on some project for the Yemeni Antiquities Authority," replied Salam.

"Did Nura say why she thought they might see her uncle as a threat?" asked Ozbek.

"Some of the more orthodox and hard-core fundamentalists felt that his research raised too many questions about the authenticity of the Koran. To them what he did was blasphemy and he was considered apostate, which meant that a case could be made for killing him. If you believe that sort of thing."

"And do you?"

Salam was taken aback. "No way. Not at all."

Ozbek made a few more notes and then said, "You told the FBI that Nura said Waleed and Omar hired an assassin. That's not exactly an easy thing to do. How'd they find him?"

"Sheik Omar arranged it," replied Salam. "The man's name was Majd al-Din. It means Glory of the faith in Islam."

"What was his name before that?"

"I don't know."

"You told the FBI that Nura believed he was from the CIA. Why?" asked Ozbek.

"She had overheard Omar bragging about him. He said al-Din was a revert to Islam."

"Revert is a Muslim term for a convert, right?"

"Yes. According to Nura, Omar was crazy about this guy because he was a typical, average-looking white guy who would never raise suspicions anywhere. He was like a chameleon that could change his appearance at the drop of a hat. He said when you sat down with him he looked more like an accountant than someone who used to kill for the CIA."

Ozbek added it all to his notebook, making sure he got everything down.

"Omar was especially amped about this guy," continued Salam, "because he'd been part of some super-secret program or unit or something at the CIA called the Transept. Does that ring any bells with you?"

Ozbek looked up from his pad, shook his head and lied. "No."

"Well, this guy al-Din is supposedly like the Terminator. He has been programmed to kill and that's all he does. Kill. Kill. Kill."

"A lot of people like to boast that they've worked for the CIA," replied Ozbek.

Salam laughed. "And those people are usually the biggest liars. The *I could tell you what I used to do but then I'd have to kill you* types."

Ozbek smiled. "So you can see why this all sounds a little over the top."

"According to Nura, Omar had been al-Din's spiritual advisor for several years. The sheik seemed to know a lot about him and his background."

"Maybe he was bullshitting."

"Maybe," said Salam. "But I wouldn't bet on it. Omar's a rough character and he's paranoid as hell. He's not going to bring a white revert into his inner circle unless he's fully vetted the guy."

Ozbek didn't like the sound of what he was hearing, and neither would the CIA. He noted a few more things and then asked, "Is there anything else you can give me about al-Din? A current address or phone number he might be at?"

"I'm sorry," said Salam as he lifted the last bite of his meal and then suddenly changed his mind and set the fork down. "Nura was killed before she could tell me anything else."

Ozbek was sorry too. "Did al-Din ever come by FAIR while Nura was there? Did she ever see what he looked like?"

Salam shook his head and changed the subject. "I'm going to prison, aren't I?"

"That's not for me to decide."

Salam was quiet for a moment. "I told the police about my dog. He only had food and water for a couple of days. Do you think they've sent anybody over to my house?"

"I'll bet they've sent tons of people to your house," said Ozbek.

Salam realized the humor in what he just said and smiled for a moment. "Ninety-nine point nine percent of the Muslims in this country are good people. They love America just like me. I was doing what I thought was right for the United States. I still think that."

"I know you do," said Ozbek as he flipped his notebook shut, "and for what it's worth, I believe you."

"So you can help me."

"I'm going to try," said the CIA operative as he stood up and walked to the door. As he reached it, he asked, "By the way, what kind is it?"

"Excuse me?" replied Salam.

"Your dog. What kind is it?"

"Chesapeake Bay Retriever."

"That's a good breed," said Ozbek. "Very loyal."

Salam nodded and watched as the man left.

• • •

Outside the interrogation room, the D.C. Metro detective handling the investigation was waiting for them. He was a hard, no-bullshit cop in his mid-fifties named Covin with a gray mustache and the build of a college linebacker. "Did you get everything you needed?" he asked.

Ozbek shook his head as he slid the notebook back into his coat pocket.

"He's full of shit," stated the detective. "Academy Award performance every time. If you listen to him long enough you actually catch yourself believing him."

"You don't?" asked Ozbek, careful not to reveal his own feelings.

Detective Covin looked at him. "Let's just say that all of this smells."

Ozbek agreed with him on that. "What kind of personal effects did he have on him when you picked him up?"

Opening the folder he was carrying, the cop read off the list. "Watch. Wallet with credit cards, bank card, cash, and a D.C. driver's license. Business card case with cards. Car keys. Cell phone—"

"We'd like to take a look at his cell phone," said Ozbek.

The detective closed the file and looked at the two CIA men. "That means you're going to have to sign the chain of evidence sheet. At this point, you've only come in and asked a couple of questions. The minute you lay a finger on that evidence, you and the CIA are permanently tied to this case.

"I was a prosecutor before I became a cop and I know what a defense attorney would do with the fact that two spooks were left alone with the suspect's personal effects."

Rasmussen resented the implication. "What are you saying?"

"I'm saying quit while you're ahead. Questioning the suspect about a possible tie to a CIA operative is one thing. Going through his personal effects is something altogether different."

"You're right," said Ozbek as he signaled for Rasmussen to back off. "We don't want to get involved with any of the evidence. That could be bad for all of us." Checking the signal strength on his cell phone he added, "I'm going to need to jump back into the interrogation room for a second."

"What for?" asked Covin.

"There's something I forgot to ask the suspect."

• • •

As Ozbek and Rasmussen left D.C. Police Headquarters and headed for their car, Rasmussen asked, "What was that last-minute question you had to ask Salam?"

"I needed his cell phone number."

"What for?"

"Plan B," replied Ozbek.

Rasmussen had a pretty good idea of what Plan B was, but he let it slide for the moment. "What's Plan A?"

"I want to run everything Salam just gave us against the Transept personnel files."

"You want to pull the files for every Transept operative who looks like an accountant and is good with disguises? That's almost every person in that program, *including* the women. They were all recruited because they were forgettable."

"I don't care. I want the whole team working on this," insisted Ozbek. "I want to know where every single Transept operative is right now—active, retired, even dead. All of them. And while we're at it, let's pull everything we have on the victim's uncle."

"Marwan Khalifa from Georgetown?"

Ozbek slid his keys from his pocket and nodded. "I want to know where he is and exactly what he's working on. If he's the target, I want to know why."

"I'll let Patricia know not to wait up," muttered Rasmussen. "For either of us."

CHAPTER 19

Jefferson was a brilliant polymath," said Professor Nichols as he set the ice bag he'd been applying to his jaw on the coffee table in front of him. "He possessed encyclopedic knowledge in a wide range of areas and was a skilled architect, archeologist, paleontologist, horticulturalist, statesman, author, and inventor. He was also an adept cryptographer who loved puzzles as well as making and breaking codes.

"He could read in seven languages and never read translations if he could read the original. In fact, he taught himself Spanish specifically so he could read *Don Quixote* on his transatlantic passage to France in 1784. He felt the book was vital to his understanding of the Muslim enemy the U.S. was facing in the Mediterranean."

"Why?" asked Tracy. "What does *Don Quixote* have to do with Islamic pirates?"

Harvath had read *Don Quixote* as a boy and hadn't thought about it much since. He did remember something interesting that he'd been taught about its author, Miguel de Cervantes, and wondered if that might have been why Jefferson had been interested in the book. "Cervantes got the idea for his novel while in a Barbary prison," said Harvath. "Didn't he?"

Nichols nodded. "Miguel de Cervantes was a Spanish soldier who had fought in many battles against the Muslims, including the Battle of Lepanto, a decisive victory for European Christians over invading Islamic forces. Though he was wracked with fever, he refused to stay belowdecks and fought admirably, incurring two gunshot wounds to the chest and one which rendered his left hand, and some say his whole left arm, useless for the rest of his life.

"After six months of recuperation, Cervantes rejoined his unit in Naples and stayed with them until 1575, when he set sail for Spain. Off the Catalan coast, his ship was attacked by Muslim pirates who slew the captain and murdered most of the crew. Cervantes and the handful of passengers who survived were taken to Algiers as slaves.

"He suffered five years of barbaric treatment under his Muslim captors. He tried to escape four times and prior to his ransom finally being paid, Cervantes was bound from head to toe in chains and left that way for five months. The trauma provided much fodder for his writing, particularly the Captive's Tale in *Don Quixote*.

"Jefferson was reading *Don Quixote* to learn more about the Barbary pirates, but right in the middle of it he discovered something else—a cleverly hidden cryptogram. It took him a while to crack it, but once he did, it revealed an incredible story hidden within the Captive's Tale."

"What was it?" asked Tracy.

"In sixteenth-century Algiers," replied Nichols, "educated slaves like Cervantes were used by their largely illiterate Algerian captors as amanuenses to perform a variety of tasks, from accounting to transcribing documents.

"It was in the house of one of the city's religious leaders that Cervantes first learned that the last revelation of Mohammed's life had been purposefully omitted from the Koran."

Just when Harvath thought the man couldn't come up with anything more astonishing, he did. "What was Mohammed's final revelation?" he asked.

"That's exactly what the president and I have been trying to find out," said Nichols. "According to Jefferson, Mohammed was murdered shortly after revealing it."

"Wait a second," said Tracy. "Mohammed was murdered? I never knew that."

"632 AD," replied Harvath, who in order to better understand his nation's enemy, had studied Islam extensively. "He was poisoned."

"Do they know by whom?"

"Jefferson believed," said the professor, "it was one of Mohammed's apostles; the men he referred to as his companions."

"Jefferson didn't exactly have access to the Internet," said Harvath. "How could he have done any substantive research on this kind of topic?"

"Per his diary," replied Nichols, "the task was extremely difficult. He did have help, though. Besides an incredible network of international contacts in diplomatic, academic, and espionage circles, the European monastic orders charged with ransoming prisoners from the Islamic nations proved very useful.

"These monastic orders were exceptional record keepers. They debriefed all of the prisoners they repatriated and recorded the accounts of their captivity verbatim. Many of these orders had representatives and in some cases even headquarters in France. Through them, Jefferson had access to an array of archives detailing what the prisoners did during their captivity, as well as what they saw and overheard.

"There were many prisoners like Cervantes who worked in the homes and businesses of their Muslim captors and picked up very interesting bits of the missing Koran story over the years. Jefferson's task was to take that information and put it together with other avenues of research he was working on to tease out a bigger picture.

"What we've been able to piece together of that bigger picture includes several references to one man in particular," said Nichols as he reached for a sheet of paper, wrote down the name *Abū al-'Iz Ibn Ismā'īl ibn al-Razāz al-Jazarī,* and held it up.

"Who's he?" asked Tracy.

"Al-Jazari was one of the greatest minds of Islam's Golden Age. He was the Islamic equivalent of Leonardo da Vinci; an incredible inventor, artist, astronomer, and highly regarded scholar who was also interested in medicine and the mechanics of the human body.

"In 1206, he published *The Book of Knowledge and Ingenious Mechanical Devices.* In it he documented an amazing host of mechanical inventions including programmable automatons and humanoid robots, but he was best known for creating the most sophisticated water clocks of his time."

"He sounds impressive," said Harvath, "but how does he fit in with the missing verses from the Koran?"

The professor put up his hands. "That's the problem. We don't really know."

"Even if you did, how could discovering something like this have any impact on fundamentalist Islam?" asked Tracy.

"Good question," replied Nichols. "You see Muslims believe that the Koran is the complete and immutable word of God. To suggest anything else is considered blasphemy and an outright attack on Islam. Nevertheless, about a fifth of the Koran is filled with contradictions and incomprehensible passages that don't make any sense.

"For example, in the beginning of Mohammed's career as a prophet in Mecca, Allah revealed to him through the Angel Gabriel the concept of living peacefully with Jews and Christians. Later when Mohammed, who had been shunned by the Jews and Christians, became a warlord and raised a powerful army in Medina, Allah supposedly revealed that it was every Muslim's duty to subdue all non-Muslims and not rest until Islam was the dominant religion on the planet."

Tracy nodded. "That never made sense to me."

"You're not alone. Part of the confusion comes from the fact that the Koran isn't organized chronologically. It's organized predominantly from the longest chapters, or suras, to the shortest. The peaceful verses from the beginning of Islam can therefore be found throughout. The problem, though, is that the violent verses take precedence due to something called abrogation."

"What's abrogation?"

"Basically, it says that if two verses in the Koran conflict, the later verse shall take precedence. The most violent sura in the Koran is the ninth. It is the only chapter in the Koran that doesn't begin with the phrase known as the Basmala—*Allah the compassionate, the merciful.* It contains verses like *slay the idolaters wherever you find them* and *those who refuse to fight for Allah will be afflicted with a painful death and will go to hell* as well as calling for warfare against and the subjugation of all Jews and Christians.

"Although it's the next-to-last chapter, it's the last true set of instructions Mohammed left to his followers and it's those verses that have been driving violence in the name of Islam ever since."

"The difficulty for peaceful Muslims who do not espouse violence," clarified Harvath, "is that they don't have a contextual leg to stand on in their religion. When Mohammed said 'go do violence' and when he himself committed violence, Muslims are not allowed to argue with that. In fact, they are expected to follow his example."

"Why?" asked Tracy.

"Because Mohammed is viewed as the 'perfect man' in Islam. His behavior—every single thing he ever said or did—is above reproach and held as the model for all Muslims to follow. Basically, Islam teaches that the more a Muslim is like Mohammed, the better off he or she will be.

"But, if Mohammed did in fact have a final revelation beyond Sura 9," said Nichols, "and if, as Jefferson believed, it could abrogate all of the calls to violence in the Koran—"

"Then its impact would be incredible," replied Harvath, who

after a pause asked, "You found all of this in Jefferson's presidential diary?"

"No," replied the professor. "The diary was only a jumping-off point. Jefferson had been on the trail of the missing revelation long before he came into the presidency and he kept working on it until well after he had left the White House.

"We've had to sort through many other Jeffersonian documents to try to find more information. The problem is that Jefferson died heavily in debt and his estate was broken up and sold. Certain key items have gone missing. That's why the president dispatched me here to Paris."

"To locate more of Jefferson's missing documents?" asked Tracy.

"In particular," said Nichols, "Jefferson's first-edition *Don Quixote*. We believe it contains handwritten notes that can lead us to what we're looking for."

"Where is it?"

The professor took a deep breath and then replied, "That's where things start to get tricky."

CHAPTER 20

THE WHITE HOUSE

President Jack Rutledge had just finished his morning briefing when his chief of staff, Charles Anderson, stuck his head back inside the Oval Office. "The Saudi crown prince is on the phone for you, sir," he said.

"Any idea what he wants?" replied the president as he walked behind his desk and sat down.

"He didn't say. Do you want me to tell him you're unavailable?"

"No. I'll take his call."

When Anderson had left the room, Rutledge picked up the phone. "Good afternoon, Your Highness."

"Good morning, Mr. President," said Crown Prince Abdullah bin Abdul Aziz from his residential palace in eastern Riyadh. "Thank you for taking my call."

"Of course, Your Highness. We are always happy to hear from our friends in Saudi Arabia."

"I trust you and your daughter, Amanda, are well?"

"We are," said Rutledge, ever mindful of the Arab custom to make small talk about the health and well-being of the conversation's participants and their respective families before getting down to business. "How are you and your family?"

"Everyone is well, thank you."

"I'm glad to hear that."

"Mr. President," said the crown prince, "may I speak frankly with you?"

"Of course," replied Rutledge.

"I understand that you may be searching for something that doesn't belong to you."

The president waited for the crown prince to elaborate. When he didn't, Rutledge asked, "Could you be more specific, Your Highness?"

"Mr. President, Islam is one of the world's three great religions. It brings comfort and solace to a billion-and-a-half people around the world. I am concerned that you may be attempting to shake the faith of those billion-and-a-half people."

"And just how exactly are we trying to do that?" asked Rutledge.

"I'm not talking about America in general," corrected the Saudi leader. "I'm talking about you specifically, Mr. President. You and the personal vendetta you seem to have against our peaceful religion."

The president reminded himself that he was talking to a foreign head of state; one whose country actively promoted and financed the radical Wahhabi ideology embraced by so many of the world's terrorists, but a head of state nonetheless. "Your Highness, you asked me if we could speak frankly, so let's do so. I have no idea what you're talking about."

The connection was so clear, it was almost as if the overweight Saudi was standing right next to the president when he said, "There is no lost revelation of Mohammed, Mr. President."

Rutledge couldn't believe his ears. *How the hell did the Saudis know what he was looking for?* "That's good to know, Your Highness. Thank you."

"Saudi Arabia has been a very good friend to the United States," cautioned the crown prince.

Sure they had. The president wanted to thank him for the fifteen hijackers the Saudis sent over on 9/11, the countless Saudi nationals who had overstayed their visas and had been picked up in the United States on terror-related charges, and numerous other examples that suggested Saudi Arabia was anything but a friend to the United States, but he kept his mouth shut. Until America pulled the oil needle out of its arm once and for all, it would have to deal politely with Saudi Arabia. "And America appreciates your country's friendship, Your Highness. I think you've received some incorrect information, though."

The Crown Prince clucked his disapproval over the phone line. "My sources are very reliable. As is my warning, Mr. President. If you want what is good for our two nations; if you want what is good for America and the billion-and-a-half Muslims of the world, you will abandon your fruitless search. The lost revelation of Mohammed is nothing more than a fairy tale. The Loch Ness monster of the Islamic world."

It was a monster, all right, thought the president, and if the crown prince was calling to dole out such "friendly" advice, it had to mean that he and Anthony Nichols were getting close. And the closer they got, the more dangerous all of this was going to be.

CHAPTER 21

The professor cleared his throat and said, "On October 27 of 2005, the worst rioting in France in the last forty years erupted and spread across the country when two Muslim teens from a poor housing complex east of Paris were killed. The teens thought they were being chased by police and attempted to hide in an electrical substation, where they were electrocuted. The riots lasted for nearly three weeks during which over nine thousand cars were torched, a fifty-year-old woman on crutches was doused with gasoline and set on fire, and weapons were fired at police, firefighters, and rescue personnel.

"An internal French investigation gave conflicting reports that the police were after two other men who were either evading an identity check or had trespassed at a building site. Either way, that differed with a statement given by a friend of the deceased teens who claimed the boys had been accused of burglary and were running because they feared interrogation."

"So what was it?" asked Harvath.

"All of it actually, but we didn't learn that until much later."

"How can it be *all of it*?" asked Harvath.

"French immigrants of North African descent who are normally Muslim are often hired as day laborers on construction jobs, much in the same way Mexican laborers are in America. Their employers pay them off the books in cash and turn a blind eye to their residency status.

"According to intelligence picked up by the American embassy in Paris, two such workers from Clichy-sous-Bois, the flashpoint of the riots, were hired to help renovate a building not far from the Luxembourg Gardens.

"During the demolition phase, the two laborers stumbled across a strange wooden box hidden behind a false wall. Though the men had no idea what they had discovered, after forcing it open they realized its contents were old and most likely valuable. So, in hopes of making a little extra money on the side, they smuggled it out of the building and began selling it off in bits and pieces in an attempt to avoid drawing any unwanted attention. It wasn't long, though, before the French security services began looking into it."

"Back up," said Harvath. *The French security services?*

"Why them?" added Tracy. "Why not the police?"

"Good question," replied Nichols as he took a sip of his drink. "What got them interested was who the box belonged to."

"Thomas Jefferson."

Nichols nodded.

"How did they know that?" asked Harvath.

"An antiquities dealer they tried to sell documents to got suspicious and contacted French authorities," said the professor.

"What was a box filled with Jefferson's stuff doing hidden in a building near the Luxembourg Gardens?" asked Harvath.

Nichols swirled the liquid in his glass. "In addition to his home on the Champs-Élysées, Jefferson kept a small suite of private rooms at the Carthusian monastery in the Jardin du Luxembourg, where he could work and think in peace. The Carthusians observed a strict vow of silence and expected their tenants to do the same. The arrangement was perfect for Jefferson.

"His house on the Champs-Élysées had been broken into three times in 1789," continued Nichols. "In fact, the robberies had gotten so bad that he had to request private security."

Tracy massaged her temples with her index fingers. "What were the robbers looking for?"

"No one knows for sure. It may have been as simple as petty theft, or it could have been government sponsored espionage. The fact is that the monastery was much more secure and it is likely that Jefferson would have felt comfortable leaving important items there."

"That still doesn't explain why the French security services were so interested in the box, or what the box was doing walled up in some building in the first place," said Harvath.

Nichols attempted to explain. "The box belonged to the third American president and many of the documents inside were encoded. The French have an obsession with codes. They never broke any of Jefferson's, so when the opportunity to get their hands on items he had encrypted popped up, they jumped on it. The only problem for them, though, was that the codes were created using an ingenious machine Jefferson had invented while living in Paris called the wheel cipher."

"What's a wheel cipher?"

"Imagine twenty-six wooden discs, like donuts or circular coasters with a hole drilled through the center of each. They were a quarter of an inch thick and four inches in diameter with the letters of the alphabet printed randomly around the edge. The donuts slid onto a metal axle, the protruding edges of which allowed it to be placed in a special rack. From there the discs could be rotated at will to spell out the desired message.

"For the message to be decoded, the recipient not only needed their own wheel cipher, but they also needed to know the order in which to place the wooden wheels along the axle. Without that information, any encoded message was useless."

"And along with the encoded documents," said Harvath, "Jefferson's copy of *Don Quixote* was in that box?"

"Yes," replied Nichols.

"What was in the documents?"

"From what we can tell, some of his early work on the missing Koran text. The bulk of what we have been able to piece together from other documents is all encrypted and our best guess is that he used his wheel cipher to do it. To unlock that information, though, we need to know how he ordered his discs."

"Which means you have a Jefferson wheel cipher," said Tracy.

"We do."

Harvath was impressed. "And the key to placing the discs on the axle is what's inside Jefferson's *Don Quixote*?"

"Yes," said Nichols. "For whatever reason—the sensitivity of the information or concern over what his many enemies might do with it—Jefferson encoded most of his research. In fact, some of the entries in his presidential diary, as well as most of the pages of notes that President Rutledge has acquired and hopes may pertain to Mohammed's missing revelation, are encoded. That's a large part of why I was hired."

"To help the president decipher the codes?" asked Tracy.

The professor nodded.

"But why would Jefferson have left the box behind when he returned to America?" inquired Harvath.

"Because," said Nichols, "when he left, he didn't know he wouldn't be coming back. He was barely off the boat back in America before George Washington asked him to accept a position as his secretary of state. Congress moved quickly to approve the appointment and Jefferson's life changed in the blink of an eye."

"But he would have sent for his things."

"Of course he did. But in 1789 he couldn't just pick up a phone. Arrangements had to be made and they took time. The French Revolution was in full swing and before he could claim his belongings from the Carthusian monastery, it had been sacked and burned by the Parisian mobs."

"And with it, presumably, the belongings Jefferson had left there," said Tracy, "including the hidden box."

"So where's the *Don Quixote* now?" asked Harvath. "Do the French have it?"

"No. The laborers suspected they were under surveillance and recruited the two teens that were killed to deliver the rest of the cache to several intermediaries.

"The boys were leaving a meeting with the laborers when the

French authorities decided to move in. They were hoping to get the two laborers who were the ringleaders, but the men gave them the slip. The boys were the next best thing. The authorities pursued the teens, but we know how that ended.

"The laborers disappeared, presumably back to North Africa. The French are rumored to have retrieved some of the documents, but they never got the book—probably because they didn't realize its significance and their focus was on the documents themselves.

"A friend of one of the teens filled in the pieces for the security services, confirming most of what they'd already learned in their investigation. A CIA operative based out of the American Embassy was having dinner with a French counterpart who filled her in on the whole case. The Frenchman thought it would be amusing to her because of the Jefferson connection. She reported back to the head of station, who briefed Langley, and the report made it to the president, who shared it with me.

"When I discovered that a rare first-edition *Don Quixote* was going to be on sale at this year's International Antiquarian Book Fair here in Paris, I contacted the dealer, and without tipping my hand, made an inquiry into the provenance of the book. He was somewhat standoffish, but the book world is filled with strange characters.

"He agreed to send me scans of the first couple of pages. There was an annotation and it looked to be a match for Jefferson's handwriting. I made an appointment to see him so I could examine the book.

"When I got there, he told me he had already decided to sell the book to someone else. Nothing I could do would persuade him. Someone had offered him a lot more money for it. The president couldn't raise that kind of money; at least not right away."

Harvath raised an eyebrow. "The president had trouble getting funding?"

"This isn't a government operation. He has been financing this out of his own pocket. I asked the dealer to agree to wait until close of business today before he went through with the other party. He gave me until three o'clock.

"I was leaving the meeting when I passed you and the bomb detonated."

"When we first saw you, you were coming out of a bookstore. Does the dealer work there?"

"No, the store has a small café in back. He wanted a neutral place to meet. He's very paranoid."

As he should be, thought Harvath. *And so should you.* Nichols was in way over his head. "Do you have any idea who is bidding against you?" he asked.

"A first-edition *Don Quixote* with all of its original mistakes that Cervantes personally corrected for the next edition? It could be any bibliophile or lover of literary history."

"Or it could be the people who have been trying to kill you," said Harvath as he looked at Tracy. "I think we need to find out."

CHAPTER 22

CIA HEADQUARTERS
LANGLEY, VIRGINIA

Y ou're sure that's the whole list?" asked Aydin Ozbek as he walked into his office with Steve Rasmussen and motioned for him to close the door.

Rasmussen shut the door and dropped onto the couch with three file folders and a legal pad. "Selleck gave it to me personally," he said as he reached over and picked up Ozbek's wooden puzzle.

Ozbek poured himself a cup of coffee and studied the printout. "He sure pulled it together fast, didn't he?"

"Make mine black," said Rasmussen when his colleague failed to offer him any.

Without taking his eyes off the list, Ozbek poured a second cup, walked to the sitting area, and set it down on the coffee table.

Rasmussen picked it up. "Oz, if you had a small fleet of Lamborghinis, you'd know where they were 24/7, 365 too. Selleck was able to crank that out so quickly because Transept is a tight operation."

"So he can vouch for all of these operatives?" asked Ozbek as he sat down.

"I wouldn't go that far," said Rasmussen. "They're all going to need to be interviewed. Hell, even the instructors for Transept will need to be interviewed. Anyone who has ever even been in the same room when the word Transept was uttered is going to get a knock on their door."

"What about this one here?"

"Which one?" asked Rasmussen as he set the puzzle down and leaned across the table to see what Ozbek was looking at.

"Matthew Dodd. Status KIA/NRL."

"I asked Selleck about that too. Killed in Action, No Remains Located."

Ozbek's brow furrowed. "If there were no remains, why wasn't he marked as MIA?"

"Modern technology, that's why. The guy was working in the northwest frontier province of Pakistan six years ago and called in an air strike. Either he was too close to the target or he fucked up the numbers. Either way the missiles landed practically on top of him and he got smoked. The Agency had a drone overhead and saw the whole thing. It stayed overhead the rest of the night but they never picked up any signs of survivors. No infrared, no nothin'. And despite how remote and hostile the area is, they eventually got a team up there the following spring, but all they found was a crater. Therefore, Killed in Action, No Remains Located."

"So what you're telling me is that one of the Agency's finely tuned *Lamborghinis* all of a sudden developed engine trouble?"

Rasmussen knew where Ozbek was going. "Doesn't make much sense, I know."

"You and I have both called in air strikes," replied Ozbek. "I usually make sure my math is right on the money."

"Agreed," replied Rasmussen as he slid one of the files from his stack and handed it to his colleague. "That's why I thought you might want to see this. It's the incident file along with the investigation's findings."

Ozbek took his time reading through it. When he was done, he closed it and handed it back. "How come our department doesn't have a file on this guy?"

Rasmussen held up his hands. "As far as the Agency is concerned, the guy's dead. Selleck said that if we wanted, he'd have the Predator footage pulled and we could watch it ourselves. Apparently, it's pretty convincing."

Ozbek shook his head. "Let me see his personnel file."

Rasmussen handed it to him.

The first thing he looked at was Matthew Dodd's official CIA photo. "The guy's definitely got Ernst and Young written all over him," he said.

Rasmussen raised a hand to his mouth and wiggled his fingers. "All the better to slip into your country undetected, my dear."

"What's behind door number three?" asked Ozbek as he finished leafing through Dodd's dossier and pointed at Rasmussen's final folder.

"Nura Khalifa's uncle, Dr. Marwan Khalifa. Naturalized American citizen of Jordanian descent, a founder of Georgetown University's Ph.D. program in Islamic studies, and one of the foremost experts on the textual history of the Koran. He also teaches in Georgetown's Department of Arabic, the Center for Contemporary Arab Studies, the Prince Alwaleed bin Talal Center for Muslim-Christian Understanding, and the Departments of History, Theology, and Government," replied Rasmussen as he handed the file over.

"That's one hell of a résumé."

"You're telling me."

"Where is he now?" asked Ozbek as he flipped through the folder.

"The answer to that question might not be exactly what we want to hear."

Ozbek looked up from the file. "Why not?"

"Salam was telling us the truth about Dr. Khalifa working on a project for the Yemeni Antiquities Authority. The thing is, he wasn't in Yemen. He was in Rome at the Italian State Archive Services."

"So at least we know where he is."

Rasmussen held up his hand. "Five days ago, they had a fire."

"Khalifa's dead?"

"According to my contacts at the Italian Internal Security Agency, the police in Rome have four unidentified bodies, all pretty badly burned. I've got our people working on trying to locate Khalifa's dental records in the States. Once we've got our hands on those, we'll shoot them over, but at this point it doesn't look good. One CFLR staff member says that Dr. Khalifa had been working late the night of the fire and no one has seen him since."

"What was he working on? What were you able to find out?"

Rasmussen nodded. "The Yemenis had uncovered stacks of old parchments and scraps of varying documents dating back to the seventh and eighth centuries. They supposedly were some of the earliest pieces of the Koran.

"The Yemenis brought Dr. Khalifa in to authenticate them. Because they don't have any decent facilities in Yemen, he'd gotten their approval to transport the find to Rome so that all of it could be photographed and preserved."

"Did any of it survive?"

"It's all gone."

"So that's it? Old bits of the Koran? That's what he had been working on? That's what his niece thought made him a threat to Islam?"

Rasmussen referred back to his notes. "Dr. Khalifa was working closely with the deputy assistant director of the Italian State Archive Services. He's the one who told the police that Khalifa was working late the night of the fire. Anyway, this guy, Alessandro Lombardi, claims that Dr. Khalifa was very excited about the find because he had discovered intriguing inconsistencies between the Koranic parchments from Yemen and the Koran that Muslims worldwide use today."

"What kind of inconsistencies?" asked Ozbek.

"Lombardi says Khalifa didn't elaborate much. But what he did say was that several of the things he had found supported another project he was working on. It was based on some story about the prophet Mohammed having a final revelation that never made it into the Koran and that he had been assassinated to keep it quiet."

"Whatever this final revelation is," said Rasmussen, "it's supposedly enough to turn the whole religion on its ear. Mohammed shared it with his apostles, but some of them didn't like it and apparently bumped him off. Mohammed knew he had been poisoned, so he summoned his chief scribe and recounted the final revelation to him in hopes that it would survive."

"And?"

"According to Khalifa, the scribe was hunted down by the men who had poisoned Mohammed. They found the final revelation hidden beneath the scribe's robes. They burned it and then chopped the scribe's head off."

"End of story," said Ozbek.

"Not quite," replied Rasmussen. "What the scribe was carrying was a copy. The killers never located the original."

"But Khalifa found it?"

Rasmussen shrugged. "Supposedly, his partner on this other project thought he had a line on it."

"Then, presuming Khalifa is dead, he might not have been the only target. Do we have a name for his partner?" asked Ozbek.

"Nope."

"E-mails? A research organization he or she belonged to? Anything?"

Rasmussen shook his head. "Lombardi said that Khalifa kept everything on his laptop."

"Which let me guess," said Ozbek, "was with him the night of the fire."

"According to Lombardi, it was."

Ozbek stood up and began pacing. "What about at Georgetown? Did Khalifa have a desktop computer in his office? What about his university e-mail account? How about his house? Phone records?"

Rasmussen looked at his colleague. "All stuff we can't have access to without permission."

"Steve, hold on. Nura Khalifa's boss, Waleed, along with Sheik Omar, began asking a lot of questions about her uncle's work, which is considered by the more hard-core Islamists to be threatening. Next thing we know, Omar has allegedly hired an assassin to remove a serious threat to Islam, and shortly thereafter it looks like the uncle has died in a fire? Does any of this look a little too coincidental to you?"

"I don't believe in coincidences."

"Neither do I," replied Ozbek.

"That still doesn't change the fact that the CIA is prohibited from carrying out domestic operations."

"If you're not comfortable—"

"I didn't say I wasn't comfortable," replied Rasmussen.

"Good. How long will it take to get everything I just asked for?"

"Including sending teams in broad daylight to Georgetown and Dr. Khalifa's residence? Several hours at least."

"Okay," said Ozbek as he pulled out the piece of paper with Andrew Salam's cell phone number written on it and handed it to Rasmussen. "That'll give us time to start working on Plan B."

CHAPTER 23

The International Antiquarian Book Fair was held every year in the Grand Palais, one of the most striking buildings in Paris. Constructed for the 1900 World's Fair, the classical palace was topped by a dramatic series of glass and steel domes. It was intended as a monument to the glory of French art and had long been one of Scot Harvath's favorite exhibition halls. Today, though, he wasn't so sure.

The Grand Palais had some of the best security guards in the world. Its basement housed its very own National Police station charged with protecting the exhibitions, as well as the vendors themselves. The annual gathering of rare-book dealers from around the world drew enormous crowds and showcased thousands of rare objects from thirteenth-century manuscripts and maps of the first Viking explorers, to the manifesto of the surrealist movement and a letter written by Niccolò Machiavelli on the publication of his book *The Prince*. It was the most important event of the year for professional and amateur bibliophiles alike. And somewhere in the building was a man who unknowingly held the key to disarming the greatest threat to Western civilization. All Harvath had to do was find him.

It was a feat much easier said than done as the rare-book dealer they were searching for, René Bertrand, was a "floater," an independent who worked the exhibition floor without a booth of his own. All they had to go on was a meeting time and place where Nichols was to present his final offer for the Jefferson *Don Quixote*. Bertrand had definitely stacked the deck in his favor.

Even with Nichols' help, the chance of finding the man among the massive crowds was slim at best. Nevertheless, the trio had to make the attempt.

The glass ceilings of the Grand Palais gave visitors the impression of walking through the world's largest greenhouse. The overcast sky above matched Harvath's mood. Every time he saw a police officer, he discreetly steered Tracy and the professor in another direction. They couldn't be too careful. There was no way of knowing if the French police were looking for them already or not. But that wasn't the only thing weighing on Harvath.

Before leaving the péniche, he'd allowed Nichols to check the balance of the bank account the president had established for him. No new deposits had been made. They had precious little to bargain with.

Published more than four hundred years ago, only eighteen first-edition copies of *Don Quixote* were known to exist worldwide. Hailed as the first "true novel," a first-edition *Quixote* was quite literally worth more than its own weight in gold.

The group spent the next twenty minutes surreptitiously weaving their way through the crowd.

Fifteen minutes before the rendezvous time, Harvath told Tracy and Nichols to stay put and did a quick sweep of the area. When he came back, they were gone. *Something wasn't right.*

Immediately, Harvath went into a state of heightened alert. His mind was full of questions as his hand slid beneath his coat and gripped the butt of his Taurus pistol. *Had the people who'd targeted Nichols gotten to them? Was it the police? Was he next?*

He fought to keep his heart rate and breathing under control. Quickly and quietly, he did another sweep. Forty-five seconds later he found them behind a booth sitting on a bench. Nichols was holding a cup of water in his left hand while his right arm was around Tracy's shoulders.

"What happened?" asked Harvath as he forced his eyes away from Tracy and kept scanning the area.

"I'm fine," she replied.

"She's not fine," said Nichols. "She's sick."

"I'm *fine*," Tracy repeated.

Harvath looked at her. "Is it the headaches?"

"She needs to see a doctor," Nichols interjected.

"I don't need a doctor. Would you two cut it out?"

Time was running out. "Can you stand up?" asked Harvath.

"Give me a minute," said Tracy. "I'm just a little dizzy. It'll pass."

They didn't have a minute. Harvath needed to make a difficult call.

Reaching into his pocket, he peeled off several euro notes and shoved them into Nichols' hand before Tracy could object. "Get her back to the boat and stay with her," he ordered. "Don't use the phone or the computer until I get back. Do you understand me?"

Nichols nodded. "What are you going to do?"

"I'm going to get that book," said Harvath as he turned and disappeared into the crowd.

CHAPTER 24

When René Bertrand appeared at the appointed time, he wasn't hard to spot. Even in the quirky world of rare-book dealers, Bertrand was a real character.

The flamboyant dandy in a white three-piece silk suit stood about five-foot-seven. The only thing thinner than his emaciated frame was the pencil-thin mustache that hovered above his almost nonexistent upper lip. His hair was parted on the left and slicked back with some sort of pomade while a pair of gray eyes darted nervously back and forth beneath two overly manicured eyebrows. A pocket watch on a gold chain sat nestled inside his vest pocket. On his feet, the rare-book dealer wore a pair of highly polished black and white spectators while a brightly colored handkerchief billowed from his breast pocket.

There were dark circles under his eyes, and given his overall physical appearance, Harvath wondered if there was more to Bertrand's paranoia than just being in possession of one of the world's most valuable books.

Harvath waited as long as he dared and then finally approached the man. "Monsieur Bertrand?"

"Yes?" the book dealer replied in heavily accented English.

Harvath had run through how he was going to play this. Nichols had explained that Bertrand was very careful. He had shown the professor only copies of the first few pages of the *Don Quixote* with its dedication from Cervantes to the Duke of Bejar, a phrase in Latin that read "After the shadows I await the light," and of course the handwriting of Thomas Jefferson.

Bertrand was certainly not going to be carrying the book with him. It would be kept someplace safe until a price had been settled upon and he had received his money.

"I work with Professor Nichols," said Harvath.

"And why is he not here?"

"He's getting the rest of your money together."

René Bertrand smiled, his teeth stained from a lifetime of cigarettes and coffee. "That is very nice, but he has yet to make me an offer I can accept."

Harvath noticed that Bertrand was perspiring. "Are you feeling okay, Monsieur?"

The smile never wavered. "The offer, please?" he asked.

"We are prepared to beat the competitive offer by one hundred thousand."

"Euros?" asked Bertrand.

"Naturally," Harvath replied. "I also have been authorized to give you this," he said as he tapped the outside of his jacket. "Ten thousand euros cash, right now, in exchange for just ten minutes of your time?"

"Ten minutes of my time for what?"

Now it was Harvath's turn to smile. "For me to explain why you should close the bidding and why the University of Virginia is the right home for this very special book."

The book dealer's heavy-lidded eyes narrowed. "And I get to keep the ten thousand no matter what?"

Harvath nodded. "No matter what."

"May I see the money, please?" asked Bertrand.

Withdrawing the envelope from his inside pocket, Harvath discreetly opened the flap and showed him the stack of bills. "Perhaps we can find a café nearby?"

Bertrand loved dealing with universities, especially American universities. In his experience, they always had much more money than sense. "There's a café not far from here," he responded. "I need to use the facilities anyway. Let's make it quick. I have a meeting with your competition in thirty minutes."

In espionage, operatives learn to discern and then play to a subject's vulnerabilities. For Harvath, René Bertrand, to employ a very bad pun, was like an open book. He stood to make a lot of money from his role in the sale of the *Don Quixote,* but ten thousand euros for ten minutes of his time was a sweetener the man couldn't say no to. Espionage was often part con game. The surest way to get people under your control was to ask them to do you a favor.

And that's exactly what Harvath had done. Now, for his plan to work, he needed to get Bertrand out of the building.

The ten thousand euros was nothing more than bait, and the book dealer had taken it. No doubt he saw Harvath as a fool, but he was about to learn who the fool really was.

The pair worked their way up the crowded main aisle to the front of the Grand Palais. They were about two hundred feet from the entrance when Harvath felt something hard pressed into the small of his back.

At the same time, a man leaned in toward his ear and warned, "Do anything stupid and I'll pull this trigger and sever your spine."

CHAPTER 25

He had appeared out of nowhere; not exactly a difficult feat at such a crowded exposition, but Harvath should have sensed his approach. He should have been more on his guard.

The man's English was perfect. Immediately, Harvath ruled him out as being French. He could have been security for Bertrand, but somehow Harvath doubted it. He hadn't yet done anything to the book dealer that would have required such a reaction. He had been waiting until he got him outside and away from the exhibition hall for that, which left only one other option.

The man must have been Bertrand's other buyer for the *Don Quixote*. "The competition" as the book dealer had put it, whom he was supposed to be meeting in thirty minutes.

Whoever this mystery man was, he had a gun to Harvath's back. And regardless of how angry Harvath was at being taken by surprise so easily, he had no choice but to follow the man's orders.

With his free hand, the gunman grabbed René Bertrand by his reedlike arm, flashed his weapon, and drew the rare-book dealer up against Harvath as he shoved the pair forward. Bertrand was terrified and barely able to utter, "You."

Harvath's mind raced for a solution: some way to distract the man behind him and grab his gun, but there was little he could do. They were in the center of a horde of people slowly shuffling their way toward the exit. He could practically feel the breath of his assailant against the back of his neck. Harvath barely had any space between himself and the people in front of him. Hoping for a space to open up in front of him and at the same moment chaos to be created as a distraction was asking for a miracle. But a miracle was exactly what happened.

Past the bobbing and weaving heads of the crowd in front of him, Harvath noticed three French national policemen standing near the exit. One of them appeared to be scanning the faces of the crowd and referring to a sheet of paper in his hand at the same time.

The gunman saw them too. He tightened his grip on the book dealer's arm and pressed his gun even harder into Harvath's back as he said, "One false move and I will kill both of you before the police even realize what's happening."

There was no question in Harvath's mind who he would rather take his chances with. He only hoped the French police were looking for him and that the piece of paper one of the cops was carrying had his photo on it.

As they got closer to the exit, the crowd in front of them began to thin out and the police began checking the faces of the people nearest to Harvath. Knowing that the gunman couldn't see his face, Harvath started rapidly moving his eyes in hopes of capturing their attention.

Glancing to his left, he saw that sweat was pouring down the bookseller's face and that he was shaking. Either he was growing more petrified of their abductor, or there was something else going on with him. It didn't take long to discover what it was.

As Harvath and the book dealer approached the police, the officer with the paper recognized them. He checked one more time and then alerted his colleagues, one of whom instantly got on his radio.

Harvath thought for sure he was the one they'd recognized, but when the men drew their weapons they yelled for René Bertrand to stop.

The gunman wasted no time. Pointing his Heckler & Koch pistol around Harvath's right side, he fired several shots in rapid succession as all hell broke loose in the lobby of the Grand Palais.

CHAPTER 26

Harvath spun and drove his elbow into the gunman's solar plexus. As the assassin fell backward, Harvath drew his weapon and looked over just in time to see René Bertrand running back into the hall.

All three cops were down. Two of them were bleeding out and Harvath feared they weren't going to make it. The third was on his radio, calling for backup.

As people ran screaming in all directions, Harvath had to make up his mind. His priority was the book dealer and after one more glance at the gunman, he took off after him.

Twenty yards ahead, he could see Bertrand, but because of the crowd he couldn't close the distance. He felt like the proverbial salmon swimming upstream. Raising his weapon into the air, he fired a shot.

Instantly, the crowd parted and Harvath raced after the book dealer. Bertrand took a sharp left, banging his shoulder into a large bookcase and knocking it over.

Harvath leapt over the spill of books and kept on, pushing people out of his way as he ran. He had to remind himself to scan and breathe, scan and breathe. He had no desire to be taken by surprise again.

Less than ten yards away from Bertrand, he noticed what he was running toward—an emergency exit.

As the book dealer neared the door, Harvath fired two shots into the frame and yelled for him to stop. Bertrand might have been foolish, but he wasn't an idiot. He stopped right where he was.

In the blink of an eye, Harvath was on him. Securing his weapon, he grabbed the book dealer by the collar and punched him hard in the gut with his other hand.

As Bertrand doubled over, Harvath kicked open the fire door and dragged the man outside.

At Cours La Reine, Harvath stopped a 1970s Renault, pulled its teenage driver out, shoved René Bertrand in, and sped off across the Pont Alexandre III bridge back toward the barge.

After ditching the car several blocks from the Quai de la Tournelle, Harvath screwed the sound suppressor onto the end of his Taurus for effect and warned the book dealer what would happen to him if he didn't cooperate. The two then covered the rest of the distance to the Sargasso safe house on foot, stopping repeatedly to duck into doorways as police cars sped past.

When they reached the péniche, Harvath opened the door of the wheelhouse and shoved René Bertrand down the stairs.

Nichols, who was in the galley brewing tea, and Tracy, who was lying on the couch, were both startled by the commotion.

"Professor," said Harvath as he slammed Bertrand into a chair at the dining room table, "I need you to find me some rope. There's probably some up on deck."

"Right away," said Nichols as he turned off the stove and disappeared up the stairs.

Tracy swung her feet onto the floor and asked, "This is our rare-book dealer I presume?"

"It certainly is," replied Harvath.

Tracy studied him. His skin was pale to the point of almost being translucent, and he was drenched with sweat. Though he kept licking them, his lips were dry and cracked. "What did you do to him?"

"Nothing. Yet," said Harvath. "I think our pal here is pretty tight with Harry Jones. Aren't you, René?"

"He's a heroin addict?" asked Tracy.

"Who had the French police looking for him at the Grand Palais. That's why you're so paranoid, isn't it, René?"

The book dealer refused to look Harvath in the eye.

"What happened?" said Tracy.

Harvath pulled up a chair and kept his eyes glued to the book dealer's as he spoke. "René and I were just on our way out of the exhibition hall to discuss our transaction when his 3:30 showed up and stuck a gun in my back."

Tracy was stunned.

"Apparently, René's clients are very protective of him," continued Harvath. "Anyway, whoever this guy was, he was marching us toward the front door when the cops spotted René and yelled for him to stop. The guy behind me fired at them and now two of the cops are probably dead and the third was wounded pretty badly."

"How did you get away?"

"Our friend René thought it would be a good idea to sneak out one of the emergency exits, and I concurred. Someone was kind enough to lend us a car, which we ditched a couple of blocks away, and here we are."

"You're sure it wasn't *you* the cops were looking for?" asked Tracy.

As Harvath was about to answer, Nichols came down the stairs with a length of rope. "Got it," he said.

Harvath accepted the rope and began binding the book dealer to his chair.

Nichols blanched, remembering his experience at the hotel. "Are you going to torture him?" he asked.

"It's going to feel like torture," replied Harvath, "but I'm not going to lay a finger on him. As soon as he's ready, Monsieur Bertrand is going to tell us everything we want to know. Aren't you, René?"

Bertrand remained silent.

Harvath patted him down and found what he was looking for. In the man's left breast pocket was an oversized silver cigarette case. Harvath opened it up and placed it on the table where the book dealer could clearly see it. He knew the stress of the Grand Palais had pushed Bertrand over the edge. Now, only inches away, was the heroin his body was crying out for.

CHAPTER 27

O f course I'm angry," said Abdul Waleed as he paced. "We agreed it would look like a murder/suicide. But Nura Khalifa is dead and Andrew Salam is still alive!"

Sheik Mahmood Omar stood from behind his ornate desk crafted of Damascus steel and gestured toward a carpet in the center of the room with large silk pillows. A tea tray had been set upon a cloth known as a *sufrah*. "We learn little from our successes, but much from our failures," offered the imam as he sat down.

"Maybe you don't understand," responded FAIR's chairman as he took a seat across from him. "Salam is going to tell the police everything, if he hasn't already. The FBI is probably already involved. Either way, somebody is going to come and question me."

Sheik Omar raised a polished serving pot and poured Arabic coffee into two, small handleless cups. The heady aroma of coffee mixed with cardamom and saffron filled the office.

"And what will they learn?" asked Omar.

Waleed wondered if the imam was losing it. *"What will they learn? Where should I start?"*

Handing his guest the traditionally half-filled cup, the sheik stated, "While the words are yet unspoken, you are master of them; when once they are spoken, they are master of you."

"Enough Bedouin proverbs, Mahmood. We need to have a plan."

Omar took a sip of his coffee. "The evidence planted at their homes and at your offices is still there?"

Waleed nodded.

"The security cameras were not functioning at the memorial?"

"Correct," said Waleed.

"Then we don't need to do anything. We have left enough to convince the authorities that Nura was meeting with Salam to tell him that their affair was over. She was ashamed at having debased herself before marriage and was going to beg her family for forgiveness. Salam decided that if he couldn't have her, then no one would."

"You underestimate the FBI."

"Do I?" asked Omar. "A woman is tragically murdered; a *Muslim* woman from the FAIR offices. There is evidence pointing to a spoiled relationship between her and the man who killed her. Unless you do something foolish, the investigation will end there."

"And what about Salam? What about his story? What about the training he received? What about my personal connection to him?" demanded Waleed.

"When the FBI asks you about those, you admit to them. You met Salam when he started attending this mosque. He was bright, charming, and extremely creative. That's why you hired his P.R. firm to work on FAIR's public and media relations. He worked closely with Nura and you suspected something more than just business might be going on between them, but you never knew for sure. She was very discreet about her private life—"

Waleed interjected, "But what about the man Salam believed to be his handler? And what about the evidence on us Salam was amassing?"

"His handler made sure Salam turned over everything each time they met. He was taught never to keep any information that could compromise him."

Waleed shook his head.

Omar set down his coffee cup. "Would you rather that the real FBI had gotten to Nura and turned her? Or any of the others we have working for us?"

"No, I wouldn't."

"Operation Glass Canyon was a brilliant idea, and our benefactors in Saudi Arabia are quite pleased. By infiltrating ourselves, we're better equipped at discovering outside attempts from Zionist groups or agencies like the FBI or DHS trying to penetrate our organizations. We also often receive better information from our spies than our most loyal people. McAllister & Associates has paid for itself several times over and is a profitable venture in more ways than one."

"But Salam is in jail. Do our benefactors know that?"

The imam shrugged his shoulders. "For every glance behind us, we have to look twice to the future. We'll find someone to replace him. Life will go on."

Waleed wished he shared the sheik's confidence. "I still think Salam knows too much and is a danger to us. He has been well trained. His story will sound too real."

"How well trained is he, really? All of the tradecraft he learned could have come from books."

"He'll lead them to Islamaburg," countered Waleed.

"Where he and other young Muslims learned how to shoot and defend themselves. So what? No laws were broken there. Trust me, Abdul, the trail is going to go cold very fast."

Waleed plucked up a bite-sized sweet from the tray and shoved it in his mouth. He always seemed to eat more when he was under stress. "What have you heard from Paris?"

Mahmood Omar chose his words carefully. There was no need to upset Waleed any further. "Things are progressing."

"So our problem still hasn't been taken care of?"

The sheik smiled reassuringly. "I have every confidence it will. Every delay has its blessings. Al-Din will be successful in Paris and then we can put all of this behind us."

•   •   •

When his audience with Omar was over, Abdul Waleed exited the mosque and headed for his car. As he crossed the street, he reminded himself to remain calm. Both the FBI and the D.C. Metro police would most likely want to ask him questions. He had thought about having some of FAIR's attorneys present, but Omar had cautioned him against it. He felt it would look too suspicious.

He needed to contact the office to see if any law enforcement agencies had called yet, or maybe had even dropped by unannounced. Omar had warned him to expect them to show up without warning to examine Nura's desk, computer, and other belongings.

Waleed climbed in his car and fished his ear bud from one of the cup holders. As he turned the ignition, he slid his cell phone from the plastic holster at his hip and turned it on. Omar had a thing about cell phones ringing in the mosque. He saw it as a personal affront to Allah. In fact, the only thing he disliked more than cell phones was dogs.

On that point, he and Waleed were in complete agreement. Cell phones were a necessary evil in modern life, but he had always agreed with the Islamic injunctions against dogs. They were impure, absolutely filthy animals and Mohammed had rightly forbade Muslims from keeping them as pets.

After plugging in his headset, Waleed pulled away from the curb and dialed his office.

The man had no idea that Steve Rasmussen had remotely accessed Andrew Salam's phone in the evidence room at the D.C. Metro Police Headquarters and had downloaded its contents.

Once Rasmussen had retrieved Waleed's mobile number, Ozbek had been able to "hot-mike" his phone—a novel form of electronic surveillance which allowed him to remotely power up the phone and activate its microphone. He and Rasmussen had heard the entire conversation with Sheik Omar.

It was the first solid lead the CIA operatives had. The covert forays into Dr. Khalifa's home and office at Georgetown had been absolute busts.

Ozbek was now on his phone issuing orders to the rest of the DPS. "That's right," he said. "I want the entire team focused on Paris. Everybody. Right now. We'll meet in the conference room for an update in an hour."

As he hung up the phone, Rasmussen looked at him and said, "None of the intelligence we just gathered will ever be admissible in court."

Ozbek knew his colleague was right.

"We've probably also just screwed the FBI on a major part of their investigation too."

That thought had crossed Ozbek's mind, but he didn't want to think about it. Instead, he turned his anger on Rasmussen. "This is twice now that you've informed me that I've stepped over the line. I get it and I don't want to hear it again, okay? The more I hear his name come up, the more my gut tells me this al-Din was an Agency hitter.

"Mahmood Omar and Abdul Waleed are dedicated Islamists that the FBI should have taken down a long time ago. Our country is at war and our job is to prevent the enemy from winning. And before you give me a speech about upholding the Constitution, I want you to take two seconds and think about what would happen to the Constitution and the Bill of Rights if America ever became an Islamic nation."

"I'm not saying any of that," replied Rasmussen. "Relax."

"I know you've got your pals at the Bureau. They're good people. But when you're fighting against assholes who only punch below the belt, you need to have a few people on your side who don't give a fuck about the Marquess of Queensberry."

"Listen," said Rasmussen. "I agree with you. There's no such thing as a fair fight. I understand that."

"But?"

"No buts. We get paid to make sausage. Nobody wants to watch it being made. They only care about how it tastes."

"So we're good?" asked Ozbek.

"We're good," said Rasmussen as he stood. "I'll see you in the conference room in an hour."

Ozbek watched him leave and hoped that if this thing got any uglier that he'd be able to count on him.

CHAPTER 28

Harvath made René Bertrand watch as he swabbed a spoon from the galley with hand sanitizer and then removed a small chunk of heroin from the man's "cigarette" case.

The drug smelled faintly of vinegar as he placed it on the spoon and added a tiny squirt of water from the book dealer's syringe. Harvath then used Bertrand's lighter to heat the mixture from underneath and pulled the stopper out of the syringe to act as a stirrer.

When it was ready, he dropped a small, wadded up piece of cotton into the center of the spoon. The cotton ball was the size of a tic-tac and functioned like a sponge; sucking up the entire mixture.

Bertrand's previously dry mouth was wet with anticipation and his eyes were glued to Harvath's every move.

After cleaning the stopper, Harvath inserted it back into the syringe. He placed the needle in the center of the cotton and drew the stopper back ever so slowly. Though the process was designed to filter out any undesirable particles from the mixture, it also served to hone Bertrand's craving.

Even though he'd done so on multiple occasions, Harvath wasn't a fan of torturing people. It had its place, but as far as Harvath was concerned it was only called for after all other reasonable alternatives had been exhausted. René Bertrand's obvious drug problem had provided him a perfect alternative to torture.

Although there probably would have been some who claimed that what Harvath was doing to the man right at this moment actually *was* torture, they'd be wrong. Harvath knew what real torture was and this wasn't it. This wasn't anywhere near it.

Harvath pulled up the right sleeve of the book dealer's suit jacket and then rolled up his shirt sleeve. Swabbing his arm with another piece of cotton that had been soaked with hand sanitizer he said, "We'll dispense with the chitchat, Monsieur Bertrand. You have something I want. The sooner you cooperate, the sooner you and Aunt Hazel here can start dancing, understand?"

Harvath watched as the man's eyes stayed locked on the loaded syringe which Harvath set down on the table. He knew that a heroin addiction was one of the worst addictions a person could have.

When Bertrand finally spoke, his voice was hoarse. "There is a special place in hell for people like you."

"Tell me where the *Don Quixote* is."

The book dealer mustered up a Gallic snort along with a contemptuous roll of his eyes. "So you may steal it from me? What an appealing offer. Is this how American universities do business today?"

This time the snort and a roll of the eyes came from Harvath. "Yeah, it's a new policy. We voted it in right after we decided to start carrying guns."

Though his blood was on fire, Bertrand didn't respond.

"René, we both know I don't work for any university. We also know you have a book that doesn't belong to you. It was stolen and I want it back."

"And who are you?" the Frenchman demanded. "My clients discovered that book. What makes you the rightful owner?"

Harvath was done screwing around with this guy. Picking up the syringe, he held it in front of the book dealer's nose and depressed the plunger, sending a stream of cooked heroin into the air.

"*Putain merde!*" the man yelled.

"Tell me where it is, René," demanded Harvath.

Bertrand refused to comply.

Harvath looked at Nichols. "Open the porthole."

"Excuse me?" replied the professor.

"Do it," commanded Harvath, gathering up the book dealer's drug paraphernalia along with the rest of his heroin.

Nichols opened the window and stood back as Harvath walked over and threw everything but the syringe into the river outside.

"Now," said Harvath as he returned to his seat and held up the needle for the muttering book dealer to gaze at. "This is all that's left. You tell me where that book is or else you can kiss this good-bye too."

To emphasize his point, Harvath depressed the plunger again, squirting more of the mixture into the air.

The book dealer fixed Harvath with a look of rage and in his heavily accented English finally said, "Enough. Stop. I will tell you where it is."

Harvath waited.

Bertrand looked at him like he was insane. "First give me the drug."

"First tell me where the *Don Quixote* is."

"Monsieur," the book dealer pleaded. "You help me and then I will help you. I promise."

"I want the book first," stated Harvath.

"Putain merde!" the man yelled again. "Please!"

Harvath raised the syringe and threatened to eject more liquid.

"I don't have it!"

"Where is it?"

"I can't get it," stammered Bertrand.

"Why not?" asked Harvath as he kept the syringe primed to spill its remaining contents.

"It is being held by a third party. They will not release the book until the money has been transferred."

"But any intelligent buyer would want to see the book firsthand before parting with that kind of money."

"But Monsieur—"

"He's right," injected Nichols. "Whoever wins the bid would be entitled to examine the book before transferring the funds."

Bertrand's face was like stone. "You must be aware that these people do not play around. If you do not pay them, there will be trouble."

"I'll take my chances," said Harvath as he lowered the syringe and let it hover millimeters above the man's arm. "Now where is the *Don Quixote?*"

The book dealer closed his eyes and exhaled. "It is being kept at a mosque in Clichy-sous-Bois."

CHAPTER 29

Having served in Iraq and other world hot spots, Tracy Hastings had an exceptional mind for operations. Right now, though, all she could do was lie on the bed in the darkened stateroom with a damp cloth across her eyes.

"Nichols was right," said Harvath as he used the computer to pull up information about the Bilal mosque in Clichy-sous-Bois. "We need to get you to a doctor."

"I told you. It'll pass," she responded.

Pushing away from the small, wooden desk he turned his chair so he could face her. "Let's drop this. Forget the president, forget the damn book; forget all of it."

Tracy removed the cloth and raised herself into a sitting position against the pillows. "You can't. Not because of me."

"The headaches are getting worse, not better. Look at you. You need help."

"So does Nichols. So does the president."

"After everything that has happened, how can you even think about the president?" demanded Harvath. "You were almost killed because of him."

"And I've let it go. Now it's your turn."

"I can't do that."

"You have to," she insisted.

Harvath leaned forward in his chair. "Tracy, I don't want my old life back. I want this life, the one I have now. I want you."

"And you've got me. I'm not going anywhere."

"You don't understand what I'm trying to do," Harvath began.

Tracy looked into his eyes. "Scot, I can't promise you that everything between us is going to be perfect. I dropped my crystal ball the day I got shot. What I can tell you is that I understand who you are. The better part of your life has been devoted to taking America's fight to its enemies, this enemy in particular. Now, without another person having to be maimed or killed, you have a chance to defeat one of the greatest threats civilization has ever seen. I'm not going to let you throw that away. I can't.

"This is what you're so good at. You know how these people play and you know how to beat them at their own game. You're angry with the president because he made some secret deal that freed a terrorist who stalked your friends and family. It's done. Get over it. This isn't about him. This is about right and wrong. And you need to do the right thing here."

"But you need help."

"Okay," she relented. "I need help. I'll get it. But I'm going to get it without you. And that's not open for discussion."

"Tracy, listen."

"Scot, if I have to get up off this bed just to beat some sense into you I will. I won't like it, but I'll do it."

Harvath smiled. Tracy Hastings was the most amazing woman he'd ever met. If they were blessed with a hundred years together, he could spend every single day of it telling her how much she meant to him without ever really coming close to how deeply he felt.

"I want to be happy and I want it to be with you. But for the two of us to work," she continued, "you can't stop being who you are."

"Even if I'm the guy who disappears for weeks at a time and can't tell you where I'm going or when I'll be back?"

"As long as it's not with a mistress, I think we'll find a way to make it work."

Harvath was at a loss.

"Now," said Tracy, sitting up straighter, "bring that laptop over here and let's figure out how we're going to get you into that mosque so you can get that book back."

CHAPTER 30

The book dealer had been careful in his dealings, very careful. Dodd had simply chalked it up to eccentricity. But it wasn't eccentricity, it was an over-abundance of caution and now he knew why.

Hacking the French servers had proven easier than he'd expected. The dossier on René Bertrand made for interesting reading. The man had a long history of offenses, most of them drug-related, but they had been escalating. Currently, the French police were looking into the book dealer's association with a smuggling ring that operated between Morocco and France. The investigation had everything: money, women, weapons, drugs, and lots and lots of people who had turned up dead.

As far as the authorities were concerned, Bertrand was definitely a person of interest, but the most telling detail, at least for Dodd, was the fact that the book dealer seemed to be reviled by everyone he had ever come in contact with.

René, the heroin fiend, needed to disappear and was desperate for money. No wonder he risked having his face seen in Paris. He needed to move the *Don Quixote* so he could cash in and evaporate. Until the police had appeared at the Grand Palais, Dodd had never suspected Bertrand had such skeletons in his closet. He should have known better.

His plan had been to make contact with the book dealer and keep active surveillance on him until Nichols showed up. At that point, Dodd had wanted to simply move in and take the man out. He could have done it a number of ways, but a knife in close would have been best.

Instead, Omar had laid out the car bombing scenario. Though Dodd strongly objected, the sheik had insisted on making a statement. The statement had failed, as had its follow-up attempt. Nichols had survived and now the book dealer and the *Don Quixote* had been taken out of play.

Omar was painfully shortsighted. He had access to unlimited funds and could have made an overwhelming preemptive bid for the book, but his desire to make his "statement" had gotten the better of him. Nichols wasn't as easy to kill as the sheik had anticipated.

Dodd had no idea who the man and woman helping him were, but he intended to see them die. Too much had gone wrong, and Dodd needed to end his string of bad luck. The most important thing, though, was getting that book.

The assassin had already tossed Bertrand's hotel room and had come up empty. Combing the man's dossier now, he searched for anything that might lead him to where the book dealer was keeping the *Don Quixote*.

Bertrand reminded him a bit of himself. He was a loner who had no family he could have left the book with. He had been living underground, moving from crappy hotel to crappy hotel, always a step ahead of the police. While Dodd didn't have to go to quite such extremes, he knew what those places were like and didn't relish the idea of having to visit each flophouse to conduct his own investigation. That said, he couldn't rule it out.

The assassin was about to log off, when something about one of the book dealer's drug arrests grabbed his attention. Bertrand was caught purchasing heroin in the violent Parisian suburb of Clichy-sous-Bois. It was the same suburb that experienced rioting after French police chased two doomed Muslim teenagers into an electrical substation. It wasn't his only arrest in Clichy-sous-Bois either.

Dodd began compiling a list of names of people arrested with the book dealer or named as being on the fringes of the police investigations. Several of them had very serious rap sheets. But more important than their criminal records was the fact that they were all of Moroccan descent and under investigation by the French internal intelligence service known as the Renseignements Généraux, or RG for short.

After spending considerable time trying to get in, Dodd realized that the RG's servers were beyond his ability to hack. He would have to satisfy himself with what he could learn about the men from the French police. Along with their mug shots, Dodd compiled a list of last known addressees, the details of their various arrests and one final scrap of information the RG probably had no idea was on the French police servers.

France's counterterrorism strategy was to disrupt violent attacks before they happened. To do that the RG had been monitoring every mosque, every cleric, and every Islamic sermon throughout France since the mid-1990s.

When the French police had mounted their own investigation of the men from Clichy-sous-Bois and had bumped up against the RG, they'd made mention of it in a memo. While details of the RG's investigation had been scrubbed, the source of overlap hadn't. The men associated with René Bertrand all attended the same mosque.

After printing out their pictures, Matthew Dodd shut down his computer and checked his watch. Depending on how long it took him to get ready and to get to Clichy-sous-Bois, he might even be able to attend evening prayers.

CHAPTER 31

W hat do we have?" asked Ozbek as he entered the crowded room and set his coffee at the head of the conference table. He'd been in his office talking with his veterinarian about his dog when the message from Steve Rasmussen came in on his BlackBerry.

"Within the last hour, there was a shooting in Paris," said Rasmussen as he gestured to the flat-panel monitor at the other end of the room. On it was a feed from a French television channel that showed police, news crews, and first responders outside an ornate building. "It happened at an antiquarian book fair at the Grand Palais. The shooter used a large-caliber handgun. He took three shots. His targets were three French police officers. Two are dead and one is in critical condition."

"If this was a Transept operative, the third cop would have bought it as well," said Ozbek.

"The hospital says he's as good as dead anyway."

Ozbek worked the pieces in his mind as he spoke. "So we've got a car bombing earlier today outside a small café well off the beaten tourist track. Then, this. Do we have a description of the shooter?"

"Not much."

"What about video? The Grand Palais must have CCTV footage."

"They do and I'm almost ready to upload it," offered Rasmussen.

"Give me the details about the shooting."

One of the unit's few female operatives, an attractive, fiercely intelligent brunette in her mid-thirties named Stephanie Whitcomb, responded, "According to preliminary reports, the shooter was seen with two other men. One is a French National and sometimes rare-book dealer named René Bertrand.

"Bertrand has a long history of drug-related offenses. He was being sought for questioning in relation to a smuggling ring out of Morocco."

"So the police spotted him at the book festival," said Ozbek, "and that's when the shooting began?"

"Correct," she replied. "The other man in the shooter's party is presumed to be an American."

"How do we know?"

"A witness overheard him earlier speaking English with a woman and a man, also presumed American. The shooter had the book dealer and the other man walk directly in front of him and probably had his weapon drawn, but hidden somehow. When the police ID'd René Bertrand and ordered him to stop, the guy started firing."

Rasmussen jumped in, pantomiming an elbow to the back of his chair. "At that point, the American turned and struck the shooter, knocking him down."

"Interesting," replied Ozbek.

"In the chaos," said Whitcomb, "the book dealer fled into the exhibit hall. The American chased after him and fired a shot from his own weapon into the air. Less than a minute later, the American fired two more shots. He then grabbed the book dealer by the neck and they were seen exiting the Grand Palais via a fire door."

"What happened to the first shooter?"

"He disappeared," she said.

"We've got our video," said Rasmussen as he directed the unit's attention back to the monitor. "According to our liaison with the French internal security service, the first shooter was very careful not to let his face be seen, but he screwed up."

The group watched as Rasmussen ran the footage and continued to narrate. "The man in the white suit is René Bertrand. The other man is our American. And right behind them is the original shooter."

Ozbek peered at the monitor. "I can't see his face."

"Keep watching," said Rasmussen.

They watched as the shooting unfolded. There were several different angles included with the feed. "Here it comes," he said. "Right as he gets elbowed by the American, he doubles over and goes down. Everyone is running by this point; mass pandemonium. But when our shooter straightens up and searches for the other two men, he accidentally reveals his profile for a fraction of a second."

"Can you enhance that?" asked Ozbek, thinking he recognized the face.

Rasmussen isolated the image and then enlarged it.

"Now run it against the Transept images. Start with our *Killed in Action No Remains Located* pal. Pull up his left side profile."

Rasmussen found it and put it up in a split screen. Nobody said a word. After a pause, Rasmussen combined the images by sliding one on top of the other. It was a perfect match.

"Ladies and gentlemen," said Ozbek. "Matthew Dodd aka Majd al-Din."

"Holy shit," replied Whitcomb.

"Holy shit indeed," repeated Ozbek as everyone stared at the screen. "Now, our next question is, what the hell is he up to?"

Rasmussen tapped a few keys on his laptop and said, "Thanks to the French, we may have an idea."

CHAPTER 32

R asmussen uploaded another stream of CCTV footage to the conference room monitor. "This is from the scene of the bombing earlier today. It was taken from a bank across the street."

The Dead Poets Society team members watched as the first car was stolen and then replaced with the Mercedes carrying the bomb.

Rasmussen split-screened the footage with a feed from another camera and while using a laser pointer said, "See these two customers sitting outside at the café? Once the Mercedes is in place, they get up and leave."

"Almost like they knew what was about to happen," said Whitcomb.

"Who are they?" asked Ozbek. "Can you enhance that?"

Rasmussen shook his head. "The footage is from a bank camera meant to monitor an ATM, not the café across the street. It gets too blurry, but it doesn't matter. Look at this." Clicking a few more keys, Rasmussen brought up the café from a different angle. "This is from a hotel security camera right up the street."

Ozbek stood up and walked over to the monitor. "Stop it right there. Can you go in tighter?"

Rasmussen did.

"That's him. Our American from the Grand Palais."

"It gets better," said his colleague. "Watch this." Rasmussen clicked his keys again and another angle came up. "This is from a second bank across the street."

Ozbek and the team watched as a mid-fifties man exited what looked like a bookstore and bumped into the American and his female counterpart. The man then walked toward the café while the

American and his companion walked in the opposite direction. Suddenly, the American seemed to notice something out of view. He then turned and ran after the man who had left the bookstore. He caught him right before the café and knocked him to the ground, covering him with his own body, just seconds before the car bomb exploded.

A hush fell over the conference room.

Ozbek was the first to break the silence. "What made the American run after the man from the bookstore?"

"No idea," replied Rasmussen. "It looks like he might have seen something—"

"Or someone," interjected Whitcomb.

"But whatever, or whoever, it was, it wasn't captured by any of the cameras. They did, though, capture this," said Rasmussen as he rewound the video feed to a much earlier point on its time code.

The team watched as a thin man in a white three-piece suit came up the sidewalk and looked up and down the street before entering the bookstore.

"René Bertrand," said Ozbek. "So he and the American were at both the bombing and the shooting. What about Dodd?"

"If he was there, he was very careful not to get recorded by any of the cameras."

Ozbek took a sip of his coffee as this new information played in his head. "What do we know about the American?" he asked. "He seems to have had foreknowledge of the bombing. But why chase the man from the bookstore down and risk exposure like that?"

"We're doing a facial recognition on him right now," said Whitcomb as she worked her own laptop.

"The American's female counterpart and the man coming out of the bookstore match the description of the duo the American was seen speaking with in English at the Grand Palais right before the shooting," said Rasmussen.

"If they were at the Grand Palais, the French should have them on video, shouldn't they?" asked Ozbek.

"They probably do, but they've got a lot of footage to comb through. It's going to take some time to find it."

"I want the faces of Ms. American and Mr. Bookstore run through the databases as well."

Rasmussen nodded. "Already on it."

"We need every scrap of information we can get," said Ozbek. "I want to know everything about these people. Who are they? Where are they from? Where have they been? Where are they now, and how the hell are they connected to Matthew Dodd? Also, I want to know what, if any, connection they have with Marwan Khalifa. That's it. Let's get to work."

Ozbek tossed his empty cup into the trash and was halfway to the door when Stephanie Whitcomb suddenly said, "I've got a hit."

Team members that had been filing out of the conference room turned and quickly came back in.

"On whom?" asked Ozbek.

"Our American," said Whitcomb. "His name is Scot Harvath. Scot is spelled with one *T*. United States citizen. Age thirty-seven. Hair brown. Eyes blue. Five-foot-ten. 175 pounds. We've got a passport number and place of issuance. I've also got a Social Security number and a handful of matches for newspaper and magazine articles for a U.S. ski team member with the same name from about twenty years ago. After that the trail goes dark."

"How *dark*?"

"This guy's a black. There's nothing else. No tax returns, nothing. I think it's been scrubbed," replied Whitcomb.

"Isn't that interesting?" replied Ozbek.

"Wait'll you see this," stated Rasmussen who had abandoned his subjects and had begun a search on Harvath through the CIA's proprietary database.

Tilting his head toward the monitor, he said, "Check it out."

Ozbek and the others watched as Harvath's passport photo materialized and then next to it, a more recent picture from what appeared to be a closed-circuit security camera.

There was something familiar about the background. "Where was that taken?" asked Ozbek.

Rasmussen looked at his CIA colleagues and then after double-checking his information replied, "Downstairs."

CHAPTER 33

As if three cabdrivers refusing to take him there weren't warnings enough, one look at Clichy-sous-Bois convinced Harvath that he'd made the right choice in leaving Tracy and Nichols back at the barge.

Not that he'd had much choice in the matter. Tracy's headache had left her immobile, and that meant the professor was the only one who could keep an eye on René Bertrand. Nevertheless, having them along in such a rough neighborhood would have been more of a hindrance than a help.

Clichy-sous-Bois was a dilapidated hellhole of poverty-stricken French housing projects that didn't even have its own Metro or RER train stop. Graffiti covered every surface and groups of tough young thugs wearing the latest gangster street wear sprouted like weeds from every corner. If it wasn't for the language difference, this could have been any ghetto back home from Compton to Queens. It was someplace Harvath definitely didn't belong.

The Bilal Mosque turned out to be a run-down, two-story warehouse attached to a butcher/pastry shop on one side and a public bath, or *hammam,* on the other. As they arrived in front, Harvath's cabdriver, a young Algerian immigrant named Moussa, offered to wait for him.

Harvath politely refused, but the man wouldn't take no for an answer. He liked Harvath. It was the first time he'd had an adult fare in his cab that didn't ask him to turn his American funk music off and who could converse with him about it at length. Anyone who knew all seven tracks of *Standing on the Verge of Getting It On* was better than all right in his book.

And though Moussa didn't live in Clichy-sous-Bois, he knew its reputation and made a persuasive argument that finding a cab once Harvath came out of the mosque would not only be impossible, but also could be extremely dangerous.

The young man was right. Harvath gave him a hundred euros and told him to stay close. The cabbie pointed to a café across the street and told Harvath if he wasn't in his taxi when he came out, that was where he would likely be.

Harvath thanked him and stepped out of the cab with the briefcase and a small rolling suitcase he had purchased in preparation for his visit to the mosque.

Leaving the barge had been one of the most dangerous parts of the operation. He no longer wondered if the police had begun circulating his picture. With the shooting at the Grand Palais, he knew they would be. He also assumed they had connected him to the bombing that morning. Therefore, purchasing some off-the-shelf items to disguise his appearance had been his first priority.

The suitcase and briefcase had come next, then a trip to one of Paris's ubiquitous art supply stores. With a visit to a used-book store and a computer equipment shop, his foray was complete and he had returned to the barge.

From his e-mail server, Nichols downloaded the high-resolution *Don Quixote* scans that Bertrand had sent him. They consisted only of the cover and the first five pages, but it would have to do. Playing with several different types of paper and the new printer Harvath had purchased, they got their work product as close to the real thing as possible.

Judicious use of the small oven in the galley added just the right patina of age to their decoy. Though it wouldn't stand up to close scrutiny, it didn't have to. It only had to allow Harvath to get out of the mosque without anyone knowing he'd made a switch. How to create the proper distraction, though, had turned out to be the hardest part of their planning.

It was Tracy who had come up with the idea and she had given Harvath instructions on how to best retrofit the device as well as the suitcase to match his needs. An auto supply store on the outskirts of Paris was his last stop before finally finding the cab that brought him to Clichy-sous-Bois.

It wasn't the most foolproof plan in the world, but no operation was ever one hundred percent airtight. You always had to leave room for the unexpected. Considering that they had little time and even less resources, it was their best hope.

Harvath doubted the members of the Bilal mosque would frisk him, but he didn't want to be carrying a weapon if they did and decided to go unarmed. If he was caught with a gun, it would have instantly blown his cover and their chance at the book would be lost.

It was in wrestling with how to play up his role as a nerdy and somewhat naïve academic that they hit upon the perfect way to pull off their plan.

Now, as Harvath approached the mosque door, he took a breath and focused on what he needed to do. Once he stepped inside that door, there would be absolutely no turning back.

CHAPTER 34

The first thing Harvath noticed upon entering the mosque was its sad state of disrepair. Though the congregation had done its best to spruce the place up, nothing could hide the fact that they were worshipping in an old warehouse that probably should have seen the better end of a wrecking ball twenty years ago. Whoever the founders of the mosque were, they obviously weren't getting any of Saudi Arabia's free-flowing cash; probably because the Bilal Mosque's version of Islam wasn't "pure" enough for their Wahhabist wing nuts.

Harvath despised the extremist Saudi state religion, Wahhabism, and how the Saudis zealously exported their poison around the globe, supporting it with billions of dollars every year.

Right behind the Wahhabis were the radical Deobandis, who controlled over fifty percent of the mosques in Great Britain and counted among their most devoutly faithful Afghanistan's notoriously evil Taliban regime.

Militant, orthodox Islam, be it of the Wahhabist, Deobandi, or any other flavor, was the biggest ideological problem the world faced. Muslims made up a majority in sixty-three countries around the globe. And of the thirty major conflicts under way in the world, twenty-eight involved Muslim governments or communities.

While people outside of Islam spoke of the need for it to reform, next to nothing was being done on the inside of Islam—where the commitment and desire really mattered. If Thomas Jefferson *had* been successful in discovering lost Koranic texts and if those texts could uncouple Islam from its militant, supremacist tendencies, then the entire world needed those texts now more than ever.

Harvath's thoughts were interrupted by a middle-aged, bearded man wearing gray trousers and a black cardigan sweater.

"As sala'amu alaikum," said the man, extending his right hand.

"I'm sorry," replied Harvath, careful to remain in character. "I don't speak French."

The man smiled. "It means, Peace be upon you. And it is not French; it is Arabic." His English was accented, but understandable.

"Oh," said Harvath, feigning ignorance as he returned the smile and shook the man's hand. "Thank you."

"How may I help you?"

"I am looking for Monsieur Namir Aouad, the mosque director?"

"And you have found him," said Aouad. "You must be Professor Nichols' assistant from the University of Virginia."

"Kip Winiecki," said Harvath recycling an old alias.

The mosque director pointed at Harvath's rolling suitcase. "Do you plan on staying with us long?"

Harvath looked at the suitcase and laughed politely. "No, sir. Professor Nichols has me booked on a flight home tonight. He wants me to begin getting things ready for the arrival of the *Don Quixote.*"

Namir Aouad was charming. Harvath had to remind himself to remain on his guard.

"I was surprised when Monsieur Bertrand told me that Professor Nichols would not be coming himself," remarked Aouad. "For something of such great value, doesn't the professor want to authenticate it in person?"

It was a question Harvath had been prepared for. "Novels in the *picaresco* style of the late sixteenth century are not exactly the professor's forte."

"Which is why he selected you?"

"Precisely," replied Harvath as he pushed the glasses he was wearing back up his nose.

Whether the mosque's director was suspicious of the response or not, he didn't let on. "You can leave your bag here," said Aouad. "No one will touch it."

Harvath didn't doubt him, but he needed it with him. "I have some materials in it I may need while examining the book."

"As you wish," said the man as he gestured toward his office.

Harvath followed. Along with the glasses and wig he had purchased, Harvath had adopted a slightly stooped posture. He completed his hopefully disarming disguise by placing a stone in his right shoe, which gave him a pronounced limp. Right now, Scot Harvath looked like anything but a counterterrorism operative.

Aouad's office was fronted by a traditional Islamic door—shorter and wider than those normally found in the West. The door seemed to be one of the only upgrades that had been made.

Inside, the office looked much like Harvath imagined it had for more than sixty years, the main furniture consisting of a cheap metal desk at one end and two metal chairs. A somewhat rusty gooseneck lamp sat atop the desk and aided the sputtering fluorescent lights hanging from the ceiling above.

Along the walls were pieces of art that incorporated Koranic verses proclaiming the glory of Allah. A collection of scratched bookcases contained multiple volumes of the Koran, the Hadith, and other Islamic texts. There was a computer, a printer, a telephone, steel file cabinets, and all of the other equipment one would expect to find in almost any kind of office.

"May I offer you tea?" asked Aouad.

"Yes, please," replied Harvath. "Thank you."

As the mosque director walked around his desk and picked up the phone, he motioned for Harvath to take a seat.

Harvath left his suitcase near the door and walked over to one of the chairs. French was his second language. He had learned it in grade school under the strict tutelage of the nuns of the French order of the Sacred Heart and he listened now with interest as Aouad requested the tea as well as two additional men.

It wasn't necessarily an unusual request, especially considering the circumstances, but what bothered Harvath was the way Aouad had looked right at him when he'd asked for the two men. It was an odd tell.

Moments later, two large men knocked and entered Namir Aouad's office. The fact that one of them was carrying a diminutive tea tray did nothing to quiet the alarm bells that began going off in Harvath's head.

CHAPTER 35

A ydin Ozbek met Carolyn Leonard at a quiet table near the back bar. The head of Jack Rutledge's Secret Service detail, she was in her late thirties, about five-foot-ten, and very fit. She wore her red hair down around her shoulders, and her understated Brooks Brothers suit concealed a .40 caliber Sig Sauer 229, two spare magazines, a BlackBerry, Guardian Protective Devices "pop-and-drop" OC grenades, and a few other tools necessary to her trade.

As a rule, Ozbek never dated women who were in the military, law enforcement, or the intelligence realm. For Carolyn Leonard, though, he'd long been willing to break that rule. She was easily one of the most attractive and eligible single women in D.C., a fact that most likely had made her rise to one of the most prominent positions in the Secret Service much more difficult than it should have been.

Despite his obvious attraction to her, Carolyn had never showed him any interest beyond friendship. It was probably for the best. Meeting up, hooking up, and breaking up would not have been conducive to the favor he needed now, even for a professional like Carolyn Leonard.

"I can't talk to you about this," she said as she pushed the small Sony Cybershot camera back across the table.

Uploading the stills and closed-circuit footage to a digital camera seemed a lot more discreet to the CIA operative than handing Leonard a big manila envelope with a couple of VHS tapes and a stack of 8 x 10 photographs inside.

"Come on, Carolyn," he replied. "I'm not asking for state secrets here. I just need you to ID the guy and answer a couple of questions for me."

The CIA operative slid the camera halfway back across the table.

She looked at him. "You're asking me to violate my oath."

"No, I'm not. I just need to know what's going on."

"Aydin," said Leonard with a smile, "you work for the CIA. Are you telling me that things have gotten so bad over there that you need the Secret Service to do your investigations for you?"

Ozbek smiled. "We're all on the same side and we all need help from time to time. Will you look at the videos again, please?"

Leonard was quiet for a moment. "I don't need to see them again."

Now it was Ozbek's turn to be quiet. He'd learned a long time ago that most people were uncomfortable with silence and would fill the void if you kept your own mouth shut long enough.

"What do you know about Scot Harvath?" she asked.

The CIA operative had been able to piece some of the information together before meeting with Leonard. "He's a Navy SEAL who was transferred to the Secret Service to help you with both antiterrorism and counterterrorism operations at the White House. He was instrumental in helping recover the president when he was kidnapped several years ago.

"He has been involved in a few off-the-books assignments and everyone who has ever worked with him considers him a top-notch operator. Other than that, nobody knows what he has been up to."

Leonard didn't say anything.

"My guess," said Ozbek, "is that maybe he was drawn over to the dark side on a permanent basis. There was mention of him being attached to something called the Office of International Investigative Assistance at DHS helping international law enforcement and intelligence agencies head off terror attacks, but that's about as far as I got. The guy doesn't seem to stay in one job very long."

"Well, you got one thing right," she replied. "He is a top-notch operator."

"So what's he doing in Paris at the sites of a bombing and a shooting today?"

"I don't know."

"Carolyn, you saw how he humped and dumped that guy seconds before the explosion. He *knew* it was going to happen. He's involved with that bombing somehow."

Leonard took a sip of her drink. "You still haven't explained what your interest is in all of this."

Ozbek knew better than to hold out on her. "The man behind Harvath in the video from the shooting—we have reason to believe he's one of ours who went off the reservation."

"You think Harvath is *working* with him?" she said, the tone of disbelief evident in her voice.

"I don't know what to think. That's why I'm talking to you. You know Harvath."

"And I know him well enough to know that he wouldn't be involved in a bombing or a shooting."

"Really?" asked Ozbek. "Then give me a plausible explanation for why I have video of him at the scenes of both."

"Jesus, Aydin. Are we really having this conversation? Harvath saved a person who otherwise would have been blown to bits in that bombing, and it's obvious the guy at the shooting had a gun on him."

"But why? Why Harvath? Why both scenes? That's what I'm trying to get at."

Leonard looked at Ozbek. "You, a CIA operative, have suspicions that Harvath is involved in black ops yet you're asking *me,* a Secret Service agent, what he's up to in Paris? Oz, let me ask you a question."

"Shoot."

"What kind of money do you guys get for chasing your tails like this?"

Ozbek ignored the sarcasm and changed his line of questioning. "The woman with Harvath, who is she?"

"She's his girlfriend," replied Leonard. "Tracy Hastings. Ex-Navy. She was an EOD tech before an IED she was defusing went off prematurely and took out her eye and part of her face."

Though the video wasn't the best quality in the world, Ozbek found it hard to believe the attractive woman he had seen had suffered such a horrific tragedy.

"You wouldn't know it by looking at her," added Leonard, somehow reading his mind. "If you've got her face on video, you should have been able to run it through all of your databases and get a match, at least for her passport photo."

When Ozbek didn't answer she said, "You didn't have a match on her, did you? Why not?"

Ozbek replied truthfully. "The video footage from the bombing wasn't good enough."

Leonard leaned back in her chair. "Imagine that."

"What about the man Harvath saved from the bomb?" asked the CIA operative.

"No idea," she replied.

Her answer came a little too quickly for his liking. "Even though the video quality was bad," he said as he picked up the digital camera and switched to the still pictures he had stored on it, "I ran his image through the database anyway."

"Standard operating procedure, I would imagine," said Leonard.

"We get paid for doing a little bit more than chasing our tails."

Leonard remained silent.

"Anyway," continued Ozbek, "we ran it and got hits all over the place. None of them were what we were looking for so we applied some filters to try to narrow it down. The one person I could tie him to was Harvath, so I started there. I ran the subject through the U.S. Navy database, the database at DHS, even the Secret Service."

"You've been a naughty boy."

Ozbek brushed off the remark. "Then on a real wild hair, I ran him through a different Secret Service database."

Leonard raised her eyebrows. "Something tells me *naughty* may not exactly be enough to cover what you've been up to."

"We got an eighty percent match on a repeat visitor to the White House, cleared and badged for all access except the situation room. Want to see his photo?" asked the CIA operative as he brought up the image on his camera.

"Not particularly."

Ozbek turned the camera around for her to see anyway. "His name is Anthony Nichols. He's a professor at UVA. He also holds an American passport and flew into Charles De Gaulle Airport from Reagan National two days ago."

"That's a hell of a coincidence," said Leonard.

"I might agree with you," replied Ozbek, "if it weren't for the fact that I don't believe in coincidences."

Leonard didn't say anything.

"Carolyn, there are a lot of dead people in Paris right now—two of them cops. The guy behind it all is very likely a former CIA operative named Matthew Dodd who staged his own death and went to ground several years ago."

Ozbek thought about mentioning Marwan Khalifa, but until he knew that Khalifa was actually dead and that Matthew Dodd had something to do with it, he thought better of it. "This guy Nichols," he said, "is in a lot of danger. More than he may know."

"Dodd is that good?"

"He was one of our best. I need to stop him, but I can't do it without your help. And no matter how good an operator Harvath may be, he has no idea what he is up against with Dodd," said Ozbek as he set the camera down in front of her.

Leonard looked at Anthony Nichols' face on the camera's display for several moments.

After asking a few more questions, she powered the camera down, and slid it into her pocket. Rising from her seat she said, "I'll see what I can do."

"Where are you going?"

"Keep your phone on," said Leonard as she walked away from the table. "I'll be in touch."

CHAPTER 36

Jack Rutledge set aside the file he was reading and removed his glasses as Carolyn Leonard knocked and entered the Oval Office.

"Thank you for seeing me, sir," said Leonard. "I know how busy you are today."

"I'm never too busy for the head of my Secret Service detail," said Rutledge as he stood and invited her to join him in one of the two chairs in front of the fireplace. "Please come in."

"Thank you, sir."

Once she was seated, the president sat down across from her and remarked, "I get lots of people every day who'd like to have five minutes with me. Not many of them are as cryptic as you are about their reasons. What's going on?"

"Mr. President, I hope you understand how seriously I take my job."

"Carolyn, if you're bucking for a raise," kidded Rutledge, "you're going to have to take it up with the director of the Secret Service."

"No, sir," replied Leonard. "This isn't about a raise."

"Then what do you need?"

"Mr. President, my job is to protect you, and I take that job very seriously."

"For which I am very grateful," said Rutledge, as he noticed her removing a small digital camera from her pocket.

Leonard smiled politely before continuing. "I would never want to jeopardize our professional relationship by overstepping my bounds—"

"Carolyn," interrupted the president. "If I think you are overstepping your bounds, I'll tell you. What's this all about? Do you need a photo for someone? You don't have to be embarrassed by that. All you have to do is ask."

The Secret Service agent glanced at the camera and then back at the president. "I wish it were that simple, Mr. President. I'm here about the gentleman you hired to be your archivist."

"Anthony Nichols?" asked Rutledge, thinking it was odd that he hadn't heard from him and yet here was the head of his protective detail bringing up the man's name. The president sat up a bit straighter. "What about him?"

"Are you aware that Mr. Nichols is in Paris, sir?"

The president shook his head and lied. "No, but Mr. Nichols is free to travel wherever he wants. He's a grown man. Why are you bringing this to my attention?"

"You were briefed on the bombing that happened there earlier today?" asked Leonard.

"Of course, but what does that have to do with Anthony Nichols?"

"He was there."

"He *was*?" Rutledge exclaimed. "Was he hurt?"

"No sir, he was very fortunate. Someone knocked him down just before the blast happened."

As the president took a moment to process what he was hearing, Leonard continued. "The person who knocked him down was Scot Harvath."

Rutledge was shocked. *"Harvath?* What's he doing in Paris?"

Leonard turned on the digital camera, selected the video clip of the shooting and handed it to the president. "This was taken at the Grand Palais in Paris several hours after the bombing."

The president watched the footage all the way through and then replayed it.

"Two of the three police officers who were shot were pronounced dead on the scene. The third passed away in a hospital forty-five minutes ago."

"My God," replied Rutledge.

"The CIA believes—"

"The CIA?" exclaimed the president.

"Yes, sir. They believe that the shooter in that clip is a CIA operative named Matthew Dodd who faked his own death and disappeared off the grid several years ago after converting to Islam."

"*Islam?*"

"Yes, sir."

"Do they know what Harvath was doing with him?"

"From the video," said Leonard, "it looks like he was his prisoner."

"Where is Harvath now?"

"According to my source, no one knows."

Rutledge reminded himself to remain calm and more importantly, quiet.

"I made a couple of anonymous inquiries through contacts I have in Paris," said Leonard. "Harvath's picture along with those of the shooter, Anthony Nichols, and Tracy Hastings are being circulated to law enforcement officers throughout France."

"Tracy Hastings is caught up in this as well?"

"Apparently, she had been at the Grand Palais with Harvath and Anthony Nichols shortly before the shooting."

"Who's the other man in the video; the man in the white suit?" asked the president.

"He's a rare-book dealer with quite a sketchy background named René Bertrand."

The book dealer? thought Rutledge. *Everything was coming unglued.*

"Why am I hearing this from you and not the CIA?"

"The CIA has a unit responsible for hunting down intelligence agents who go missing. The man who heads the unit is an acquaintance of mine," said Leonard.

"That still doesn't explain why he came to you with this."

"He knows Professor Nichols has visited the White House on several occasions. He also knows of course that Harvath worked here. He's looking for information that might lead to the capture of his rogue operative and he thought I could help him."

The president raised his eyebrows. "Which means what?"

"As I said, sir," replied Leonard, "I take my job very seriously. I do not discuss what goes on inside your administration."

Rutledge felt the knot in his stomach loosen ever so slightly. "I appreciate your professionalism, Carolyn. What else can you tell me about what happened in Paris?"

"My contact says the CIA has reason to believe that Nichols is involved in something that certain fundamentalist Islamic figures find very threatening; something they may be willing to kill for in order to keep quiet."

"Does your acquaintance know who this Matthew Dodd is working for?"

"He wouldn't say," replied Leonard. "To tell you the truth, I think he might have been holding out on me."

"Why?"

"From what I gathered, he has been putting his fingers into pies here at home, which is something that the CIA is forbidden to do. He did tell me, though, that Matthew Dodd is one of the most dangerous operatives the Agency has ever fielded. He doesn't know what Harvath's involvement is in all this, but he's concerned that Harvath doesn't know the seriousness of what he's up against with Dodd."

Rutledge took a second to let it all sink in and then stood. "Thank you for bringing this to my attention, Carolyn," he said. "I haven't spoken with Scot Harvath recently—"

"I'm sorry to interrupt," interjected Leonard politely, "but I actually heard a rumor that Harvath had a nasty run-in with someone and actually retired over it. Is that true?"

"I can't comment."

"I understand, sir," said the Secret Service agent, who then shook her head and laughed. "Whoever would allow an operative like Scot Harvath to hang up his jersey has got to be a complete fool, right?"

"If I hear from Professor Nichols," replied the president, "I will definitely make sure to pass along your warning."

Leonard recognized the signal that their meeting was over and stood as well. "There has got to be some way to get a warning to Harvath too. He needs to know what's going on. Isn't there anybody who can get in touch with him?"

"If I can think of anybody, I'll get on it right away," said Rutledge as he held out his hand. "Thank you for coming to see me."

Leonard accepted the president's grasp and offered up her other hand to accept the digital camera back.

"May I hold on to this for a little while?" he asked as he saw her to the door.

"Of course," she replied.

As soon as Leonard was gone, President Jack Rutledge crossed back to his desk and snatched up the telephone.

CHAPTER 37

PARIS

The men Namir Aouad had called into his office were each at least six-foot-three and well over two hundred and ninety pounds.

They had jet black hair and close-cropped beards. Their dark eyes were alert and wary. One of the men had a long hooked nose that resembled a vulture's beak while the other's looked misshapen, probably from having been broken multiple times.

Aouad issued a fresh set of commands in French. Big Bird, as Harvath had nicknamed him, set the tea tray down on the mosque director's desk and poured the steaming mint liquid. In the man's enormous hands, the pitcher looked like a child's toy.

The other man stood near the door at rigid attention, his hands clasped in front of his privates like a soccer player waiting to absorb a free kick. His eyes never drifted from Harvath. There were moments, during pauses in the conversation, where if Harvath strained his ears, he thought he could hear the air whistling in and out of the man's malformed nasal cavities.

Clichy-sous-Bois was a tough area, and Harvath couldn't help but wonder what else mosque director Namir Aouad was into besides being a middleman for stolen first edition *Don Quixote*s.

As he and Aouad made small talk over their tea, Harvath remained purposefully vague. His was a hastily created identity and the last thing he wanted to do was blow it by getting trapped in a subject he should have been an expert at.

Tea was a traditional show of good faith on Aouad's part. Refusing him could have been seen as an insult. It was important to make the man as comfortable as possible.

Luckily, Aouad was a soccer fan and Harvath followed the sport closely enough to be able to converse on that subject until they were finished.

Once Big Bird had cleared the tray, Harvath lifted his briefcase and set it upon Aouad's desk. "Shall we get started?" he asked as he popped the latches and began to withdraw the items he would pretend to use to authenticate the *Don Quixote*.

"Of course," said the mosque director as he nodded to one of his men. The man with the whistling nostrils approached one of the steel file cabinets, pulled out a long drawer and removed a battered wooden box about the size of a small portable typewriter. He approached the desk and handed it to Aouad who thanked him and told him to wait outside the door with Big Bird.

The mosque director set the box down on his desk, raised its thick lid, and said, "It's all yours. At least it *will* be, once payment is made."

Harvath smiled and stepped around the desk. Immediately, he was struck by the fact that it was some sort of puzzle box.

When Scot was little, his father had brought him back multiple puzzle boxes from Japan, some with over a hundred moves necessary to open them. Harvath loved them and so had his father, who was an avid woodworker. The boxes had always seemed a strange metaphor for their intricate and complicated relationship.

Though Jefferson's puzzle box was in a state of disrepair, there was no mistaking its exceptional joinery and that it had been crafted from a collection of fine hardwoods. At one point the box had most likely been polished to a fine sheen and its brass hardware to a noticeable luster. It definitely would have been a handsome and practical addition to the accoutrements Jefferson kept in his offices at the Carthusian monastery.

It had been marred, though, by time and the conditions under which it lay hidden. It also bore unsightly gouge marks where a screwdriver or worse yet, a hammer and chisel or pry bar had been used to force it open.

As Harvath ran his fingers across the front surface, he discovered a barely discernible, inlaid monogram that bore the initials *TJ*.

Harvath and his father had attempted crafting rudimentary puzzle boxes of their own, but certainly nothing as beautiful as Jefferson's. It took Harvath back to the woodshop in his family's garage and he wondered what his father would have thought of being able to run his hands along a work of art that had once belonged to such a notable American.

Harvath's interest in the puzzle box was not lost upon Aouad. "The box is also available for purchase. For an additional fee, of course."

"I'll be sure to let the university know," said Harvath as his eyes fell upon the object of his assignment.

Sitting in the center of the box, the book lay wrapped in a long strip of muslin discolored with age. Carefully, Harvath removed the book and set it upon the desk. "Do you mind?" he asked as he reached right across Aouad's chest and adjusted the gooseneck lamp to better the lighting.

"Be my guest," said the man as he stepped around to the opposite side of the desk to give Harvath more room to work.

Harvath spun his briefcase around and removed a pair of white cotton gloves. Now, a portion of Aouad's desk was obscured from the mosque director by both the lid of Jefferson's box and of Harvath's briefcase.

Aouad watched as Harvath laid a small jeweler's mat on the desk and then delicately unwound the strip of fabric from the tome.

As Nichols had warned him, the book was in poor condition. Harvath tsked loudly and shook his head as he explored its original limp vellum binding.

"Had the book been in perfect condition," offered the director, concerned that Harvath was mounting a case for a lower offer, "the price would have been much higher."

Harvath ignored him and continued his examination. The book was exactly the size the professor had said it would be, but it was heavier than they had expected.

Harvath placed the series of images which had been e-mailed to Nichols off to the side of the box and gently opened the more than four-hundred-year-old book to its first page.

Readily visible were the first edition hallmarks Harvath had been told to look for. There was the dedication to the Duke of Bejar, a descendant of the royal family of the ancient kingdom of Navarra, as well as the Latin phrase, "After the shadows I await the light."

He compared the images to the aging book before him and then slowly turned to its twenty-sixth chapter. Nichols had instructed him that only the first edition bore a description of Don Quixote forming a rosary from his shirt tails. In subsequent editions it was changed to "oak galls" in order to appease seventeenth-century Spanish censors. Someone who truly knew how to authenticate the book would have known to look for this and Nichols had made sure that Harvath, who spoke limited Spanish, knew exactly where to find it.

It took him several minutes, but Harvath finally found it. It was amazing. Out of an original four hundred copies of *Don Quixote* only eighteen first editions were known to still exist. What Harvath now held in his hands was the nineteenth.

It was an incredible discovery made even more remarkable by its provenance and the secrets it promised to unlock. Harvath was left with only one final item to authenticate.

Jefferson was known to insert his private mark, or more accurately his initials, at very precise locations in his books. At that time, signature marks were placed on the bottom of certain pages to help guide the bookbinder in the proper assembly or "gathering" of a manuscript, as it used to be called, into book form.

Each section of a book was issued a different signature, normally letters which progressed in alphabetical order. Jefferson's mark consisted of writing the capital letter *T* before the signature letter *J*. And at the printed signature letter *T*, he would follow it with his own letter *J*.

Harvath took his time as he patiently looked for both marks. His heart beat faster as he found the handwritten *T* mated to the publisher's *J* and then the handwritten *J* following the printed *T*. This was Thomas Jefferson's *Don Quixote*. Harvath was sure of it. There were notes on multiple pages, but he had no idea which contained the secret to the order of the wheel cipher discs. That would be for Nichols to unravel.

Harvath forced himself to take a breath. This was the hard part. Placing the book upon the jeweler's mat, he cautiously reached into his briefcase with his other hand.

Suddenly, a piercing siren erupted from the other side of the room.

CHAPTER 38

Namir Aouad spun toward the door. He was startled and had no idea what was happening.

Within seconds, Big Bird and Whistles had burst back into the room, their hands menacingly hovering inside their jackets.

Harvath shook his hands in the air as he limped around the desk. "My fault," he yelled as he wobbled to where the men were gathered around his suitcase. "I'm sorry."

He removed his gloves and fumbled with the combination lock on the outermost zippered compartment while the deafening shriek continued. Other people from the mosque were now sticking their heads in the director's office to see what was going on and Aouad yelled at Big Bird to shut the door.

Finally, Harvath got the combination lock open and unzipped his bag. Fishing out a device the size of a garage door opener he depressed a series of buttons and the earsplitting alarm stopped.

"Wow," said Harvath as he swung the device from the lanyard he had attached to it. "Can you imagine what would have happened if that had gone off while I was on the airplane? Maybe I should take the batteries out."

Big Bird and Whistles glared at him.

Harvath held the object up a little higher so they could see it better. In reality, it was a poor man's car alarm that was made to be clipped to a visor. It reacted to breaking glass, movement in the vehicle, or in

Harvath's circumstance the panic button on a remote key fob from across the room. With Tracy's help, he had been able to boost the sensor and replace a small part of the suitcase material to look like a patch, but which in reality helped the key fob to connect with the alarm. "You hang this on your doorknob," lied Harvath, "in case someone tries to get into your hotel room."

"Monsieur Winiecki, are you quite finished?" asked Aouad, who had already returned to his desk to make sure nothing had happened to the *Don Quixote*.

"Not really," said Harvath as he hobbled back.

"Please hurry up. Evening prayers will be starting soon."

Harvath put his gloves back on, pushed his glasses back up the bridge of his nose, and squeezed past the mosque director.

He focused on the book's title page, comparing it repeatedly to the image that René Bertrand had e-mailed to Nichols.

Finally, Harvath closed the book, delicately rewrapped it in the faded strip of muslin, and placed it back inside Jefferson's box. Closing the lid, he gathered his items and began placing them into his briefcase.

"And?" said Aouad, his eyebrows raised. "Are you satisfied?"

"With the item's authenticity, yes. But its condition leaves much to be desired."

"Monsieur Winiecki, as I said—" began the man.

Harvath held his hand up as he closed the lid of his briefcase. "The price reflects the book's condition, I understand. I can tell you that neither Professor Nichols, nor the university, is going to be happy with what I have seen here tonight."

Namir Aouad was no fool and he smiled. "Monsieur, you and I both know that your university is going to be thrilled to have this book."

Harvath didn't reply.

"I'll tell you what. For an additional twenty thousand, I would be happy to include this handsome wooden box."

"Five," replied Harvath as he watched the director run his hand over its lid.

"Fifteen," countered Aouad.

"Ten and that's my last offer."

The mosque director held out his hand. "It is acceptable," he said.

Harvath shook the man's hand and then picked up his briefcase. "I'll inform Professor Nichols and he will have the university wire the money to René Bertrand's account."

"Excellent," replied Aouad as he walked his guest to the door and helped him retrieve his rolling bag. "I believe you have a cab waiting?"

The man was well informed. "I do."

"Wonderful. Then I will wish you a bon voyage and as soon as Monsieur Bertrand informs us that the funds have been received, we will arrange to have the book *and* the box delivered to Professor Nichols."

Harvath nodded and followed Whistles and Big Bird to the front of the warehouse. The mosque was beginning to fill up.

Harvath smiled at Aouad's two goons as they stopped the torrent of people flooding in so that he could exit the front door. Once again, the men just glared at him.

Outside on the pavement, the evening air was chilly and crisp. As Harvath exhaled, he could see his breath. Gripping the handles of his briefcase and suitcase, he looked both ways before crossing the street.

The cab was still there; parked only a few lengths away. When Harvath reached it, he saw that it was empty and he made a beeline for the café. The sooner he got off the streets, out of Clichy-sous-Bois, and back to the Sargasso safe house, the better he was going to feel.

Harvath entered the run-down café and paused to allow his eyes to adjust to the poor lighting. The scent of apple-flavored tobacco filled his nose as his eyes began to pierce the semi-darkness. Men sat on cushions around low tables paying their bills, draining coffee cups, and taking final tokes on hookah pipes before heading off to evening prayers.

At the end of the *comptoir,* Harvath saw his driver, Moussa. The young man was standing not far from an older man in a knit cap with a bushy red beard.

As Harvath approached, the man in the cap looked up and their eyes met. There was something familiar about him. It was more like a feeling, but Harvath couldn't place it. The wheels in his brain spun, trying to figure out how he knew the man. There was something about his eyes.

Suddenly it hit him—*the Grand Palais!*

Harvath had already dropped his suitcase and was charging for the door when Matthew Dodd reached under his shirt and pulled out his weapon.

CHAPTER 39

Had Harvath had more time beforehand, he would have thoroughly scouted Clichy-sous-Bois before ever approaching the mosque. Having a "rabbit hole," as it was known in tradecraft terms, where he could safely disappear and change his appearance would have been invaluable. But at this point all he had were his instincts and they told him to run like hell.

Hitting the pavement outside the café, Harvath cut back across the street and used the people entering the mosque for cover. He had no idea why he thought it would work. If this really was the shooter from the Grand Palais, he'd already gunned down three cops. What would a bunch of civilians matter?

They probably wouldn't, but they would afford Harvath some cover and make him harder to target and so he ran straight for the crowd and plunged into their midst on the sidewalk in front of the Bilal.

A million questions like *Who the hell was this guy?* and *How had he found me?* were pounding on the door of Harvath's mind but he refused to devote any attention to them. Right now his entire mind had to be focused on staying alive.

He didn't need to look over his shoulder to know that the shooter was right behind him. Out on the street, Harvath was still a sitting duck, so he did the only thing he could—he plowed his way back into the mosque.

There was a murmur of dissent from the men as Harvath continued pushing, jabbing, and shoving his way through the crowd. Indignation rose as he grew even more aggressive.

Men cursed at him in French and Arabic—one even spat, but it had little effect. The Secret Service had taught him how to fight his way through a crush of people and he was exceedingly good at it.

Two men made the mistake of trying to block Harvath's path. He had no time to negotiate with them. The man closest to him received a knee strike to the common peroneal nerve in his upper thigh, rendering him unable to stand. Harvath then rammed his shoulder into him, tumbling the man into his associate as he fought his way deeper inside the mosque. All the while, he kept a death grip on his briefcase.

Suddenly, men began shouting behind him and then he heard gunfire. The mob of worshippers panicked. The shouts turned to screams.

As the panicked mass crushed forward, Harvath's eyes searched for a way out. The only chance he had was to find an exit of some sort at the rear of the mosque, but nothing short of a bulldozer was going to clear the way fast enough. If he didn't do something soon, he was going to be trampled and possibly even killed.

Fighting his way out wasn't an option. The people around him were packed too tight. They were nothing more than sheep and Harvath had learned a long time ago that sheep had only two speeds— graze and *stampede*. And once the stampede started, the only thing that could save you was to get the hell out of its way.

As the crowd surged deeper still, a three-paneled screen was knocked to the floor. That's when Harvath saw his way out—a recessed doorway that had been hidden by the screen.

Using all of his strength, Harvath moved laterally through the throngs of terrified people to get right up against the wall.

Planting one foot in front of the other, he kept a tight grip on the briefcase as he fought his way back to the door.

By the time he got there, Harvath discovered a father and his young son seeking sanctuary, pressing themselves into its whisper-thin recess.

The father's hand was on the doorknob and he rattled it as Harvath approached, demonstrating that it was locked.

Harvath signaled for the man to move and slammed the bottom of his foot into the door, which splintered and gave way with a crack. As it did, Harvath yelled for the father to get his son inside. He followed right behind and was greeted by damp air and the faint scent of chlo-rine from the bathhouse.

Harvath closed the door behind them and wedged a thin piece of lumber beneath the handle in hopes of keeping it shut. At least long enough for him to get away.

When he caught up to his fellow evacuees, he looked at the father and asked in French where the exit was.

The man shrugged and gestured around the narrow passageway with palms upturned.

The time for Harvath to get away was now, while chaos still reigned inside the mosque. Having switched the real *Don Quixote* with the fake he, Nichols, and Tracy had created, all that mattered was that he get it out of Clichy-sous-Bois and back to the barge.

He realized that if there was an exit at the back of the mosque, most of the people running in that direction would get out that way. That made chances pretty good that Harvath could exit the back of the bathhouse and get somewhat lost in the crowd as they all spilled out into the neighborhood.

The only problem was that the shooter was probably thinking the exact same thing. Though he'd have less cover going out the front door, it was the option that made the most sense.

Making his way through the *hammam,* Harvath found the reception area and the front doors. He checked for any signs that they were wired to an alarm system. The last thing he wanted to do was draw any more attention to himself.

As he began to unlock the doors, he decided to remove the *Don Quixote* from the false bottom he'd created in his briefcase and tuck it into the waistband of his trousers.

He was in the process of balancing the briefcase on the door handles when a noise from behind caused him to turn.

As he did, he was hit in the chest and blown through the doors.

CHAPTER 40

CIA HEADQUARTERS
LANGLEY, VIRGINIA

So that's it?" asked Aydin Ozbek as he gripped his telephone. "He just kept the camera and said nothing?"

The CIA operative listened to Carolyn Leonard for a few more moments in dismay. The call was winding down as Stephanie Whitcomb poked her head inside Ozbek's office. He held up his index finger indicating he was almost finished.

"Yeah, I understand," he said into the telephone. "I appreciate your trying. If you come across anything, please let me know."

After hanging up, Ozbek turned his attention to Whitcomb, who stood in the doorway with a folder tucked under her arm. "What's up?" he asked.

"The FBI agents interrogating Andrew Salam want to access some of our database information."

"Why?"

"The more they talk to him, the more they believe that maybe he didn't kill that woman at the Jefferson Memorial," she said.

"No kidding. I told them the same thing, but what's that have to do with accessing our databases?"

"Using Salam's description of his handler, they pulled photos of their own people going back twenty-five years, loaded them onto a laptop and worked them into a digitized mug book."

"And they got nothing," replied Ozbek.

Whitcomb looked at him. "What does that tell you?"

The CIA operative rolled his eyes. It was a stupid question. "Ah, that whoever recruited him wasn't really an FBI agent?"

"But what if he *was* an intelligence operative who just worked for another agency?"

Ozbek picked up his pen and tapped it on his desk blotter. "The FBI would be able to get whatever they wanted from DEA, DHS, DOJ."

"But not CIA. Not without asking us first."

"Whoa," cautioned Ozbek. "Maybe the Bureau's okay with flashing pictures of their people at Salam, but there's no way in hell we're going to do that. We can't."

"That's exactly what I said. No dice."

"So why are we even talking about this?" asked Ozbek, who was anxious to get back to work.

Whitcomb drew the file folder out from under her arm. "The Bureau guys are smart. They came up with a compromise."

"Like what?"

"They brought Salam an Identi-Kit and just sent over this composite," she said as she pulled a page from her folder. She held it up for Ozbek to see. "They want to know if we can search our databases for any candidates that might be a match for this guy."

Even with Whitcomb standing across the room in his doorway, Ozbek recognized the likeness immediately. Matthew Dodd's face wasn't one he was ever going to forget.

CHAPTER 41

CLICHY-SOUS-BOIS

Harvath hit the ground with Big Bird's two-hundred-ninety-plus-pound frame right on top of him. Aouad must have discovered his switch of the *Don Quixote*.

With the briefcase still clenched in his right hand, Harvath swung at the giant's head, but was a second too slow. Big Bird raised his left arm and blocked the blow, forcing Harvath to swing with his other hand.

He connected with the man's jaw, but his attacker barely even flinched. As Harvath pulled back for another strike, Big Bird unloaded with both of his enormous hands.

The man drove two quick punches into Harvath's ribs, knocking the wind out of him. As Harvath gasped for air, he kept trying to use his legs to lift his body up, but with Big Bird sitting on top of him, it was like being pinned underneath a truck.

The giant threw another combination of punches that sent an intense wave of pain radiating throughout his body.

Harvath responded with another left and connected once again with the man's head, but it had no effect whatsoever. It was like trying to melt an iceberg with a hairdryer. Still fighting for breath, Harvath took another shot to his ribs as he tried to figure a way out.

Thinking he might have noticed a weakness when he had first tried to clobber the giant with his briefcase, Harvath drew it back and swung again.

Sure enough, as Big Bird raised his arm to block the case, he lowered his head beneath the level of his arm and that was all that Harvath needed to see. He absorbed two more blows before he could launch his counterassault.

Summoning what few reserves of strength he had left, Harvath let the briefcase fly.

This time, when Big Bird raised his forearm and lowered his head, Harvath was ready for him.

As the man's head came down, Harvath's came up and the pair met with a sickening crack of bone against cartilage. There was a spray of blood as Harvath tore open a wound that ripped through the top of Big Bird's beak and into his forehead.

The giant roared in pain as his hands flew to his face and Harvath wasted no time in going to work on him.

With his breath coming in such shallow gasps, Harvath had trouble gathering his strength. Pulling the briefcase back, he took advantage of the fact that the giant's eyes were flooding with blood and couldn't see what was coming.

The briefcase nailed the man square in the temple. His hands dropped from his face and he sat there for what was only a second or two, but what for Harvath felt like an eternity, before he slowly keeled over to his right and collapsed into the center of the street, unconscious.

Harvath struggled to roll out from underneath the man, but as he did, he was greeted by a new vision just as terrible. Whistles was coming right at him with a pipe in his left hand.

Sitting up with the briefcase clasped to his chest, Harvath tried to stand, but his legs wouldn't obey. Trying to get Big Bird off of him had been like doing a million squat thrusts and his legs were like rubber. The best he could manage was a feeble scoot on his ass toward the other side of the street.

When his back hit a parked car, he knew that was as far as he was going to go. Even if Whistles was only half the fighter Big Bird was, Harvath was a dead man.

If only he had brought a weapon with him. A knife, pepper spray, anything would have been better than nothing at this point.

When Whistles saw that Harvath couldn't stand, he smiled. His mouth was filled with bad teeth and though he knew it was impossible, Harvath almost thought he could smell the man's rancid breath from across the street.

There was no doubting the giant's intentions as he drew back his pipe and ran forward into the street.

The situation was close to hopeless, but Harvath refused to go down without a fight—even a half-assed one.

As he drew back one of his legs to deliver a kick to the man's knee, there was a scream from off to his left and two flashlights rushed toward him.

At first, Harvath thought it was the police. The *f* word floated to the forefront of his mind, but evaporated in a haze of tire smoke and a squeal of brake pads as the trunk of Moussa's taxicab slammed into Whistles.

The young Algerian had the rear passenger door open and was yelling for Harvath to get in before the giant's body even hit the ground.

Harvath staggered inside and collapsed on the rear seat, his briefcase still clasped in his right hand.

Moussa reached back and after closing the door, sped down the street and into the night.

CHAPTER 42

As they drove back to Paris, Moussa asked nothing more than where Harvath wanted to be taken. The man probably had a lot of questions, but to his credit he kept his questions to himself and allowed Harvath to close his eyes and rest.

Per his passenger's instructions, Moussa headed his cab for the Ile Saint-Louis. They came in via the Pont Marie and maneuvered through the tiny streets down the Rue Boutarel to the Quai d'Orléans. From there, Harvath had a clear view across the Seine to the péniche that functioned as the Sargasso safe house. He asked Moussa to pull over.

Handing two thousand euros over the seat, Harvath said, "This should cover the repairs to your taxi." He then reached for the door handle. "Good-bye, Moussa. Thanks for your help."

The young Algerian turned to say something, but his passenger had already exited the cab.

Harvath walked down to the water, slid the *Don Quixote* into a plastic bag he found in a trash can, and then ditched the briefcase. Being careful to remain in the shadows, he watched the barge for the next twenty minutes.

During that time, he did a lot of thinking. Foremost in his mind was the question of who the people were on Anthony Nichols' tail and how they had tracked Harvath to the Bilal Mosque. He planned on making it one of the first questions he asked the professor once he returned to the boat.

When Harvath was convinced that everything appeared okay, he crossed the river by the Pont de la Tournelle and observed the barge for several more minutes from the other side before finally descending to the quai.

Harvath slipped inside the wheelhouse and quietly descended the stairs. He found René Bertrand right where he'd left him, tied to the dining room chair. His head was slumped forward and he appeared to be either asleep or passed out. Nichols was in the galley with his back turned and Harvath caught him by surprise.

"You scared the life out of me," he said as he turned around, his hand clasped to his chest. "Did you get it?"

Harvath held up the plastic bag. "How's Tracy?" he asked.

Nichols drew a deep breath and set the mug he was filling with hot water onto the counter. "She's gone."

"*Gone?* What do you mean she's gone?" demanded Harvath as he abandoned the galley and headed toward his stateroom.

Flipping on the lights, his eyes were drawn to the empty bed. He pushed open the bathroom door only to find it empty as well. "How long?" he asked as he heard Nichols pad into the room behind him.

"At least an hour," he responded.

"Did she say where she was going?"

"She said she needed to see a doctor and that you would understand."

Harvath set down the book and then opened the false panel and removed the box containing the pistol.

Nichols sensed what Harvath was thinking and added, "She also said she didn't want you coming after her."

"Every police officer in this city has our pictures by now," said Harvath as he withdrew the weapon and tucked it into his waistband. "How far do you think she's going to get?"

"Probably not far and I think she knows that. I also think she feels that she was only slowing you down by staying here."

"You do, huh?" Harvath replied rudely.

"Scot, her headaches were worse than she was letting on," stated Nichols.

"So you're a doctor now?"

"She didn't want to put you in a position of having to decide between her and what we need to accomplish."

Harvath looked at Nichols. "What *we* need to accomplish?" he repeated.

"She said you weren't going to be happy about it."

"You know what? Don't tell me what my girlfriend thinks or feels anymore, okay?" snapped Harvath as he crossed to the tiny desk, fished the headset out of its drawer, and powered up the laptop.

The professor realized they were done talking and quietly backed out of the room.

Harvath chose an e-mail address from the host of anonymous accounts he maintained and sent a message to both Ron Parker's cell phone and his desktop.

It took some time before he appeared in the video chat room.

"You look like shit," said Parker as he came on line from the Sargasso conference room in Colorado. He was in his late thirties, about Harvath's height with a shaved head and a dark goatee.

Parker was normally a wiseass until he understood the severity of a situation, so Harvath ignored the remark. "What took you so long?"

"I was doing a training exercise with SEAL Team 10 on the other side of the property, and my Ducati only moves so fast. What's up? Your message said it was urgent."

"Tracy's gone."

Parker straightened up and leaned forward into his camera. "What happened?"

"She left while I was out. She said she needed to find a doctor."

"For what? Is she injured?"

"She's had headaches. Bad ones, apparently."

"What do you mean *apparently*?" asked Parker. "You don't know?"

"She didn't want me to know," replied Harvath. "She'd been taking painkillers under the radar."

"If you sit tight, she'll probably come back in a bit. Don't worry."

"Ron, I *am* worried. Every cop in this city has to be looking for us. You've got contacts here that I don't. How quickly can you find out where she is?"

The video chat room was not as fast as Harvath would have liked and it took a moment for Parker's response to be piped back.

"I'll reach out to my guys now, but Tracy could be anywhere— a hospital, a doctor's office. I'll try my embassy sources first. We'll see if anyone contacted them looking for a referral."

"No," replied Harvath. "No one from the embassy. I want this kept off their radar screen."

"That might be tough."

"Why?"

Parker adjusted his camera so Harvath could see the owner of the Sargasso Intelligence Program, Tim Finney, who was sitting off to his side.

Finney was a former Pacific Rim shootfighting champion now in his early fifties who towered over Harvath by at least seven inches and rang in at an impressive two hundred fifty pounds of solid muscle. He had intense green eyes and, like Parker, his head was completely shaved—a similarity that Harvath had often attributed to Finney's resort having the world's laziest or most uncreative barber. But despite his size and his reputation as an absolutely ruthless, no-holds-barred fighter in the ring, Finney, like Parker, was one of the best friends an honest man could ever have.

Finney held up a pink telephone message sheet while Parker said, "Gary Lawlor is looking for you. He's called twice already. He says he has a message from the president."

"Why would he call you two?"

Finney took the microphone away from Parker and said, "Don't be an idiot, Scot. He knows damn well there's only two numbers you dial when you're in trouble and since his phone hasn't been ringing, it isn't hard to figure that you reached out to us. Now what should we tell him?"

"How much does he know?"

"He knows you're in Paris."

"How does he know that?" asked Harvath.

"He says that's what the president wants to talk to you about."

Harvath had told Nichols not to make any calls or to use the computer while he was gone. He wondered if the professor had disobeyed him. He doubted it. More than likely, the French had already ID'd him and had contacted the president. Either way, things were now even more screwed up than before.

"Gary asked if we were putting you up," continued Finney, "and how he could contact you."

Harvath had no desire to hear what the president had to say. "What'd you tell him?"

"We told him that *if* we heard from you, we'd tell you to check in with him."

"Did he buy it?"

Finney put his hands up. "I've got no idea, Scot. He's your boss."

"*Was* my boss," clarified Harvath.

"Whatever. Why don't you call him and ask him yourself?"

"I'll think about it," he lied.

"Well think about this. You're in the shit *way up* past your eyeballs, and so is Tracy. I don't think we've got a rope long enough to throw to you. You might want to put your pride on the back burner and think of someone other than yourself for a minute. Gary Lawlor and President Rutledge might be the only people who can help untangle this mess."

Finney was right, but Harvath was hardheaded enough to not want to admit it.

When he didn't reply, Parker took the microphone back and said, "I'll get back to you as soon as we have something. In the meantime, get yourself cleaned up." Then the feed from Sargasso went dead.

CHAPTER 43

Harvath had always had a good relationship with Gary Lawlor. The former FBI deputy director had been a close friend of the Harvath family for almost as long as Scot could remember. And when Scot's father, a SEAL instructor, had died in a training accident in California, Gary had become like a second father to him.

When President Rutledge had decided to mount the Apex Project to battle terrorists on their own terms, he wooed Gary away from the Bureau to put him in charge. Though they often butted heads in their attempts to get results, Scot and Gary worked well together.

Even so, Harvath had not spoken with Lawlor since he and Tracy had left D.C. To a certain degree, he felt guilty about that. Gary had always been there for him and his mother. He was tough, but also fair, and had pulled Harvath's bacon out of the fire too many times to remember. Harvath owed him a lot more than a phone call right now.

It was just one of those things that had gotten away from him. The longer he put off calling, the harder it was to do it. Gary was a real by-the-book kind of guy. Though his job was to be as unconventional as the terrorists he was charged with hunting, there was still an ingrained sense of due process and fair play that had been instilled in him over his lifelong career at the FBI. He had gotten better about it, but only because he'd learned to save his questions until Harvath was done with an assignment or to not even ask them at all.

Scot had known that when he did finally reconnect with Lawlor, the conversation wasn't going to be about the weather or the places he and Tracy had visited. He wasn't much for BS. Harvath knew

Gary would stick him with tough questions about when he was coming back and what he was planning on doing in the future. That was probably one of the biggest reasons Harvath had been avoiding him. Until he had answers, the last thing Scot had felt like facing was questions.

But things had changed and Finney was right. Whatever message or marching orders Lawlor might have for him from the president, Harvath had no choice but to shelve his animosity and put Tracy's welfare first.

Routing through a series of anonymous proxy servers, Harvath tapped into one of his VoIP accounts and dialed Gary's cell phone back in D.C.

The man answered on the first ring. "Lawlor," he said, a faint metallic hum to his voice.

Harvath cleared his throat. "Gary? It's Scot."

"Are you okay?"

"I'm fine."

"Good. You've got every police officer, gendarme, and intelligence operative in France looking for you right now. Do you know that?"

"Popularity is a real pain in the ass," replied Harvath.

Lawlor chuckled for a moment and then was serious again. "You've got big problems, my boy."

"You wanted me to call you so you could tell me things I already know?" The words came out harsher than Harvath had intended, but he made no effort to pull them back.

"A bombing this morning. A shooting in the afternoon. What do you have planned for this evening?"

"How about a stampede at a local mosque?"

"Don't jerk me around," replied Lawlor.

"Fine, I'll come up with something else," said Harvath. "What do you want?"

"You drop off the grid for months. No good-byes, no nothing. Just left your BlackBerry and credentials behind along with a smartass note that says *gone fishing* and now you've got the nerve to act like I'm interrupting your vacation."

Harvath fought back the urge to defend himself and instead tried to think of Tracy. "You're right. I'm sorry. I should have contacted you."

"You're damn right you should have," replied Lawlor. "You're lucky the president feels beholden to you. No other operative would have been allowed to just disappear the way you have."

"You could have found us any time you wanted. We've both been using our own passports."

"Give me a break, Scot. Tracking you has been like playing whack-a-mole. One day you pop up on the grid entering a foreign country and then there's nothing for three weeks or a month till you pop up someplace else just long enough to cross another border and get your passport scanned."

He was right. Harvath and Tracy had not gone completely to ground, but the only trail they had been leaving to follow was dust. "I needed some time off to think."

"Well, time's up. You have to get back to work," said Lawlor. "The president needs your help."

Harvath reminded himself to keep the volume of his voice under control. "I don't work for him anymore. And with all due respect, I don't work for you either."

"In that case, you can have all the time you want to think. French prisons are very lonely places—especially for a foreigner."

"The bad-cop routine doesn't really work with me, Gary. You should know that."

"And you should know that the evidence the French have on you does not look good. It could take a couple of years before the investigation into all of today's events is complete and the case against you is finally brought to trial. You might get your day in court, but under their antiterrorism laws, you're going to sit in a cell counting the months until it comes. And while you sit there, it'll be as an American tied to a bombing that killed multiple French citizens and a shooting that resulted in the deaths of three French cops. It's not going to be like shacking up at the Ritz."

Harvath started to speak, but Lawlor plowed right over him. "And what about Tracy? Do you want to put her through the same thing? Is that the kind of man you are?"

"Let's leave Tracy out of this," said Harvath.

"Too late. She's in it. Just as deep as you are. Probably even worse now. Are you even aware that the French have taken her into custody?"

Harvath's stomach dropped. He wasn't surprised, but it didn't make having it confirmed any easier to take. "Where?" he asked.

"She showed up at a Parisian hospital about an hour ago and turned herself in."

"Is she okay?"

"She's undergoing a medical evaluation," replied Lawlor. "The police have her under guard."

Harvath was quiet for a moment and then said, "How did you find out about it?"

"The French have video of you at the bombing and the shooting at the Grand Palais. Because of your involvement the president brought me in to help contain things."

"What about Tracy?" asked Harvath, more concerned about her welfare than his own. "What's going to happen to her?"

"They're going to arrest her, book her, the whole deal, but her medical treatment is their first priority. She's undergoing a CAT scan now."

"Where? What hospital?"

"No way," replied Lawlor. "You wouldn't get within two blocks of it."

"Don't be so sure."

Lawlor knew he was right, but that wasn't the point. "Okay, you could get to her, but it's not worth the risk, not right now. She's being taken care of. As head of DHS's Office of International Investigative Assistance, the president has me helping the French coordinate their investigations into the bombing and the shooting at the Grand Palais."

"I want to talk to her at least."

"Not a chance. For all intents and purposes, she's in French custody now, and just because she happens to be in a hospital doesn't mean she magically gets afforded any more special treatment than if she was in a jail cell. Besides, I already tried to call her. The French cops took the phone out of her room. They claim they don't want her colluding with anyone."

"That's nuts. You know we had nothing to do with any of this," said Harvath.

"Well, the French have lots of video that makes them believe otherwise."

"Rutledge has to help us out of this," demanded Harvath. "Or at least, Tracy. He owes her that much."

"We'll talk about the president in a minute," said Lawlor. "First I want you to take me through everything that has happened. From the beginning."

Harvath's old life had sucked him back in so far he couldn't even see daylight. With Tracy now in French custody, there was nothing he could do to fight it anymore. He took a deep breath, readjusted himself in his seat to help take some of the pressure off of his battered ribs, and started to speak.

CHAPTER 44

There are a lot of photos in there," said Aydin Ozbek. "Take your time."

"Nope," replied Andrew Salam, turning the laptop around. "That's him."

"You're sure?" asked Rasmussen.

"Positive. That's the man who recruited me."

Ozbek looked at Rasmussen and then turned his eyes back to Salam. "I know you've been through this extensively with the FBI, but we need you to go through it with us once more. We need to know how you communicated with him. When and where did you meet? Did he ever come to your home, your office? Did you ever go to his home or office? All of it."

"You know who this guy is, don't you?" asked Salam. "He's CIA, isn't he?"

"Let's just take this one step at a time," said Rasmussen.

"Fuck *one step at a time*," retorted Salam. "You know I'm telling the truth. My recognizing this guy *proves* it."

He studied the faces of the men sitting across from him. There was something about all of this that he couldn't quite grasp. Then suddenly, it hit him. "Holy shit. My handler is your assassin, isn't he? He and al-Din are the same person. That's why you're back here talking to me."

"We don't know any of that for sure," replied Rasmussen.

Salam laughed. "All along, the FBI has been panicked that he was one of theirs and now it turns out he's one of *yours*."

"We're still putting this together—"

Ozbek interrupted his colleague. "The man you ID'd in that photo is Matthew Dodd. He faked his death and disappeared a little over five years ago."

"About the time he converted to Islam," offered Salam.

"If what you've told us is accurate, then that does seem to fit the timeline."

"As does recruiting me and setting up the Glass Canyon operation."

Ozbek nodded, slowly. "Give or take."

"Then that's it. You've got your proof," stated Salam. "I'm innocent. You can get me out of here."

"Identifying Dodd as your handler is one thing. Proving he was, as well as proving that someone other than you killed Nura Khalifa, is something else."

"But you can help me," insisted Salam. "If you tell the FBI that Matthew Dodd was my handler, it'll help prove that I'm telling the truth."

"We don't have to tell them anything," replied Rasmussen.

Ozbek waved him off. Putting his elbows on the table, Ozbek clasped his hands together and rested his chin on his thumbs. "We might be able to help you," he said, thinking, "but first you have to help us."

"With what?" asked Salam.

Rasmussen looked at him. "Don't be stupid, Mr. Salam."

Once again, Ozbek waved him off. "We've got a pretty good idea where Dodd is. We may even know who his target is—"

"Is it Dr. Khalifa?" interrupted Salam. "Was Nura right about it being her uncle?"

"We have reason to believe that Dr. Khalifa is already dead and that there may be another target."

"So Nura was right," said Salam, more to himself than to the CIA operatives.

"We don't know that Dodd killed him," replied Ozbek. "Not for sure. Not yet. But we believe that there is something larger at play here, and we need to know what that something is."

Salam looked at his interrogator. "And you think I can help you figure it out?"

"Maybe, maybe not," said Ozbek. "But you might be able to point us in the right direction."

"By giving you the same information I gave to the FBI?"

Ozbek nodded.

Despite having been duped by his so-called FBI recruiter, Andrew Salam wasn't stupid. In fact, he was far from it. "How do I know that you won't take the information I give you, find Dodd and feed him into a wood chipper somewhere, then deny we ever had this conversation?"

"You don't really have much choice," said Rasmussen. "You're going to have to trust us."

Salam laughed once more. "Yeah, right. The way I see it, I've got lots of choices. I can talk to the FBI, D.C. Metro Police, or wait until I'm finally given a lawyer and then talk to the press. If anybody doesn't have much of a choice here, I think it's the CIA."

Rasmussen was ramping up with a retort, but Ozbek pointed toward the door. "I'll meet you at the car."

"What?" replied Rasmussen.

"Let us have some time alone," said Ozbek. "Go get a cup of coffee or something."

Rasmussen sat there for a moment in disbelief. Then, with a grunt, he stood and exited the interrogation room.

Once the door had closed, Salam said, "I thought you guys were okay at first, but he's starting to turn into an asshole."

Rasmussen's specialty was operating in the field, not an interrogation room, and Ozbek let the remark go unchallenged. Reaching into his jacket he removed a new digital camera and powered it up. "The last time we were in here you asked about your dog," he said as he handed the device to him. "I thought you'd want to see these."

Salam's face softened as he scrolled through the pictures. "So the police did take care of him."

"Not really," said Ozbek. "They were a lot more concerned with ripping your house apart. They were going to put him in the pound, but I got it all sorted out. He's with one of your neighbors now."

"Which one?" Salam asked apprehensively.

"The older guy across the street."

"Who? The veteran with the P.O.W. flag?"

"Yep," said Ozbek. "Any problem with that?"

"No," replied Salam. "He's a good guy. He did a couple of tours in Vietnam. I don't think he cared for me much when I moved in, but he came around and has always been polite. Thanks."

"You're welcome. Now—"

"What's your thing with dogs anyway?"

"I've got a black Lab."

"Nice dog," said Salam. "Smart."

"Yes, they are," replied Ozbek. "Listen, Andrew, you need to know that the FBI has uncovered e-mails between you and Nura Khalifa as well as some other pieces of evidence that suggest you two were having a relationship."

"That's ridiculous."

"The evidence suggests that Nura had met with you to tell you that the relationship was over."

"But there was no relationship," insisted Salam. "It was strictly professional."

Ozbek shrugged. "I'm just telling you what I've heard."

"What *other pieces of evidence* do they have?"

"Whatever they are, it seems to point to an *if I can't have her no one can* motive for murder."

"But I didn't kill her. We were attacked. I told you that. I'm not an idiot. If, and the key word here is *if,* I was going to kill somebody, do you think I'd be dumb enough to choose a location where I'd have to disarm Park Police security cameras? I couldn't even do that if I had wanted to.

"You have to believe me. Nura and I were *both* targets. They wanted us dead and when I survived they planted all of that BS information to make it look like we had a relationship and that I wanted to kill her because she was going to leave me."

"That's a lot of work," said Ozbek.

"So is knocking out surveillance cameras at the Jefferson Memorial."

Ozbek couldn't argue with that.

"These people aren't the turban-wearing morons most of our politicians think they are," continued Salam. "They're extremely sophisticated, and have resources you can't even begin to imagine. If you knew the places their operatives had wormed their way into, you wouldn't be able to sleep at night. They have armies of sympathizers, legions of apologists, and one of the best crafted public relations and media strategies ever created. These people make the Nazis look like amateurs.

"This is the most dangerous threat this nation has *ever* faced, and yet I'm going to hang for trying to do my duty as an American to take them down. This isn't justice, it's bullshit."

Ozbek looked at him. "You're right. It is bullshit."

"So you believe me, then?"

Ozbek nodded. "But I have to be honest with you. There is a limit to how much we can do for you. This investigation belongs to the FBI and D.C. Metro. The CIA has no official role in it whatsoever."

"What about Dodd? Capturing him would change things, wouldn't it?"

"Probably," replied Ozbek, "but he could turn around and cut a deal with the CIA to give them something of greater value."

Salam shook his head. "And I'd still be screwed."

"It happens. I just want you to be aware of that."

"Thanks a lot."

"Andrew, you're in a tough position. Based on how the deck is stacked against you, nobody would blame you at this point for clamming up and waiting for a lawyer."

"Why are you telling me all of this? If I go to the press about Dodd, it could be very embarrassing for the CIA."

"They're big boys and girls," said Ozbek. "They've got people who know how to handle spin."

"But still," replied Salam, pressing his point.

"You're a good guy, Andrew. Somebody screwed you big time, yet you've cooperated every step of the way with us. And I think you've cooperated because you know you haven't done anything wrong. More importantly, you know what you were doing was for the good of your country and that's what honorable people in this nation do.

"I can't promise I can unfuck everything you're in, but if you help me, I *will* promise that I'll do everything I can to track down Matthew Dodd and make sure that he and his Islamist pals won't do any further harm to America."

Salam thought about it. It didn't take long. He knew what the right thing to do was. "Take out a pen," he said. "You're going to need it."

CHAPTER 45

PARIS

Dodd had found the director of the Bilal Mosque in his office. "The police are on their way!" he screamed at Dodd in French after the assassin had kicked in his door and entered his office.

"They'll come all right," replied Dodd as he closed the door behind him, "but not until they have amassed many men. Your neighborhood doesn't exactly have the best reputation. Frankly, the police are just as terrified of coming here as everyone else."

Namir Aouad eyed the intruder's weapon. "What do you want?"

"Why was the American here?"

"What American?"

Dodd removed the suppressor from beneath his shirt and screwed it onto the threaded barrel of his pistol. "Why was he here?" he repeated.

"I don't know what you are talking about," Aouad stammered.

The assassin didn't like being lied to. He raised his H&K and fired, slamming a round into the wall just above the mosque director's head. "Tell me why the American was here or I'll find something other than the wall for my next shot."

Aouad studied the man's thick beard, clothing, and distinctive Islamic cap. "You look like a Muslim."

"I am."

"Then you cannot shoot me," declared Aouad. "It is forbidden for a Muslim to harm another Muslim."

For a moment, Dodd's mind drifted to his deceased wife and child and what he imagined their deaths had been like. His eyes then went cold. "When you choose to aid an infidel over another Muslim, you are no longer a Muslim."

"I have not aided any infidels," protested the director.

"Tell me about René Bertrand."

Aouad's eyes looked up and to the right. "I do not know this man."

Dodd had his pistol up before the man had even finished his lie. He pulled the trigger and drilled a round through the mosque director's shoulder.

Aouad screamed in pain as his hand flew to the wound. Within seconds, a dark, moist stain began to spread across his sweater. He drew his hand back and almost passed out from the sight of the blood. "The American came for the book," he wailed. "He came for the book."

The assassin was amazed. "Bertrand left the book with you?"

"Please, I need an ambulance," pleaded the injured mosque director.

"You'll need a hearse if you don't answer my questions," threatened Dodd.

"I was holding the book for its owners."

"You mean the men who stole it," clarified the assassin.

The mosque director nodded eagerly. He was losing a lot of blood and did not want to be shot again. "Please! I need an ambulance," he repeated.

Dodd wasn't paying attention. He was too preoccupied with his own thoughts. The assassin was stunned that the book had been in the mosque all this time. If only he had known! "We would have paid you much more money for that book."

Aouad was confused. "You?"

"Yes, you idiot," yelled the assassin as he raised his pistol again. "Who was he? How did Bertrand make contact with him? I must have that book."

Aouad was starting to feel dizzy. "It's gone. The American stole it," he said pointing at the wooden box on top of the file cabinet.

The assassin crossed to the cabinet.

"Please," moaned Aouad. "Let me call an ambulance."

"Shut up," snapped the assassin.

He opened the lid and looked inside. An old volume lay on top of an aged piece of cloth. The cover was rough and faded.

Dodd was an expert on many things, but rare books wasn't one of them. He only had the recollections of what René Bertrand had e-mailed him to go on. As he opened the *Don Quixote* and scanned the first several pages, he couldn't understand what the mosque director was talking about. They looked exactly as he remembered them.

Leafing beyond those pages, though, he soon figured out what had happened. The first few pages had been glued into the book instead of being stitched. *It was a fake.*

"You fool," he roared as he turned to face Aouad.

The mosque director opened his mouth to reply only to have the enraged assassin fill it with four rounds from his silenced pistol.

Matthew Dodd waited for his breathing to come back under control and then wiped his prints from all of the surfaces he had touched. Stepping out of the director's office, he exited the mosque and stepped into the street.

He blamed Omar for this, all of it. If only the man had listened to him from the beginning, this business with the book would have already been finished.

A cold rain began to fall again, but it did little to cool Dodd's anger. Nichols and his people had the book now. The assassin could lay the blame anywhere he wanted, but in the end, he had failed and he didn't like the taste of failure, especially when something so significant was at stake.

Dodd started walking. He needed to get himself under control. As he walked, he was so busy fuming that he almost missed the dark blue Opel driven by two North African–looking men as it sped past him.

Deciding that it wasn't a threat, the assassin filed the car and its two occupants away in the back of his mind and turned his attention to what he was going to do about that book.

Up ahead, the Opel turned the corner and disappeared from sight.

CHAPTER 46

By the time Dodd got to the corner, he had come to the conclusion that if Nichols and the book hadn't already left the country, they would very soon. The assassin was mulling how he might still head him off, when he arrived at the corner and the hair on the back of his neck stood straight up.

Whether he saw the double-parked Opel or the fixed stock of the H&K MP-5A2 being swung at his head first made no difference. Dodd's instincts had already taken over.

As if two pins had been pulled, the assassin's knees folded and his entire body dropped. His right fist exploded outward and connected with his attacker's testicles. With the first of the two North African–looking men doubled over, Dodd grabbed the other's pistol and wrenched his wrist outward. The man's body followed and as it did, the assassin whipped his suppressed pistol out and put one shot behind the man's ear, killing him instantly.

Turning just as the other man raised his weapon to fire, Dodd pulled his trigger again, placing the round just beneath his assailant's nose.

It was a finely tuned spectacle of death for which Dodd had few peers. As the second man's corpse hit the ground, the assassin's breath and heart rate were already coming back down to normal. Killing was not an emotional experience for Dodd, it was physical.

The assassin scanned up and down the street for witnesses. Not seeing any, he approached the running car and popped its trunk. Quickly, he gathered up each of the dead men and dumped them inside along with their weapons.

Going through their pockets, Dodd fished out two sets of credentials identifying them as Renseignements Généraux agents. They were tasked to the *Milleux Intégristes Violents* or Violent Fundamentalist Environment Unit responsible for monitoring French mosques.

Dodd closed the trunk, opened the driver's side door, and slid inside. There were two bags on the back seat containing high-tech surveillance equipment. Mounted between the two front seats was a small computer known in law enforcement parlance as an MDT or Mobile Data Terminal.

Like any police squad car, the MDT was tied into a wireless network that allowed RG agents to run names, photos, and other information as well as communicate with dispatch and headquarters personnel.

The assassin pulled up the last series of communications. The two agents he had just killed had been assigned to observe the Bilal Mosque and videotape worshippers as they were leaving Friday prayers. They were on their way to the mosque when the shooting there was reported.

Dodd had underestimated the response time of the French authorities. He knew the RG didn't have enough manpower to monitor all 1,700 mosques and places of Muslim worship every day, so when he cased the Bilal for surveillance shortly before entering the café across the street and didn't see any, he had assumed it wasn't on the RG's list for that night.

That didn't mean there couldn't have been undercover operatives inside the mosque, though, but in the pandemonium that had ensued, they would have been hard-pressed to ID him as the shooter unless they had been standing right next to him and even then, he was wearing a disguise.

Nevertheless, someone had given the RG a description of him, and the two dead operatives had started looking for him the moment they got the call. Their hastily mounted ambush had been a very bad idea and it was going to cost the RG more than just two dead agents.

Having tried earlier to crack the RG's servers without any luck,

Dodd now had an open door. He pulled up all of the alerts that had been issued since the bombing that morning and studied them.

In minutes, he was able to put together a picture of just about everything the French police and intelligence agencies knew.

He noted that he had slipped up at the Grand Palais and had been caught on video, but it was only his profile. The authorities had perfect shots of Nichols, as well as the man and woman who were helping him.

With this much of a manhunt on for them, they wouldn't even be able to hop on a skateboard without being stopped.

Still, the man in the café who was working with Nichols had been smart enough to disguise himself. He'd also been clever enough to slip away from the stampede in the mosque. Dodd needed to reassess who he was up against. Nichols had help and it was well trained help. This wasn't something that had been planned for.

The assassin scrolled to the most recent alert and learned to his surprise that the woman had been apprehended.

Her name was given as Tracy Elizabeth Hastings, age twenty-seven, American citizen. The alert revealed that she was being held, pending medical treatment, at the American Hospital of Paris.

Dodd thought for a moment about going to the hospital but then changed his mind. Though he could probably slip inside undetected, the risks associated with getting to the woman and smuggling her out were far too great.

Even if he were successful, what would he do with her? Trade her for the book? What if Nichols had already copied the information from it that he needed? There were too many unknowns.

Nichols was where Dodd's focus needed to be. And before the assassin decided what to do about him, he needed to have the best view of the battlefield available. He needed to know as much of what Nichols knew as possible. *But how to do that?*

Dodd's eyes looked up to check his mirrors and the rest of his surroundings and then fell back to the MDT. As they did, something about its rugged, rubberized casing caught his attention.

It reminded him of the laptop he had taken from Marwan Khalifa just after killing him in Rome and gave him an idea.

Careful to cover his tracks through a series of intermediate servers, the assassin searched the Internet for any news of Khalifa's death.

Reports of the fire at the Italian State Archive Services were available in several Italian dailies, and while a handful of the articles mentioned bodies having been discovered at the scene, there was nothing yet that identified one of them as being that of Dr. Marwan Khalifa.

With that knowledge, Dodd began formulating a plan. He remembered the e-mail Nichols had sent to Khalifa. If Nichols was successful in getting back to the United States, there was every reason to believe that he still planned on keeping his appointment with Khalifa at the Library of Congress on Monday.

CHAPTER 47

Tell me everything you know about him," said Harvath as he chased two aspirin with a glass of water.

Bertrand had been moved to one of the vacant staterooms so Harvath and Nichols could speak in private.

"Where should I start?" replied the professor. "Marwan Khalifa is one of the most respected Koranic scholars in the world. He's a Georgetown professor and we had worked together before, which made him a perfect choice for this project."

"When had you worked together before?"

"About five years ago. Right after 9/11, I wrote a paper about the

First Barbary War and America's introduction to Islamic terrorism. Marwan helped me with some of the finer points of Islamic history."

"When was the last time you spoke with him?" asked Harvath.

"I sent him an e-mail shortly before I left for Paris to confirm a meeting we have Monday in D.C."

"How much did he know about what you were working on for the president?"

"Everything," stated Nichols. "He was practically my partner on this project. He knows more about the Koran and its history than anyone else I can think of."

"And the president was okay with this?" asked Harvath.

"Of course. In fact having a scholar of Marwan's standing on board will lend much needed weight to this discovery."

"Why would you and the president need any additional weight?"

Nichols looked at him over the top of his mug. "First of all, the president doesn't want any recognition for the discovery."

Harvath chuckled. "Almost every single violent conflict around the world right now involves Muslims, yet with this discovery virtually overnight, all of these conflicts have the potential to come to a halt and Jack Rutledge won't want to take any credit for it? Please."

Nichols thought Harvath was being rather disrespectful, but he chose not to engage in an unproductive confrontation. "The president is worried that his involvement might politicize the discovery and detract from its true importance.

"If we find what I think we are going to find, there will be many elements within Islam who will do everything they can to discredit the discovery."

"You mean the radical fundamentalists," said Harvath.

Nichols nodded. "They won't go easily and unfortunately, they are masters at perverting the truth and creating conspiracy theories. The president decided it would be best if he wasn't seen to have any involvement with this at all. The last thing he wants to do is empower the Islamists."

"If this turns out to be that threatening, orthodox Muslims are not going to take it lying down."

"No, they won't. The Danish cartoon riots were nothing compared to what this will look like. It will be an outright attack on their legitimacy, and they will do everything they can to discredit it. What's more, as crazy as it sounds, they have God on their side."

"What do you mean?" asked Harvath.

"The mere suggestion that the Koran is incomplete runs absolutely counter to what every Muslim is taught. To accept the premise that the Koran is incomplete would mean accepting that it is not perfect. And from there it is not a huge leap to wonder what else might be incorrect or incomplete about their holy book.

"It's a test of faith that many, no matter how moderate, may not want to accept," said Nichols.

"So how do you win? Just go public with the information and hope that the truth wins out?"

"That's what we've been wrestling with. The Islamic regimes that could be most helpful in publicizing this message will probably be threatened as well. Most likely, they're going to be lining up to discredit the find."

"So then how do you win?" repeated Harvath.

Nichols set his mug down, took a deep breath, and said, "This is where we have to trust the moderates and by that I mean the *true* moderates, like Marwan. If the reform movement doesn't come from within the Islamic faith, it will never be accepted as legitimate. We in the West can demand reform all we want, but we can't force it upon the Muslim community. But if we can get to the bottom of what Jefferson was after, we will be handing the moderates the biggest broom they've ever had with which to sweep clean."

Harvath wished he shared the man's optimism. "Who else besides Marwan and the president know about what you're working on?"

"No one," replied Nichols.

"No assistants? No grad students? No girlfriend?"

"Don't I wish," said Nichols as he rose and crossed to the galley.

"Where did you do your research?" asked Harvath.

The professor filled the kettle with water and turned on the stove. "Everywhere. The UVA library. Monticello. The Library of Congress."

"The White House?"

"Off and on," said Nichols. "I also brought a lot of source material home with me, but per the president, I didn't keep any handwritten notes. All of my work was kept on a flash drive."

"Where is it?"

"Hidden in my office."

Harvath shot him a look.

"Very well hidden," he added.

"Is it encrypted?" asked Harvath.

"I used an open-source, on-the-fly encryption program called TrueCrypt. Even if I was forced to give up the password, it provides two levels of plausible deniability. The president signed off on it."

"Did you pay any research firms to conduct research on your behalf?"

"Again, no," said Nichols. "I bought articles about Jefferson off the Web and paid for them with my own credit card and reimbursed myself out of the account the president had established for me. Any books I needed and didn't want to check out of the library, I purchased over the Internet and paid for the same way."

"Chat rooms? Lectures you attended? Other scholars you reached out to besides Marwan?" inquired Harvath.

"Nope," said Nichols as he retrieved a spoon from a drawer in the galley.

"Then Marwan has to be your leak. Whoever is on your tail is there because he said the wrong thing to the wrong people."

"That's impossible. Marwan wants this project to be successful just as much as we do."

Harvath was about to reply when the laptop in his stateroom started beeping with an incoming call.

CHAPTER 48

The caller ID on the incoming VoIP call showed up as *unavailable*. Having given the number for this account to only one person, Harvath assumed it was Gary Lawlor. He was wrong.

"Hello, Scot," said the voice as Harvath put his headset on and accepted the call. "It's been a while."

Not long enough, thought Harvath as he recognized the voice of President Rutledge. Several emotions coursed through his body, including anger at Lawlor for blindsiding him with this phone call. "Hello, Mr. President," he said flatly.

Rutledge had no reason to expect a warm reception after what Harvath had been through. "We need to talk."

"Yes, we do," replied Harvath, unashamed of his priorities. "What's being done for Tracy?"

The president looked down at the update Lawlor had handed him before initiating the call. "She has experienced some swelling of the brain. That's where the headaches have come from. The doctors think it may have been brought on by stress. They are starting her on medication and will keep her for observation."

"What are you specifically doing to help her?"

"Everything I can," said Rutledge, "and in exchange, I need you to help me."

Harvath was silent.

Rutledge waited for him to respond and when he didn't, the president said, "I know you disagree with the way I handled things and I know you hold me responsible for what happened. I can live with that. But what you need to understand is that I made my decisions, as I always have, based on what I believed to be best for our country."

"People I care about were killed; even more were injured," countered Harvath. "A terrorist with a vendetta against me was freed from Guantánamo and when he came after the people I care about, I was told to stand down and not do anything about it."

"And for that I am truly sorry, but it was a choice I had to make. We need to move past it."

"You'll forgive me, Mr. President. I have a problem getting over things that fast."

Rutledge's blood pressure was starting to rise. "Do you want me to give you an order? Is that what this has to come down to? My God, if we can't come together to fight these people what's going to happen to our nation?

"Listen, you can dislike me all you want, but I know you dislike the enemy more. I also know that no matter how hard it has ever been, you've never said no when your country needed your help."

Rutledge took a long pause before continuing. "Scot, my presidency has been underwater from the beginning. It has been overrun by fundamentalist Islam since the day I took office. I have been hobbled by an inept, PC, partisan Congress more concerned with covering their own asses than doing the heavy lifting that needs to be done for America.

"I have green-lighted more off-the-books operations than any president in history. Why? Because this Congress, Republicans and Democrats alike, doesn't have the guts to focus on the true threat our nation faces. They want to play their fiddles while Rome burns, but we've got a chance to be successful in spite of them.

"I have spent two terms in office unable to take my eye off the war with fundamentalist Islam. I have no delusions about my legacy as president. I know I won't be remembered for much, if anything at all, and I can accept that. At this point, I'm beyond worrying or caring about it.

"But what I am worried about is doing everything I can with the limited amount of time I have left to help shore up our nation and weaken the enemy. No matter who succeeds me in this office, Democrat or Republican, they are going to get the shock of their life when they try to hit the ground running and realize that the best they can do is try to give up as little ground to radical Islam as possible. We have a chance to change that."

Harvath studied the pistol sitting next to the computer. Beneath it was the list of hospitals he thought Tracy might be in.

He hated being put in this position and resented the hell out of everyone involved, including Tracy, for putting him there. But regardless of how he felt about Rutledge and what had gone on between them, he couldn't turn his back on what needed to be done. At the end of the day, Harvath always did the right thing. It was who he was, no matter how many times he'd been kicked in the teeth for it.

Finally he replied, "What do you need me to do?"

Rutledge's sense of relief was evident in his tone of voice. "First, we need to get you up to speed on everything that has happened including who we believe is targeting Professor Nichols."

"And then?"

"Then we need to figure out how the hell we're going to get you and that book out of the country and back home as quickly as possible."

CHAPTER 49

Anthony Nichols had arrived in Paris on a commercial flight, and that was exactly how Rutledge had planned on getting him back to the United States. There had been no margin of error built into the plan in case things went wrong. It wasn't how a proper operation was run, but Harvath couldn't blame the president. Rutledge wasn't an operator.

He was, though, extremely tight when it came to operational security. Normally, that was a good thing, but in this instance it meant that there were scant few resources he could tap for help.

After his last phone call with Gary Lawlor, Harvath had learned two things. The first was that Dr. Marwan Khalifa had been fully vetted by the president and neither he nor Lawlor believed the Koranic scholar had anything to do with the attempts on Anthony Nichols' life. For now, Harvath was going to have to take them at their word.

The other thing was that President Rutledge wasn't going to be able to get him and the professor out of the country any time soon. Harvath knew that the longer they remained in France, the greater their chances were of getting caught. He had to come up with his own plan and once he did, the first call he made was to Finney and Parker at the Sargasso Program.

"Yeah, we've got a cobbler in Paris," replied Tim Finney. "But she doesn't just play both sides of the fence, she plays both sides of the porch, the driveway, the front yard—"

"I get it," interrupted Harvath. "How good is she?"

"Excellent and she charges like it too."

"I'm going to need two passports right away, tonight."

There was a loud noise as Finney pursed his lips and sucked in a big breath of air. "That's going to be expensive."

"I know," replied Harvath. "Good, fast, and cheap—pick any two."

"Do you want them to be U.S.?"

"No. The French are going to be scrutinizing American passports very closely. Make them Canadian. Entrance to France seven days ago. Medium amount of international stamps and travel visas, all to first- and second-world countries. We'll also need a couple of credit cards. Brand doesn't matter. We'll take whatever blanks she has."

"What about photos?" asked Finney.

"I'm going to get to work on those now," said Harvath. "I'll post them in the usual place along with aliases and physical descriptions."

"Okay, I'll get on this right away. I'll have her put it on my account and we'll settle up later. You do have access to funds, right?"

"Yes," replied Harvath, remembering the private account the president had established for Nichols. "I'll make sure you get reimbursed."

"It's not that I don't like you, Scot," said Finney. "It's just that we're talking about some pricey work here."

"Understood."

"The passports will be left at a dead drop. As soon as they're ready, she'll let us know where you can pick them up. How about on your end? Anything else you need?"

Harvath prioritized the other items in his mind. "We're going to need a private jet as soon as the passports are ready," he said. "Preferably something with a discreet pickup service."

"Destination?"

"Montreal for the flight plan, but once we're safely on our way, we'll need to change for D.C."

"That's doable," said Finney.

"And one other thing," replied Harvath. "I've got a problem bound and gagged in one of the staterooms that needs to be dealt with, but not until we're gone."

Finney didn't like the sound of that. "Dealt with how?"

"Somebody just needs to open the cage and let him out. Chances are the cops will pick him up within half an hour. By that point, I don't care what he does or says."

"Is he dangerous?"

"Only if you're a bag of heroin or a fashion editor."

"Okay," said Finney. "I'll have someone check in on him once I know you're out of French airspace. That's it, then?"

"That's it," replied Harvath.

• • •

Two hours later, Harvath was back aboard the péniche. With him was a digital camera he had lifted off a tourist near Notre Dame and several plastic bags filled with items he and Nichols would need to disguise themselves.

Once they had taken each other's picture in front of a plain white wall, Harvath uploaded them to the draft folder he used to communicate with Parker and Finney. He'd already provided names and physical descriptions for the bogus passports. Now, all they could do was wait.

An hour later, Harvath heard from Ron Parker. "The car will be there to pick you up at 0500. Your private charter to Montreal is all booked."

"What about the dead drop for the passports?" asked Harvath.

"Your driver has been instructed to take you to the Paris Marriott Champs-Élysées. The bell captain's name is Maurice. You give him the James Ryan alias from your new passport and he'll hand over two suitcases. Inside are dirty clothes and assorted toiletry items just in case somebody decides to give you a closer look. One of the bags has a piece of yarn tied to the handle. Inside, you'll find an envelope with the passports."

Harvath had to hand it to him, Parker and Finney thought of everything.

• • •

When they arrived at the Marriott Champs- Élysées shortly after five a.m., Harvath found the bell captain, gave him the James Ryan name as well as fifty euros, and retrieved the bags.

Back in the car, he removed the passports and looked them over. Finney's cobbler was a true artist. The documents were impeccable.

He committed his stamps and visas to memory and then quietly quizzed Nichols to make sure he had done the same.

At Paris–Le Bourget Airport, they were met by a representative from the charter company who saw to their bags and accompanied the pair to passport control.

Harvath had instructed Nichols to appear tired and disinterested. He had cut the professor's hair very short and had him shave off his beard. His face had been darkened with toner while Harvath wore a new wig and glasses. He also now sported a mustache.

The passport control officer took his time studying their documents. Harvath grew concerned and debated whether he could subdue the officer and still be able to get Nichols on board the plane and take off. They were the only ones there at the moment and Harvath gave himself fifty-fifty odds of being successful.

Thankfully, he didn't have to do anything. The jet rep was on a first-name basis with the officer and chided him into hurrying it up. With a dismissive wave of his hand, the officer stamped the passports and handed them back.

Within five minutes, they were on board the aircraft, and as the main door was closed, Harvath breathed a sigh of relief. Ten minutes more, with well deserved drinks in hand, the pair was airborne and headed for the States. The hardest part, though, was leaving Tracy behind.

Harvath had been against it, but he knew there wasn't anything he could do about it. To his credit, the president had already started the diplomatic wheels rolling. It was now Harvath's turn to perform.

As the ground disappeared beneath the Bombardier Global Express XRS jet, Harvath left Nichols on the couch and walked back to the sleep suite in the aft cabin. Lying down on the bed, he closed his eyes and tried to rest. He had a very bad feeling that things weren't over yet—not by a long shot.

CHAPTER 50

BALTIMORE, MARYLAND
SATURDAY

Matthew Dodd's balls weren't simply big, they were enormous. Fooling the CIA into thinking you'd been killed was one thing, but living within fifty miles of Langley was the absolute height of hubris and Aydin Ozbek was positive that it was exactly what would lead to Dodd's downfall.

The assassin had been very careful about covering his tracks, but not careful enough. Most of the dead drops and meeting places Dodd had established with Salam while posing as his FBI handler were in and around Baltimore. That had gotten Ozbek to thinking.

Why Baltimore? The most logical answer was because Baltimore was not D.C. There were too many people who could have recognized Dodd there. What's more, Salam had ID'd Dodd directly from his CIA service photo which meant that Dodd had never disguised himself when they were together. The assassin was smart enough to know that few disguises held up under close scrutiny over long periods of time. So the more Ozbek thought about it, the more Baltimore made sense. Not only was it close to D.C., but it was probably easier to get lost in than anywhere else within an hour's drive.

At the DPS office, Ozbek had his team map all of the dead drop locations and all of the rendezvous points Salam could ever remember having been to. There were a couple of dead drops in D.C., but those were only set up for emergencies.

The prevalence of activity in the Baltimore area made Ozbek certain that it was Dodd's main base of operations. He had to be living somewhere close by.

Though he held out little hope of finding him, Ozbek ran title searches under Dodd's name and any known or suspected aliases, including his Muslim name, Majd al-Din. When those came up empty, Rasmussen half joked that it wouldn't have been beneath the assassin to buy something under the names of Sheik Omar, Abdul Waleed, or even Andrew Salam himself. Those names turned out to be busts as well, as were any real estate holdings titled under any of Omar's mosques, FAIR, or the McAllister & Associates front.

More than likely, Dodd was renting something under a false name they didn't know of, which made it all but impossible to trace him.

Or so they had thought.

It was Stephanie Whitcomb who had suggested they dredge the credit bureaus and Web-based tenant screening services. If Dodd was renting, unless he was living in an absolute fleabag, his landlord would have run a background check on him.

Their search resulted in three hits in the Baltimore area. Two belonged to a pair of female roommates who were interns at the Foundation on American Islamic Relations and the third was a man named Ibrahim Reynolds who listed the Um al-Qura Mosque in Falls Church, Virginia, as his employer.

A little further digging revealed that the original Ibrahim Reynolds, whose name and social security number were bogusly listed on the rental application, had died at two months old in San Diego, California. It was the break they had been looking for.

And as a reward, Ozbek had decided to let Whitcomb come along when they hit Dodd's apartment even though Rasmussen had been dead set against involving her.

Had Ozbek been able to see what was coming, he would have agreed.

CHAPTER 51

As far as any of them knew, Matthew Dodd was still in Paris. At least he had been as of the shooting the previous day. Nevertheless, they weren't taking any chances.

Just before 4 a.m., Ozbek pulled his black GMC Denali over to the sidewalk and dropped off Whitcomb. Once she was out, he pulled away and headed west.

The apartment they believed belonged to Dodd was in the southeast part of Baltimore just north of the Fells Point area. And though they all thought it, none of them commented on the irony of the neighborhood being known as Butchers Hill.

Since it was assumed an attractive young woman would be less suspicious, Whitcomb was given the job of surveilling as much of the area as possible before Ozbek and Rasmussen went into the apartment.

They picked a spot at the top of the street where she could have an unobstructed view of his apartment, yet would be concealed if anyone looked out the window in her direction. She was using Ozbek's own thermal imaging system, which despite being an early generation, would still allow her to "see" through several inches of concrete.

Her encrypted Motorola radio was outfitted with a bone mike that she inserted in her right ear. They looked like the earpieces newscasters or Secret Service agents wore and were much less obvious than throat mikes.

The radio was activated by a small transmitter button that Whitcomb wore around her left index finger and which she had covered with a Band-Aid. This would be a totally silent operation. Similar to a SWAT team entry, communication would be facilitated by clicks from the transmitter button.

While Whitcomb got into place, Ozbek and Rasmussen waited in the Denali a block away. Rasmussen thought about raising his objection to bringing Stephanie along again, but decided to let it go. Ozbek was the boss, and he wasn't going to change his mind. Oz had explained to Whitcomb that what they were doing was off the books and technically against the rules, but she'd agreed to come along anyway. She was not only an action junkie, she was a big girl and could make up her own mind as to what she did and didn't want to do.

Nevertheless, Rasmussen wasn't exactly thrilled to be part of an ever-widening band of lawbreakers from the CIA. The Agency had had enough trouble with its image of late. It didn't matter that what they did, they did for the greater good. The press and a majority of the morons in Congress were constantly busy tearing them new assholes and painting them as monsters.

Rasmussen's thoughts were interrupted when Whitcomb clicked that she was in place and that the apartment and the street were all clear.

Unable to find a parking spot anywhere, Ozbek positioned his Denali in front of a hydrant and cut the engine. He and Rasmussen hopped out, and casually made their way toward the three-story brick building.

Half a block before they got to the entrance, they turned right and headed into an alley.

At the rear entrance of the building, Ozbek removed a lock pick gun while Rasmussen unholstered his .45 caliber HK USP tactical pistol and affixed its suppressor.

It took Ozbek less than a minute to open the door at which point he removed his Beretta 92 FS, attached its suppressor as well, and stepped inside.

The apartment believed to be Dodd's was on the top floor facing the street. Ozbek signaled Rasmussen, who headed into the main hallway toward the front stairs.

Ozbek counted to ten and then crept up the moldy back stairwell.

As he neared the third story, he depressed his own transmit button for a final sit rep from Whitcomb.

She toggled back the all clear just as a gloved hand dropped in front of her face and clamped down across her mouth.

CHAPTER 52

Dodd sank the straight razor in deep and drew it in one fluid slash across the woman's throat, severing both her carotid arteries and her windpipe.

Quickly, he disconnected her bone mike and transmitter.

As the woman bled to death, the assassin lowered her body to the ground and stripped off her shirt to get to her bulletproof vest. It wouldn't be a perfect fit, but it was better than nothing.

She carried a Glock 19, a sound suppressor, and two additional mags, but no identification whatsoever. Though Dodd couldn't be certain, he felt confident that she was CIA. The only question was how many others had she come with?

After putting on her bloodstained vest, Dodd clipped the woman's radio to his belt, inserted the earpiece, and wrapped the transmit button around his own left index finger.

As he zipped up his jacket, he studied the thermal imaging device. It was a nice piece of equipment, expensive. Whoever this woman was, Dodd was now even more convinced that she was CIA. The only reason you didn't carry ID was if you were working undercover and nobody but CIA would be working undercover with gear like this. This kind of device screamed high-end law enforcement or intelligence operation.

Dodd raised it to his eyes and studied his apartment. He counted two heat signatures inside. Slowly, he scanned the rest of the area.

Three people was an odd number to be traveling with, even for the CIA. If it hadn't been for the illegally parked vehicle he'd seen when coming back from the airport, he might never have noticed the woman surveilling his apartment.

Dodd knew most of the cars in his neighborhood, which made the ones that didn't belong there stand out even more. The black Denali had Virginia license plates and had been parked in front of a hydrant. Everyone on Butchers Hill knew how tough it was to find parking, and they also knew how merciless the police were in ticketing and towing. Whoever owned that vehicle was obviously a newcomer to the neighborhood or in a big hurry.

What also had caught Dodd's attention was that a light rain had fallen at some point during the evening. All the cars had dry spots underneath except for the Denali, which meant that it had been recently parked. Holding his hand above the warm hood was the only confirmation he needed.

The assassin retrieved the long straight razor he carried in his shaving kit. It didn't take him long to find and dispose of the spotter. Now it was time to eliminate whoever was inside his apartment.

Certain that his adversary felt that they had the outside covered, Dodd crossed the street and headed for his front door. Tucking the imaging device under his arm, he screwed the suppressor onto the Glock and slid the spare magazines into his waistband so he could get at them quickly if he needed to.

Dodd unlocked the front door and slipped inside. He knew every creak in every stair up to his apartment and ascended like a ghost.

He kept his eyes peeled for any portable intrusion detectors that may have been placed along the stairwell, but saw none. Near the final landing, he raised the imaging device to his eyes and once more searched for the forms inside his apartment. He found them just as he set foot on the third floor.

Moving into the hallway for the best possible shot, Dodd leveled his weapon at the drywall and began pulling the trigger.

CHAPTER 53

O zbek had no idea what had happened until he heard Rasmussen yell, "I'm hit," and then things all around him started exploding.

He leapt into the bathroom and dove into its cast iron tub just as rounds began pinging off of it. Whoever was shooting at them was doing so with a suppressed weapon and was firing right through the drywall. Activating his bone mike, he said, "Raz, how bad are you hit?"

"Bad," replied Rasmussen. "Motherfucker shot me in the leg! It's bleeding all over."

Both men were wearing low profile cargo-style pants by Blackhawk Industries that included a revolutionary integrated tourniquet system. "Clamp it," ordered Ozbek, though he knew Rasmussen was probably already doing it.

He could hear Rasmussen shout from the other room as he lifted the flap on his pants and spun the carbon fiber bar that tightened a cord in the fabric around his upper thigh and cut off the blood flow. The pants had been designed to help minimize loss of blood and get you back in the fight as fast as possible. Everyone on Ozbek's team wore them and had trained with them extensively.

Ozbek was about to confirm that Rasmussen had activated the tourniquet when he heard another series of rounds drill into the apartment.

"Son of a bitch," groaned Rasmussen over his mike.

"Take cover," ordered Ozbek.

"I did," his colleague replied. "This asshole knows exactly where I am."

Ozbek was about to climb out of the tub when silenced rounds started pinging off it yet again. *How the hell does he know exactly where we are?*

He looked up to see if there were any cameras that might tell him how the shooter was pinpointing their locations and then his heart dropped into his stomach. *The thermal imaging device.*

Ozbek clicked his transmitter in rapid succession. *Nothing.* He tried to raise Whitcomb once more, and when he received seven clicks to the tune of Shave-and-a-haircut-two-bits he knew that Whitcomb was dead. He also knew that he and Rasmussen were both sitting ducks. The shooter not only had the imaging device, he had Whitcomb's radio. What he didn't have, though, was their alternate frequency.

Ozbek didn't need to tell Rasmussen to switch freqs. He'd heard the same thing and was already on their alternate channel.

"He's got the imaging unit, doesn't he?" whispered Rasmussen, his voice strained. He didn't bother to ask about Whitcomb. He didn't want to know the answer.

"Yes," replied Ozbek as he looked up at the bathroom mirror hanging on one hinge. Through its broken glass, he could see where the rounds had come through the drywall. "He's firing laterally in four-to-six-inch patterns."

"What do you want to do?"

Ozbek needed to come up with something fast. If he and Rasmussen fired blindly into the hallway, their rounds would penetrate the apartments on the other side and very likely kill innocent people. If they sat there and did nothing, though, they were as good as dead and Dodd would get away.

If only the shooter couldn't see them.

Suddenly, Ozbek knew what they had to do. "Raz," he said over the radio, "is there a thermostat out there?"

Rasmussen scanned the walls with his flashlight until he found it. "Yes."

"Can you get to it?"

"I don't know."

"What do you have for cover?" asked Ozbek as he turned on the cold water in the tub.

"The couch."

"You've got to reach that thermostat. We need to get the heat up as high as possible."

Rasmussen studied the distance and gave the couch a nudge with his shoulder. It moved but only barely. He tried again, harder this time, and it moved a little bit more. On his third shove, bullets came through the wall all around him.

Rasmussen yelled out loud as he planted his good leg and pushed the couch with all of his might. It moved more than he expected and shot off at an angle jamming up against a bookcase.

Crawling behind the length of the couch, the injured CIA operative got his hands behind the bookcase and pulled as hard as he could, sliding it away from the wall, careful not to tip it over. Finally, he had it far enough out that he could snake behind it and reach the thermostat on the other side.

Pushing himself up on his good leg, Rasmussen reached out as far as he could and flipped the temperature gauge as high as it would go.

He dropped back to the floor as more rounds pierced the bookcase and drilled into the wall where he had just been standing.

"It's done," said Rasmussen.

"Hang in there," replied Ozbek as he slipped fully clothed and with his body armor into the tub that was rapidly filling with bone-chilling water.

There were multiple risks to what Ozbek was doing and he was aware of them all, but he was also aware that he had no choice. The key was in discerning the proper moment to get out of the tub.

Even if the heating unit was only adequate, the small apartment shouldn't take long to heat up. The longer he waited, the better chance he had of his plan working, but that held true for the shooter as well.

Ozbek knew there was only so much of a drop in body temperature he could expect in a short amount of time, but every little bit would help. Being an older generation, the imaging unit had its limitations. Ozbek needed to get his temperature as close to the apartment's as possible, thereby rendering his heat signature as near to invisible as possible. Once he did he would have to move fast.

From the reports he was getting from Rasmussen, the shooter seemed to be focusing entirely on the wounded man. Three more waves of fire had come through the wall, splintered the bookcase, and slammed into the couch.

The shooter had apparently given up on Ozbek for the time being. By taking out Rasmussen in the living room, he'd then be able to enter via the front door and take Ozbek out from inside the apartment.

Ozbek knew they couldn't wait any longer. "Raz," he said into his mike. "How hot is it out there?"

"I can't see the thermostat, but it's getting hot," he replied.

"Okay, I'm going off comms and coming out. Don't shoot me."

"Roger that," replied Rasmussen.

Ozbek pulled out his earpiece and then submerged his head beneath the water for as long as he could.

Breaking the surface, he quickly soaked a towel, draped it over his head, and slid out of the tub.

CHAPTER 54

Ozbek didn't wait to see if the shooter was going to start firing at him. He knew that his body heat would begin rising soon.

He rushed into the living room with his pistol up and at the ready. At the door, he crouched down and reached up with his left hand to grab the handle.

When the door released, he pulled it back slowly, just enough to squeeze through, and then swung into the hallway.

He found the shooter halfway down the hall with the thermal imaging unit pressed up against his face. Ozbek pulled his trigger. The man stumbled backward and as the imaging unit fell to the ground, Ozbek saw the face of Matthew Dodd.

He pulled the trigger again, punching another two rounds into the man's chest and sending him tumbling backwards.

As Dodd fell, he squeezed the trigger of his own weapon, splintering the doorframe just above Ozbek's head.

Ozbek rolled back into the apartment and called for Rasmussen to come give him cover fire. Risking a peek into the hallway, he snapped his head back inside just as two more of Dodd's rounds came blistering toward him.

Ozbek waited a beat and then stuck his gun around the doorframe and pulled the trigger.

Once more, he called for Rasmussen and once more he stuck his head into the hallway. This time, he saw Dodd racing into the rear stairwell. Ozbek fired, but the man disappeared from view.

When Ozbek glanced back in the apartment and saw Rasmussen's condition, he knew he had to get him medical attention soon. There was also Stephanie Whitcomb to consider. For all he knew, she could still be alive outside, barely clinging to life.

Even so, Matthew Dodd was too damn close to let get away.

Ozbek looked at Rasmussen and said, "I'll be right back," as he jumped up and charged into the hallway.

He reached the rear stairs and took them three at a time. He landed hard on the first landing and peered around the corner. There was no sign of Dodd, and Ozbek launched himself down the next set of stairs.

It wasn't until he was almost at the second-floor landing that he noticed how dimly lit it was. *Dodd had shattered the overhead lighting.*

Racing toward a field of broken glass, as well as a possible ambush, Ozbek grabbed the banister and tried to halt his forward trajectory.

Losing his balance, he slid down the stairs sideways. He landed hard on the second-floor landing where the broken glass dug into his left leg and shoulder.

Ignoring the pain, Ozbek swung his pistol down the next set of stairs and kept moving. When he got to the ground floor, he carefully opened the back door and stared out. There was no sign of the assassin.

Ozbek wanted to continue the chase, but he had no idea in which direction the man had fled and he also had two operatives down.

Pulling pieces of glass from his flesh, Ozbek hurried back up the stairs to Dodd's apartment. He needed to get Rasmussen to a hospital and hoped to God that Stephanie Whitcomb wasn't going to need to be taken to a morgue.

CHAPTER 55

WASHINGTON, D.C.

It was just before nine-thirty in the morning local time when the Bombardier jet touched down at Ronald Reagan National Airport.

A Signature Flight Support representative met Harvath and Nichols at their plane. She helped steer them quickly through the private aviation passport control and customs area, and when the men politely declined complimentary breakfast and hot showers, she escorted them outside to where a gray Buick was waiting for them.

The men threw their bags in the trunk and Harvath slid into the front passenger seat next to the driver, while Nichols climbed in back.

"How was the flight?" asked Lawlor as he pulled away from the curb.

"Beats a cold C-130 any day of the week," replied Harvath as he peeled off his disguise and introduced Anthony Nichols.

As they merged onto the George Washington Memorial Parkway, Harvath asked about Tracy.

"The doctors at the American Hospital have been in touch with her surgeons back here," said Lawlor. "They still have her under observation."

"Has the swelling gone down?"

"Not as much as they would like. They've started her on a new medication."

Harvath didn't like the sound of that. "Is she in any pain?"

Lawlor shook his head. "Apparently, the pain is the one thing they have managed to get under control."

"Have you spoken with her?"

"No, but someone from the embassy has. She's hanging tough and not telling anyone anything."

Harvath looked out at the sailboats and other watercraft dotting the Potomac despite overcast skies. "How are the French authorities treating her?"

"Her medical treatment is still first and foremost. But with three cops dead and a bunch of civilians killed and wounded at the bombing, there are certain elements pressing to be allowed to interrogate her."

"I suppose I can understand that," Harvath admitted.

"The sooner we accomplish things on our end," replied Lawlor, "the sooner we can give the French enough to hopefully get Tracy released."

"Hopefully?"

"You know what I mean," grated Lawlor.

The men rode the rest of the way in silence.

• • •

Forty minutes later, Lawlor swung the car off the road and rolled to a stop in front of a nondescript, padlocked gate. "Do you want to do the honors?" he asked, holding up a key.

Harvath took it and stepped out of the car. It was a bittersweet feeling to return home after all this time without Tracy.

Harvath unlocked the gate and pushed it open wide enough for Lawlor to drive through.

Pulling even with Harvath, Lawlor rolled down his window. "Do you want to get back in, or do you want to walk?"

"I think I'll walk," said Harvath.

He noticed the sign for his alarm company lying in the weeds and replanted it, then swung the gate shut behind him.

He watched as Lawlor and Nichols disappeared down the winding, tree-lined drive and began walking.

Bishop's Gate, as the property was known, was a small, eighteenth-century stone church that sat on several acres overlooking the Potomac River, just south of George Washington's Mount Vernon estate. It was the twin of a small church in Cornwall called St. Enodoc.

Bombarded during the Revolutionary War because of its status as a haven for British spies, Bishop's Gate lay in ruins until 1882, when the Office of Naval Intelligence, or ONI, secretly rebuilt it and turned it into one of the ONI's first covert-officer training schools.

Eventually the ONI outgrew the Bishop's Gate location and the stubby, yet elegant church with its attached rectory was demoted to a document storage site before being cleared out and abandoned.

As a token of his appreciation for everything Harvath had done for his country, President Rutledge had deeded Bishop's Gate in its entirety to Scot in a ninety-nine-year government lease with a token rent of one dollar per annum. All that was required of Harvath was that he maintain the property in a manner befitting its historic status and that he vacate the premises within twenty-four hours if ever given notice, with or without cause, by its legal owner, the United States Navy.

It had been more than fifty years since the Navy had any use for Bishop's Gate other than as a file graveyard, yet Harvath had been overwhelmed by the president's gift. Not including the garage, the unique house formed by the church and the attached rectory came to over four thousand square feet of living space. All Harvath had to do was make sure the grass was mowed and his dollar-a-year rent was paid on time.

As he walked down the driveway, he was reminded of the president's generosity and how much they had been through together over the years. Though he still harbored resentment over how he had been treated, he wondered if Tracy had been right. Maybe it was time to forgive Jack Rutledge and move on.

Emerging from the final twist of the wooded drive, Harvath laid eyes on his house. Bishop's Gate was even more beautiful than he remembered.

Lawlor and Nichols were standing outside the front door waiting for him.

"You've got a key," said Harvath as he approached. "What are you standing out here for?"

"It didn't seem right," said Lawlor. "It's your house, after all."

Harvath took the key from Lawlor and unlocked the sturdy front door. As he walked in, he was greeted by the solid scent of stone and timber.

Hanging on the wall in the vestibule was a beautiful piece of wood he had discovered in the rectory attic carved with the Anglican missionaries' motto TRANSIENS ADIUVANOS—*I go overseas to give help.*

He had discovered it on his first visit, and it had struck him as a sign that he and Bishop's Gate were meant to be together. It was prophetically fitting for the career Harvath had chosen for himself.

For a moment, he was reminded of why he had devoted his life to combating the terrorist threat to America at home and overseas.

He was also reminded of Tracy and how rather than make him choose between her and aiding the president, she had selflessly removed herself from the equation. Harvath allowed himself a sliver of belief that maybe he could have both the career he wanted and a fulfilling family life.

"What did you and Tracy do with Bullet?" asked Lawlor who had followed Harvath inside and interrupted his train of thought.

Nichols asked, "Who's Bullet?" as he admired the extraordinary old church.

"Biggest dog you've ever seen in your life, even as a puppy," replied Lawlor. "They call them Caucasian Ovcharkas. The Russian Military and the former East German Border Patrol loved them. Fast as hell, smart and incredibly loyal. Those things can weigh upward of two hundred pounds and they stand over forty-one inches at the shoulder."

Nichols let out a whistle of appreciation.

"Finney and Parker have him," replied Harvath.

"Those guys are good pals," said Lawlor with a laugh. "Dogzilla is probably eating them out of house and home."

"Where'd you find a dog like that?" inquired Nichols.

Harvath looked up the stairs toward the bedroom he'd been sleeping in when Tracy had been shot and said, "Don't ask."

Harvath wasn't in the mood to discuss his odd acquaintance with a dwarf named Nicholas who dealt in the purchase and sale of highly classified information and who was known throughout the intelligence world as *the Troll*.

"I put groceries in the fridge," stated Lawlor. "Let's get some coffee on and talk about what we need to do."

"Sounds good to me," replied the professor.

"I'll be there shortly," said Harvath as he walked away. He needed a few more minutes alone to gather his thoughts and process being home before he would be ready to talk about what would come next.

CHAPTER 56

Lawlor was a master with Tracy's French press, something Harvath had never gotten the hang of. He didn't know if it was because he was too lazy to bother with it or if he just liked watching Tracy go through the effort for him.

Either way, by the time Harvath came into the kitchen, Lawlor was pouring three steaming cups of fresh coffee. He took his and sat down at the table where Nichols and Lawlor joined him.

Nichols was the first to speak. "So I understand that this is now my new home?"

"For the time being," replied Harvath as he took a sip of coffee.

"What about all of my research materials? My books? My toothbrush even?"

"Make a list and we'll get it for you," said Lawlor.

Harvath held up his hand as he set his coffee cup down. "This guy Dodd is good, Gary, very good. We have no idea where he is or who he's working with. He could have already left Paris and be on his way here for all we know. Professor Nichols needs to be protected 'round the clock."

Lawlor nodded. "You're right," he said. Turning back to Nichols he added, "Scot will get you everything you need. You and I will stay here."

"We also need to lay some ground rules," said Harvath.

The professor looked at him. "Like what?"

"For one, no phone calls, no exceptions. Gary will set you up on a secure server for e-mails. Follow his protocols and don't deviate.

"Two, you are not to leave the property under any circumstances. If you want to take a walk, Gary or I will go with you. We need to know where you are at all times. Understood?"

Nichols nodded.

"Good," said Harvath. "You can work in my study. Gary will get you settled in. In the meantime," he added as he leaned over to his breakfront and removed a pad and pen from one of its drawers, "let's get cracking on the list of things you need from your apartment as well as your office in Charlottesville. The sooner I get that trip out of the way, the better I'm going to feel."

• • •

Nichols was still working on his list when Harvath topped off his cup with more coffee and left him in the kitchen with Lawlor.

Scot walked down the narrow stone hallway from the rectory and took one of the discreet side doors that opened into the little church.

In its day, Bishop's Gate must have been a real espionage paradise because beneath its sturdy foundation, it was replete with secret rooms and passages. Harvath was amazed that the ONI had never discovered them. Then again, maybe they had, but out of respect had left them untouched.

Harvath, though, had seen their incredible potential and had put the best of the passages and subterranean chambers to use.

He had uncovered them when trying to move the baptismal font to the other side of the church. The font contained an intricate locking mechanism that took Harvath an entire week to repair. Once he had it working, he discovered that the church's stone altar could be moved forty-five degrees, revealing a narrow set of circular stairs that led into an area Harvath fondly referred to as his "crypt."

Harvath winced as he squeezed down the stairs and remembered what a royal pain in the ass it had been getting all of the materials down there. But it had been worth it. Here, Harvath stored the tools of his trade.

A hidden ventilation system assured a constant flow of fresh air which concealed dehumidifiers dried and circulated. The crypt maintained a constant temperature and electricity was provided via a set of rechargeable marine batteries which powered the overhead lights.

Harvath flipped on the light switch and the long, slightly rectangular room was bathed in a fluorescent glow. Steel racks lined each wall, while a wide stainless steel table ran down the center of the room.

Scot Harvath had a lot of friends, both within the special operations community and within the community of those dedicated to providing America's top operatives with all the gear and equipment they needed to get the job done and get it done right.

A fellow SEAL who had started the world's preeminent tactical equipment company, Blackhawk Industries, made sure that Harvath had every item they had ever made. Harvath had introduced them to a brilliant young frontline doctor who had designed a new battle dress uniform with built-in tourniquets that was going to revolutionize what military and law enforcement members wore into battle. Blackhawk had snatched the doctor up and now hanging in one of Harvath's steel cages were several pairs of new tourniquet pants, which every military expert was saying was the greatest battlefield innovation since body armor.

Beyond Harvath's collection of Blackhawk Warrior Wear, Under Armour clothing, demolitions gear, communications equipment, night vision accoutrements, his pistols and his knives was finally, his heavy equipment.

Next to his Beretta, Benelli, Remington, and Mossberg shotguns were two pristine Robar RC 50 rifles and hanging next to those works of art were his heavy-use items.

Having contributed multiple design suggestions to H&K while with the SEALs' Dev Group, Harvath had one of almost every Heckler & Koch machine and submachine gun model produced in the last twenty years. He also had variants of M16 Clinic's awesome Viper.

While they were all exceptional, Harvath's most lethal, most effective and most accurate piece came out of a quiet, sophisticated shop in

Leander, Texas, called LaRue Tactical that stamped all of their gear *Live Free or Die*.

Harvath's pal and his dog's namesake, Bullet Bob Herrington, had turned him on to Mark LaRue, and no matter what crazy requests Harvath had ever thrown at his shop, the folks at LaRue Tactical had always come back with something better than he had asked for. Many people joked that Mark was a Texas version of James Bond's Q and that as a proud Texan, maybe his codename should be BB-Q. LaRue Tactical was a SEAL and Delta Force–preferred supplier, and it was easy to understand why.

Harvath reached over and took down his custom built, short-barreled LaRue M4 "stealth" tactical rifle. It looked like an ordinary door-kicker weapon, but it was anything but. It was so incredibly accurate that with the right high-powered optics on it Harvath could shoot three-inch groups at six hundred yards.

With an Aimpoint CompM4 red dot sight system for day-to-day usage, a Xiphos NT rail light, and an FSL Laserlyte laser, the weapon was one of his most prized possessions. In honor of Harvath's Norseman call sign, Mark LaRue had laser-engraved the magazine well with the mythological hammer of Thor, the Norse god of thunder.

For his sidearm, Harvath selected an HK 45 caliber USP Tactical, 230-grain Winchester SXT&P ammo and extra mags along with Gemtech suppressors for both weapons. He then unfolded a cleaning mat on the table and set about cleaning and oiling each weapon to make sure they were in absolutely perfect working order.

After loading several black polymer Magpul magazines with twenty-eight rounds of 77-grain Black Hills Mk262 ammo, he loaded the tactical rifle, its suppressor and mags into a special case while everything else went into a low-profile, Blackhawk messenger-style over-the-shoulder bag. Harvath then shut down the lights and exited the crypt.

After putting the altar back in place, he assembled his gear near the front door and walked back into the kitchen. Professor Nichols was at the stove scrambling eggs while Lawlor sat at the table reading his handwritten list.

"Is that it?" Harvath asked as he entered.

Lawlor pushed the piece of paper to the edge of the table and took off his glasses. "That's it," he said.

"Do you want breakfast before you go?" asked Nichols as he lifted Tracy's cast iron skillet off the stove.

"Sure," replied Harvath, hoping that he wouldn't need any of the equipment he had just spent all that time assembling.

Nevertheless, *Better to have it and not need it* was one of Harvath's favorite maxims. Actually his favorite maxim was *Better to have a lot of it and not need it,* but that was beside the point. If anything happened, he wanted to make sure that he was prepared.

CHAPTER 57

Even though it was Saturday, Harvath hadn't been able to find parking right away. Like any college campus, street parking at UVA was on a first-come-first-served basis. As a result, he ended up having to park several blocks away from the Corcoran Department of History.

He didn't mind. After the drive down, it felt good to get out and stretch his legs. It also felt nice to be on a university campus again. He was surprised to see how busy and vibrant it was even on a weekend.

After a short walk, Harvath arrived at a three-story brick building called Randall Hall. Nichols' office was on the second floor, and Harvath used the keys the professor had given him to let himself in. He was quite surprised at what he found. It was a lot different than he had expected.

Instead of vintage academia, the décor was quite stylish. The furniture was sleek and modern. Oil paintings of early American scenes were interspersed with tasteful black-and-white photography. Nichols was turning out to be somewhat of an iconoclast.

The focal point of the room was a stunning, dark wooden Bauhaus desk positioned in front of the windows with a ribbed leather desk chair and matching blotter. A vintage 1930s black Bakelite telephone retrofitted for modern use sat next to a sleek Apple computer. The desk was polished to such a shine that Harvath could actually see his reflection in it.

Wooden file cabinets ran the length of one wall while bookshelves ran the length of the other. There were the requisite historical texts one would expect to find in the office of a Jefferson scholar, as well as tomes by leading Democratic authors from the last several decades. Removing a couple of them, Harvath noticed that many had been signed. It was an impressive collection.

He tracked down the two Jefferson volumes the professor had asked for and slid them into his bag.

In the far corner of the room, just as Nichols had said it would be, was his blue KIVA-brand athletic bag with a tennis racquet and info on UVA's Snyder Tennis Center sticking out of it. Though Nichols claimed he was the only one with keys to his office, Harvath had worried that his choice of a hiding spot for his flash drive might have been a little too attractive for thieves.

Unzipping the main compartment of the bag, Harvath removed a pair of shorts and a Clinton/Gore T-shirt, and then found what he was looking for.

Pulling the plastic lid off a can of tennis balls, he dumped them into his hand. He had to give the professor credit. In practice, it actually was a rather ingenious way to hide his flash drive. Harvath probably never would have looked there. He found the razor-thin incision in the last ball and ripped it the rest of the way open.

As well as being especially skilled at taking lives, they were exceptional stalkers who could seemingly appear and disappear at will. At least that was how things operated in the Middle East. In the United States, it was a bit different.

While the two men were of average height and unremarkable facial features, their Arab appearance made it harder for them to blend into American crowds, even on a diverse campus like UVA. What's more, they were stalking a professional—someone who instinctively checked for tails.

Failing to kill Andrew Salam when Hamza and Rafiq had had the chance was an unforgivable offense. Salam should have died alongside Nura Khalifa. The only thing that had redeemed the two Saudi operatives in Sheik Omar's eyes was the exceptional job they had done planting the evidence of a failed relationship between the young man and woman.

Mistakes did happen, but that was not what Hamza and Rafiq were being paid for. Omar had brought them to America for results. He would not react well to another failure, which was all the more reason they had to succeed now.

Monitoring Randall Hall and Professor Nichols' campus apartment had been a tedious chore, but Omar had insisted on it. The operation in Paris had been a total failure and the sheik was beyond angry.

Al-Din, Omar's American assassin, had e-mailed the sheik French security-cam photos of the man and woman who had been helping Nichols. Hamza and Rafiq had been told by Omar in no uncertain terms what he expected them to do if they came across Nichols or any of his associates.

Hamza had been surveilling Randall Hall when the man had shown up. After checking his photo against the one he'd been given by Omar, he called Rafiq and instructed him to pick up their car and get over to Randall Hall as soon as possible.

They both carried pistols, but they were for self-defense only. Even suppressed firearms made noise and could draw unwanted attention.

The flash drive had fit perfectly inside. So snug was it that som
could have bounced the tennis ball and not even heard the device
tling within. Harvath removed the drive and slid it into his pocket.
had at least a two-hour drive in front of him and he still needed
swing by Nichols' house to pick up his clothes, as well as some oth
items. Exiting the professor's office, he pulled the door shut an
locked it behind him.

Once outside, Harvath headed toward the central part of campus
where his SUV was parked.

He entered the dramatic, colonnade-lined commons known as the
Lawn. At the very top was the Rotunda, the architectural and intel-
lectual heart of UVA, which Jefferson had designed himself and based
upon the Pantheon in Rome.

The thought of the Pantheon brought back a flood of memories for
Harvath. The last time he had seen it he'd almost been killed.

With that realization, a strange feeling washed over him. It took
him a moment to realize that the feeling had nothing to do with cheat-
ing death all those years ago in Italy. It had to do with right here and
right now.

As the hair on the back of his neck stood up, Harvath's hand slid
into his bag and searched for the butt of his Heckler & Koch.

Somebody was following him.

CHAPTER 58

Hamza Ayyad and Rafiq Sa'id were no strangers to killing.
Ex–Saudi Intelligence operatives, they had been steeped
in every facet of tradecraft and the black arts known
to man.

Any killing these men did was usually up close and personal, with their bare hands or a wide variety of quiet weapons like knives, needles, karambits, or any one of dozens of everyday items.

Just by how the man acted and carried himself while walking into Randall Hall, Hamza could tell that he was a professional. He was fit and agile, his eyes wary and alert. Though he dressed down with the clothes he wore, the man also had a formidable build. Even with the element of surprise, Hamza knew he would not be an easy kill. Too many things could go wrong and that was something they could not afford. That was why he had called for Rafiq. Together, the two of them could take him down without incident.

That was until he had suddenly left the building.

The man had been inside for less than ten minutes. As Hamza waited and then fell in a safe distance behind him, he used his Bluetooth headset to carry on a conversation with Rafiq and keep him informed of their position.

Dressed in jeans and hiking boots with a windbreaker over a denim shirt, Hamza carried a small backpack to better blend in with the student body population. It was a beneficial side effect of the 9/11 attacks that while Americans might be more suspicious of people who appeared to be Muslim, they had tied themselves in such politically correct knots that even campus police, fearing professional and personal discrimination lawsuits, would think four times before questioning someone who looked like Rafiq or Hamza. As a result, the two Saudi hit men had been able to roam the UVA campus with impunity.

Now, their problem was how to apprehend their target. Snatching someone off a crowded public street in Riyadh or Medina was extremely complicated. In America, it was all but impossible. The target would either have to be coerced into their vehicle or forced into an isolated area where he could be taken out.

Hamza was weighing the possibility of getting in close enough to use his knife when the subject suddenly turned.

CHAPTER 59

After doubling back, twice, Harvath began to believe he had imagined the whole thing. Nobody was on his tail.

When he was within half a block of his SUV, Harvath checked his six one more time, and decided to go for it.

With one hand on his remote key fob and the other gripped around the butt of his HK inside his bag, Harvath quickly closed the distance to his black Chevy Trailblazer.

After checking the street for suspicious vehicles, he scanned the sidewalks in all directions and then approached his SUV. He checked the cars parked both in front of and behind his. Then, pretending like he was going to cross the street, he stopped short, popped the lock on his truck, opened the door and hopped in.

As fast as he could, Harvath slid the key into the ignition and fired up the engine. His eyes flicked back and forth from the mirrors to the sidewalks on both sides of him. There was a white minivan coming from the end of the block behind him and he kept his eyes glued to it as he backed up his SUV in anticipation of vacating his parking spot.

Behind the minivan was a blue Nissan, several car lengths back, which must have discovered someone else leaving their spot as the driver had come to a stop and had applied his right turn signal indicating his intent.

Harvath waited for the minivan to pass him and then he turned his front wheels out toward the street and began to exit the space.

No sooner had he done so than the blue Nissan slammed into the side of his SUV, thrusting its nose back into the space and pinning his door shut. Running up hard on his passenger side was a short, dark-skinned man in a windbreaker and blue jeans. As he ran, one of his hands disappeared beneath his jacket.

Harvath got his head down just as a storm of bullets raked his Trailblazer.

The shots were being fired one at a time, probably by the driver of the Nissan and probably via a semiautomatic pistol of some sort. These guys apparently hadn't come loaded for bear. They were going to regret that.

Harvath reached behind his seat, flipped up the lid on his Storm case and snatched his modified LaRue M4.

By the time he was back, the guy in the windbreaker already had his weapon out and was firing rounds through his windshield. Harvath leveled his sights and returned fire.

With the suppressor affixed, the weapon was amazingly quiet in comparison with the weapons his attackers were using.

Harvath's rounds found their mark and he put two tight groups into the chest and head of the man in the windbreaker. He then swung the weapon to his left.

Jabbing the M4 through his broken window, Harvath ignored the rounds coming at him from the Nissan and depressed his trigger. When he hit the final round, he dropped his spent magazine and reloaded with a spare from the reserve carrier in record time.

After whipping his head around in search of any additional threats, Harvath fired fifteen more rounds into his attackers' vehicle and then exited the passenger side of his SUV.

As he crept to the back of his Trailblazer, his head was on a swivel. *Scan and breathe,* he told himself. *Scan and breathe. Don't get taken by surprise.*

His weapon was up and in the firing position as he slipped out from behind his vehicle and approached the blue Nissan. All around him, UVA students were screaming and running for cover.

When he drew even with the driver's side window he saw that the driver had sustained multiple shots to his head and torso and was definitely dead.

In the distance, Harvath could hear the staccato cry of approaching police cars. He opened the Nissan's door and pulled the driver's corpse out onto the street. He patted him down, but didn't find any identification. He assumed it would probably be the same for his partner lying dead on the sidewalk.

Harvath swung his head around once again and this time caught some imbecile with a camera phone actually trying to take his picture. Without even thinking, he raised his weapon and pointed it at him. "Drop it," he ordered.

The terrified student did as he was told.

"Now get lost," ordered Harvath.

As he watched the idiot take off, he walked over and retrieved the phone. The sound of police cars was getting closer. Harvath didn't have much time.

Hopping in the still idling Nissan, he threw it in reverse and backed up enough to be able to get his SUV out. Then, careful not to leave any prints, he did a quick sweep of the car for anything that might tell him who these guys were or who they worked for—visors, center console, glove box; all of it was empty.

After retrieving the man's weapon, Harvath jumped out and used the camera phone he had confiscated to take two quick pictures of the driver and then one of the license plates.

He repeated the process with the corpse in the windbreaker, who as he had suspected wasn't carrying ID either, and then pitched the men's guns into the back of his Trailblazer.

Using two ratty towels he kept in back, he quickly wrapped them around his front and rear license plates and hopped into his SUV.

Screaming out of the parking space, he put as much distance between himself and the University of Virginia as fast as he could.

CHAPTER 60

W hat's he doing here?" said Abdul Waleed as he walked into Sheik Omar's office.

Matthew Dodd, his face badly scratched, was sitting on the couch. *"As sala'amu alaikum,* brother," he replied. Even though he'd been wearing the female CIA operative's vest at his apartment when he'd been shot, his chest still hurt like hell. It was difficult to speak or breathe deeply.

Waleed hesitated a moment and then replied, *"Walaikum as sala'am."*

"Our operation in Paris was unsuccessful," stated Omar. "There are other problems as well."

Waleed's eyes shot back to Dodd. This was not what he needed to hear right now. He had spent the morning getting grilled by the FBI about Nura Khalifa and Andrew Salam. His nerves were shot. Pointing his finger at Dodd, he said, "All of the problems have been your fault."

"Stop," ordered Omar as he waved the director of FAIR to a chair. The sheik didn't want another fight in his office. He'd already gone apoplectic with Dodd and his blood pressure was just now finally coming back under control. "When what we want doesn't happen, we must learn to want what does."

More proverbs, thought Waleed. "Mahmood, the FBI know everything."

"Everything?" questioned the sheik. "I don't think so. They know only what Andrew Salam has told them and Salam is a liar and a murderer."

"But even liars sometimes tell the truth," replied Waleed, tossing a desert proverb right back into the imam's lap. "I'm telling you the FBI believes what Salam is telling them."

"How can you know this?"

"Because I saw it on every one of their faces. I heard it in their voices; in every one of their questions. They know what we have been doing. And what they don't know, they assume and their assumptions are correct!"

"Calm down," said Omar. "We need to remember to believe what we see and lay aside what we hear."

Waleed shook his head in disgust. "We have underestimated them."

"They have no evidence. The American people will never allow a Muslim witch hunt. Islamophobia, remember?"

"Omar, listen to me. The American people are not with us. They are afraid of us. But they are more afraid of being politically incorrect, and we have made that work for us. Make no mistake, though, there is a limit even to that, and we are getting very close to having overplayed our hand. If we are not absolutely careful, absolutely vigilant, the tide of political correctness will turn against us."

The sheik laughed.

"You think this is funny?" asked Waleed.

Omar looked at the man. "You overestimate the people of this nation. They are soft and stupid. The reason political correctness and multiculturalism exists is because they are too lazy to hold others to what it once meant to be an American. This nation is dying and we are not the problem; we are the solution. Islam—true, pure Islam—is what will save America."

"If Paris was a failure, though, there may no longer be a true, pure Islam. Not as we know it at least."

"Paris was unsuccessful because we overreached," said Dodd as he looked at Omar. "That is not going to happen anymore."

The inference was clear and Waleed found it quite bold. Dodd was blaming Omar for what happened in Paris. Looking at the sheik, Waleed said, "You mentioned other problems. What *other* problems?"

"The CIA located my apartment in Baltimore," replied Dodd.

"How?"

"I don't know. It doesn't matter. What matters is that as a result, one of their operatives is dead and another is wounded. It will be chaos at Langley."

"What matters," clarified Waleed, "is the timing of all of this. The information had to have come from Salam."

"But he had no idea who his handler was," interjected Omar. "He believed he was working for the FBI."

"Abdul is right," said Dodd as he tried to unravel it. "Somehow the authorities were able to make the connection. It had to have come from Salam."

"You need to disappear again," stated Waleed. "Go anywhere. Just get out of the country and stay hidden."

Omar held up his hand. "Not yet. Not until his work here is done."

"What work? The professor who was assisting Marwan Khalifa? Anthony Nichols?" asked Waleed.

The sheik nodded.

"Let your talented Saudi operatives handle him. No, wait, I forgot. They're the reason Salam is still alive in the first place."

Omar's blood pressure was rising again. He didn't need Waleed's sarcasm. He was just about to rebuke the man when the telephone on his desk rang. Picking it up, he listened for a moment and then hung up. Reaching for his television remote he said, "There's been a shooting at the University of Virginia. A bad one. Apparently, it is all over the news."

CHAPTER 61

With the windshield missing and bullet holes on each side, Harvath knew he wouldn't make it very far in his Trailblazer. After several minutes of driving, he discovered a heavily wooded access road that bordered the 573-acre Boar's Head Inn Resort.

Harvath pulled off the road and drove as far as he could into the woods before shutting down the engine. Sticking to the trees, he crept around the edge of the golf course until he reached the inn. The valets were extremely busy, and it didn't take Harvath long to find what he was looking for.

A queue of cars, with their keys in the ignitions, sat waiting to be parked. Harvath never liked doing things the hard way if he didn't have to. Walking up to a green Volvo sedan like he owned it, Harvath slid inside, started it up, and pulled away from the inn.

It took him a few moments to get his bearings and find the access road, but once he did, he drove straight to the spot in the woods where he had hidden his Trailblazer.

Harvath took the license plates off his SUV and transferred everything, including all of the weapons, into the trunk of the Volvo and then carefully made his way home.

• • •

"I'll send a team down to pick up your car and have them drop the one you borrowed where it'll be found," said Lawlor as Harvath removed the last of his gear from the Volvo. "I'll get to work on the police at UVA as well."

Harvath reached into his pocket and removed the memory card from the camera phone. "This has photos of the two men I shot," he said as he handed it to Gary, "as well as a picture of their license plate."

"The car's probably stolen, but we'll run it anyway. Do you need anything else while I'm out?"

Harvath shook his head.

"Okay," said Gary as he got into the Volvo. "I'll requisition a car for you and be back by seven so you'll have plenty of time to make it into D.C."

Harvath watched as Lawlor drove off from Bishop's Gate. A visit to the White House was about the last thing he was in the mood for. He had not seen Jack Rutledge face-to-face since shortly after Tracy's shooting and had no desire to see him now. It had been Harvath's idea for Nichols to remain in seclusion and work on the missing Koranic texts at Bishop's Gate. But to do that he needed Jefferson's wheel cipher and the other documents the president had in his possession. And though Rutledge could have given them to Gary to bring back to Bishop's Gate, the president had insisted that Harvath come and pick them up personally. It seemed that like it or not, Harvath was finally going to have to face Jack Rutledge.

After checking on Nichols and giving him the flash drive as well as the other items he'd collected from his office at UVA, Harvath walked into the kitchen. Putting on water for coffee, he suddenly thought better of it and turned it off.

He'd been on edge for the last several hours. His nerves were raw and his jet lag was kicking in. He didn't need to be downing cups of coffee; what he needed was rest.

Harvath headed upstairs and, ignoring the picture of him and Tracy on his nightstand, lay down on his bed and closed his eyes. He worked on quieting his mind and clearing it of all thoughts.

Slowly he was able to disconnect until he finally stepped off the edge into a deep, dreamless sleep. He stayed in that state for several hours until he was awakened by the sound of Lawlor coming back down the driveway.

Though his body fought him on it, Harvath dragged himself out of bed and into the bathroom. He took a long, hot shower, letting the water beat down on his neck and shoulders.

When he'd had enough, he threw the temperature selector all the way to cold and stood there for as long as he could. The shock was better than a double espresso.

Climbing out of the shower, Harvath shaved, dried his hair and then picked out a suit. It might have been Saturday, but he was going to the White House to meet the president and he would dress appropriately.

When he was dressed, he followed the smell of coffee down to the kitchen. Lawlor was working his magic again with the French press.

"Any news on Tracy?" he asked.

"No," replied Lawlor as he handed him a cup. "But the two guys you laid out at UVA have come back with interesting backgrounds."

"Such as?"

"Apparently, they're Saudi nationals with several aliases. Some of the information suggests they may have been with Saudi Intelligence."

"Were these guys being run by the Saudis?" asked Harvath as he took a sip of coffee. "Or were they freelancers like Dodd?"

"Based on the crown prince's interest in what the president has been up to, we think the Saudis were running them," said Lawlor. "My guess is that they were sitting on Nichols' office and his apartment in case he showed up. I don't think they followed you to UVA. I think they were already there."

"Me too," said Harvath.

Lawlor handed him a set of car keys. "Black Tahoe outside. I had the OnStar and the other GPS gear removed."

"Thanks."

Harvath slid the keys into his pocket and took his coffee cup with him into the church. After sliding back the altar, he walked down into the crypt and laid out two pistols, his tactical rifle, and a handful of frag grenades.

While he didn't plan on encountering any trouble on his quick round-trip to the White House, he'd felt the same way before leaving for UVA.

But unlike his trip to UVA, this time, he was going to be bringing back a critical package and he had no intention of letting anyone but Anthony Nichols get their hands on it.

CHAPTER 62

THE WHITE HOUSE

Carolyn Leonard met Harvath at the vehicle entrance on 17th and Pennsylvania Avenue. The president had instructed that Harvath be cleared all the way through and not searched. Knowing Harvath and the nature of the work he did for the president, Leonard assumed it was because he would be coming armed; probably heavily armed.

After the retractable bollards had been lowered and Harvath had driven through, Leonard hopped in the passenger seat and rode with him through one more checkpoint before having him park between the Treasury Department and the East Wing on East Executive Drive.

"Should I leave my nine iron in the car?" asked Harvath as he patted his side.

"If it was up to me, yes, but the president has made it clear that you have a full pass. So it's your call," she replied as she climbed out.

Harvath preferred to have at least one weapon under his control at all times. Not that anyone was going to break into his vehicle on the White House grounds and sabotage his gear, but being just a little bit paranoid was what kept people in his line of work alive. He decided to retain his sidearm.

Leonard radioed that they were on their way in and Harvath walked alongside her across the street.

It was a strange feeling being back at the White House. Harvath had spent many nights in the residence while on the president's Secret Service detail and it was eerie how quiet the building could be—almost like a church.

There was no staff visible as they made their way into the main elevator and Leonard pressed the button for the third floor. "Solarium?" ventured Harvath.

The woman shook her head in response.

When the elevator opened on the third floor, Harvath heard the crack of billiard balls and had his answer. Leonard led him across the central hall to the game room on the south side of the residence.

As they approached, Harvath studied the president's detail agents standing at their posts outside—one male, one female. Harvath didn't recognize either of them. They gave him the same considered once-over he had bestowed many times upon Rutledge's visitors as a Secret Service agent. He knew that they lived by the maxim: *Be polite to everyone you meet, but have a plan of how to kill them.* It was a habit Harvath still employed to this day.

"Excuse me, Mr. President," said Leonard as she knocked on the game room door. "Scot Harvath is here."

Rutledge, his sleeves rolled up and his tie discarded, leaned his cue against the Brunswick pool table and replied, "At last, somebody who can hold their own in here. How are you doing, Scot?"

"I'm fine, sir," said Harvath as he met the president halfway and they shook hands.

"Would you like a beer?" asked Rutledge, as Leonard left the room and closed the door behind her.

Harvath tapped his hip, indicating he was carrying his weapon.

"Watching your waist?" joked the president as he walked over to a small refrigerator and opened its door. "How about a Diet Coke?"

"That would be great," replied Harvath. "Thank you."

Rutledge pulled out a can of Diet Coke for Harvath and a bottle of St. Pauli Girl for himself and opened them up. He handed the can to Harvath and clinked his bottle against it. "Cheers."

"Cheers," Harvath replied.

"Did you know that President Lincoln was a confessed billiards addict?" asked the president.

"No, I didn't," replied Harvath, who had played pool once or twice with Rutledge on the road, but never in the White House game room.

"Lincoln called it a health-inspiring, scientific game that lends recreation to an otherwise fatigued mind. Why don't you choose a cue and we'll lag for break."

Harvath took a sip of his Diet Coke, removed his jacket, and then selected a cue. He beat the president just barely on the lag and was given the honor of the break.

They settled on a straight game of eight ball. Harvath had learned a long time ago that the key to a clean break was the same as a good shot off the golf tee. It was all about a smooth backswing and clean follow-through.

Drawing the cue back farther than most in order to put extra power into his shot, Harvath struck the cue ball and sent it rocketing forward. There was an impressive crack as the cue met the other balls, sending three spinning into pockets.

After a short run of the table, Harvath scratched and handed control over to the president.

"I've been waiting for this meeting for a long time," said Rutledge.

Harvath leaned on his cue and took another sip of his Diet Coke. Though he made up his mind to let bygones be bygones, the air was still thick with tension. "I know you have, sir," he replied.

"Scot, I need to tell you in person how sorry I am for what happened. If I had known any harm was going to come to you or the people you care about, I would have warned you."

"Mr. President," Harvath began, but Rutledge stopped him.

"I made a deal with terrorists," he continued, "and you personally suffered because of it. Though they violated the nature of the agreement, I still held you back from getting involved and protecting those around you. That was wrong, and I take full responsibility.

"You have proven yourself time and again to this administration and to your country. I have repeatedly told you what an asset you are, yet when my back was against the wall I shunned your help and forced you to decide between protecting the people important to you and being labeled a traitor and I'm sorry for that."

After his phone call with the president from Paris, Harvath hadn't expected the subject to be brought up again. The president's humility spoke to the strength of character that Harvath had always admired in him.

Rutledge came around to Harvath's side of the table and extended his hand once more. "I only want you to take it if you truly accept my apology."

Harvath didn't need to think about it and he didn't need to hear any more. Firmly and without hesitation, he gripped the president's hand and forgave him.

"Good," said Rutledge as he lined up his next shot. "Now that we've got that out of the way, I can give you what you came for."

CHAPTER 63

Aydin Ozbek sat in his house alone with the lights out and only a bottle of Maker's Mark to keep him company. It had been one of the worst days of his life.

Rasmussen's gunshot wound was more serious than he had thought. Without the tourniquet pants he would have bled out and died in the apartment. He was lucky to be alive.

Then there was Stephanie Whitcomb. Her throat had been slashed ear-to-ear. When Ozbek found her, she was already dead. There was nothing he could have done to save her.

Her body lay in the back of his truck under a blanket while he transported Rasmussen to the nearest level one trauma center and dumped him at the Emergency Room entrance.

It was cold, but necessary. Raz would have done the same thing had the situation been reversed. It was better if only one of them was compromised and had to deal with all the BS that came with seeking treatment for a bullet wound. It was also better that the Denali with Stephanie Whitcomb's body in back not be discovered either.

Bruce Selleck, the NCS Director, had gone absolutely ape shit when Ozbek had called him and explained why he needed to see him at Langley as soon as possible.

When he showed up and Ozbek told him what had happened, Selleck gave him the ass-chewing of his life. Ozbek deserved it. He had overstepped his authority in a big way. They had one dead operative and another in the hospital, and the entire undertaking threatened to burn the Agency to the ground.

Running ops on American soil was completely forbidden. It didn't matter what the prize was. Ozbek had colossally fucked up.

The Agency had to bullshit the hospital on Rasmussen's gunshot wound to avoid an investigation and deal with Whitcomb's murder and what to do with her body. The woman had a family, friends. She couldn't just vanish. Besides, that wasn't how the CIA liked to do business.

Selleck debriefed Ozbek himself and then sent his "good for nothing" ass home and told him not to come back to work until the Agency decided what it was going to do with him.

As if that wasn't enough, there was a message waiting for Ozbek on his voice mail when he got back to his house. It was the vet. Shelby had succumbed to her cancer and had passed away. Ozbek was crushed.

Though there was nothing else he could have done for his dog, he hadn't wanted her to die without him. He had been selfish in making her hang on this long. He should have ended her suffering days, if not weeks, ago.

And though he knew it was shallow to dwell on his dog's passing, the pain he felt was simply training wheels for having to deal with Stephanie's death.

The shock from it all was starting to wear off and he had no intention of facing the guilt over her murder by himself. That was why the Maker's Mark sat on the table in front of him.

He had already passed through the first stage of grief—denial. *This can't be happening* raced through his mind repeatedly as he drove Stephanie Whitcomb's body back to Virginia.

Then came the anger stage. Ozbek was masterful at that one. He had a lot of anger and he wasn't stingy with it. It was misplaced, he knew, and Selleck almost punched his lights out for trying to project some of it in his direction rather than at himself.

From anger, Ozbek moved to the third phase—bargaining, except his deal making with God had a vengeful twist. He offered God anything He wanted, as long as Ozbek could be allowed to settle the score with Matthew Dodd.

By his third drink, he had become quite persuasive and was actively engaging God out loud, iterating point by point why he should be given the opportunity to kill an animal like Dodd, when his phone rang.

"You sound terrible," said one of Ozbek's DPS operatives named Beard. "Did I wake you up or something?"

"Or something," replied Ozbek. "What's going on?"

"Two things. We put tripwires on Marwan Khalifa's e-mail accounts like you asked and we just got a hit."

Ozbek set his drink down. "Inbound or outbound?"

"Outbound."

"So he's alive."

Beard paused a moment. "That's the second thing. The Italians have ID'd Khalifa's body with the dental records we sent them. He's dead. They're positive."

"So what's with the e-mail?" asked Ozbek.

"Somebody appears to be using it to pose as him."

"Pose how?"

"Apparently," replied Beard, "Khalifa had an appointment on Monday morning at the Library of Congress. Whoever's posing as Khalifa has moved the appointment up to tomorrow in Annapolis."

"You're sure this wasn't some e-mail that was typed previously and somehow was just delayed in being sent?"

"Nope. There have been two exchanges in the last hour."

"Who is he communicating with?" asked Ozbek.

"Anthony Nichols."

It has to be Dodd, thought Ozbek as he stood up so fast he almost knocked his table over. *He's posing as Khalifa so he can draw Nichols out.* "Does anyone else know about this?"

"No," said Beard. "You're the only one."

"Keep it that way," replied Ozbek.

"What are you going to do?"

"Never mind," he ordered. "Just get me copies of everything right now."

"Right away," replied Beard.

Ozbek hung up the phone and screwed the cap back on his bottle of Maker's Mark.

Not only did the Lord work in mysterious ways, he thought to himself, *but He was also incredibly fast.* He would have made an exceptional CIA operative.

CHAPTER 64

Harvath returned to Bishop's Gate and found the professor in his office. "You're still up?" he asked.

"Lots to do," replied Nichols, who then nodded at the manila envelope and soft canvas bag Harvath was carrying.

Approaching the desk, Harvath set the envelope down, opened the mouth of the bag, and withdrew a beautiful wooden box similar to the one the *Don Quixote* had been kept in at the Bilal Mosque in Paris.

It was crafted from the same hardwoods and included Thomas Jefferson's inlaid initials. Harvath set it on the desk. "The president said you would know how to open it."

"One of Jefferson's many secrets," replied Nichols as he delicately went to work. He noticed Harvath admiring the box. "A piece of art, isn't it?"

"It is," said Harvath.

"Are you familiar with puzzle boxes?"

"I had a few of them as a kid," he replied. "My father and I even made a couple of our own together. Nothing as beautiful as this, though."

"What was he like?" asked the professor as he slowly unlocked one of the side pieces and then proceeded to the next link in the sequence.

Harvath smiled. "He was tough as hell. But my mother and I knew he loved us—a lot."

"He passed away?"

"A while ago," said Harvath. "Just after I got out of high school. He was a SEAL instructor. He died in a training accident."

The professor looked up from the box. "I'm sorry about that."

"So am I."

Moments later, Nichols depressed the inlaid initials and tilted open the lid. The interior of this box was lined with velvet and upon it sat Jefferson's wheel cipher.

Nichols removed the device, set it reverently upon the desk next to the *Don Quixote,* and then, almost as an afterthought, handed the box to Harvath to examine.

For several minutes, neither of the men spoke. At last, Harvath broke the silence. "So you've got everything you need now. It should be simple from this point forward," he said as he handed the puzzle box back to the professor.

Nichols laughed. "We've come a long way, but I've learned that nothing about Thomas Jefferson is ever simple. He has been referred to as the Great American Sphinx. It's one of the best descriptions I ever heard of him. The same author also made a brilliant comment that when you study Jefferson's face on the nickel he always looks to the left. As a Democrat, I take great pride in that."

This time Harvath laughed. Though they had met under less than ideal circumstances, he had grown to like the professor a lot.

"Anything new on Tracy?" he asked.

Harvath shook his head. "Not really."

"I'm sorry to have dragged you both into this."

"It's not your fault. What matters now is that you decipher the Sphinx's code," said Harvath with a grin. "If he really did discover missing texts from the Koran and those texts could help moderate Muslims to reform Islam, we need to find them."

"Speaking of which," replied Nichols, "I received an e-mail from Marwan Khalifa."

There was that name again, thought Harvath. Even though the president had vouched for him, Harvath had his reservations. "What did he want?"

"He just got back from the project he was working on overseas. We were supposed to meet Monday at the Library of Congress to put our heads together on everything, but Marwan thinks he has found something useful in his research and wants to meet tomorrow instead."

Harvath was apprehensive. "Where?"

"That's the thing. Marwan is worried that someone may be following him. He doesn't want to come into D.C. He doesn't even want to go home. He's staying in a hotel and wants to meet near there; where he knows the area and feels comfortable."

"Where's that?"

"Annapolis."

Harvath knew Annapolis pretty well. "Where exactly does he want to meet?"

"In typical Marwan fashion," said Nichols, "he has chosen a location rich with symbolism and more than a hint of irony."

CHAPTER 65

The United States Naval Academy was located across the Severn River from the Naval Surface Warfare Center along the banks of the Chesapeake Bay.

Referred to by some as *The Boat School* or *Canoe U, The Academy,* as it was more appropriately called, was the undergraduate college responsible for educating future Naval and Marine Corps officers. It was also home of the Navy football team.

Though Harvath had done his undergrad work at the University of Southern California he had been to the academy a handful of times. On three of those occasions, he had eaten at the academy's private Officers' & Faculty Club. At the end of each meal he had walked east across the street and down a simple brick pathway to admire the oldest military monument in the United States.

Known as the Tripoli Monument, it was sculpted in 1806 to commemorate the heroes of the first war against the Barbary pirates. Echoing seventeenth-century allegorical style it was made of the same Italian Carrera marble used by Michelangelo. Its central feature was a tall "rostral column" identical to the one used in Rome's Colosseum. It was studded with the carved prows of enemy ships and capped with a majestic American Eagle.

The square pedestal upon which the column rested depicted the turbaned heads of Islamic pirates.

Around the outside of the monument were a winged angel representing Fame and a female scribe representing History recording the deeds of the brave American heroes who fought against the Muslims. Commerce was shown honoring the heroes' role in preserving America's right to trade unmolested by the Muslim pirates in the Mediterranean, and finally a maiden with two young children at her feet represented America.

Upon the monument were carved the names of six heroes, cited by Congress for their gallantry, who took brave action on *"the shores of Tripoli"* against the Muslim pirates before Tripoli's "pasha" finally relented.

It was a moving tribute to the brave Americans who stood toe-to-toe with Muslim fundamentalists. Before being moved to the academy, the monument had actually stood in front of Congress. There were many, including Harvath, who thought it should be moved back there as a reminder to the nation's elected officials of the true nature of the enemy America faced today and the need to stop putting politics and political correctness above principles.

As optimistic as Harvath tended to be, he knew there wasn't a chance in hell the monument would ever be relocated back to Congress. In fact, there was a movement being spearheaded by a high-ranking Muslim Pentagon official named Imad Ramadan to have it destroyed because it was "offensive" to Muslims and more particularly to Muslim sailors of the U.S. Navy. Ramadan claimed it was beneath the country's dignity to denigrate Muslims in such a fashion.

Harvath had met Ramadan twice while working at the White House and had thought he was full of shit. From what he could remember, the man had been born somewhere in the Middle East and had immigrated to America for college, after which he spent two decades with the Air Force before joining the Department of Defense. Though his position involved defense affairs, the only affairs he seemed concerned with were those of Muslims—American or otherwise.

He had come as part of a Pentagon delegation to discuss Muslim outreach programs with the president, who had been wise enough to distance himself from the groups Ramadan was trying to get invited into the oval office for cozy photo ops.

Like many Islamic apologists, Ramadan seemed to be in a state of perpetual outrage. Coming on the heels of his orchestrating the firing of the Defense Department's Islamic jihad specialist for telling the truth about Islam and how it inspires violence, his call to tear down the Tripoli monument rang absolutely hollow. The majority of the people engaged in the war on terror wondered how this Islamist in sheep's clothing was able to keep his job, especially at a place like the Pentagon. The running joke was that if Ramadan had his way, pretty soon you wouldn't be able to make it past the E ring without first taking a foot bath.

Harvath tried to push the irritation from his mind and glanced at his Kobold. "Your pal Marwan is late."

"He'll be here," said Nichols.

Standing next to the monument on the manicured grounds between the Naval Academy museum and the admissions office, Harvath felt like a sitting duck. His eyes kept sweeping the windows, doorways, and rooftops searching for anything unusual; any sign of trouble.

The O&F Club was known for its Sunday brunch and because of the exceptionally agreeable weather this morning, there were lots of people walking past the monument.

"We'll give him ten more minutes," replied Harvath. "That's it."

Nichols nodded and went back to scanning the faces of the people as they walked by.

Suddenly, Harvath's earpiece crackled to life. "Heads up," said Gary Lawlor. "You've got somebody headed in your direction across the grass from the south. Blue jeans, dark tennis shoes, hooded black sweatshirt with a bag slung over his shoulder."

Harvath turned. "I've got him," he replied. "Stay sharp."

"Roger. Standing by."

Harvath looked at Nichols and said, "Get behind me." He then reached under his coat and drew his weapon, careful to keep it concealed.

He didn't like any of this. The man in the sweatshirt had his hood up over his head so that his face couldn't be seen. Instead of using the brick walkway, he was cutting across the lawn. Whoever this guy was, he wasn't a pro. No one would have announced themselves like that. Nevertheless, Harvath was definitely on his guard.

As the man approached, he slowly removed his hood. He was of average height and bland features. He had short hair and wore glasses. If Harvath had to guess his age, he'd put him somewhere in his thirties. "Is one of you guys Anthony Nichols?" the man asked.

"I'm Anthony Nichols," the professor replied before Harvath could stop him.

At that moment the man slid his hand into the bag hanging across his shoulder.

"What are you doing?" demanded Harvath, his finger tightening on the trigger of his weapon.

The man looked at him like he was nuts. "I was told to come here and ask for an Anthony Nichols and then give him an envelope."

With one eye on the man with the bag, Harvath quickly scanned their immediate area. He was about to ask him who had sent him when Lawlor's voice exploded over his earpiece. "Scot! Watch out!"

CHAPTER 66

A new man burst out of a small group of people passing the monument and Harvath was just able to cover Nichols and knock him to the ground before the figure barreled into the hooded man with the bag.

Harvath had no idea what was happening. All he knew was that the new man was straddling the chest of the man with the bag and had a suppressed Beretta pressed up underneath his chin. That made him a threat.

Harvath's training as a Secret Service agent was telling him to get Nichols the hell out of there, but he wanted answers. Ignoring Lawlor's repeated demands to know what the hell was happening, Harvath pulled his pistol from beneath his jacket and pointed it at the man with the Beretta. "Drop your weapon," Harvath ordered.

The man with the Beretta ignored him. With his free hand, he pulled a folded piece of paper from his pocket and shook it open. From where Harvath was, he could see it was a picture of some sort. The man studied the face on the paper against the visage of the man underneath him. "Who the fuck sent you here?" he demanded as he scanned the area looking for heaven knew what.

"Drop your weapon," Harvath ordered once more.

"I work for a messenger service," stuttered the man with the bag. "I was told to come here and drop off an envelope."

Harvath had had it. "Drop your weapon or I'll shoot."

The man relaxed his grip so that he was only holding the weapon via his index finger in the trigger guard.

"Now set it down," ordered Harvath.

The man did as he was told.

"Now get the hell off that guy."

The minute people had seen the weapons, they had cleared out of the area. Harvath knew that momentarily USNA Police would be all over the place.

"Don't you want whatever this guy has in his bag?" asked the man after he set down his gun.

Harvath couldn't believe the balls on this guy. "I want you off of him and on your knees," he ordered. "Right there. Hands behind your head."

"I'm a friend of Carolyn Leonard's," the man said.

"Gary," Harvath said over his radio. "I need you over here now."

"On my way," replied Lawlor from his hide site.

Harvath turned his attention to the hooded messenger. He actually did want to see what the man had for Nichols. "Very slowly," he said as he trained his pistol on him, "open the top of your bag."

The messenger did as he was told.

"Now," continued Harvath, "lean forward, stick the bag out as far as you can, and shake the contents onto the ground."

When the items spilled out, most of them the personal effects of the messenger, it wasn't hard to spot the small, padded envelope with Nichols' name written across it in thick, black ink.

"That's it. I'm just a messenger. Seriously," he said.

Harvath believed him, but he still frisked him and had him sit tight. Next he turned his attention to the other man. "How do you know Carolyn Leonard?"

"I'm the one who tipped her that Matthew Dodd was hunting you in Paris."

"You know who we are?"

"Scot Harvath and Anthony Nichols," replied the man. "But anything else should be discussed away from here," he added as the sound of sirens grew closer. "I don't want to spend the day being interrogated by the cops."

"Where are you parked?" asked Harvath.

"Close," replied the man.

A few minutes later, Harvath and Nichols climbed into the man's black SUV. As it started up and pulled away from the curb, Harvath pulled out his BlackBerry. Keeping his weapon trained on the driver, he dialed Carolyn Leonard's number.

When she answered he said, "Carolyn, it's Scot Harvath. I have somebody here who says he's a friend of yours." Looking at the man he demanded, "What's your name?"

With his eyes sweeping for any signs that the police were following them, he replied, "Aydin Ozbek. I work for the CIA."

CHAPTER 67

Harvath didn't know whether to laugh and admire the man's audacity, or break his jaw for using them as bait.

"So you knew Marwan Khalifa was dead, that Dodd was most likely the person using his e-mail account, and yet you decided not to give us any heads-up whatsoever?" asked Harvath.

"If I had, you wouldn't have gone to the meet," replied Ozbek.

"Of course we wouldn't!" exclaimed Nichols.

Harvath didn't need the professor's help on this. "Just check that thumb drive," he said.

They were sitting in a small Internet café in Virginia. Leonard had vouched for Ozbek over the phone, but Harvath had insisted on a visual. His cell phone didn't have a camera, so the final ID was achieved via a webcam at the café. The other reason Harvath had selected the café was because of the content of the envelope the messenger had brought for Nichols—a large-capacity flash drive.

"I'm telling you," said Ozbek. "You were set up. Right down to the messenger. You think it was a coincidence that he bore such a resemblance to Dodd?"

Harvath looked at him. "Maybe from where you were standing, but from where I stood, he was an average, unremarkable guy. I think you overreacted."

"He picked that guy in order to flush us out."

"Us?" said Harvath. "I was standing out in the open already."

"He wanted to see if anyone was on to him and if so, how many people they saw fit to send after him. Everything Dodd does has a reason. Trust me."

"If all of that's true, then you played right into his hands by jumping that messenger, didn't you?" said Harvath.

Ozbek ignored the remark. "That flash drive is a trap," he stated. "You know it is. Why would you want to keep it?"

"There's no harm in seeing what's on it. It might have material that was supposed to convince us that he really was Khalifa."

"To what end? You said yourself that in the e-mails he sent Professor Nichols he was probing, trying to figure out how far along you are with your own assignment. I'm telling you that flash drive is trouble."

"Listen," said Harvath, "the drive could very well contain a Trojan horse of some sort. I agree. That's why we're using a public computer. If the drive is an attempt to sneak in and snoop around, we don't have to worry about it."

Nichols looked up from his terminal and said, "Everything looks like it's in Arabic. I can't read any of this."

"Let me see," said Ozbek.

While Harvath was a proficient Arabic speaker, his reading ability had never been as strong as he would have liked. "Be my guest."

Ozbek studied a few of the files for a moment and then asked, "What's the Great Mosque of Sana'a?"

"It's a project Marwan was working on in Yemen," replied Nichols. "It was a trove of documents, scrolls, and pieces of parchment believed to have been from the earliest Korans known to Islam."

"There are descriptions of digital pictures and other items referenced as having been 'archived' or 'preserved.' Is this what he was working on in Rome?"

Nichols was still in shock from having learned that his friend and colleague had been killed, and his voice shook when he spoke about him. "He told me that it was one of the most exciting projects he had ever been involved with. He kept saying that the timing had been divinely ordained. I was miles away from anything in my research at the time, but he was confident that our two projects were going to come together at precisely the right moment and that what had been uncovered in Sana'a would lend even more legitimacy to the project I was working on."

"And what exactly have you been working on?" asked Ozbek. "I understand why a Muslim radical like Dodd would want to kill Marwan Khalifa, but why you? Why go through so much trouble to kill an expert on Thomas Jefferson?"

Nichols looked to Harvath for whether or not he should answer that question.

"Not here," replied Harvath.

"Where then?" Ozbek asked.

"You'll see when we get there. In the meantime, I want all those documents printed out before we leave. I'm not letting that flash drive touch any of our computers."

CHAPTER 68

It was several hours later when Ozbek took a break from the reams of Arabic documents he was studying from the mysterious flash drive and came into the kitchen.

"How's it going?" asked Harvath. He was sitting at the kitchen table going over some information Nichols had brought in for him to look at. He filled him in that Lawlor had finally smoothed things over at the academy and was on his way back. He had taken a statement from the messenger, but it didn't look like the man was going to provide any information that could be useful.

Ozbek pulled a beer out of the fridge, and Harvath signaled that he'd take one as well. He knew that having one of the operatives under Ozbek's command killed and another put in the hospital with a very bad gunshot wound had been extremely hard on him. Green Berets were tough, but they were also human and cared deeply about the people they fought and served alongside.

"Khalifa was definitely onto something," said Ozbek, referring to the documents that had been printed from the flash drive as he joined Harvath at the table. "The problem is that the information is incomplete. He talks about certain pieces of manuscript, but there's no backup for it, no source."

"Are you surprised?" said Harvath as he took a sip.

"Not really. It's just enough information to whet your thirst, but nowhere near enough to quench it."

"A hearty fuck-you from Mr. Dodd and his Islamist friends."

Ozbek nodded and took a pull from his beer. "Considering the Italian State Archives all but burned to the ground, Khalifa's copies of the Sana'a find are probably all that's left. So if Dodd does have

Khalifa's computer, we can forget about any of it ever seeing the light of day."

"Which makes the professor's work even more important."

"You know," said Ozbek as he leaned back in his chair and stretched his legs, "this whole Jefferson story is amazing. If it's true, Khalifa's work really wouldn't have mattered anyway. I mean it would have been a nice complement, but an actual missing revelation from the Koran that Mohammed's closest confidants assassinated him over will be earthshaking in and of itself."

Harvath agreed. "If it's handled properly, it could tank the fundamentalists and propel the moderates into true control over their religion. The war on terror could be all but won."

Ozbek nodded knowingly and took a sip of his beer. "Despite how confusing and contradictory I find that religion, I've worked with lots of good Muslim people. Frankly, I don't think it can ever hack off the Islamist cancer without a huge bombshell being detonated from within. I really hope Professor Nichols finds what he's looking for."

"Speaking of which," replied Harvath as he picked up several of the pages Nichols had decoded and given him to study, "I think he's getting very close. Have you ever heard of a Muslim inventor named al-Jazari?"

CHAPTER 69

Harvath reached for a box of matches from the study's mantelpiece. It was going to be a cold night. If he didn't start a fire now, the room would never get warm. It was both a drawback and part of the charm of living in such a historic structure.

Once the fire was going, Harvath took a seat near the desk where the professor was working, picked up the puzzle box, and asked, "Now that you have decoded some of Jefferson's notes, how does al-Jazari fit into all of this?"

Nichols scanned several pages on the desk until he found the one he was looking for. "Al-Jazari's work was well known throughout the Islamic world and his inventions were highly coveted. Like da Vinci, al-Jazari relied on patronage as well as commissions for his livelihood.

"Also like da Vinci, al-Jazari was a dedicated man of science. Even as early as the twelfth century, Muslim scientists and academics were aware of multiple errors throughout the Koran such as Mohammed's incorrect explanations of the workings of the human body, the earth, the stars, and the planets, which he had communicated as being the true words of God. There were also the satanic verses."

Harvath knew all too well about the satanic verses. Desperate to make peace with his family's tribe, the Quraysh, Mohammed claimed that it was legitimate for Muslims to pray before the Quraysh's three pagan goddesses as intercessors before Allah.

But when Mohammed realized what he had done and how he had compromised his monotheism to get his family's tribe to join him, he took it all back and claimed the devil had put the words in his mouth. The abrupt about-face acted like gasoline being poured on a smoldering fire with the Quraysh and remained a fascinating retraction, which many throughout history, Salman Rushdie included, have found quite notable.

"There is belief that, like da Vinci," continued Nichols, "al-Jazari was skeptical of the infallibility of the faith that dominated the society in which he lived.

"Supposedly, when al-Jazari first learned the story of Mohammed's final revelation and its exclusion from the Koran, he became obsessed with finding it."

"And did he?" asked Harvath.

Nichols took a breath. "According to what Thomas Jefferson uncovered, yes, he did."

Harvath waited for the professor to continue.

"Al-Jazari's notoriety and not insignificant celebrity provided him access to anyone and everyone throughout the Muslim world. He traveled far and wide and met with Muslim heads of state as well as their ministers, scientists, and court officials, as well as merchants, pirates, traders, and numerous scholars.

"By al-Jazari's time, Mohammed's final revelation was thought by many who knew the tale to be no more than a myth; more fiction than fact. If such a thing truly existed, why hadn't it been brought to light?

"Al-Jazari supposed that if Mohammed had indeed had a final revelation that got him assassinated, then there still could have been forces in the Muslim world that would kill to keep it quiet. If these same forces got their hands on it, the revelation would undoubtedly be destroyed.

"So al-Jazari went looking among the people most likely to know about the revelation and where it might be hidden—the scientists and scholars of his day. The more he probed, the more he believed the secret was being kept alive somewhere.

"It took him many years, many journeys, and many intrigues but al-Jazari finally located it—the original copy of Mohammed's final revelation as dictated to his chief secretary and sealed by the prophet himself shortly before he died."

"Where did he find it?" asked Harvath.

Nichols shook his head. "I haven't decoded that part of Jefferson's notes yet. What I have decoded, however, says that al-Jazari was so impacted by what he read that he was moved to make sure the revelation was preserved and passed on to those who thirsted for the truth.

"The Islamic tradition is pretty well known for the penalty it imposes on those who blaspheme Islam or apostasize themselves from the faith."

"Death," replied Harvath.

"Exactly. There are many lay people and scholars alike, both within and without the Muslim community, who feel that the pure, orthodox Islam of the fundamentalists could never survive outside the context of its seventh-century Arabian origins. Apply twenty-first-century science, logic, or humanistic reasoning to it and it falls apart.

"They believe this is why Islam has always relied so heavily on the threat of death. Question Islam, malign Islam, or leave Islam and you will be killed. It is a totalitarian modus operandi that silences all dissent and examination, thereby protecting the faith from ever having to defend itself.

"It's no wonder that those who knew about Mohammed's final revelation were so careful not to reveal it."

"But al-Jazari did," said Harvath, "right?"

"Yes," said the professor. "Even if it might not ever be widely disseminated, al-Jazari wanted to make sure that those Muslims who sought the truth about their religion and its patriarch would always be able to find it; even if they had to work hard to do it."

"I'm guessing that Jefferson had to work hard at it too."

"According to his journals," replied Nichols, "the task was extremely difficult. He did, though, have one of the best resources in the world at his disposal: the United States Marine Corps."

"To the shores of Tripoli," Harvath said as he remembered their conversation in Paris.

"Precisely," replied Nichols. "In his diary, Jefferson recounted how in 1805 he sent Army officer William Eaton along with a contingent of Marines under Lieutenant Presley O'Bannon to attack Tripoli and depose the pasha, who had declared war on the United States. It was America's first battle to take place on foreign soil.

"Eaton recruited the pasha of Tripoli's brother, Hamet, the rightful heir to the Tripolitanian throne who was in exile in Egypt, to aid in a little eighteenth-century regime change. Their target was the wealthy and highly fortified port city of Derna.

"After an hour of heavy bombardment from the USS *Nautilus, Hornet,* and *Argus,* under the command of Captain Isaac Hull, Hamet led his soldiers southwest to cut off the road to Tripoli while the Marines and the rest of their hired mercenaries attacked the harbor fortress.

"Many of Derna's Muslim soldiers were terrified of the Marines and quickly retreated, leaving their cannons and rifles unfired.

"Through the chaos and pandemonium in the streets, a small unit of Marines split off from their colleagues on a top secret assignment from President Jefferson. Their job was to infiltrate the governor's palace. There was a small snag, though.

"Over the objection of Lieutenant O'Bannon, Hamet and his Arab mercenaries had identified the governor's palace as their second objective after securing the road to Tripoli.

"O'Bannon's contingent of Marines was told they had to get in and get out before Hamet and his men arrived. Their primary objective was to recover a very important item for the president."

"Let me guess," said Harvath. "This very important item had something to do with al-Jazari."

Nichols nodded. "The Marines fought run-and-gun, as well as hand-to-hand, battles all the way to the governor's palace. Like their fellow Marines fighting at the harbor, their bravery was unparalleled and would set the standard for every Marine action from then on.

"Within an hour and fifteen minutes of the initial ground assault, Lieutenant O'Bannon raised the American flag over the harbor fortress. It was the first time the stars and stripes had ever been flown over battlements outside of the Atlantic. Shortly thereafter, O'Bannon's covert Marine unit returned, having successfully completed their assignment.

"After holding the city and repelling a counterattack, Eaton wanted to press farther into Tripoli, but Jefferson held him back, preferring instead to conclude a peace treaty and secure the release of all Americans being held in Tripoli, in particular the crew of the USS *Philadelphia*, which had run aground in Tripoli Harbor eighteen months before.

"Though Eaton, like O'Bannon and his Marines, returned home a hero he always felt that Jefferson had sold him out. He never knew of the Marines' covert operation and the real reason for attacking Derna.

"An interesting footnote is that after the victory, Prince Hamet presented Lieutenant O'Bannon with a scimitar used by his Mameluke tribesmen in appreciation of his courage and that of his Marines. This is the model for the saber the Marines still carry to this day."

Harvath stood up, set the puzzle box on the desk, and walked over to place another log on the fire. "Even as a Navy man," he said, "I'm willing to admit that the Marines have an impressive lineage.

"What's interesting, though, is that I've never heard about the covert operation at Derna."

"Nobody has," replied Nichols. "Not even Congress. I just decoded Jefferson's writings about it. Per his orders, the Marines took the secret with them to their graves."

"So what about the item they were sent to retrieve from the governor's palace in Derna? What happened to it?"

The professor swept his hand over his notes and replied, "That's the mystery we need to unravel."

CHAPTER 70

W e now know," said Nichols, "that what lay within the governor's palace had been created by al-Jazari, had something to do with Mohammed's final revelation, and had supposedly been there since Cervantes was a prisoner in neighboring Algiers. We also know that O'Bannon's Marines succeeded in finding it and bringing it back to Thomas Jefferson. What it specifically was and what happened to it from there is what we need to find out.

"And," said Nichols as he looked over the desk cluttered with books and papers, "the answer lies somewhere in here. I hope."

Harvath smiled at him. "Then you'll find it. In the meantime, I'm cooking tonight. Do you want to eat with us in the kitchen, or are you going to eat in here?"

The professor thought about it for a minute. "I'm going to keep working."

"Understood. I'll bring a plate in for you."

"And some coffee please," said Nichols as Harvath left the study.

• • •

Lawlor was sitting at the kitchen table with Aydin Ozbek when Harvath walked in. "While I don't mind another set of experienced hands," said Gary, "what this operation really needs is a lawyer."

"That rough at UVA, huh?" replied Harvath as he walked over to the fridge and started pulling things out.

"Nothing compared to Paris, but it was still rough. The cops were plenty pissed off."

"Any word on Tracy?"

"Someone from the embassy is staying in the room with her now."

Harvath set a head of lettuce on the counter and turned. "Why? What's wrong?"

"Nothing's wrong, the French were just getting a little overzealous in wanting to question her. Some of them feel she's had enough time to rest and be on her pain medication and that there's no reason she shouldn't be talking. Her doctors don't like it, though. They don't want her exposed to any stress until they can get the brain swelling completely stopped. The French authorities were getting a bit too pushy, so the doctors tried to bar them from her room. When that happened, the French threatened to move her out of the American Hospital to another that would be more cooperative.

"Tracy's doctors reached out to the embassy and they now have someone in her room around-the-clock to run interference and act as a buffer."

"Do you think that's going to work?" asked Harvath, concerned for Tracy.

"For now, yes."

Harvath didn't want to ask about later. He just wanted Tracy back home. He found the iPod he had used before Tracy bought him the bigger and better version he'd left behind in his hotel room in Paris and dropped it into the audio station near the stove.

Tracy loved listening to Pachelbel's Canon in D when she cooked. He was tempted to play that now, but knew it wouldn't do much to brighten his mood. He needed something else; something more upbeat.

Scrolling through his list of artists, he pulled up the Zapp Band, and as "More Bounce to the Ounce" began to play, he started cooking and tried to forget about his problems for a while.

Later, once dinner was finished and all the dishes had been cleaned and put away, Harvath brought up one last point of business for the evening. After learning everything he had about Matthew Dodd, he thought it made sense to post a watch. Lawlor and Ozbek agreed and Harvath divided up the shifts. He would go first, then Ozbek, and then Lawlor.

With everything decided, Lawlor took Ozbek upstairs to get him settled while Harvath made his rounds. He closed the drapes in the study and restricted Nichols to a small desk lamp.

Moving through the rest of the rectory as well as the church, Harvath made sure all the doors and windows were firmly closed and locked, then he set the alarm and settled in for his shift.

There were about a thousand things he would have liked to have done on his laptop, but he didn't want to ruin his night vision. He needed to be able to sit inside his dark house and look out the window and discern things unimpeded. The laptop would have only hampered his ability to see and also would have silhouetted him in the glow of his screen, making him a prime target if anyone wanted to take a shot at him. Not a smart thing to do.

Instead, Harvath sat quietly in the dark with his LaRue M4 across his lap, and thought about everything that had happened.

• • •

At the end of his watch, he woke Ozbek and passed the figurative baton. He filled him in on the alarm system and then checked on Nichols. The professor was several cups into the pot of coffee Lawlor had brewed for him and didn't show any signs of slowing down any time soon. *So much for jet lag,* thought Harvath as he walked upstairs to his room.

After brushing his teeth with nothing more than a small night-light to illuminate the bathroom, he took one final look out the windows before going to bed.

He had absolutely no idea that out in the darkness, a pair of eyes was staring right back at him.

CHAPTER 71

Even though he knew he couldn't be seen, Matthew Dodd didn't move a muscle; he didn't even breathe. With his night-vision monocular pressed up against his eye, he studied Scot Harvath until the man stepped back from his window and disappeared from view.

Dodd lowered his monocular and looked at his Omega. It was just past the hour. The men inside were apparently taking shifts. That was fine. He could wait.

Leaning against a tree at the edge of Scot Harvath's property, Dodd retrieved a bottle of water from his backpack and took a long swallow.

In his mind, he replayed the last conversation he'd had with Sheik Omar. Despite the man's past assurances that he would allow Dodd to handle the problem as he saw fit, Omar had tried to take control again. He wanted Nichols killed and if that meant killing the man who was protecting him, as well as any civilians who happened to get in the way, then so be it. Delicacy and finesse were alien to him.

Dodd had tried to explain that killing Nichols wouldn't solve their problem. Jack Rutledge would simply find someone else to do the work. They needed to gather intelligence. They all knew what Mohammed's lost revelation was rumored to contain. They also knew that if it was revealed, true, pure Islam would cease to exist.

The focus now needed to be on how much Nichols knew and how close he was to discovering the prophet's final revelation.

The assassin knew from his prior surveillance that without the *Don*

Quixote, Nichols had no hope of success. Then the professor had located it and despite all of Dodd's efforts, he was now using it to complete his work.

Be that as it may, before the meeting in Annapolis, Dodd had learned by posing as Khalifa in his e-mail exchange with Nichols that the book had not provided immediate answers. The professor was still connecting the dots and fitting the pieces together. Yet despite that candor, Dodd felt that the man had not been completely forthcoming with everything he knew. That's when he had hit upon the idea of the flash drive.

It had been infected with a sophisticated Trojan horse that was virtually impossible to detect. Called an "echo program," as soon as the drive was connected to the professor's computer, the program would have inserted itself inside. Then, the next time the professor went online, regardless of whether or not the flash drive was still connected, the contents of his computer would have been compressed and transmitted to Dodd.

The echo program would have kept on transmitting information such as key strokes, Web searches, e-mails, and newly saved files every time Nichols went online. The program would have also given the assassin remote access to the professor's computer, including the ability to control any attached peripherals such as a webcam or microphone.

Unfortunately, the drive had been activated only once, at an Internet café outside Annapolis. Dodd credited that misfortune to the presence of the CIA operative who had been at his apartment two nights before.

The assassin had waited for the device to be activated again, but it never happened. That was okay, though, as the CIA operative had made a tragic mistake in Annapolis that had blessed the assassin with a contingency plan.

Dodd had done more than just send a messenger to the Naval Academy. He had been there as well, watching. The professor was working with two men—the man from the Grand Palais whom Dodd had seen again at the Bilal Mosque and another, older man. The older man had tried to remain out of sight, but Dodd had made him early on. He stood around afterward to watch him flash some sort of credentials and handle the academy police officers; eventually leaving in the front seat of one of their cruisers. Dodd had no idea, though, who he was.

Then there was the CIA operative. Dodd hadn't seen him until he leapt out of a group of people to knock the messenger to the ground, but he had known he was there. He had seen his Black GMC Denali.

It was the same Black GMC that had been parked near his apartment in Baltimore two nights ago—its engine warm to the touch and the pavement beneath it wet. The man hadn't even bothered changing license plates. He must have assumed that Dodd had neither noticed his vehicle before their run-in, nor remained behind afterward to watch him put his injured colleague in the front seat and the lifeless body of his female colleague in the cargo area in back.

Discovering the CIA operative's vehicle at the Naval Academy had been an unexpected dividend. Dodd had arrived with a small transmitter just in case Nichols' car presented itself, which it never did. The black Denali turned out to be the next best thing.

Dodd had been operating by the CIA maxim that action begets intelligence. His plan all along had been to flush Nichols into the open in order to glean information from him. Tracking him back to where he was staying had been icing on the cake. Now, all he had to do was pick the right time to enter the house.

CHAPTER 72

The assassin had watched the man from the Grand Palais take the first four-hour watch and then the CIA operative the second. The third would be the older man. That was when Dodd would make his move.

Based on the sign at the front of the driveway, it wasn't hard to figure out who provided alarm coverage to the small estate. It took the assassin about an hour after tapping into the phone line to create a digital intermediary between the house and the alarm company via his laptop.

As the second shift ended, Dodd watched through his night vision device as the younger CIA operative was replaced by the older man. The man entered the kitchen, put on coffee, and then moved from room to room with some sort of tactical rifle, ostensibly making sure everything was still secure.

When he returned to the kitchen, he set his weapon on the table and remained still.

The assassin removed a Powerbar from his backpack, opened it, and took a bite. As he watched the man inside the house, his mind began to drift to his dead wife and child. He had been warned about the damage that reviewing the police file on the accident could cause but not having been at either of their funerals, he had needed closure. Now, when he thought of them, all he could see was the twisted hulk of steel that had been their car and the bloody, lifeless bodies of the two beautiful souls that had meant more to him than anything else in the world.

The accident photos snapped through his mind—one after another after another—in a sick, never-ending loop. It was all he could remember when he thought of them. He could no longer access who they were, who he was, before the accident. Even that had been taken from him.

Dodd didn't want to think about them now and forced himself to focus on something else. He needed to concentrate on what he came to do.

Half an hour later, the man got up again and did another sweep of the house and then returned to the kitchen. Dodd remained in place, watching.

At the top of the hour, the procedure was repeated. It was all that the assassin needed to see. He had no doubt the man would keep getting up to sweep the structure every half hour.

Leaving his hide site, he crept back to his laptop. The Achilles' heel of most home defense systems was their alarm. Few people could afford truly impregnable, unhackable setups. Even the most sophisticated operatives were limited by what their budgets allowed and often chose industry stalwarts like Brinks or ADT.

Dodd had cracked some of the best security systems in the world and while this one was good, it wasn't impossible. Activating several strings of code, he stared intently at his laptop as the alarm system invisibly shut down. To anyone monitoring at the alarm company or anyone in the house looking at the alarm panel, nothing would appear to have changed. It was now time to make his approach.

The assassin had seen enough of the house to know that the perimeter was ringed with motion sensors that would have been separate from the main alarm. When tripped, they would activate exterior lighting and probably sound some sort of audible warning inside.

After he returned to his hide, he observed the house for several more minutes to make sure nothing had changed. Confident that everything was as he had left it, Dodd removed two canisters from his pockets and moved forward in a low crouch.

When he had gotten as close as he dared, the assassin slowly moved his face from side to side as he searched for any indication of a breeze.

Dead calm.

He looked at his watch. It was time. Popping the first canister, Dodd stood just long enough to overhand it toward the far side of the rectory. He followed suit with the second canister, locked in his bearings, and then waited.

A thick, specially engineered fog designed to defeat motion sensors and thermal imaging devices began to engulf the old stone building, as well as the grounds in front of it.

This close to the Chesapeake, fog was not unusual. It was the perfect cover and the assassin used it fully to his advantage as he maneuvered his way to the front door.

Locating the knob, he removed a set of picks and went to work on the locks. As the last one released, he drew a suppressed Walther P99 and slipped inside.

The interior smelled like coffee and wood smoke. Dodd checked the alarm panel and smiled. Everything was perfect.

Glancing at his Omega again, the assassin strained for any sound of the man on watch. There was nothing. At this point, he was most likely in the church, or already on his way back. After making sure there were no other sounds of life from upstairs, Dodd moved into the kitchen to wait for the older man to return.

He didn't have to wait long. When he entered, the assassin acted without hesitation.

CHAPTER 73

H arvath awoke to the sound of his doorknob slowly turning. Grabbing his pistol from on top of the nightstand, he leapt out of bed and shot across the room to the wall near the door.

Flattening himself against it, he watched as the knob stopped turning and the door began to quietly swing open. Twisting his torso, Harvath drew his pistol to his chest and allowed his left hand to hover slightly in front of his body.

As a figure appeared in the doorframe, Harvath grabbed a handful of shirt, pushed his gun into the man's face and spun him a hundred and eighty degrees into the room. He slapped up hard against the wall where his head hit with a sharp crack. At that moment he suddenly realized who it was.

"Are you crazy?" snapped Harvath as he let go of Nichols. "I specifically warned you against doing things like this. I could have killed you."

The professor was seeing stars, but he ignored them. "Gary's down," he said in a panicked whisper.

Immediately, Harvath's mind went back into danger mode. "Where is he?"

"The kitchen. There's blood all over the floor."

Harvath was about to respond when he heard the creak of a floorboard outside the room. He raised his index finger to his lips and then held his hand out signaling Nichols not to move. The man nodded and pressed himself up against the wall.

Harvath heard another board groan. It was closer this time. He raised his pistol and prepared to fire.

A fraction of a second later, Ozbek spun into the doorway, his pistol up and ready to fire. When he saw Harvath, he lowered his weapon. "What the hell is going on?" he asked.

"Gary's been hit in the kitchen," replied Harvath.

Ozbek stood back so Harvath could pass. "Let's go."

Harvath ordered Nichols to stay put and lock the door. Then, he and Ozbek made their way toward the staircase.

It was shades of Tracy's attack all over again and Harvath struggled to keep the images of coming down the same set of stairs to find her lying in a pool of blood from taking over his mind. There was a threat in his house and if he didn't keep it together, he was going to get himself killed.

Harvath slammed an iron door down in his mind and focused on what needed to be done.

He and Ozbek covered each other as they swept down the stairs. In the vestibule, Harvath noticed that not only was the front door ajar, but the alarm keypad showed the system was still armed and fully functioning. Obviously, that wasn't the case.

Harvath signaled to Ozbek and they crept down the narrow hall to the kitchen. Even before they got inside, Harvath could make out Lawlor's shoes and the cuffs of his trousers.

Cautiously, the two men inched into the kitchen checking every possible point of concealment until they were satisfied it was clear. Ozbek then stood guard as Harvath rushed to Lawlor.

A pool of blood had spread out on the floor beneath his head. Harvath's throat tightened as he reached for Gary's carotid in the hopes of finding a pulse.

To his relief, he found one. Lowering his ear, he noticed that he was still breathing.

As best he could, Harvath scanned his face and neck for any signs of an entry or exit wound. There were none. Snatching a kitchen towel from the oven door, he gently slid it under Gary's head. There was nothing more he could do for his friend until he caught whoever was in his house.

Standing up, Harvath saw the tactical rifle sitting on the counter.

The magazine had been removed and placed alongside it, as well as the round that had been in the chamber. *Very strange.*

Harvath snatched up the round and tucked the magazine into his back pocket so the weapon couldn't be used against them. He then rejoined Ozbek, and the two men swept the rest of the house.

Arriving at the study, Harvath knew that whoever had broken in was now long gone. The desk that Nichols had been working at was almost completely bare. All of the papers, Nichols' laptop, his notes, as well as Jefferson's puzzle box with his wheel cipher had vanished. The only things remaining were a stack of general reference books on Jefferson.

Harvath didn't need to see any more to know what had happened. Matthew Dodd had found his house. The only question he had at this point was *how.*

It would have to wait, though. Harvath left Gary with Ozbek and Nichols, grabbed a flashlight, and headed outside. The materials that had been taken were beyond priceless. Even though he was certain Dodd was long gone, maybe he had left behind some sort of clue. With so much at stake, Harvath couldn't just let him vanish.

Harvath swept the grounds until he found an area of bent grass and underbrush where the assassin must have been hiding. It was perfectly clean and devoid of anything useful.

Harvath traced the man's path back toward the main road to the spot where he must have tapped into the Bishop's Gate alarm system. While Harvath could have someone out to dust for prints, he doubted Dodd would have been careless enough to leave any. Besides, he didn't need some technician telling him what he already knew. Matthew Dodd had broken into his home, he was certain of it. The information Harvath most needed was where Dodd had gone.

Harvath kept searching until Gary's ambulance arrived, but he didn't find anything else. Dodd had disappeared.

With the theft of all the Jefferson material, Harvath and his colleagues, not to mention America, had been dealt a staggering setback.

CHAPTER 74

UM AL-QURA MOSQUE
FALLS CHURCH, VIRGINIA

Dodd had gone to great pains to try to explain to Sheik Omar that professional assassins did not kill indiscriminately. They killed only when necessary. But it was an exercise in futility. Though Omar was a devout and exceedingly intelligent man, he was incapable of grasping subtlety.

He and Waleed hated nonbelievers more than anything else—and this included Muslims who didn't follow their purist interpretation of the Koran. Nonbelievers were considered *kuffar* and deserved to die.

Waleed was more pragmatic and would have understood the dangers inherent in trying to stumble through a dark house he wasn't familiar with to attempt to kill everyone there. Neither man, however, would have understood why Dodd chose to strike a target across the back of the head with the butt of his pistol rather than kill him. So instead, he lied.

Sheik Omar sat at his desk, spinning the wheels of Thomas Jefferson's cipher device, which rested upon the *Don Quixote*. "What about the others inside the house? Are they dead?"

"With the time I had available it wasn't feasible," replied the assassin.

Waleed stopped leafing through the pages. "You had all night."

"I could have had two nights. It still would have been very problematic."

Omar raised his eyebrows. "Why?"

"Whoever these men are, they are highly trained operatives."

"Even so," interrupted Waleed.

Dodd raised his voice and rolled right over him, "I wouldn't expect you to understand what situational awareness means."

"They had no idea you were coming. You said so yourself."

The assassin had never liked Abdul Waleed. Nothing would have made him happier than to crush the man's windpipe. "Killing a professional takes much care and attention to detail, especially when you intend to kill him on his own ground. Too many things can go wrong if you aren't properly prepared."

"So by your own admission, it isn't *impossible,*" stated Waleed as if he had scored a decisive debating point.

Dodd turned his gaze to Omar. "We have everything now. They have nothing. That was my assignment and I completed it."

"No," said Waleed from the couch. "Your assignment was—"

"Be quiet," ordered Omar raising his hand. He shifted his eyes from the wheel cipher to Dodd. "The dogs may bark, but the caravan moves on."

The assassin looked at him. "Meaning?"

"Meaning, you cannot remove from their minds what they have already learned. Don't assume that because you have taken away their material that you have taken away their will. They'll keep going."

Dodd tried to interrupt, but Omar stopped him. "How do you know they even need this material anymore? Maybe they already have everything necessary to locate the final revelation."

The assassin didn't need to look at Waleed to know the man was gloating.

"We need to know," said Omar, "beyond any doubt that the threat has been completely neutralized."

"What do you want done?"

Handing over everything that had been taken from Bishop's Gate the sheik said, "You need to solve this riddle and make sure the final revelation is never found."

Dodd reached out for the items, but as he tried to take them, Omar hung on to them just a moment longer. "Make sure there are no mistakes," he added as he let them go.

CHAPTER 75

Explain to me why Jefferson didn't just come right out and say what this thing was and where it was hidden," asked Ozbek as they drove south toward the last person who might be able to help them.

Nichols didn't answer. He was in a state of shock. Sitting on his lap was the folder he had taken to bed last night. Inside were two centuries-old documents—all that remained of his research. One looked like a blueprint and the other a mechanical schematic of some sort. The writing on each was only partially decoded. Had the professor left them in the study, they, like the wheel cipher and the *Don Quixote,* would be gone as well and they would have had nothing at all to go on.

The professor was reliving in his mind how he had been on his way back to the study after only a couple of hours of sleep when he had found Gary Lawlor on the kitchen floor. Ozbek had to repeat his question two more times before he got his attention.

"Excuse me?" replied Nichols.

"Why didn't Jefferson just spell everything out? Why go to all this trouble?"

"He had a lot of enemies."

"Including Congress," added Harvath, "who went back to an appeasement policy of paying off the Muslims once Jefferson left office."

"What was the last phrase you decoded?" asked Ozbek.

Opening the folder, Nichols fought back the car sickness that always overtook him when he tried to read while driving and replied, "It says that the prophet's final revelation lies with the scribe."

"With *the* scribe," repeated Harvath unenthusiastically from the front seat. "Not *his* scribe?"

Nichols shrugged. "It says *the.*"

"So what does that mean?" asked Ozbek. "Was that Jefferson's way of saying the secret died with Mohammed's scribe?"

"Without the wheel cipher and the rest of my notes," he replied, "it could mean anything."

"What do you think it means?"

"Based on the little we have, I can't be sure."

"But what we can be sure of," stated Harvath, "is that it won't take Dodd very long to figure out where we're going. They have all of it now—your computer, your notes, the wheel cipher, everything."

"If this even means anything," replied Nichols as he held up the folder.

Harvath wasn't listening. His mind had drifted to Gary. Together with Ozbek, they had supported his neck and had log-rolled him to assess his injuries. Head wounds were notorious for the amount of blood they produced, but even so, when Harvath saw that the man hadn't been shot, but merely clubbed, he was shocked. Harvath couldn't understand why, especially after considering all of the people that Dodd had already murdered, Gary hadn't been killed.

Shortly before the ambulance arrived at Bishop's Gate, Gary regained consciousness. Having the good sense to be glad that he was still alive never occurred to him. He was too pissed off that Dodd had been able to sneak up on him. He may not be a spring chicken, but he was very good at what he did, and Harvath could tell he was embarrassed. The last thing Gary ever would have wanted to appear was old. In the world of counterterrorism, operators needed to possess both brains and physical ability. Any suggestion that you weren't up to snuff in either department was cause for concern, and Gary knew it.

Within minutes of coming to, he wanted to take control. Though both Ozbek and Harvath assumed he had a skull fracture, he pushed them away and struggled to sit up. Gary was at his best managing difficult situations.

He demanded a full rundown of what had happened. Harvath knew better than to deny him.

Once he had a picture of what they believed had taken place and he understood the extent to which their operation had been compromised, he started issuing orders. Chief among them was the edict that Harvath would not ride to the hospital with him. Time was everything at this point.

Harvath knew he was right. The only question was what their next move should be.

Having finally discovered the small tracking device after sweeping his Denali, Ozbek was very much in favor of throwing hoods over the heads of Sheik Omar and Abdul Waleed, dragging them back to Harvath's, and applying pressure until they gave up all that they knew.

The idea did have a certain appeal to it, Harvath had to admit, but they were going to get only one chance to confront those two. He preferred to relegate kidnapping them to Plan B. Right now, the best possible outcome would be to get to the prize before Dodd. Hooking the jumper cables up to Omar and Waleed could very easily buy Dodd the time he needed to beat them to Mohammed's final revelation. And once that happened, regardless of what Omar and Waleed might tell them, the chances were very good that Dodd would disappear and along with him the revelation.

Harvath swung out from behind the slow-moving car in front of them and pushed down hard on the accelerator.

CHAPTER 76

Susan Ferguson, the curator for Thomas Jefferson's Monticello, met them a quarter mile past the estate in the circular blacktop drive of the International Center for Jefferson Studies. She was a tall, attractive brunette in her early forties casually dressed in blue jeans and a fleece with a walkie-talkie clipped to her waist.

When the professor climbed out of the truck, the two shared an affectionate hug. "It's good to see you, Anthony," said Ferguson.

"You too, Susan," he replied. "Thanks for coming in on your day off."

"Well, you said it was urgent." Ferguson's voice trailed off as she noticed both of the well-built men Nichols was traveling with get out of the vehicle behind him. They had *cop,* or *soldier,* or something she couldn't exactly describe written all over them. Though she didn't see any weapons, she had a feeling that they were armed. "What's going on?" she asked.

Nichols pointed to his companions and said, "Susan, I'd like to introduce you to Scot Harvath and Aydin Ozbek."

"Pleased to meet you," said Harvath. Ozbek stood to the side and nodded politely.

Ferguson looked at Nichols and waited for a further explanation.

"It's a long story," he said. "Maybe we can talk on our way inside?"

The woman hesitated for a moment and then gave in. As they walked, Nichols gave her the short speech Harvath had rehearsed with him in the car about how he was working for a wealthy businessman who was obsessed with security. By the time they reached the library building, the woman seemed less tense about the armed men accompanying her friend and colleague.

Harvath reached over and helped hold the door open as everyone filed inside.

The main wing of the Jefferson Library was a dramatic two-story arcade punctuated by rows of polished bookcases and curved beams of matching wood across the ceiling capped off by a dramatic wall of mullioned glass at the far end.

Pointing to one of the library's several work tables Ferguson said, "Okay, let's see what you've got."

Nichols removed the file folder from under his arm and produced the two yellowed documents. The curator pulled out one of the chairs, sat down, and removed a pair of glasses from her pocket. "You're positive these are authentic Jefferson?" she asked as she put her glasses on.

"Positive," replied Nichols.

She studied each of them for a few moments. "None of this writing makes any sense."

"They're encoded."

"Have you been able to decipher any of it?" she asked.

The professor shook his head. "Only partially."

"Interesting. Very interesting. Where did your client get these?"

"He has been a collector of Jefferson documents for many years," replied Nichols. "He has resources most would kill for."

"That must be nice," said Ferguson, who then stood up. "I'll be right back."

"Where are you going?"

"I want to gather a few reference materials. There's something familiar about these drawings."

The curator disappeared and came back a few minutes later with a stack of books and a handful of other items, including an oversized magnifying glass. Setting everything down on the table, she picked up the magnifying glass and returned to her investigation.

Harvath kept a watchful eye over her and Nichols while Ozbek kept an eye on the door.

Ferguson made notes on a small pad as she flipped back and forth through the pages of her reference books. Occasionally, she would stop to ask Nichols a question and then would return to studying the documents.

It went on like that for over half an hour until she removed her glasses and set them on the table.

Nichols stopped pacing and came over to the desk. "Well? What do you think?"

Tucking a loose strand of hair behind her ear, the curator looked up at him. "This first set of drawings here," she said, pointing at the paper, "is mechanical. They appear to be schematics of some sort."

"I figured as much. Do you have any idea what for?"

Ferguson smiled. "With Jefferson, it could be anything. The man was constantly inventing things. The handwriting and drawing techniques definitely seem to be his, but this first page is odd."

"How so?" asked the professor.

"This is a cutaway of some sort focusing on a very unique set of gears. In all of Jefferson's mechanical drawings, I've never seen gears that look like this. Also, gears are normally housed out of sight. You don't usually see them. Yet these gears are intricately stylized and decorated.

"Also the schematic seems more like a set of directions for switching out or maybe rebalancing the gears. Does that make sense?"

Nichols shook his head. "Not really."

"There's something else," said Ferguson as she handed the professor her magnifying glass. "If you look very closely at this particular gear here, you can see that it's different from the ones above it."

"It is?" said Nichols as he took the magnifying glass from her and looked where she was pointing. "I thought they all looked the same."

The curator shook her head. "For the most part, they do, but the decoration changes ever so slightly on this one and its shape seems a little different than the others."

"You're right," replied the professor.

Harvath had been listening to the exchange and approached the table. "May I?" he asked.

Nichols handed him the magnifying glass.

Harvath had not seen either document until a couple of hours ago and even then—in the wake of the break-in, with what had happened to Gary and deciding to leave for Monticello—he had not studied them that extensively and certainly not with a magnifying glass.

After studying the drawing of the gears for a few more seconds he called Ozbek over. "Take a look at this," he said as he handed him the magnifying glass.

"What do you think?" asked Harvath as Ozbek studied the drawing and more importantly the gear in question. "Is that a rendering of the Basmala?"

Susan Ferguson didn't know who Harvath and Ozbek were, but they definitely weren't just the bodyguards. Her curiosity, though, was piqued. "What's a Basmala?"

"Every sura or chapter of the Koran except for the ninth," explained Harvath, "begins with the phrase *In the name of Allah, the Most Gracious, the Most Merciful.* In Arabic that phrase is known as the Basmala and it can be rendered artistically in different ways."

"And that's what's on that gear?"

Harvath looked at Ozbek, who nodded.

"You said that the ninth chapter doesn't start with 'Allah the Most Gracious, the Most Merciful.' Why not?" asked Ferguson.

"It's Mohammed's next-to-last known revelation and contains the most violent passages in the Koran. The peaceful passages that Muslims point to as indications of how tolerant and gentle their religion is come from the early part of Mohammed's prophetic career only to be abrogated by the verses in sura nine."

"So Jefferson was sketching a set of gears with Arabic writing on them?" said the curator, more to herself than anyone else.

"Do you know if Jefferson owned any Arabic or Islamic instruments or objects?" asked Nichols.

Ferguson shook her head. "Just the Koran that the Library of Congress has now."

"Are you aware of him being given anything by the Marines or more specifically by a Lieutenant Presley O'Bannon after the First Barbary War?"

"No, I'm not."

"Do you know if Jefferson ever referenced an inventor from the Islamic Golden Age named al-Jazari?" asked Harvath.

Ferguson paused. "What the hell is this all about?"

There was silence around the table.

"Unless you answer the question," said the curator, "I'm not going to be able to do anything else for you."

This time it was Harvath who looked at Nichols for guidance. He knew the professor had a lengthy history with her, but what Harvath needed to know was if Susan Ferguson could be trusted.

When the professor nodded, Harvath began speaking.

CHAPTER 77

Scot gave Susan Ferguson as many details as he dared, and as he spoke, the curator of Monticello sat riveted.

When he was finished, there were undoubtedly a million questions she wanted to ask, but Ferguson stayed focused. "So what you're looking for is a mechanical item that uses gears, which was designed by this al-Jazari, and was brought back to Jefferson by the Marines who were at the Battle of Derna in 1805, correct?"

Everyone nodded as the curator reached for the other document and then said, "We also have a second set of drawings that look like architectural details of some sort."

"Carpentry work?" said Harvath.

"Definitely carpentry work."

"Does it look familiar at all?" asked Nichols.

Ferguson examined it under her magnifying glass again. "Monticello was a woodworker's paradise. Jefferson designed every frieze, every cornice, and every pediment himself. They're everywhere."

"So you don't recognize it, then?"

The curator reached for a book titled *Les Édifices Antiques de Rome* and opened it to page fifty. "This is a detail of the Corinthian temple of Antoninus and Faustina in Rome. Jefferson based the frieze in the entrance hall on this design."

Harvath looked at the Jefferson drawing and the page in the book side-by-side. "They're nearly identical."

Ferguson nodded. "You said this Islamic inventor was famous for his clocks?"

"Yes," answered Harvath. "Why?"

"Because," replied Nichols, "the entrance hall is the location of Jefferson's Great Clock."

Ferguson looked at him. "Which has never been removed from Monticello since its installation in 1805."

"We need to see that clock," said Harvath.

"But it didn't come from an Islamic inventor. It was built by a clockmaker in Philadelphia named Peter Spruck."

Nichols recognized a book about Monticello that was sitting on the table and picked it up. He flipped through it until he found the section regarding the Great Clock. "Spruck might have built it," he replied, "but Jefferson designed it, right down to the size of the gears and how many teeth each one has."

"When was it built?" asked Harvath.

Nichols searched for the exact date. "1792. Three years after he returned from Paris."

Harvath looked back at Susan Ferguson and repeated, "We really need to see that clock."

The curator looked at her watch. "Monticello opens to the public in half an hour. We need to be fast."

CHAPTER 78

Even though Harvath had been based in Virginia as part of the Naval Special Warfare Development Group, he had never been to Monticello. As a child, he'd grown up seeing it on the back of the nickel, as well as on the two-dollar bill up until the mid-seventies. It was a magnificent piece of American history that he'd always regretted never having visited.

Once a sprawling plantation of five thousand acres upon an 850-foot peak on the outskirts of Charlottesville, Monticello took its name from Italian for *little mountain*. Designed completely by Thomas Jefferson, it was the only private home in the United States to have been designated a World Heritage Site.

Susan Ferguson had called ahead so that when they arrived at Monticello less than five minutes later, they were allowed to drive straight up to the main house.

Harvath parked as close as he could and they all jumped out. Beneath the Northeast Portico they got their first view of the Great Clock. It was mounted above a lunette window and a pair of French doors.

Ferguson had explained on the way over that the clock had two faces, one outside which showed just the hour, while another inside the entrance hall indicated hours, minutes, and seconds. What she hadn't mentioned was that it was mounted more than fifteen feet off the ground.

Nevertheless, what grabbed Harvath's attention was the hour hand. Its tip was in the shape of a heart while its tail was in the shape of a crescent. Whether it was meant to represent Islam or not, Harvath couldn't be sure, but it was too much of a coincidence to discount. Looking over at Nichols, he could tell that the professor had noticed it as well. "We're going to need a ladder," he said as he and Nichols continued to look up at the clock.

"Mr. Jefferson already saw to that," replied Ferguson as she removed a ring of keys from her pocket and unlocked the French doors.

The dramatic entrance hall was two stories tall, with an upper balcony connecting a wing on each side. Its floor had been painted grass green and the entire space looked like a mini-museum of its own with maps, antlers, paintings, bones, busts, fossils, animal hides, Native American artifacts, and other objects that had appealed to Jefferson.

Once the group was all inside, they turned and looked up at the interior face of the Great Clock which was housed in a wooden box.

Its face was black and its hands, numbers, and ornamentation were a brassy gold. Upon it rested a classic pediment and behind that a frieze similar to the one in Nichols' drawing.

A series of cannonball-like weights suspended on ropes that moved up and down through holes in the floor allowed for the precise measurement of time, including days of the week, which were indicated by small signs attached to the weights on the south side of the entrance hall.

In the corner to his right, Harvath noticed a wooden ladder that stretched almost to the ceiling.

"The clock needs to be wound with a special key once a week," said Ferguson. "We still do it the same way, just not normally with our display ladder."

Harvath stared up at the clock face and noticed that the tail of its second hand was also in the shape of an Islamic-style crescent.

Ozbek helped bring the ladder over and gently leaned it against the wall. "All right," said the curator once it was in place. "Who's going up for a closer look?"

Harvath stepped forward and with Ozbek steadying the ladder, climbed up. Eye-to-eye with the clock, he noticed that the hours were Roman while the minutes of the hour were Arabic.

After a cursory review of the outside, Harvath began to remove the housing.

"Please be careful," cautioned Ferguson.

It took him several minutes to figure out how to get it all the way off and when he did, he handed it down to Ozbek who set it carefully on the floor and went back to holding the ladder. The entire inner workings of Jefferson's Great Clock were now exposed.

"Do you see the gear?" asked Nichols. "Is it there?"

There were plenty of gears, but nothing that resembled what was in the schematic. Harvath looked down at the curator and asked, "Is there any way we can stop this for a minute?"

Ferguson looked at her watch and then out the window where visitors were already starting to mill about and gather near the portico.

"Susan?" Harvath repeated. "I need to stop this clock for a minute."

The curator took a deep breath. "Okay. Here's how you stop it."

Once all the movement had ceased, Harvath was able to reach his hand inside and better examine the mechanics.

He wasn't having any luck. He asked Nichols to hand up the schematic and he checked each gear against each of the gears in the drawing.

He then had Nichols hand up the architectural drawings and

compared them to the carpentry work around the clock and the entablature along the wall. It was close, but not perfect. *It had all seemed so right, but yet they were missing something.*

"We open the doors in two minutes," said Ferguson. "Do you see anything at all?"

"Nothing," replied Harvath as he handed the diagrams back down to Nichols.

With the curator walking him through it, Harvath restarted the clock and then replaced the housing. He climbed down the ladder and hung it on the nearby wall.

"I don't understand it," said Nichols. "It seemed like the perfect fit."

Harvath borrowed the architectural detail again and looked at Ferguson. "Maybe this diagram is the clue to what we're looking for. If Jefferson drew it, he probably drew it for here, right? So what should we do? Go room by room? I know the second and third floors aren't open to the public. Maybe we should start up there."

"Or the stone weaver's cottage," offered Nichols.

"There wouldn't be carpentry like this in the stone weaver's cottage," said Ferguson as she bit the inside of her cheek in thought. She then pulled the walkie-talkie from her belt, changed its channel, and spoke into it. "John, this is Susan. Do you copy?"

A moment later, a man's voice came back over the radio. "Go ahead, Susan."

"Do we have Paul Gilbertson on the docent schedule today?"

"Who's Paul Gilbertson?" asked Nichols.

Ferguson motioned for him to hold his question.

A moment later, the voice replied, "Yes, we do. He's leading the architectural study tours."

"Will you please ask him to meet me up at the main house right now? Tell him it's urgent."

CHAPTER 79

P aul Gilbertson was a large, Santa-like figure in his early seventies with a full beard and glasses that dangled from a cord around his neck. His hands were rough and his fingers looked like thick pieces of rope. A Leatherman tool hung from a nylon sheath on his belt.

He accepted the architectural schematic from Nichols and put his glasses on. With the tip of his tongue between his teeth, he made sucking sounds as he studied the drawings. After turning the document around in his hands he said, "Even without knowing what all of the coded words mean, this definitely looks like Jefferson's handiwork. They have Palladio written all over them," and then he went back to making the noises with his tongue.

Harvath looked at Ferguson. "What's Palladio?"

"Andrea Palladio was a Renaissance architect. Jefferson was completely self-taught in architecture and referred to Palladio's four books on the subject as his bible."

A couple of minutes later, as if being led by the drawings, Gilbertson walked away. The rest of the group quickly followed.

They entered the dining room and watched as Gilbertson scrutinized the woodwork around the doors and windows.

As they did, Harvath discovered a clever revolving serving door. It looked like a regular door, but it didn't have hinges. Instead, it had a rotating pin, fastened at the top and bottom in the center of the door. Food apparently could be loaded on to shelves affixed to the back of the door and then it would be turned outward to present the food to the dining room without a servant ever having to enter.

As Harvath spun the door back to its original position, Gilbertson shook his head and said, "This isn't a diagram for door surrounds *or* molding."

"What is it then?" asked Nichols.

The docent moved away from the window and crossed to the wall. "One of these," he said.

"A fireplace?" replied Harvath.

The man nodded. "I think it's a design for a mantelpiece."

Nichols looked at him. "Are you sure?"

"To be completely sure," he replied, "I'd need a full drawing, not just a sectional. But with a full drawing, almost anybody would be able to tell what they were looking at."

"Why do you think it's a mantelpiece?" asked Harvath.

"The diagrams are of very specific pieces that require sophisticated joinery," replied Gilbertson as he signaled for Harvath to follow him. Walking over to the side of the fireplace, he said, "It reminded me a lot of this mantelpiece."

"Why?" asked Harvath.

"Watch."

Harvath looked on as Gilbertson opened one of the mantelpiece's panels to reveal an ingenious hidden compartment. Inside was a rope and pulley system.

"What is it?" he asked.

Gilbertson smiled. "It's a dumbwaiter for wine. There's one on each side of the fireplace. Jefferson designed them himself. Right beneath us is the wine cellar. When more wine was needed, a slave in the cellar would place a bottle in the box and send it up."

"So you think this set of drawings is for a fireplace dumbwaiter system?"

"It does appear to have an attachment point for a rope and pulley system, similar to this mantelpiece, but with such a limited diagram it's hard to tell," said the docent. "If I had to guess, I'd say that what you have there is a sectional view of a mantelpiece that has some secondary purpose."

"Speaking of which," said Nichols, "when we came in here, you didn't go straight over and show us the fireplace. You studied the doors, the windows, and the ceiling first. Why?"

Gilbertson held up the document. "The frieze Jefferson drew here looks just like the one from the Corinthian temple of Antoninus and Faustina in Rome. Susan was right to take you to the entrance hall first. But it's this smaller design at the bottom of the page that made me think of this room.

"Look at the entablature around the ceiling in here," he said, pointing up. "Jefferson used rosettes and bucrania or ox skulls."

Everyone looked up.

Harvath was the first to glance back down at the paper. "But that doesn't look like the drawing. This has a woman's face."

"But what's next to the face?"

Harvath looked closer. "Vines?"

"Flowers," said Gilbertson. "It's the edge of a bucranium. Ox skulls draped with flower garlands were a popular sacrificial motif for Roman altars. They became popular again for adorning Renaissance buildings."

"Did Jefferson use bucrania anywhere else here at Monticello?"

"He did. In his bedchamber and in the parlor," replied Gilbertson, "but not with faces. The only place faces appear anywhere similar to this is in the frieze in the Northwest Piazza. It was modeled on a frieze from the Roman baths of Diocletian."

"May I see that again please?" asked Susan Ferguson.

The docent handed her the page.

Nichols was about to say something when he noticed the intense look on his colleague's face as she analyzed the document.

"Now there could have been a design like this here at Monticello at one point in time," stated Gilbertson, "but I don't know of it. That doesn't mean that it didn't exist, though. You may want to speak with one of the librarians about their collection of Jefferson's notes and letters. They can be excellent research resources. In fact—"

Ferguson suddenly interrupted him. "No, Paul. You're right. This motif wasn't designed for Monticello."

The docent was surprised by her certitude. "It wasn't?"

"No, Jefferson designed it for his other plantation, Poplar Forest."

"How do you know?"

"Several of the entablatures there were also based upon an ancient frieze from Diocletian's Roman baths. They had human faces interspersed with three vertical bars, but Jefferson decided to add some whimsy and directed his craftsmen to include ox skulls."

"And the mantelpieces?" asked Harvath.

"Poplar Forest has fifteen," offered Ferguson.

Harvath smiled. "That's got to be it."

"The only problem with that," said Gilbertson, "is that Poplar Forest was gutted by fire in 1845. Only the walls, columns, chimneys, and fireplaces are still original."

CHAPTER 80

Poplar Forest was located in Bedford County just southwest of the city of Lynchburg, Virginia. Even with a heavy foot, it took Harvath nearly an hour in waning rush-hour traffic to make the eighty-mile drive.

As they drove, Nichols filled them in on the big picture points he knew about Poplar Forest.

"Jefferson referred to Poplar Forest as his 'most valuable possession' and began building the house there in 1806, shortly after the First Barbary War.

"It was his retreat where he was free to carry on his favorite pursuits—thinking, studying, and reading. His parlor, which also doubled as his study, housed over six hundred books in multiple languages by authors such as Aesop, Homer, Plato, Virgil, Shakespeare, and Molière.

"The house at Poplar Forest was considered the pinnacle of Jefferson's architectural genius. Based upon the design principles of Andrea Palladio, Jefferson constructed the all-brick home in the form of a perfect, equal-sided octagon, which appealed to his love of mathematics. Inside, the home was divided into four octagonal rooms surrounding a central dining room that was perfectly cubed.

"With triple-sash and floor-to-ceiling windows, as well as a sixteen-foot-long skylight in the center of the house, every space was flooded with light. And though the idea was to create a simple, informal country retreat, the entire home, right down to its kitchen, was a state-of-the-art masterpiece."

The fact that Poplar Forest was closed on Mondays wouldn't have stopped Harvath from finding a way to get inside, but Susan Ferguson had called Poplar Forest's director, Jonathan Moss, who agreed to drive over from Roanoke and meet the men there.

Turning right off Bateman Bridge Road at the entrance of Poplar Forest, Harvath followed the long driveway for a mile before it ended near the front of the house. Theirs was the only vehicle there.

"Looks like we're here first," stated Nichols. "Should we take a look around?"

The three men climbed out of the SUV, briefly stretched, and then began walking. As they circled the main house and the newly reconstructed service wing, the professor shared the handful of additional modern details he knew about Poplar Forest. In particular, he described how it had been rapidly degrading until 1983, when a nonprofit corporation was formed to buy it and the surrounding five hundred acres. Over the next twenty-five years the corporation painstakingly researched and restored the estate to its original condition.

After fifteen minutes of sightseeing, they heard a car door slam shut. Poplar Forest's director had arrived. With Nichols and Ozbek right behind him, Harvath turned and headed back to where they had parked.

Jonathan Moss was the skinniest person Harvath had ever seen. Standing about five-foot-eleven, with dark hair and a pronounced Adam's apple, the man looked to be about fifty and reminded Harvath of Washington Irving's Ichabod Crane.

Moss gathered packets of information from the trunk of his car, slammed the lid, and walked up to the north portico where Anthony Nichols introduced himself and facilitated the rest of the introductions.

After shaking hands, Moss passed a packet of Poplar Forest information to each of his visitors. "I hope your trip doesn't turn out to be a waste of time," he remarked as he led the men toward the pine front doors, which had been painted to replicate the color and grain of mahogany, just as in Jefferson's day. "As I understand was explained to you, much of the house was destroyed by fire in the 1800s. I think we've done an exceptional restoration job, but I don't know how much help that is going to be to you. All of the original woodwork was burned, including the mantelpieces."

Moss opened the doors and once everyone was inside, he had his guests follow him down the narrow entry corridor to the dining room at the center of the house.

Harvath looked up at the light slicing through the pitched glass panes of the skylight. The entablature depicted bucrania and a variety of human faces, but didn't look like their architectural renderings.

The professor produced the documents and set them on the table for Moss to study. As he did, Nichols ran through the same questions they had addressed with Susan Ferguson back at Monticello.

"I don't know what to tell you about the gears," said Moss. "We have a few mechanical items here that Jefferson designed such as the polygraph for making copies of the letters he wrote, but nothing with an extensive gear system like this."

"Any Islamic instruments like clocks or other mechanical items from the Arab world?" asked Nichols.

The director shook his head. "Nope."

Moss continued to answer in the negative on questions about Lieutenant O'Bannon, al-Jazari, and anything having to do with the First Barbary War.

Just as Paul Gilbertson, the docent from Monticello, had done, Moss suggested that there could be some answer in Jefferson's voluminous correspondence of more than twenty thousand letters written during his lifetime.

Nichols had already wrung Jefferson's correspondence dry. He also had access to items Moss had never and would never see. If there was an answer to be found, it was here. It had to be. "What about the architectural sketches?"

Moss positioned the page in front of himself and after studying it a moment stated, "Susan said one of her docents believed this was a schematic for part of a fireplace mantel, correct?"

"Correct."

"During our restoration, we restored fourteen of the fifteen brick fireplaces themselves."

"Why not the fifteenth?"

"It was the only one that didn't need it."

"Where is it?" asked Harvath.

Moss held up the Jefferson architectural drawing and replied. "In the same room whose entablature depicted ox skulls and the Roman goddess of wisdom and learning, Minerva." Pointing to the door in front of them, he said, "The parlor."

CHAPTER 81

As Moss led them into the space that had served as Jefferson's parlor, as well as his library and study, the first thing Harvath noticed were the ox skulls and depictions of Minerva around the edge of the ceiling.

Studying the period furnishings, Harvath asked, "What was originally beneath this room?"

"The wine cellar," replied Moss.

Paul Gilbertson had pointed out in the drawings what appeared to be an attachment point for a rope and pulley system, similar to what was used in Jefferson's dumbwaiter at Monticello.

Now, that same schematic had led them to Poplar Forest and a room above a wine cellar with the only fireplace in the house from Jefferson's time that had never needed to be renovated.

Harvath wondered why. Maybe its construction was purposely different from the others; better, stronger for some reason. He also wondered if maybe the secret they were looking for wasn't necessarily hidden within the mantelpiece, but that the mantelpiece had simply acted as a gatekeeper.

Originally, Harvath had thought the architectural schematic represented some sort of twist on a puzzle box—a diagram that indicated how to manipulate pieces in the correct order which would in turn unlock a panel and reveal whatever Thomas Jefferson was hiding.

Moss pointed to the fireplace on the east side of the room and said, "That's it there."

Harvath, Nichols, and Ozbek walked over and examined the mantelpiece.

The professor wasn't very excited. "If whatever it was, was ever here, it's gone now," he stated.

"Maybe not," replied Harvath as he turned to Moss and asked, "Was there a dumbwaiter in this room that would have allowed for wine to be brought up from the cellar?"

The Poplar Forest director shook his head. "I'm afraid not."

"You never saw any holes in the floor in here or anything like that which could have been part of a rope and pulley system; even if they could have been part of a system of counterweights for a clock of some sort?"

"None at all. We replaced the floors throughout the house. If there had been holes like that, we would have seen them."

Harvath went back to examining the mantel, in particular where it butted up against the wall.

"What are you thinking?" asked Nichols.

"I'm thinking of a baptismal font in a church I know of," said Harvath as he leaned his shoulder into the mantel and tried to give it a shove.

"What does a church have to do with what we're looking for?" asked Ozbek.

Harvath borrowed the architectural document from the professor and set it atop the mantel. "Paul Gilbertson at Monticello said he believed this was a cutaway drawing of a mantelpiece, right?"

"Right."

"Well, what if it was more than that? What if the movable joinery was actually a type of combination lock?"

"Like the puzzle box," said Nichols, a note of excitement in his voice.

"What puzzle box?" asked Ozbek.

The professor pantomimed a small box with his hands. "They're boxes Jefferson was fond of which required pieces to be manipulated in a particular order to get them to open. He kept the wheel cipher in one of them."

"And the *Don Quixote* we found in Paris," added Harvath.

"What difference does it make, though?" said Ozbek. "The original mantelpiece is gone."

"But not the fireplace," replied Harvath as he pointed to the drawing. "Gilbertson said he believed this was an attachment point for a rope and pulley system."

"There was no dumbwaiter here, though."

"No holes in the floor either," added Nichols.

Harvath looked at them. "What if it wasn't for a dumbwaiter system? What if it was for something else entirely?"

"Like what?"

"I'll tell you as soon as we move this mantelpiece."

CHAPTER 82

Moss' eyes popped out about as far as his Adam's apple when Harvath explained what he wanted to do.

"I'm sorry," said the director, "but the Corporation for Poplar Forest would never allow that."

Nichols pulled his wallet from his pocket. "What if I was willing to pay for putting everything back exactly the way it was afterwards?"

"I'm sorry, professor, but we can't just allow one of our mantelpieces to be ripped away from the wall."

"I'd also be willing to make a contribution," said Nichols.

Moss pursed his lips in thought. Looking at the architectural document the professor was holding in his hand, he asked, "What about that?"

The professor held it up. "What about it?"

"Seeing as how it has such an intimate connection to Poplar Forest, what are the chances of it being donated to our collection?"

"I think I might be able to convince its owner to consider loaning it on a long-term basis."

"And the other document?" asked the director. "With the Arabic writing?"

"It would depend on your cooperation."

"Very well," replied Moss. "It's imperative that mantelpiece come off as delicately as possible. Do we understand each other?"

"Of course."

"We're going to need some tools," said Harvath.

"We have plenty of those," replied Moss. "Follow me."

•   •   •

Half an hour after Moss stopped complaining about the damage Harvath and Ozbek were doing to the mantelpiece as well as the plasterwork around it, they had it separated and leaned up against the adjacent wall.

Nichols and Harvath stood next to each other and examined the brickwork of the fireplace.

"Let me see the diagram again," said Harvath.

The professor handed it to him as Harvath rubbed his finger over a hole in one of the bricks that had been filled with mortar.

"Why do you suppose this is here?" he asked.

Nichols shrugged. "Maybe it was an anchor point for the mantel-piece."

"That's what these are here," said Harvath as he pointed to similar features on both sides of the firebox.

Walking back to the tools Moss had helped them gather, Harvath removed a cordless drill and inserted a narrow masonry bit.

"We only talked about removing the mantelpiece," objected Moss. "We never discussed drilling into the bricks."

Harvath looked at Ozbek, who was standing near Moss. The

former Special Forces soldier put his hand on the director's shoulder and said, "Let's indulge him a little."

After securing the bit, Harvath set to work drilling out the mortar.

It took over ten minutes and when the hole was finally clear, two things were readily apparent. Not only was this not an anchor point, but the hole was deep, very deep.

Harvath sent Ozbek and Moss in search of something solid that they could slide down the hole and probe with. They came back five minutes later with an oak dowel rod half an inch in diameter.

Placing the tip just inside the hole, Harvath fed it forward until it wouldn't go any further. He gripped the thin rod with both hands and tried to force it further down, but nothing happened.

Ozbek walked over to the toolbox, retrieved a hammer, and brought it back to Harvath.

Steadying the rod, Harvath tapped it with the hammer. When nothing happened, he gave it another tap and followed it with another, harder and harder each time, but to no avail.

"What exactly are you trying to—?" began Moss, but Nichols signaled for him to be quiet.

Harvath drew back the hammer once more and swung it with considerable force.

There was a crack as the hammer splintered the rod, but there was also something else—a faint sound of brick grating against brick as the rear portion of the fireplace pivoted open on a central pin, just like the revolving serving door in the dining room at Monticello.

CHAPTER 83

T he original mantelpiece must have been attached somehow to a rope system which burned in the fire," said
Nichols.

"Leaving the hole, which not knowing what its true purpose was, someone had plugged up," replied Harvath as he crouched down and stepped into the fireplace.

The wall was solid brick and it took some force to get it the rest of the way open. Harvath removed his Night-Ops flashlight from his pocket and cast its bright light into the alcove behind the fireplace. In the center was a weathered captain's chest.

Grabbing it by one of its handles, Harvath slid the chest out of the alcove and into the room. Wiping the lid clean of dust and soot he noticed an engraving—*Captain Isaac Hull, United States Navy*. Hull had commanded the USS *Argus* and had helped plan the historic attack on the city of Derna in the First Bar-bary War.

The chest wasn't locked and as Nichols, Ozbek, and Moss gath-ered behind him, Harvath carefully raised its lid. Inside was an object about the size and shape of a hat box with a peak in the middle. It was wrapped in what looked like waxed canvas or sail cloth.

Harvath reached inside and picked it up. It felt solid and very heavy. Concerned that the aged lid of the captain's chest might not be able to support its weight, Harvath took the object over to the parlor's desk and unwrapped it.

It was absolutely extraordinary. Sitting atop a twelve-inch-high, perfectly round metallic drum was a four-inch-tall figurine. It was crafted in the form of a bearded scribe who was sitting cross-legged, complete with turban, robes, and a quill in his outstretched right hand. The scribe had been painted with an enamel of some sort and appeared incredibly lifelike.

Engraved in a circle around him were what appeared to be the hours of the day. Everyone was speechless.

Moss was the first to say something. "Al-Jazari?"

Nichols nodded.

"Is it a clock?" asked Ozbek.

"I think so," said Harvath as he inspected the device.

He examined it from every angle, but couldn't find a way to access its inner workings.

He then attempted to manipulate the scribe and discovered that it was hinged and could be tilted back about forty-five degrees, but for what purpose, no one understood.

When next he tried to gently twist the figure and nothing happened, he tried pushing it down like a child safety cap on a bottle of pills. Suddenly there was a *click* and the top of the clock popped loose.

Harvath had Nichols hold the flashlight as he removed the top and looked inside.

The elegance of the workmanship was astounding. Harvath couldn't believe he was looking at something that was not only designed, but fabricated and assembled over eight hundred years ago.

"How does it work?" asked Moss.

"It was probably powered by water," replied Nichols, "at least when it came to telling time."

"But something tells me this device does a lot more than just tell time," said Harvath as he looked at the underside of the lid and found a small pocket.

Sliding the tips of his fingers inside, he coaxed out a delicate gear that was identical to the one in the mechanical schematic. Panning the light over it, he located the Basmala.

Without needing to be asked, Nichols retrieved the mechanical diagram and set it on the desk next to the device.

Harvath took a deep breath and reminded himself to go slowly. He needed to take great pains not to damage anything while remembering each move he made in case any of them were incorrect and he had to back up and do something over again.

He wished that Tracy could have been there. Despite what had happened to her in Iraq, as a Naval EOD tech she was exceptional at handling this exact kind of situation. Harvath's hands were not made for this type of work.

Even so, he wouldn't have wanted anyone else in the room doing what he was doing right now.

Nichols held the light steady as Harvath tried to reposition the gears as Jefferson had indicated in his diagram. He had no idea what kind of metal or alloy they had been crafted from, but they were incredibly clean and free of rust even after hundreds of years.

It took him twenty minutes, but as he positioned the Basmala gear, he finally fully exhaled for what felt like the first time. His sense of relief, though, was short lived.

As he snapped the gear in place, something within the device sprung loose. The entire inner mechanism, which rested on a series of small legs inside the housing, dropped a quarter of an inch. One of the razor-sharp gears nicked the tip of Harvath's left thumb.

Cursing, Harvath snatched his hand back. It was already starting to bleed.

"Are you okay?" asked Nichols.

"I'm fine," said Harvath as he untucked his shirt and used the bottom of it to apply pressure to stop the bleeding.

Ozbek walked over to the toolbox and tossed Harvath a tube of Krazy Glue. "Here," he said, "use this."

Harvath employed his teeth to help unscrew the cap and then applied some of the compound to his wound and pinched it shut.

Turning his attention back to the device, he noticed that when the mechanism had dropped, a hidden door on the side of the housing had opened. Protruding from it was a small handle. It reminded Harvath of the crank for a child's jack-in-the-box.

"I think I know how we're supposed to power this," he said.

CHAPTER 84

A s Harvath turned the tiny handle, they all watched the scribe circle and glide across the top of the drum. It was amazingly graceful and fluid, but no one had any idea what its purpose was.

"How many letters are there in the Arabic alphabet?" asked Nichols as he withdrew a piece of paper from his folder.

"Twenty-eight as far as basic letters are concerned," replied Ozbek. "Why?"

"This could be some sort of code. Maybe Scot's winding the handle too fast. Let's slow it down and watch what the scribe does in relation to the hour markers."

"But there are only twenty-four of those."

"Can't hurt to try," replied the professor.

Harvath thought he was right and began turning the handle more slowly.

Each time Nichols thought the scribe was pointing to a specific number, he wrote it down. The more Harvath watched, though, the more he had the feeling this wasn't about numbers.

Tucking his shirt back in, he noticed the blood on it and that gave him an idea. Turning to Nichols, he said, "Give me that piece of paper for a second."

As he did, Harvath grabbed his Poplar Forest information packet and spread its contents on the desk.

Crouching down so that he could have the device at eye level, Harvath stacked several of the brochures until they came to just beneath the level of the scribe's quill. He then tilted the scribe back, slid Nichols' piece of paper atop the brochure and then put his thumb in his mouth and pulled the dried Krazy Glue off his skin with his teeth.

After wetting the scribe's quill with his blood, Harvath tilted him back down. With the nib against the paper, he started turning the handle again. As he did, Arabic writing began to materialize on the page.

"My God," said Nichols.

"You mean Allah, don't you?" joked Ozbek as he slapped Harvath on the back. "Well done."

Harvath smiled. Looking at Jonathan Moss, he asked, "Do you have any bottles of writing ink anywhere?"

Moss was so amazed it took him a moment to register Harvath's request. "Yes we do," he finally said. "I'll go get some."

As he left, Harvath wrapped the bottom of his shirt around his bleeding thumb again.

"You know," remarked Ozbek, "Saddam Hussein had a whole Koran written in his own blood. I thought SEALs were supposed to be tough guys."

Harvath mumbled a good-natured "Fuck you" as he opened the tube of Krazy Glue again with his teeth and resealed his wound.

"I can't believe it," said Nichols as he stared at the scribe clock.

"Believe it," replied Harvath who retrieved the page from beneath the scribe's quill and opened the lid to look inside again. "When Moss gets back, we'll reset it and get the whole message from the beginning."

"I only wish Marwan could have been here to see this."

"I know," said Harvath as he put his hand on the professor's shoulder and they stood there admiring the machine and the awesome impact it was going to have.

• • •

Five minutes later, Poplar Forest's director walked back into the room. The first thing Harvath noticed was that his hands were empty and he had a look on his face like he was being chased by the Headless Horseman himself. Harvath was about to ask him what was wrong when he noticed someone behind him.

Susan Ferguson began sobbing as she appeared in the doorway with a suppressed weapon tight against her head held by none other than Matthew Dodd.

Harvath and Ozbek drew their pistols.

"Easy, gentlemen," said Dodd with a smile. "Now, drop the guns on the floor and kick them over here."

When the men hesitated, Dodd readjusted his aim and shot Jonathan Moss through his left shoulder.

The Poplar Forest director screamed in agony.

"Weapons on the floor and kick them over here now," yelled Dodd.

Harvath and Ozbek reluctantly complied. Neither of them had even a halfway decent shot. If they'd had, they would have taken it, but as it was, Dodd was using both Susan Ferguson and the doorframe to his utmost advantage.

"Good," said Dodd, who then shouted at Moss, "Get over here and pick those up."

The man was crying and rapidly going into shock. His right hand was clamped down over his shoulder which was becoming soaked with blood.

Dodd repeated the command and punctuated it by firing a round into the floor near Moss' feet.

The director stumbled over to the weapons and picked them up. Remaining near the floor with his head down, he handed them up one at a time to Dodd.

"Now go get that clock," ordered the assassin, "and all the papers on that desk."

Harvath was standing in front of the device, with the back of his legs pressed up against the desk. As Moss approached, Dodd indicated with two quick flicks of his weapon for Harvath to move out of the way.

Harvath knew better than to tempt Dodd. Lowering his hands against his sides, he gestured for Nichols to move to his left, closer to Ozbek. Once Nichols had done so, Harvath followed.

"Bring it here," said Dodd as the director closed the lid and then struggled to pick the device up.

Wrapping his good arm around it, the man pinned the al-Jazari clock to his chest, grabbed all the papers, and slowly brought everything back over to the assassin.

As he drew even, Dodd motioned for him to stand in the room behind him. Once Moss had passed, the assassin looked straight at Harvath and Ozbek. "I've got what I came for," he said. "Whether anybody dies today is up to you."

"We're not even, Dodd," replied Ozbek. "Not by a long shot."

"Should we settle up right now?" asked the assassin as he pointed the pistol at the CIA operative's head.

Nichols looked like he was gearing up to say something and Harvath stepped on his foot to keep him quiet.

"Get moving," Dodd said as he placed the pistol back against Ferguson's head and began to back out of the room.

"What about them?" asked Harvath, referring to the two captives. "You don't need to take them with you."

"No, I don't," Dodd replied, "but I'm going to."

"The man needs medical attention."

The assassin stared at Harvath. "He'll live as long as nobody tries to follow us."

"Nobody is going to follow you," said Harvath.

Tightening his grip on Susan Ferguson, the assassin motioned for Moss to start walking and he slowly backed out of the room.

Once he had disappeared from view and they heard the door at the front of the house slam shut, Ozbek said, "Let's go. Come on."

"He's got two hostages," replied Harvath.

"I understand that, but we can't just let him disappear with that device."

"It's no good to him anyway."

"What do you mean?" said Ozbek. "All he has to do is slide some paper in there, ink the quill and crank the handle."

"It won't work without this," replied Harvath as he held up the Basmala gear. His fingertips were bloody from having blindly pulled it from the machine behind his back while Dodd's attention was on collecting their weapons from the floor.

"He still has Susan and Jonathan, though," protested Nichols. "He'll kill them."

"I don't think he'll kill them," replied Harvath as he once again used his shirt to stem his bleeding.

"Why? Because he didn't kill Gary?" challenged Ozbek.

Harvath looked at him. "That's exactly why. If we let him go, Moss and Ferguson have a much better chance of surviving and you know it. I want this guy too, but let's be smart."

"Fuck 'smart.' We're wasting time."

Harvath knew Ozbek had lost a member of his team and had another in the hospital because of Dodd, but getting more people killed wasn't going to fix anything. "Listen to me. Don't let your desire to make Dodd pay for what he did to your people cloud your judgment."

Ozbek knew Harvath was right, but it pissed him off. Picking up the hammer, he threw it at the fireplace.

Nichols was about to register another objection when they heard the front door crash open and Jonathan Moss begin screaming for help.

En masse, they ran to the front of the house where Moss lay on the threshold bleeding. "I need a doctor," he cried.

"What happened?" asked Harvath. "Where did they go?"

"I don't know. The man told me to turn around and then they just disappeared!"

Ozbek held out his hand to Moss. "Give me your car keys."

"Aydin, no," ordered Harvath, but it was too late.

Ozbek pulled the keys from Moss' jacket pocket and ran for the parking lot.

There was no use in trying to stop him. Instead, Harvath handed Nichols Moss' cell phone and had him call 911 while he tore open the man's shirt to assess his wound and rig a makeshift pressure bandage that would slow the bleeding until help arrived.

Moments later, Ozbek reappeared. "Your car and Moss' are out of commission," he said to Harvath. "All of the tires have been slashed."

CHAPTER 85

WASHINGTON, D.C.
TWO DAYS LATER

Harvath had decided it was best to stay away from Bishop's Gate until a much better security system could be installed. He had returned only once to gather up some things and then camped out at Gary Lawlor's place in Fairfax.

Though Gary was still in the ICU with a skull fracture, he'd made Harvath give him a full oral debriefing and a written one as well. Harvath knew it would be delivered to the president. He hadn't thought anything further of it until he received a call from Rutledge asking him to come to the White House ASAP.

Harvath hoped that it wasn't bad news, and that if it was that it didn't involve Tracy. He knew from experience, though, that when the president called and told you to get into his office double quick, it wasn't because you'd won the lottery.

Carolyn Leonard met Harvath at the Southwest Gate and escorted him past security and into the West Wing. "This is your second visit in less than a week," she said as they walked. "Does this mean we're going to start seeing more of you around here?"

"Maybe," Harvath replied, more amenable than he had been in a long time to the idea.

At the Oval Office, Leonard checked with Jack Rutledge's secretary and then knocked. When the president answered, she let Harvath in and closed the door behind him.

Rutledge stood from behind his desk and met his guest in the center of the room. "Thanks for coming, Scot," he said as they shook hands.

The president pointed toward the couches, indicating they should sit there.

Once they were seated, Rutledge said, "It's been a rough handful of days."

The president was obviously concerned with their newly mended fences and was downplaying events.

Though Harvath hadn't asked for the assignment, he'd accepted it and therefore win or lose, the responsibility for it was his. "I'm sorry, sir, but 'rough' doesn't do it. I failed and I apologize."

Rutledge leaned over to the coffee table and lifted a leather folder. "I read your briefing. Do you have the Basmala gear?"

Harvath withdrew an envelope from his breast pocket and handed it to him.

Lifting the flap, the president removed the gear and held it up so that he could look at it. "Amazing. And it was at Poplar Forest all this time."

"I just wish we could have learned what the final revelation was," said Harvath.

Rutledge set the tooth-studded piece of metal down. "Because of the personal nature of the presidential diary, Anthony Nichols was never allowed to see it in its entirety. I can tell you that Jefferson's research led him to believe that Mohammed's final revelation was the only one to have come directly to him from God, not through the angel Gabriel. In a nutshell, if you believe it, Mohammed was told that war and conquest were not the answers. He was told to put down the sword and live peacefully among peoples of other faiths. Jefferson commented that it sounded similar to the conversion of Paul, though Mohammed wasn't leaving Islam for Christianity. He was just hanging up his sword and encouraging his followers to do the same."

Harvath was stunned.

"Pretty significant revelation," said the president. "Isn't it?"

"It is. And considering the fact that such a large degree of the Muslims' income was based upon looting and plundering, as well as extorting protection money from Christians and Jews who chose not to convert to Islam, it would have wiped out a sizable source of revenue for their economy. It would have collapsed. No wonder his own people wanted to assassinate him."

"Well, without the Basmala gear, the al-Jazari clock won't do much more than tell time now," replied Rutledge. "If it hasn't already been destroyed."

"What about Mahmood Omar and Abdul Waleed? You didn't have any luck squeezing them?"

"Aydin Ozbek is a good operative," said Rutledge, "but he was operating way outside the law. We can't legally use anything he gained to go after those two."

Harvath was loathe to make such a suggestion, but he felt it had to be said. "I wasn't necessarily proposing a Marquess of Queensberry approach."

"I understand," replied the president. "I also agree. The two gentlemen in question have been watched very closely and we're also looking into their ties with Saudi Arabia, but as far as we can tell right now they haven't come into possession of the al-Jazari device."

"Which means Dodd must still have it."

"We'll get to Dodd in a minute," said the president. "As per the two dead Saudis from UVA, for whom the crown prince is going to be made to answer for, we were able to link them via DNA discovered in their car, as well as additional evidence at the Jefferson Memorial, to the murder of Nura Khalifa, and what has now been classified as the attempted murder of Andrew Salam.

"Mr. Salam was freed last night and is continuing to cooperate with the FBI and D.C. Metro Police."

Harvath already knew that Susan Ferguson had spent an evening gagged and handcuffed in a rest stop bathroom outside D.C. before being discovered, so he turned his attention to someone else. "How's Ozbek's operative, Rasmussen?" he asked.

"He's going to be fine. He'll probably be out of the hospital by the end of the week."

"What about Ozbek?"

The president was quiet for several moments. "Like I said, he's a good operative, but somebody died under his command in an unsanctioned assignment. From what I've been told, he's an asset we don't want to lose and I have echoed those sentiments to DCI Vaile."

"So he's still with CIA? They didn't let him go?"

"No, he hasn't been let go. Officially, Ozbek is on unpaid leave from CIA pending a disciplinary review. Unofficially, he is continuing his unsanctioned surveillance of Omar and Waleed, but let's talk about Tracy for a minute."

This was the topic Harvath was most apprehensive about getting to. He felt certain the other shoe was about to drop and that it was going to be full of bad news.

"The French are playing hardball," said Rutledge, "big time. To tell you the truth, I can't say that if the situation was reversed we wouldn't act the same.

"They're aware of the fact that we know more than we're letting on. The only way they'll cooperate with us is on a quid pro quo basis. They won't consider turning Tracy over until we give them something of equal or greater value."

"Like what?" asked Harvath.

"Like Matthew Dodd."

"But we don't even know where he is."

"That's about to change," replied the president.

Harvath leaned forward. It was the first piece of good news he had heard in days.

"We just learned that Dodd used a satellite phone to contact Omar. He was smart. He kept the call short in order to make it difficult to trace."

"But you did," said Harvath, "correct?"

"We know he was calling from somewhere outside the United States."

"That's it?"

The president held up his hand. "The Defense Department has a new satellite program that we've started using in Iraq and Afghanistan, to track high-value targets who make short SAT phone transmissions. The secretary of defense has his best people standing by. If Dodd uses his phone again, we'll be able to pinpoint his whereabouts no matter how short the call."

"What do you want me to do?" asked Harvath.

"I have a plane at Andrews ready to go. When we find out where Dodd is, I want you on it. I'm authorizing you to do whatever is necessary to recover the al-Jazari device. Once we have what we need, we can get to work on finalizing Tracy's exchange. Any questions?"

Harvath shook his head and stood.

As he was nearing the door, the president stopped him. "By the way. Your report mentioned that before Dodd took the device, you managed to get a small bit of writing out of it."

"Yes, sir," replied Harvath. "Just one word."

"What was it?"

Harvath looked back across the Oval Office and said, "Peace."

CHAPTER 86

VIRGIN GORDA
BRITISH VIRGIN ISLANDS

Located on the North Sound of the small island of Virgin Gorda was one of the best-kept secrets in the world. Accessible only by sea, the Bitter End Yacht Club was the last island outpost before the open waters of the Atlantic.

It was where Matthew Dodd and his wife, Lisa, had spent their honeymoon and to where Dodd had now returned.

He had flown into Tortola's Beef Island airport and walked the three hundred yards to Trellis Bay where the boat he had chartered was waiting. Though he could have taken the high speed ferry to Bitter End, Dodd didn't want to mingle with other people. He had come to be alone.

After leaving Poplar Forest, he had come to a painful conclusion. Just as he had duped Andrew Salam, he himself had been duped. He had been playing with fools; engaging in business with men who weren't properly equipped to further Islam's aims. The entire religion was being subverted by men who pursued Islamic supremacism at all costs. They were neither worthy of the fealty Dodd had sworn to them, nor were they worthy of their exalted positions as spokespersons and representatives of true Muslim faith in America. They hungered for power under the guise of Islam rather than for the sake of Islam. They were apostate.

Dodd was also beginning to believe that in this grand struggle there was no "right" side to be aligned with after all. Maybe there were only right actions.

•   •   •

The assassin checked in at the front desk with only a backpack slung over one shoulder. The cottage built above the beach looking out over the aquamarine Caribbean water was just as he remembered it. Nothing had changed. As Dodd quietly unpacked his few possessions, he thought about the better times in his life.

He remembered Lisa's love of snorkeling and her delight over the Bitter End's brilliant array of wrasses, damselfish, and parrotfish. He smiled as he recalled the hours she had spent among the colorful sponges and corals just offshore.

Removing his clothes, the assassin slid into a pair of trunks and walked down to the beach. He'd dealt with sand extensively over the last several years—in his hair, in his eyes, his food, his weapons, but not between his toes where it really belonged. It felt good as the warmth radiated up through his body.

Dodd walked into the wet sand and allowed the sea to lap at his feet. Slowly he moved forward until he was up to his waist in the warm water.

After marking the time on his watch, he submersed himself beneath the surface and began swimming.

He pulled with long, powerful strokes for over half an hour. When he stepped back onto the beach, his breathing was shallow and his pulse rapid. His mind felt clear and sharp.

Outside the cottage, he cleaned the sand from his feet and then opened the screen door and stepped inside.

He stripped out of his swimsuit and rinsed off in a hot shower. With his hair slicked back and a towel wrapped around his waist, he retrieved his backpack, a glass, and walked out onto the wraparound veranda.

He placed everything on the table, sat down, and powered up his satellite phone. As it worked to establish a signal, Dodd opened one of the bottles of Arundel rum he'd bought at the airport in Tortola and poured three fingers into his glass. He and Lisa had gone through at least two bottles of it during their honeymoon.

The brown liquid burned as it went down and though it had been years since he had had a drink, the taste and the sensation were pleasant and familiar, like coming home.

His Koran should not have been sitting right there next to a bottle of alcohol. He knew that, just as he knew that he should not begin drinking again. Alcohol had only added to the darkness and despair of losing his wife and son, but here he and his Koran were anyway.

He had prayed relentlessly for guidance, but none had come. After retrieving the al-Jazari device, he had studied his heart and made his plans accordingly.

The assassin looked down at the glass in his hand and laughed. Though he was far from soft, he certainly wasn't exhibiting much self-discipline at the moment.

Islam *was* the answer for America. He felt more certain of that than anything else. He was just without any idea of how to bring such a shift about.

Nevertheless, he knew that Omar with his hate-spewing mosques and Waleed with his laughably corrupt Foundation on American Islamic Relations were all standing in the way of the truly good work Islam could do in America. The two men were not part of the solution. They were abominations and unquestionably part of the problem.

Dodd poured himself another drink. He sipped slowly at it as he watched the minutes tick away on his watch.

At the appointed time, he picked up the satellite phone and dialed Sheik Omar's private number.

Omar picked up on the first ring. "Is that you, Majd?" he asked.

"It is I," said the assassin.

"Allah be praised. We have been so worried about you since your last call. We barely had any time to speak. Did you find it? The invention of al-Jazari?"

"I did."

"Allahu Akbar, my brother. Allahu Akbar." The sheik was over-joyed. "Allah's work—our work is now secure. Allahu Akbar!"

"Are you at your desk?" asked Dodd.

"Of course I am. You've called me on my private line."

"And Abdul is with you?"

"He is sitting right here," replied Omar. "Just as you requested. When can you bring us the device?"

Dodd had no intention of staying on the phone any longer than he needed to. "Stay right there and don't move," he said. "I will call you back in thirty seconds."

Omar, though frustrated, respected the need for security. What's more, he was so happy with his assassin that at this point the man could have asked anything of him and he would have gladly obliged. "I understand," he said. "We will be right here waiting. *Allahu Akbar. Allahu Akbar!*"

Dodd hung up with the words *Allahu Akbar,* God Is Great, ringing in his ears.

A man of his word, the assassin began dialing the digits almost immediately, except they weren't for the sheik's private line. They belonged to a cell phone attached to an improvised explosive device that had been hidden behind Omar's desk.

CHAPTER 87

BITTER END YACHT CLUB
THE NEXT EVENING

As the last rays of daylight faded, Scot Harvath watched Matthew Dodd drain the final drops out of the bottle he was drinking and stumble inside his cottage.

Having watched the man drink himself into a stupor, Harvath liked his odds. It didn't mean the assassin wasn't still dangerous, but it did mean his reflexes and his situational awareness would be significantly dulled.

Harvath put away his binoculars and grabbed his dry bag, grateful to finally be going topside. Though he had rented a sizable sailboat for the operation, being cooped up belowdecks with not much of a breeze for the better part of the afternoon was not his idea of the perfect Caribbean getaway.

Needless to say, he was here to work, not to play. But a luxury yacht beat any of the snake-, scorpion-, or bug-infested hide sites he'd been forced to endure over the course of his career. Life, especially an enjoyable one, was all about perspective and as Harvath checked the restraints in the cabin he had prepared for Matthew Dodd, he reminded himself of that.

Darkness was settling in as Harvath stepped outside and took a deep breath. The evening breeze felt great against his sweat-soaked body. Quickly, he wiped himself down with fresh water and then tossed his gear into the Zodiac RIB he'd kept moored on the opposite side of the sailboat.

After casting off, he started the engine and moved toward shore, the noise from the small outboard engine just one of several that would be making their way in from the deep water harbor to the Bitter End for cocktails and dinner.

Harvath pulled the boat onto the beach just out of sight of Dodd's cottage and unloaded his dry bag and a small beach towel. The .40 caliber suppressed Glock 23 he had been issued for this assignment was meant to be a tool of last resort. Plan A was a new waterproof TASER that had been developed for the SEAL teams along with a potent drug cocktail that would keep Dodd sleeping like a baby until Harvath could get him back aboard the sailboat and out into the ocean where he'd be able to start his interrogation.

As Harvath got closer to the cottage, he stopped to listen for signs of what was going on. The last he had seen of Dodd, the rogue CIA operative had come back onto his veranda with another bottle and had round two of the drinking Olympics well under way.

Keep going, my friend, Harvath had thought to himself. *You're only making it easier.*

The cottages were built on stilts with wooden staircases on each side of the verandas. Based on how Dodd had positioned himself to look out over the harbor, Harvath decided to come up the south set of stairs and hit him from behind.

Stopping once more at the bottom of Dodd's staircase, Harvath listened. There was the sound of glass on glass as Dodd poured another drink and then silence.

With the beach towel over his arm and the Glock hidden beneath, Harvath crept soundlessly up the sun-bleached stairs of the cottage.

When he stepped onto the veranda he moved to the wall and kept himself pressed up against it as he continued forward.

He reached the first set of windows, their sheer curtains moving in and out with the breeze. Looking through the bedroom, Harvath could see Dodd's outline through the open doors on the other side silhouetted by the faint glow of light from the harbor.

The assassin's back was to him. It was time.

Harvath ducked beneath the windows and stood up on the other side. At the corner of the cottage, he listened and with nothing changed, he raised his weapon and stepped out directly behind Dodd.

As he did, Dodd shot out of his chair and leapt to his feet, but the reaction had nothing to do with Harvath.

CHAPTER 88

Harvath was surprised to see one of the Defense Department's highest-ranking officials, Imad Ramadan, standing at the other end of the veranda with a suppressed SIG Sauer pistol in his hand.

He was a balding, barrel-chested man of average height in his mid-fifties with a thick gray goatee and dark eyes.

"You're a long way from D.C., Imad," said Harvath, his Glock up and at the ready.

Upon hearing the voice from behind, Dodd spun to see who it was and almost lost his balance. He had to reach out and grab the table to keep from falling over. Even then, he was so drunk he couldn't stop swaying.

"Whoever you are," said Ramadan, "none of this concerns you."

"Why? Is this an official Defense Department matter now?" asked Harvath as he adjusted his aim. The levels of government the Islamists had been able to infiltrate and the degree to which they were working together was astounding. Nevertheless, Harvath had no reservations about killing him if he had to. The Navy would probably even give him a medal for it.

"I'm going to guess," continued Harvath when Ramadan didn't answer, "that the Defense Department has no idea you're here. Somehow you wormed your way into the loop and were able to access Mr. Dodd's classified whereabouts. So where does the defense secretary think you are? Sick day?"

"Shut up," replied Ramadan.

To his list of unsavory accomplishments as an Islamist apologist and enabler whose loyalty was to Islam above all else, the United States could now add *traitor*. Harvath wanted to choke the man with his bare hands.

Looking at Dodd, Harvath saw that he was still swaying slightly from side to side. "What happened to the device you took from us at Poplar Forest?" he asked.

Dodd was silent for a moment. Finally, he slurred, "I took care of it."

"What do you mean?" demanded Ramadan.

"I did what was right."

"Right for whom?"

"Right for my religion."

"*Your* religion," exclaimed Ramadan. "What are you talking about?"

"What did you do with it?" interjected Harvath, who knew all too well that this was not the right way to conduct an interrogation. "Where is it?"

"Who cares where?" Dodd slurred.

More people than you can possibly imagine, thought Harvath, but he didn't want to get into that argument. What he wanted were answers, and so he changed tack. "What about the *Don Quixote* and everything else you took from my house?"

"It's all gone."

That was exactly what the president had been afraid of and if the truth be told, so had he. There was zero incentive for Dodd and his extremist cohorts to hold on to any of the materials that so threatened them. All the same, Harvath needed to be absolutely certain the assassin was telling the truth and for that he needed Dodd all to himself, someplace quiet, preferably out in open water on his sailboat. First, though, he had to deal with Ramadan. "Put your weapon down, Imad," he ordered. "Right now."

The Pentagon official ignored him. Instead he asked Dodd, "Are you aware that Sheik Omar and Abdul Waleed were killed in an explosion yesterday?"

"Yes," mumbled Dodd, his eyes glassy.

"I thought so," replied Ramadan as he tightened his grip on his pistol.

"Imad, I'm not going to give you another warning," said Harvath. "Drop your weapon or I'm going to drop you."

Again, Ramadan ignored him and posed another question to Dodd, this time using his Muslim name. "Majd," he said, softer, as if addressing a small child, "has the al-Jazari device been disposed of properly?"

Harvath watched as Dodd's swaying grew worse. His lips were moving, but no sound was coming out. Though the swaying was due in large part to the amount of alcohol he had consumed, there was an additional reason for it.

Many Muslims rocked back and forth during their prayers. Harvath had seen it again and again in mosques and also with suicide bombers right before they blew themselves up.

Harvath refocused on Ramadan. "How did you know about the al-Jazari device? What's your connection to all of this?"

"Do you think Sheik Omar and Abdul Waleed were just two men working all alone? This is much bigger than you will ever know."

Harvath didn't doubt that, but his attention was focused on Ramadan's eyes. They had changed and his expression had become more resolute. He was going to kill Dodd even if it meant he would be killed as a result. Harvath could feel it. He had no choice but to act.

Harvath began applying pressure to his trigger just as Dodd rocked backward once more and suddenly came forward in an explosion of movement. He threw the wooden table in front of him into the air.

Ramadan was barely able to get a shot off before Dodd and the table were on top of him.

Harvath fired as well, but it was too late. Dodd was dead. A single round from Ramadan's weapon had drilled through his nose and out the back of his head. Harvath's shot had been equally well placed. Imad Ramadan's lifeless body lay on the veranda, the weathered floorboards turning bright red with his blood.

CHAPTER 89

St. Martin

It took Harvath less than a day to sail from the Bitter End to St. Martin—the nearest overseas administrative division of France. En route, he contacted the president to give him a full debriefing on everything that had happened and to strategize what their next course of action should be. Like it or not, and neither Harvath nor the president did, the al-Jazari device and all of the promise it contained was lost. They needed to focus on moving forward.

Though Rutledge didn't expressly request the disposal of Ramadan's body, Harvath knew how to read between the lines. The president didn't want what little time remained in his administration to be taken up by a scandal. The Pentagon official was a traitor to his country, and now he was dead. As far as the president and Harvath were concerned, justice had been served.

Harvath thought it a fitting end that Imad Ramadan should go the way of the al-Jazari device, though he doubted the device had been torn apart by Caribbean reef sharks.

•   •   •

When Harvath arrived in St. Martin, his contact from France's *Direction de al Surveillance du Territoire,* also known as the DST, which was the counterintelligence/counterterrorism branch of the French national police, was extremely unhappy at being presented with the dead body of Matthew Dodd.

After the Paris bombing and the killing of three French national police officers, the French were justifiably out for blood.

The DST operative, a rather intense man about Harvath's age, asked how the hell they were supposed to put a corpse on trial. Harvath appreciated his anger and held his own in check in order to not make things worse.

He knew it looked bad. Dead men tell no tales, and this American ex–CIA operative had been whacked by Americans before being turned over to the French. The DST man had every reason to be suspicious.

The man's anger continued to build. Not only did this put their whole agreement in jeopardy, but maybe he was going to have to take Harvath into custody as well too. He wasn't shy about revealing the fact that he was armed. So was Harvath, but he kept that to himself.

Harvath offered the man the only other thing he had. Through avenues the CIA wouldn't divulge, and which Harvath assumed was code for Aydin Ozbek's off-the-books operation, they had managed to acquire a list of the Muslim extremists Dodd had worked with on the car bombing in Paris.

The DST operative asked if his agency could have a clean exclusive on the list, meaning it could take full credit for developing the names on the list and trust that the CIA would stay quiet. Harvath assured him they would. That left only one problem.

The Frenchman sitting aboard Harvath's boat had been assigned the job of personally telephoning the president of France once he had Dodd in his custody. The fact that Dodd was dead, and had been killed by the Americans no less, would not go over well. It quickly became apparent that his biggest concern was the French president's reputation for shooting his messengers.

Harvath reached below the bunk Dodd's corpse was lying on and withdrew Imad Ramadan's pistol. Handing it to the DST operative, Harvath said, "If you hadn't reacted so quickly, he would have killed us both," and fell silent.

The intelligence agent processed the angles. "I'm going to need to make a couple of phone calls," he said, "but I believe we may be able to work this out."

Harvath could see the wheels turning in his mind as he ran through the list of people he would invite to his Legion of Honor ceremony.

They met forty-five minutes later at a nearby beach where Harvath quietly brought the body ashore and helped load it into the intelligence agent's trunk.

As the man prepared to leave, Harvath put his hand on his car door and said, "There's one other thing I'm going to need."

●　　●　　●

"It's her," said Harvath as Tracy Hastings climbed out of the DST operative's car and began walking down the dock. It was the second delivery the DST agent had made that day.

Thanking the president, Harvath disconnected the call and set the encrypted satellite phone down.

Hopping onto the pier, he made a beeline straight for her. Despite everything that had happened, she had a smile on her face that cut right through him. She was still the most beautiful woman he had ever seen.

Chucking decorum, Harvath ran for her.

When they met halfway in the middle of the dock, they wrapped their arms around each other so tightly that he was afraid he was going to crush the air from her lungs.

"Don't ever leave me like that again," he said.

Tracy untangled her arms and reached up to hold Scot's face with both of her hands. "I love you," she said.

"I love you too," he replied. "But don't ever—"

Tracy kissed him before he could finish his sentence.

Finally, Harvath broke their embrace and asked, "How are you feeling? Are you okay? The flight was all right?"

"The flight was fine," said Tracy. "I'm fine. The swelling is all gone. I'm just supposed to watch my stress."

Harvath smiled and hugged her again. "Do you think you can handle being out on the water?"

"What kind of question is that to ask a United States Naval officer?"

"The S.S. *Harvath* is a tight ship," he replied. "I'm very picky about my crew. I only sail with the best."

Tracy laughed and conspiratorially looked over both shoulders. "I don't exactly see people lining up for the job."

"Actually," said Harvath, "the rest of the crew is already aboard."

"The *rest of the crew*?"

Turning around to face the boat, Harvath placed two fingers in his mouth and whistled.

In a blinding flash of white, Bullet appeared from belowdecks and started barking.

"We've got two weeks until the president wants me back in Washington," he said. "Where do you want to go?"

"I don't care," Tracy replied as she grabbed his chin for emphasis, "as long as we're the *only . . . ones . . . there.*"

EPILOGUE

A ndrew Salam and his dog stepped inside from the rain, and he searched through his coat closet for the ratty old towel he used to clean the dog's paws. Once all the mud was gone, he kicked off his running shoes and followed his dog into the kitchen where he filled his bowls with food and fresh water.

Grabbing a bottle of Evian from the fridge for himself, he spun off its cap and chugged half of it down in one long swallow. It was good to be home and even better now that his life was starting to get back to normal.

The FBI had asked him to come to work for them, but Salam's heart wasn't in it. Not right now at least.

Picking up the remote, he turned on the kitchen television set and tuned to one of the cable news channels. Some political pundit was droning on about "change" and the upcoming presidential elections. Salam paid no attention to it. He just liked having the TV on for background noise.

Taking his bottle with him, he walked over and sat down at his kitchen table. He had a stack of mail he'd yet to go through that had been growing higher with each passing day. Most of it was junk mail, but there were probably bills in there too, and he prided himself on settling his debts on time.

As he began sifting his way through, a very unusual envelope caught his attention. It bore the return address of a hotel he'd never heard of along with a postmark from the British Virgin Islands.

Carefully, Salam opened the envelope and removed a piece of paper. Taped to the center was some sort of locker key and below it a note. The handwriting was familiar and as he read the words, his heart stopped in his chest.

Andrew,

I know you will do the right thing with this.

Matthew Dodd (aka Sean Riley)

AUTHOR'S NOTE

The idea for this novel had many parents, so to speak. It was born in part from an *Atlantic Monthly* article by Toby Lester entitled "What Is the Koran?" I had discovered the piece while doing research on another novel and had tucked it away for future use. When I came across an article written by Gerard W. Gawalt, formerly of the Library of Congress, entitled "America and the Barbary Pirates: An International Battle Against an Unconventional Foe," I started wondering if there was a way I could combine the historical relevance of the Koran with Thomas Jefferson's experience with the Barbary pirates to create a thriller that would be relevant today.

In writing this novel, I have created a work of fiction based largely on fact. That said, I have taken creative license in some areas and will attempt to list them here.

Mohammed's lost revelation as depicted herein, as well as al-Jazari's preservation of same, is of my own making. The plot device of Mohammed being assassinated by one of his companions is also of my own making (though there is evidence that Mohammed was assassinated). The concept of abrogation and everything else related to the Koran in this novel is true.

The cipher found by Jefferson in the first edition *Don Quixote* is fictional. Cervantes, though, did suffer horribly during his captivity and much of his experience in the Muslim dungeons of Algiers greatly influenced and figured prominently in his work.

Thomas Jefferson did keep a suite of rooms at the Carthusian Monastery in Paris while U.S. minister to France and invented his Cipher Wheel during this time.

Of the fifteen fireplaces at Poplar Forest, one was indeed left unrenovated, but is located in the room used by Jefferson's grand-daughters, not in his library/parlor. Some of the entablature details, as well as Poplar Forest's hours, have been changed to suit my purposes in this novel.

The weapons, equipment, and other gear used by Scot Harvath, Aydin Ozbek, et al., including the revolutionary new Integrated Tourniquet System clothing, are current and accurate.

ACKNOWLEDGMENTS

More than ever, I want to thank my beautiful and brilliant wife, Trish, for all of her love, support, and assistance with this novel. She is my muse, my best friend, and one of the most amazing people I have ever known. Without her, none of this would be possible. Thank you, my love.

I also could not do what I do without you, **my readers.** Thank you for all of your wonderful e-mails, your appearances at my signings, and all of the wonderful word of mouth you have given my novels. The reason my work has grown in popularity is because of you.

My good friend, **Scott F. Hill, PhD,** was once again one of my most invaluable assets in crafting this novel. His sharp mind is exceeded only by his warm friendship and deep sense of patriotism. Thank you for everything.

James Ryan (not his real name) operates in some of the darkest and most dangerous corners of the world. The things he shared with me during the writing of this novel made me incredibly grateful that our nation has such men and women of character, integrity, courage, and ability willing to make such exceptional sacrifices. If Mr. James Ryan ever shows up on your doorstep it is either the best day or the last day of your life. "TIA" my friend. Thank you and bless you for everything you have done for me on and off the field.

Much of this novel has been influenced by the erudite writing, commentary, and courage of **Robert Spencer,** who generously assisted me in my research. I am indeed honored to call him my friend. He suffered weekly telephone and e-mail bombardments during my writing and research and always did so with brilliant responses and good humor. Robert, I am much obliged.

One of the greatest rewards of my career has been getting to meet people whom I deeply respect and admire. As I have gotten older, I realize that outside my military, law enforcement, and intelligence contacts there aren't many people who both "talk the talk" and "walk the walk" as well. **Glenn Beck** is definitely one of those people. When you have a friend who sets the bar so high for himself, it is impossible not to constantly strive to raise your own even higher. Thank you for everything, my friend. You have been an inspiration.

I am also incredibly fortunate to have a key group of warriors with whom I not only share ideas and frank debate, but also friendship. My novels wouldn't be what they are without them. They inspire and guide my work not only by what they say, but also what they do. Each has contributed in too many ways to mention. They are: **Tom Baker, Steven Bronson, Jeff Chudwin, Rodney Cox, Thomas Foreman, Chuck Fretwell, Frank Gallagher, Steve Hoffa, Mike Janich, Cynthia Longo, Ronald Moore, Mike Noell, Chad Norberg, Gary Penrith, Rob Pincus,** and **Mitch Shore**—as well as all of my other brothers and sisters out there who asked that they not be named in this book for their own safety. Thank you for all you do for us. Stay safe.

As I have said before, without the fabulous **bookstores, online retailers,** and the **Atria/Pocket sales staff,** you wouldn't be holding this in your hands right now. I am extremely grateful to all the people who have worked so hard to build me as an author and who strive to make every book more successful than the last. It is a team effort, and along with **Jeanne Lee,** the **Atria/Pocket art and production departments,** and the **Simon & Schuster Audio family** I couldn't hope to be aligned with more creative, intelligent, and truly nice people in the publishing business.

Daniel Pipes consulted with me at the very beginning of the novel and I am quite grateful for his insight, generosity, and advice.

Dr. Rusty Shackleford and his team are a force to be reckoned with. Though few know who they really are, many know the incredibly dangerous and important work that they do every day. Thank you for everything.

Thanks as well goes to **Anna Berkes,** Research Librarian at Thomas Jefferson's Monticello; **Anna McAlpine,** Director, Public Relations & Marketing at Thomas Jefferson's Poplar Forest; and **Clark Evans** of the Library of Congress.

In Washington, D.C., I am grateful for the assistance of my friends **David Vennett, Patrick Doak,** and my new Beltway "insider," **Tim Holland.**

I also want to thank **Richard and Anne Levy** for their help as well as that of our shared foreign intelligence asset, **Alice.**

The continued help and support of two of my best sharpshooters, **Tom and Geri Whowell,** is also deeply appreciated.

Thanks as well go to **Danielle Boudreau** of Bombardier Business Aircraft, the **United States Park Service,** and the **DC Metropolitan Police Department.**

I am exceptionally fortunate to be on a powerhouse publishing team surrounded by brilliant people. That team is led by the incomparable **Carolyn Reidy.** As our professional relationship has grown, so too has our friendship. Carolyn, it is both an honor and a pleasure working with you.

Judith Curr and **Louise Burke** are two of the best and brightest in the publishing business. I'm not only lucky enough to call them my publishers, I also get to call them my friends. Every year that I work with Louise and Judith is more enjoyable than the last. Thank you both for all you have done for me.

My amazing editor, **Emily Bestler,** offered superb guidance every step of the way and helped me reach further with this novel than ever before. Emily, I am more appreciative of you than you will ever know. Thank you for everything.

My outstanding literary agent, **Heide Lange,** continues to play a vital role in my writing career. Thank you, Heide, for your intelligence, wisdom, and creativity, as well as your abiding friendship.

Gary Urda, Lisa Keim, and **Michael Selleck** are three more exceptional talents in the Simon & Schuster family whose acumen and dedication to my books is felt and appreciated on every page. Thank you.

David Brown is my remarkable publicist, who continues to amaze me as he leaps tall buildings in a single bound and makes it look so easy. David, you will always be #1 in my book and I am very thankful to have you on my team.

Laura Stern, Sarah Branham, Mellony Torres, Karen Fink and everyone else at S&S have my deep gratitude for the incredible amount of work they put into every book we publish. Again, it is truly a team effort and I am very thankful to be a member of the Atria & Pocket families.

I also want to thank everyone at **Sanford J. Greenburger Associates** for all that they do for me throughout the year, including the exceptional **Teri Tobias** and the dynamic duo of **Alex Cannon** and **Jennifer Linnan.**

In the trenches of Hollywood, you want an attorney who knows where the bodies are buried. If he's also a brilliant negotiator and one hell of a great guy to be around, then you've hit the jackpot. **Scott Schwimer** is not only all of that, he's also one of my best friends. Thanks, Scottie.

Turn the page to enjoy special bonus material from
Brad Thor's instant *New York Times*
bestselling thriller

NEAR DARK

PROLOGUE

A cold rain slicked the poorly paved streets. Aging Russian hydrofoils banged against rotting piers. Crumbling French architecture struggled with leaks. Life in Vietnam's third largest city was miserable. Inclement weather only made it worse. Andre Weber couldn't wait to leave.

Looking at his host, he commented, "Counting machines are quicker."

Lieu Van Trang smiled. "But they are far less attractive."

Weber shook his head. Trang was known for his eccentricities. A coterie of young women, stripped naked so they couldn't steal while tallying his money, was completely on brand. It was also a total waste of time.

Electronic currency counters could have done the job six times faster and would have eliminated any human error. They also didn't steal. But Trang liked to play games. He liked to fuck with people's heads. He knew his visitors wouldn't be able to take their eyes off the girls.

As far as Weber was concerned, it was unprofessional. They were here to conduct business. There was a shit ton of money on the table and that's where his team's focus needed to be. The girls were distracting. Even he was having a hard time not looking at them. And if it was difficult for him, it had to have been almost impossible for his men.

This was not how he liked to do things. Weber preferred encrypted communications and washing money through shell corporations or cryptocurrencies. Trang, on the other hand, was old-school. So old-school, in fact, that he refused to conduct any business electronically. Everything was in cash and everything was face-to-face.

The two couldn't have been further apart in their approach. Even in their appearances they were strikingly different. Weber, the Westerner, was tall and fit. With his short hair and his expensive, tailored suit, he looked like a young banker or a hedge fund manager. Trang, thirty years his senior, was impossibly thin with long gray hair, a wispy beard, and translucent, vellumlike skin that revealed a network of blue veins.

The only thing they shared in common was a lust for money and a talent for taking care of problems. While Weber didn't want to be here, he had been paid a huge sum of money, a sum equal to what Trang's girls were currently counting out, for this assignment.

When all was said and done, it would be the highest-value contract killing ever to hit the market. It had already been deposited in a secret account and would be payable on confirmation of the subject's demise.

But like Weber, Trang was just a middleman—a headhunter, skilled in identifying the right professionals for the right jobs. His fee, payable up front, was a fraction of what the successful assassin would receive. It was quite fair as he was taking only a fraction of the risk.

Anyone whose murder commanded that sort of a price had to be very dangerous and *very* hard to kill. Trang would have to take extra steps to make sure none of this blew back on him.

Once the girls had finished counting the money and had confirmed the total, he dismissed them. Every set of male eyes, including Trang's, watched them as they filed out of the room. Several of Weber's men shifted uncomfortably as they adjusted erections.

"One thousand dollars each," said Trang, enjoying the men's pain. "Best money you will ever spend. I will even throw in rooms for free."

The man had just collected a ten-million-dollar fee, yet he wasn't above pimping out his girls for a little bit more. He also wasn't shy about his pricing. *One thousand dollars?* No matter how good they were, Weber doubted they were worth a thousand dollars—not even for all of them at the same time. Trang was as shameless and as sleazy as they came.

It was time to wrap things up. Weber didn't want to stay a minute longer than he had to. Removing the folder, he handed it over.

Slowly, Trang leafed through it, employing the freakishly long nail of his right index finger to turn the pages.

When he was done, he closed the dossier and asked, "So what can you tell me about the client?"

"Only that it's someone you don't want to fuck with."

"Apparently *somebody* fucked with whoever it is or you wouldn't be here opening this kind of a contract. What transgression, what sin, could be so egregious that it would call for a one-hundred-million-dollar bounty on a man's head?"

Weber had his suspicions, but as his employment had been shrouded in secrecy and also handled by a cutout, he couldn't say for sure. Not that he would have, even if he had known. He prided himself on discretion. It was a necessary part of his business and absolutely critical in his line of work. The kind of clientele who hired men like him didn't appreciate loose talk. It was the surest way to a very similar sort of contract.

Weber changed the subject. "How long?" he asked.

The Vietnamese man arched one of his narrow eyebrows. "To complete the contract? That's like asking how long is a piece of string. Every professional is different. Each has a different way of going about their craft."

"The client wants it done quickly."

"I have a list of certain professionals in mind. I guarantee you that any one of them will be eager for the job. With a fee like this, whoever I task won't drag their feet."

"Task all of them," said Weber.

"Excuse me?"

"You heard me. Task them all. Whoever gets to him first, and kills him, wins. That's what the client wants."

Trang smiled again. "He really did fuck with the wrong people, didn't he?"

Weber nodded and, standing up from the table, prepared to leave.

"Is there anything else you can tell me?" asked Trang. "Anything that's not in the file?"

"Only one thing," Weber replied, as a torrent of rain slammed against the windows. "Don't underestimate Scot Harvath. If you do, it'll be the last mistake you ever make."

CHAPTER 1

L ooking back on it, Scot Harvath probably shouldn't have punched the guy. Flipped him on his ass? *Sure.* Put his wrist into a painful, yet harmless joint lock? *Even better.* But uppercut the guy so hard that he knocked him out cold? *Not one of his better decisions.*

And therein lay the problem. Lately, Harvath seemed to be out of the good-decision-making business altogether.

Forget for the moment that the other guy had it coming. A wealthy Wall Street type, he appeared to take great pleasure in verbally abusing his female companion. The more the man had to drink, the worse it got. It was uncomfortable for everyone sitting nearby. What it *wasn't*, though, was any of Harvath's business.

People got into relationships for all sorts of reasons. If she was willing to sit there and get berated by some jackass, that was her problem.

At least it had been until she took off her shawl. The moment she did, everything changed.

On such a warm evening, in the resort's open-air lounge, it had seemed odd to be wearing a wrap. Then Harvath noticed her bruises. She had tried to conceal them, but to his discerning eye they were unmistakable, running up and down both arms. Apparently, Wall Street could get rough with more than just his words.

In Harvath's book—hell, in any decent human being's book—men who beat women were scum. Did this guy need to be taught a lesson? *Absolutely*. Did Harvath need to be the one doing the teaching? *That was debatable*. Karma would catch up with the guy eventually. It was one of those things from which you could run, but never hide.

Nevertheless, Harvath felt for the woman. Maybe it was all the cocktails he had consumed that were talking. Maybe it was the amount of personal trauma he had unsuccessfully been trying to escape. Either way, the emotional and physical pain radiating from her was undeniable.

And so, when Wall Street next popped off, Harvath didn't even think. He just reacted. Standing up, he walked over to their table. Her problem had just become *his* problem.

"That's enough," he said.

"Come again?" the man replied, an angry look on his face as he rose to confront Harvath.

"You heard me. Leave the lady alone."

"Mind your own business," Wall Street snapped, giving him a shove.

That was when Harvath laid him out.

It was a dramatic escalation of the situation and drew a collective gasp from the other guests. The punch could have killed him. Or, he could have hit his head on one of the tables as he fell. A million and one things could have gone wrong. Thankfully, nothing did.

And while Harvath could have made the legal case that Wall Street had made contact first, it hadn't come to that. He wasn't interested in involving police or pressing charges. That didn't mean, though, that it was over.

The staff at Little Palm Island Resort liked Harvath. He was a repeat customer known for his easy smile and engaging sense of humor. But on this visit, something was off. Something had happened to him; something unsettling.

He was withdrawn and quiet. A dark cloud hovered over him wherever he went. He rose early to work out, but other than that spent the rest of his time drinking, heavily.

Had the resort been empty, the management might have been able to ignore his self-destructive behavior. It wasn't empty, though. It was at full occupancy and none of the upscale clientele wanted to spend their luxury vacation watching a man drink himself to death in the bar.

Harvath didn't care. He knew his alcohol consumption was dangerous, but after everything he had been through, all he wanted was to be released—released from the guilt, the shame, and the pain of what had happened.

The real problem was that there wasn't enough booze in the world to wash away what had happened. His wife, Lara, was dead. His mentor, Reed Carlton—a man who had become like a second father to him—was dead. And one of his dearest colleagues, Lydia Ryan—who had stepped up to helm his organization when he wouldn't, was dead. All of them had been killed in an effort to get to him and he hadn't been able to do a single thing to stop the carnage.

With all of his training, with all of his counterterrorism and espionage experience, he should have been able to protect them. At the very least, he should have seen the attack coming. But he hadn't.

Helpless to save them, he had been forced to watch as they were murdered. Horrific didn't even begin to describe it. The physical torture he was subjected to afterward paled in comparison.

Dragged by a foreign intelligence service back to their country for interrogation and execution, he had managed—through sheer force of will—to pull himself together long enough to orchestrate his own escape. Then, on behalf of Lara, Reed, and Lydia he had carried out his own bloody revenge.

It turned out to be a devastatingly empty accomplishment. He felt no better at the end than he had at the beginning. It gave him no pleasure; no satisfaction. In fact, it had only hollowed him out further—eating away at him like an acid—dimming the already sputtering flame of humanity that remained.

Losing the people closest to him—simply because he had been doing his job—was the absolute worst-case scenario someone in his line of work could ever expect to face. It was worse than torture or even death—fates he would have gladly suffered if it meant that Lara, Reed, and Lydia could have all gone on living.

Instead, he was the one expected to go on living. He would have to "soldier on," carrying the pain of their murders as well as the guilt of knowing that the deaths were his fault.

• • •

And so, once he had completed his revenge, he had traveled to Little Palm Island—a place where he had found solace in the past. This time, though, rejuvenation lay beyond his grasp. He was simply too broken; too far gone.

The only comfort he could find was when he'd had so much to drink that he was simply too numb to feel anything. He would get to that point and keep going until he blacked out. Then he would get up and do it all over again.

If not for his long runs in the sand and punishing swims in the ocean, he would have begun drinking at sunrise. As it was, he was still hitting the bottle well before noon. For someone with such a distinguished career; someone who had given so much in the service of others, it was no way to live.

But Harvath didn't care about living. Not really. Not anymore. While his heart continued to pump alcohol-laden blood throughout his body, his ability to feel anything, for anyone, much less himself, was gone. He had given up.

As such, he wasn't surprised to learn that he had eventually come to the point where he had worn out his welcome at Little Palm Island.

Considering his sizable bar tab, the manager had made him a deal. In exchange for cutting short his stay and departing immediately, a portion of his bill would be comped. Harvath agreed to cut his losses and move on.

Packing his things, he rode the polished motor launch back to Little Torch Key, revived his abandoned rental car, and drove until he came to the end of the road in Key West.

There, in a less touristy part of town known as Bahama Village, he took the first room he found and paid for two weeks, up front, in cash.

The carpet looked to be at least twenty years old—the paint even older. The whole place smelled like mold covered up with Febreze. He was a world away from the high-thread-count sheets and hibiscus-scented air of Little Palm Island. Like Icarus and his melted wings, the once "golden boy" of the U.S. Intelligence Community had come crashing down to earth. Cracking a window, he opened his suitcase.

Having served as an elite U.S. Navy SEAL, it had been drilled into him to properly maintain and stow his gear. After hanging several items in the closet and placing the rest into a battered chest of drawers, he carried the wrinkled Ziploc bag he was using as a shaving kit into the bathroom.

There, he lined the contents on the shelf above the sink and stared at himself in the mirror. He looked terrible.

Though his five-foot-ten-inch body was still muscular, he had lost weight. His sandy-brown hair might have been sun-bleached and his skin tanned a deep brown, but the cheeks of his handsome face were sunken and his once sharp, glacierlike blue eyes were tired and bloodshot.

If any of his friends could see him, his transformation would have been shocking. Decay was a powerful force. Once set in motion, it went quickly to work.

Returning to the bedroom, he walked back over to the suitcase. There was only one item remaining—a photograph in a silver frame. It was his favorite picture of Lara. She stood in a sundress, her long dark hair falling across her shoulders, with a glass of white wine on his dock overlooking the Potomac River in Virginia.

Lara's parents were Brazilian and she had grown up speaking both English and Portuguese. After her first husband had drowned, she said she had been plagued by a feeling known as *saudade*.

When he asked her to translate it, she had said there wasn't really an equivalent. In essence, it was a longing for someone or something you know you will never experience again. She had been terrified that Harvath, the first man she had loved since her husband's death, was going to cause her to relive those feelings.

As a police officer, she had understood that the majority of people were sheep—gentle creatures largely incapable of protecting themselves. To defend them from the wolves of the world, they needed sheepdogs. As a homicide detective, she further understood that sheepdogs would never be enough. The world also needed wolf hunters—brave souls willing to go into the darkness to take down the wolves before they could attack. That's what Harvath was—a wolf hunter. And that's what had scared her.

While he claimed to want a family more than anything else, he continued grabbing the most dangerous assignments that came his way. He would leave at a moment's notice—sometimes for days, weeks, or even months at a time.

He was working for a private intelligence agency named after his mentor: The Carlton Group. It had been tasked with providing the CIA room to breathe as it rebuilt itself into a leaner, better-focused, and more efficient organization along the lines of its predecessor—the OSS.

To many D.C. insiders, it felt counterintuitive to approach America's modern, rapidly evolving threats by looking to the past. But to those spearheading the renovation, they knew that's where the answers lay. The Agency was dying—choking on its own bureaucracy. Like a hot air balloon falling out of the sky, the only way to fix it was to toss anything and everything that was unnecessary overboard.

By stripping it down to its bare essentials, they could focus not only on what needed to be done, but also the best ways to do it. For far too long, brave men and women at the CIA had been prevented from doing their jobs by risk-averse middle managers more concerned with their next promotion than with conducting the nation's most dangerous business.

But, like any large, government entity gorging itself on ever-increasing budgets and layers upon layers of self-inflicted rules, regulations, and red tape, many things at the CIA weren't going to be easy to change. They were going to take a lot of work, a lot of patience, and a lot of time—during which the threats to America were only going to grow deadlier. Enter The Carlton Group.

As the man who had come up with the idea and had created the CIA's Counterterrorism Center, Reed Carlton had seen the writing on the wall long before most. When he finally tired of no one on the seventh floor listening to him about what was coming, he left and started his own endeavor. He staffed it with highly accomplished, former intelligence and Special Operations personnel. Carlton had a scary eye for talent. And, as with everything else in his career, he had been way ahead of the curve.

During the Agency's struggle to remake itself, some of its riskiest, most sensitive work was quietly contracted out to The Carlton Group. Just as they were picking up speed and more jobs were being funneled their way, they received dreadful news. Reed Carlton—the heart, soul, and brains of the entire organization—had been diagnosed with Alzheimer's.

Once he had gotten over the initial shock, he had only one request—that Scot Harvath, his handpicked successor, the man he had poured all of his wisdom, experience, and know-how into, give up field operations and take over the running of the business.

In a move that stunned everyone, Harvath had said no. It didn't matter how much Carlton threatened or cajoled his protégé, the answer remained the same. At least it had been until the Old Man, as he was known by those closest to him, had brought Lara into it.

He knew how much Harvath cared for her and her four-year-old son, Marco. He knew it was only a matter of time before they settled down and became a family. He also knew that no matter how often Harvath said that was what he really wanted most in life, it wasn't true. Not completely.

Harvath had an addiction. He was addicted to the lifestyle—the constant scrapes with death and the heroinlike highs that came from the massive adrenaline dumps they provided. And like any drug addiction, it needed to be constantly fed and continually took more than the last time to reach the same high. It also had the same outcome waiting for him at the end. Sooner or later, it would take his life.

Harvath was no ordinary junkie, though. He was highly intelligent, which meant he was exceedingly good at coming up with justifications for not getting out. *No one was as experienced, nor as skilled as he was. No one had the human networks he had. No one was as good at developing assets. No one was willing to take the risks that he did. No one could adapt as quickly on the ground.* And on and on.

It was all true, but it didn't mean that others couldn't be groomed to do the same—and that was precisely what the Old Man had wanted him to do. Harvath had stayed in the game far longer than was safe. He put way too much at risk each time he went into the field. In a word, it was *selfish*. The fact that he depended on a cocktail of performance-enhancing drugs just to remain at peak performance should have been a bright neon sign blasting the message that his days were numbered.

The Old Man's admonishment to think of Lara and Marco had pissed Harvath off. It was emotional blackmail and a professional low blow. It angered him most, though, because he knew Carlton was correct. He needed to make a tough decision. But like any junkie, he would first try to negotiate his way out of it.

Despite what the Old Man thought, Harvath honestly believed that he had several more years left of kicking in doors and shooting bad guys in the head. The sports medicine group he had found that rehabbed top professional athletes and Tier One operators had been a godsend. If not for them, he might have been reluctantly inclined to agree with Carlton that it was time to move from playing to scouting and coaching.

The docs and exercise physiologists he worked with, though, had upped his game to levels he hadn't even thought possible. Through their program, he was stronger, faster, and had better reaction time than he'd had in his thirties. The advances they had developed were incredible. So, with all due respect to his mentor, he had proposed a compromise.

Instead of abandoning operations altogether, he had spent half his time in the field and half his time at The Carlton Group incubating new talent.

This was not the outcome the Old Man had been gunning for. He needed somebody steering the ship on a full-time basis. He also knew Harvath—maybe better than anyone else. He knew that if he gave him an ultimatum, Harvath would jump ship and freelance for whoever would pay his quote—and with his skillset, there were plenty of opportunities. He might have been able to get him blacklisted at the CIA, but the Brits or the Israelis would have scooped him up in a heartbeat.

Whether Harvath would have agreed to work for a foreign service was an unknown. In the end, like a son, the Old Man wanted to keep him close. He wanted to know that the ops that Harvath undertook were as well planned and professional as possible. If he kept him in-house, he could guarantee that they would be—something he couldn't say if he let him put himself on the open market.

This left Carlton with the problem of who would actually run the organization. After discussions with the President and the Director of the CIA, he was given permission to approach the Agency's Deputy Director, Lydia Ryan. She had been an exceptional intelligence officer and understood the game from top to bottom. Lydia was an excellent hire.

The Old Man, despite having Alzheimer's, was a walking history of the espionage business. He knew where all the top secret "bodies" were buried. Lydia and Harvath had taken turns sitting with him, recording every piece of valuable information he had stored in his brain before it all slipped away.

When his capacities began to fail and he started revealing some of his sensitive exploits to his housekeeper and friends who would call up or drop by to check on him, Harvath decided it was time to silo him.

Carlton's fondest memories had been of spending summers at his grandparents' cottage on Lake Winnipesaukee in New Hampshire. It was off-season and easy for Harvath to find an available home for rent. As the oldest memories were usually the last to disappear, he thought it would be a comfortable and familiar place for Carlton.

With the President's approval, a team of Navy corpsmen—all with top secret clearance—was detailed to the Old Man. On rotating shifts, there was always one in the house. Harvath flew up to see him as often as possible.

He had just returned from a particularly harrowing assignment overseas, during which he had made up his mind about what he wanted. While he couldn't promise that he would retire from fieldwork anytime soon, he knew that he loved Lara and her son and would for the rest of his life.

Following a romantic meal, he had walked her down to the dock and had proposed. She had lovingly and excitedly accepted.

Knowing that the Old Man was slipping away, Harvath had asked her to elope with him. He wanted to get married at the cottage, quietly, by his bedside. Ryan would be their witness.

Lara knew how much Reed Carlton meant to her fiancé. She had come to love him like a father as well. Including such a special man in such a special moment was the right thing to do. And so, she had agreed.

To keep it under wraps—until they could do a big church wedding with Lara's family, his mom, and all their friends present—they hired a local judge to conduct the ceremony in private.

Everything had been perfect. The Old Man had even been more engaged and energetic than they had seen him in long time.

Harvath couldn't have asked for anything more. The walks around the lake with Lara, the laughter, the lovemaking; those couple of days—from the secret wedding until the attack—had been the happiest he had ever known. Then it had all come crashing down.

After the murders, the torture, his escape, and fighting his way across a frozen foreign landscape to freedom, much of who he had been was stripped away.

Since the funerals, his colleagues had backed off, showing their respect by giving him space and letting him grieve.

Nevertheless, he couldn't shake the feeling that someone had been keeping tabs on him. He figured it had to have been somebody from the office. They were more than just coworkers, they were family. And spies, after all, never stop spying—especially on each other.

They all knew where he had been staying. In fact, a colleague had done him a favor by shipping a suitcase full of his clothes down to Little Palm Island in advance of his arrival.

But now that he had decamped for Key West, he'd be harder to find. Harder, but not impossible.

He still had his phone, which never left the room and which he only turned on to scroll through photos, old texts, and voice messages from Lara. Lest anyone catch him while the phone was on, he had it set to "Do Not Disturb," disabling the chime and sending any new calls straight to voicemail.

Once his unpacking was complete, he had spent the next several days making the rounds of local watering holes until he finally settled on one. Not that his standards were particularly high. They weren't. All that mattered was that the air-conditioning was cold, the bar quiet, and the clientele a particular class: hard-core, professional drinkers who just wanted to be left alone.

The place he ultimately selected was a quintessential dive bar. Dimly lit, with blacked-out windows, its air was redolent of urinal cakes, spilled beer, and wasted lives.

Nobody paid him any attention. In fact, no one had given him so much as a second look. It was the perfect hole in the wall to continue his slow-motion suicide.

And though he could have continued to drink top-shelf as he had at Little Palm Island, he instead went for the worst stuff they had. He wanted it to burn all the way down. He wanted to torture himself. Glancing around, it was pretty obvious that he hadn't cornered the market in self-loathing.

Imagining the backstories of the people he was drinking "with" didn't take too much creativity. All of them had been drawn to the southernmost point in the U.S. by something. There were probably more than a few failed marriages, failed businesses, and outstanding warrants in the room. Anything was possible. They didn't call Key West a "sunny place for shady people" for nothing.

The bartender was an attractive woman in her forties. Twenty, even ten years ago, the top bars on the island would have been cutting each other's throats to hire her. She was not only sexy, but she was also adept at slinging drinks. More importantly, she knew when, and when not, to make conversation.

When it came to Harvath, she could tell that he was not looking to talk. He was polite, and tipped well, but he kept to himself.

He came in every day with a newspaper he barely read, sat in the same scarred booth where he ordered the same drink over and over, as he stared toward the front door. It was as if he was waiting for someone. But whoever that someone was, they never came.

She felt sorry for him. He was handsome, close to her age, and a man who obviously needed to be put back together. She had always been drawn to guys who were screwed up. "Broken Bird Syndrome" a friend had once called it.

He wasn't like the other customers. He seemed like a "somebody." Somebody, who at one point in his life, had prospects; potential. She had a lot of questions. *Where had he come from? What was he doing here? How long was he going to stay?* Most of all, she wondered what he was like in bed.

When it came to her advances, though, the man was immune. Whoever had wounded him had done a bang-up job.

Still, she liked having him around. There was something comforting about his presence. The strong, silent type—he struck her as a guy who could handle himself.

Maybe he was an ex-cop, or possibly ex-military. It didn't matter. All she knew was that having him in the bar made her feel safe.

Not that a lot of bad things went down in Key West. But, like every other resort town fueled by alcohol and an "anything goes" attitude, sometimes things got out of control.

It was at that moment that the door opened. And as it did, no one inside had any idea how out of control things were about to get.